Salsa
with the Pope

Samantha Wren Anderson

Copyright 2015 Samantha Wren Anderson
All rights reserved

Review

"Anderson's humorous prose…accurately describes being young and single in New York…readers will enjoy its element of escapism…engaging romance boosted by a fun main character and her baseball-playing love interest." —Kirkus Reviews

Synopsis

'What have I accomplished?' So questions Samantha Wren Anderson on her 33rd birthday. The list is short, as she's still struggling with her acting career and a walk to the altar—please, even a date at this point is a novelty. But all that changes when she meets Alan. Suddenly Samantha has a romantic boyfriend who is—even better—a playwright. Life seems perfect.

That is until Sam breaks a fellow classmate's foot in Salsa class (with her favorite purple stilettos), gets looked over for a great role in a play (that Alan wrote!), has her gall bladder removed (yuck), and has to deal with phone conversations with her mother and grandmother that border on insanity.

The ultimate challenge comes in the form of writing a one-woman show though. A dream of Sam's, she completes the play and revels in its success. Suddenly, she feels that she is becoming the self-reliant woman she has always wanted to be. She can run marathons, she can face her demons...enter Darren James. Baseball's answer to stud, this tall, dark, and handsome player dances a mean Salsa and sweeps Sam right off her feet. Now the only question remaining is...Alan? Darren? A life of celibacy...

PROLOGUE

Spring 2006

I scurry down the street as fast as I can, having no particular place in mind, only knowing that I can't go into that party. My own party and I'm a no show. Can't be helped. I need to be away from here. Away from him. *And* him. Far away. To think. To sort my thoughts.

The tears start falling as I near the avenue. I will them to stop. PLEASE. Just 'til I can get myself back to my apartment. Then you can wail and thrash about all you want, I promise myself. I round the corner in search of a cab. Not a one. Surprising for this hour on a Sunday night.

I start walking aimlessly. I can't believe this. For this to happen and…well, there's a Starbucks. That's something you can always count on. No matter where you are…Harlem; on a deserted island off the coast of Antarctica…there's a Starbucks and somehow that makes me feel a little better. I'll just pop in for a cool drink, sit down and calmly figure this out.

I open my bag for a tissue and items start popping out all over the sidewalk. My hairbrush, perfume, and two tampons make their way out before I can stop them. Of course, what one would call 'a nice breeze' comes along at just that moment and carries one of the tampons off down Chambers Street. I recover the remaining items best I can and wipe my face on my sleeve. These are party clothes that will never see the party, I reason, so who cares about a spot of snot on my jacket.

Just as I am approaching my salvation—aka Starbucks, a tall lanky gentleman in a tux approaches me.

"Lose this?" He asks.

His accent is British. He is holding up a tampon…presumably the one that got away.

"Never seen it before," I mumble, continuing to walk.

"Oh, come on now, saw you goin' after it like it was your long lost chap," he tells me.

"Look, mister, I don't know who you are, or what you want, but I don't have a need for a used tampon."

"Well, it doesn't exactly look used, now does it, in the traditional sense I mean."

He displays the wrapped tube between his fingers, as if it's the next item up for bid at Sotheby's. I turn away disgusted, more because of his maleness than because of the tampon. I mean it's just a tampon. My tampon. Rather, my former tampon.

I look straight ahead and continue to put distance between us.

"Just…buzz off."

Okay, admittedly lame, but in a pinch, it still carries some punch—no?

"Ah, come on now, I've come all the way from England to meet a woman just like you," he shouts to me, arms raised over his head, as if ruling a field goal kick as good.

"I doubt it," I say under my breath, though were I in a better mood, I might pursue that thought.

He is tall, dark, and handsome. I just happen to have my fill at the moment with tall, dark and handsomes. Nope, no room on my dance card for another. Perhaps if he returns in say…2025. I should have this all sorted out by then.

I walk into Starbucks, survey several empty tables and breathe a sigh of relief. The last thing I need is to be crammed into a corner seat with someone's elbow and cell phone conversation inhabiting my space.

Note to Self: Sunday nights at Starbucks, practically empty.

I order a Venti Vanilla Crème and take a seat at a small table in the corner. I dump all my stuff onto the opposite chair and heave my body down, as if it weighs 500 lbs. That's what it feels like. Like I'm lugging around two tons of shit.

I take a long swig of my drink, allow the sugar to hit me and consider…how did this happen? What have I done to deserve this?

CHAPTER 1

Spring 2003

It was three years ago, mind you, when all the trouble began.

I open my eyes to white popcorn. The kind that's on the ceiling. I stare at it for a moment and then I remember. In a panic, I reach down and place my hand between my legs...somewhere that it's been before, but not for this specified purpose. I feel for her—fearing the worst, but no, there she is...my tootle. All intact too.

I was worried for a moment there. You see, I had this really odd dream that Criss Angel—you know that crazy magician man—well, I had a dream that he made my tootle disappear. I know ladies, that there are times that this could seem like a good idea...a particular time of month comes to mind, but to lose your tootle FOREVER? Now let's not get cuckoo here.

Now the real question is 'what exactly did he want tootle for' (yeah, I know, it seems pretty obvious, 'so he could get some anytime he wanted', yeah, well, I'm pretty sure that's already the case and those tootles are attached to actual breathing people and not just some random tootle floating around without a host, if you know what I mean). No, there must've been a really good reason...He wanted to levitate tootle? He wanted to study the female genitalia that is tootle? He wanted to give a tootle transplant to someone (now that one makes me cringe...my tootle with another host! Ugh!)

A ringing phone stops my obsessing over my lady-part. Though it would appear a good thing, don't be too certain. It's well-wishers. Again. 'Go away,' my mind tells them. My voice tells them nothing.

I pick up the damn phone.

"Hello." I use a sick psycho-Betty Crocker sing-song voice in the hope of scaring the caller away. It's my mother. Too bad. Doesn't work on repeat callers.

"You sound cheerful," she says.

Do I? Cheerful enough to hurl my lifeless existence into the Hudson. I keep this to myself and say instead, "And why wouldn't I be. It's my day."

"Yes it is. Happy Birthday, Samantha," she says before launching into the entire birthday chorus at high volume.

I pull the phone away from my ear and think, thirty-three years. I have inhabited the earth thirty-three years. I make a mental note of all my accomplishments. This takes quite a few moments, not because the list is particularly long, but rather because I am having a hard time coming up with a single achievement. Okay, there was Dave when I was nineteen, and though I would measure the relationship as a turning point in my life—aren't all first loves—it ended, so really that could be construed—to a pessimist, which I am not—as a failure.

Okay, how about switching gears here...career accomplishments. There have been dozens of callbacks—a great thing these second auditions are in an actor's life—not as good as actually booking the job, playing the role, GETTING PAID—things a pessimist would cue on, but not being one, I wouldn't really know.

I tune in and my mother is now helping me question my life. Again.

"I'm not saying that you shouldn't keep auditioning and trying to make it, Sam, but maybe, just maybe it's time to get a *real job*." She whispers this as if breaking the news this way will somehow make it hurt less. It doesn't. "You're thirty-three now and not getting any younger." She must have realized her strategy wasn't working, as she blurts this out for the whole world to hear.

Maybe, just maybe, she is where I get my *non*-pessimistic attitude.

"I know, Mom. I know."

"I mean you've got your degree. Now why not use it," she tells me.

My degree. There. There's an accomplishment. A huge achievement. A Bachelor's Degree. *In Communications*, a pessimist might point out, but I will stand by my great achievement. Hey, I graduated Summa.

My mother's voice drones on, "I mean are you ever going to even consider it? It's not for me now. Even though you are my only shot at grandmahood."

Grandmahood? Is that even a word?

"I'll survive. I'll get by," she says slightly thick in the throat.

Oh joy—the ever-present martyr…hmm…perhaps this is where I get my propensity for drama…

"But are you sure you don't want kids? I mean take your time now deciding. It's just that you don't have forever."

As much as I'd love to say that my mom is just prattling on like she does—she has a point. When am I going to settle down and find my path?

I am doing everything in my power to become a working actor. And I'm good, I have a nice look and on the surface—and to all of my family in Ohio—you'd think it would be a piece of cake, a slam dunk. As my grandmother keeps asking, "Sammy, have you looked into soap"—no, she's not suggesting that I reek, but rather that I should audition for the 'soaps'—my grandmother has an issue with pluralism and diction…basically the entire English language, but that's a whole 'nother story all together. Incidentally, the few times I have been on 'soap' she wanted to know why I didn't wave to her and why those other people were standing in front of me…well, I didn't wave for the obvious reason and the other people, well, we call them the stars of the show…this explanation eluded my grandmother, as she could not figure out why anyone would want to see 'one of them stars' more than me, her beloved granddaughter. Now if only she were in casting.

People think that if you're good and you're not half-bad-looking, the acting biz should be a cinch. The problem with that is, in New York City, there are half a million people trying to do that same thing—and many are good and not half-bad-looking—so that makes things a teeny-tiny, itsy, bitsy bit HARDER.

So, no, no I'm not planning to work pointless jobs, commute from New Jersey, and count my pennies forever. Of course not. But I'm not ready to give this up either. Not yet.

I am less concerned about the other end of it. The personal side of it. Thirty-three years old and still not married. Not divorced or even widowed. Just single. Still.

I just figured that I would meet someone like they do, in some unsuspecting manner—in a supermarket (though I don't do too much supermarketing), at a friend's party (though I can't remember the last time one of my friends had a party), or possibly through mail order. I haven't ever actually heard of mail-order-groom, though mail-order-bride is quite notorious and with the Internet being what it is, I reason groom-order is probably available now. Possibly for a price. But still. Say a little dark-haired sexpot from Spain who speaks little English or a maybe too-tanned surfer from the west coast…or both. Why limit oneself.

"Okay Mom, I hear you. Thank you. I love you." See, I'm gracious to a fault. And this usually gets me off the phone.

"Okay Sam. Have a good birthday. And be careful."

"Always Mom. Always."

CHAPTER 2

I'm in the middle of becoming a great actor—taking a Script Analysis class, the first in a long time—and preparing for the 'industry night', whereby agents and casting directors come and view the class for potential clients. Actually, that was the big selling point on taking the class. I wanted to be 'discovered'. Okay, admittedly I was too old to be 'discovered' but I would settle for 'glimpsed'.

I am late. Shocking. No matter how early I start, I always end up late. It's making me rethink the whole 'getting up three hours before an appointment' thing. Might as well just jump up ten minutes before I have to leave and be late that way. At least I wouldn't be sleepy and cranky too.

I hurry up the four flights of rickety stairs carrying a mass of papers and a pissed off point-of-view. I'm just coming from a casting director's office. That's why I'm late. This time. And though that would seem like great news, it's anything but. Bastards.

I enter the class, winded, but still able to vent. Truth be told, no matter how winded I am, I can always find the breath to vent. It's a female prerogative.

"I can't believe these people! They have the audacity to call you with *no* notice and then, *then* they make you pay for your own copies," I say to no one in particular. "$26.50 at Kinko's and I didn't even have the cash. I had to charge it! Oh, I better book this job. Unbelievable those..."

"Samantha, you okay?" Alan, our teacher asks, while trying to hold back a chuckle. He told us all to call him by his first name, which as it turned out was lucky for us because his last name was something like, Dalalllaieeririssj.

I smile. Was I just talking out loud? Of course I was. I was venting.

"Uh, fine. I just...oh, sorry."

Alan laughs and a few of the others join him. He comes over and stands behind me, putting his hands on my shoulders and says, "You're alright now. You're amongst friends."

I don't have any particular feelings about Alan one way or another. I mean I don't know him. Don't know if he's straight or gay, single or married, or otherwise attached. I only know that I'm pretty impressed with his teaching.

He is a playwright who co-wrote an Off-Broadway play and has another slated for Broadway. That's the rumor. So, needless to say, when he asks me to stay after class to read a few of his new monologues, I'm flattered. At first I wonder if he's just trying to lift my spirits. But no. That was ages ago, my venting...okay, two hours ago. But still in the past.

As I pace around the room and read his words, I feel special. I'm not crazy about the actual monologue. But I still feel privileged. I construe this gesture as him thinking that I'm a good actor. One that he can trust with his work. And to me, there is no greater compliment.

About an hour later, our session ends and we make our way down to the street.

He says, "So, uh, you have some problems with the boys, huh?"

Is he flirting with me? Is this his way of asking if I have a boyfriend? Not knowing what he's really asking or how I feel about it, I venture a very innocent, "What do you mean?"

"Well, I just figured your choice in monologues was..."

"Oh, that," I say quickly. The monologue I picked for class is a woman confronting her batterer husband. Not like that's any indication that I have problems with men...okay I have problems with men...mainly not meeting enough of the right ones.

Needing to be bold (or just pretending to be) I say, "I find all men fall into one of three categories: taken, gay, or assholes. Which one are you?"

Take note that the categories were not romantic, faithful or fun...

He looks me straight in the eye and says solemnly, "None."

I find this hard to believe, as yes, I was saying it to be cool, to illicit a response, but truthfully, I really did find all men to be taken, gay, or assholes.

Alan graciously offers his services (teaching services...get your mind out of the gutter) for upcoming auditions and monologues. As I am seeing the Bastard Casting People in two days, I am in desperate need of private coaching. We agree that we'll speak tomorrow to set up a time and place to go over the scripts.

So expecting Alan's call, I think nothing of our phone conversation the next day. Until the end of it, that is.

"Uh, Sam," (he calls me Sam, not Samantha—a clue that I obviously miss) "I have, uh, three questions to ask you."

Will you be the lead in my upcoming Broadway production? Would you consider a month in Paris? Which do you prefer Cartier or Harry Winston? I'm not sure what he's going to ask, but I'm pretty sure it won't be that.

"Uh, okay," I say, my stomach doing a somersault.

He starts, "One. Would it be inappropriate for me to ask you out?"

I'm not at all sure how I feel about this guy. But he seems interesting. He seems to know a lot about the business. It's not like I have guys beating down my door at the moment. Why the hell not?

"We only have one more class, so I don't think it's such a biggie," I tell him after a moment's deliberation.

"But the date would be before the next class," he says.

Hmm, intriguing...now why would that be?

"That's fine," I tell him.

He goes on. "Do you have a really fancy dress?"

I lie. "Dozens."

"Would you be my date for the Drama Desk Awards?"

DING! The mother load!

Allow me to explain...the Drama Desk Awards are second to the Tony Awards. They celebrate Broadway and Off-Broadway theatre and Alan is nominated for two of these awards. Intriguing indeed.

"Okay." I hold my breath.

He tells me that he'll see me tomorrow for our private coaching session. I murmur a good-bye and explode once I hear the disconnect. I yelp and skip around the apartment—not such a large distance, but still skipping at my age.

I sleep little that night, between tossing and turning and having ghoulish nightmares. The scariest is the one where I'm served with mayo on whole wheat to the Bastard Casting People. Ahhhhhh!

The following day I make sure I look divine when I arrive at Pam's place. This is where Alan and I are meeting to rehearse. Pam and Liza run LP, the production company that is sponsoring the Script Analysis class, so she offers her apartment frequently to friends and colleagues.

The apartment is gorgeous. Spacious. A *real* one bedroom. We're talkin' New York City here—where an apartment with its own toilet is considered luxury.

As I take a seat at the table, pull the materials out of my bag, and ready myself, the queasiness returns. Faced with the scripts in hand and my coach/suitor I am battling nerves of two kinds.

The 'oh, I'm acting in front of someone' kind—though truthfully how much fun is it to act with no audience—and the 'oh, here's a guy that just asked me out' and that's giving me nerves of a more severe kind. The throw-up kind. Not that I'm planning to vomit, but I like to leave my options open.

I'm intimidated—that's what it comes down to—in the work especially. As Alan and I go over the scenes, I'm having a hard time focusing. I'm so consumed with what he thinks of me that I can't really live in the scene. My mind keeps telling my person, "You suck."

And suck I do. Or at least that's the impression I get from my audition the next day. The Bastard Casting People are rude and quiet...but on the plus side, they're not slathering on mayo trying to sandwich two slices of whole wheat around me, though as bad as this feels, they might as well be.

*They're the ones losing ou*t, I remind myself unconvincingly, as I trek to the nearest Ben & Jerry's. One day, they'll all be pursuing me and I'll remember this day and I'll simply look at them and say, "Pass."

Ooohh, can't wait for that day.

CHAPTER 3

"Damn." I say it aloud, though there's no one around to hear me. Anne-Marie, my girlfriend and Salsa sister—not my kin sister, though I often wish she were—just called to tell me she can't make class tonight. It's the one commitment I never miss—Salsa Tuesdays.

This is my third go 'round with Level One—I blame my non-Hispanic heritage on this…in fact, I think white folks should get a discount on repeat course levels…I mean it's not our fault we were born without rhythm, is it?

I sling my gym bag onto my shoulder and head out. I can't miss class. Not when I'm finally getting it. In fact, I'm one of the better ones in the group. I keep my previous attempts at Level One to myself and let them think I'm a natural…what's the harm?

I arrive and greet my fellow dancers. There's Martha, she's about seventy-five with really sagging skin, but she's a doll. She really has fun with the class, though she can't keep a beat to save her life.

"Oh, hey Jorge," I say to the young stud hovering near me. He's Latino, which would make you think he should be teaching the class, not paying for Basic. But that's not always the case. Anne-Marie is Columbian and she can't dance Salsa well at all. She's had to take Basic twice, so I don't feel quite so bad about my third go 'round.

Carlos, our instructor comes in and begins going over our steps. "One, two, three, five, six, seven."

We follow our steps in the full-length mirror in front of us.

"Okay, form a circle, women on the inside, men on the outside."

This is where we partner up. We only dance two minutes with one partner before moving on to the next...makes me feel kind of slutty.

Carlos says we're ready for some music. Yeah! I love me some Salsa (the dancin' kind....well, I love the eatin' kind too, but I'm kinda busy here...maybe later).

I have my Salsa groove on tonight. I am flying. I feel like shouting 'Hola,' that's how into the music I am. I dance with Pete, then Jorge and Carlos—and I'm actually keeping up with him—then it's Frank's turn.

Frank is a bit of a goober. He is corporate dweebie, doesn't talk that much, and when he does, it's hard to hear him. He almost whispers. He's pretty good at Salsa though. I just concentrate on the dance and don't worry about the lack of conversation.

That is until Frank screams, "God dammit, oh my fuckin' God, you've, Ahhhhhh, broken my foot."

I look around, hoping that he's talking to someone else. Nope. It's me. I've broken his foot. Well, not his whole foot, but at least parts of it. Oops.

"Are you alright?" I say, my face turning the color of a tomato.

I haven't seen my face, mind you, but I feel it. Hot and sweaty with embarrassment.

Before Frank can tell me that of course he's not alright, Carlos turns off the music—my beautiful Salsa music—and comes over to us.

"Frank, what seems to be the problem," he asks in a calm smooth voice. See, everyone knows there's a problem, not because there was screaming, but because it was Frank's voice and we all heard it loud and clear. Clearly a problem.

Frank grimaces and hops again on one foot. He looks like he just might cry.

"I think, I think she broke my foot. She stepped on it with, with, those..." he points accusingly at my purple stilettos—shoes reserved only for Salsa class. I am hurt. He has insulted my shoes. I just might cry too.

Salsa with the Pope

"Okay, well, why don't you sit down for a moment and we can see if anyone can help you get to the hospital to have it checked out."

Carlos helps Frank to the bench, while I stand completely still. I need to do something, but what... Oh, okay. (Big exhale) I'll go.

"I can take Frank to the hospital. I mean, I was his partner at the time of the *incident*." I say it just like they do on *Law & Order*. I don't want to admit guilt here. There could be ramifications. Ramifications that I'm not in the mood to deal with—or more accurately can't afford to deal with.

Carlos helps me get Frank into a cab. We head to NYU Medical. I am uncomfortable. Probably the most uncomfortable I've ever been. The guilt is starting to affect me. Oh, no.

"Frank, I am so sorry. If I was the cause of this...unfortunate mishap, I really didn't do it on purpose. I was just so into—"

"I know that," he says in an almost audible whisper. "It was an accident. Accidents happen."

See, even he knows accidents happen. I start to feel the guilt float away.

Then he places his hand over mine. Uh, yuck.

Fortunately we arrive at the hospital at just that moment. I throw all the bills from my wallet at the cab driver and help Frank into the Emergency Room, paying close attention to where he places his hands.

I leave him on a plastic chair and approach the desk. I am handed a clipboard with forms to fill-out. I hand them over to Frank.

"Oh, right," he says and pulls out his wallet. He pulls out two insurance cards. Hallelujah.

He completes the forms as I gaze around the room at all the sick people. There is a lot of blood and crying and suffering going on in this room. And it's Salsa Tuesdays. Hardly seems fair to be missing it, but I suppose sometimes we have to lend a helping hand. Okay, it's my fault. OKAY, it's *my fault*. I'll admit it. But only to myself.

I take Frank's paperwork up to the desk and take a seat near him (adjacent—safer this way). We make some small talk. The weather, the class, our jobs. Then—

"Uh, yeah, well," he clears his throat, "I've noticed you in class. I mean," he clears his throat, "I've had my eye on you for quite some time," he clears his throat, "and I've been meaning to ask you," he clears his throat.

"Would you like some water," I blurt out. It seems like a nice gesture on my part. It also seems like a survival tactic, as I don't like where this conversation is heading—please, please don't ask me if I—

"Would you like to go out sometime?" He finally gets it out.

I wish I could say that I didn't hear him. For some reason, he started to speak louder, like the spiked heel in his foot, forced out a blockage that had been living in his throat for centuries. Whatever the reason, it is a bad thing. I liked Frank so much better when he was Dweebie Whisperer. And not asking me out.

"Uh, well, Frank," I start, but am saved by someone in blue scrubs saying, "Frank Oppenheimer."

I love this person, whoever he is. I turn to the man, and give him a full-on smile. He looks at me like he thinks perhaps I am in need of a Psych Consult, but when Frank manages to get himself up—I am too busy smiling to be bothered with Frank now—the blue scrubbed man forgets all about me and has eyes only for his patient.

I help Frank get to Blue Scrubs and off they go. I take this opportunity to look into my wallet, my empty wallet. I take out my Metrocard, a one month unlimited, that has a day left on it, so if Frank can hurry it along and get out of here by midnight—roughly one hour, forty-two minutes, he will have a free subway ride home—on me. Otherwise, well…I can't really say. Of course I'm not considering the fact that Frank will be walking on one foot and the subway will be a difficult way to travel. But, hey, that's all I've got—besides my new monthly metrocard that I clearly need. Besides, his foot problem does not equal a payment of a whole month of free subway rides. I'm sorry, but it just doesn't. I spent my last dollars on the cab ride here. He can't expect me to pay for two cabs in one day! Come on.

I know that it's bad of me to leave him here alone. But I can't risk that he'll remember where we left off and ask me out again, and if there is even one iota of guilt still lingering, I may just say yes. And I can't chance it. I can't be trusted. I have to get out of here and pronto.

I leave the Metrocard and a nice note at the nurse's station.

So much for Salsa Tuesdays. Now I'll have to switch days. Damn.

CHAPTER 4

"Hey," I say to Alan.

I'm at work and he's on the phone.

"Hey yourself. I was thinking, maybe we should get together before the awards. I mean, just to break the ice."

Was he asking me out on another date? Before we even had our first date? I must really be desirable. Or he wants to see if he needs to find a replacement for me before Awards Day. Either way, I'm up for it.

"Okay. Sounds good. When and where?" I say.

"How about tonight? I can pick you up at your job."

It is Friday night. Not having previous plans will make me look desperate. Then again, tomorrow I have to shop for my dress for the Awards, so I guess it's now or never.

I look down at my attire. Dress-down day at work. I look like a construction worker in my faded jeans and oversized man's shirt. Whatever. This will just make me look that much better in my formal. *Right*.

"Sounds good," I tell him.

I primp for nearly a half-hour before we meet, but nothing's gonna change this lumberjack uniform I'm sportin'. I give up and head to the lobby of the building.

Waiting there is a clean shaven man who resembles Alan, but I have to do a double-take to be sure. Normally, he wears a goatee, which is pretty sexy. I also saw him sport a beard on occasion, but clean-shaven? Never. And I never want to again, that's for sure. His face is massive-looking without hair.

We hug each other awkwardly and set off to the theatre.

"This is supposed to be really good," I say as we make our way to the Screening Room.

"*Laurel Canyon*, yeah, I think it's gotten good reviews," he adds.

We have almost forty minutes before the movie starts, so we decide to sit in the bar and have a drink.

"What would you like?" Alan asks me.

"I don't drink," I tell him.

"Nothing. Ever?" he teases.

I laugh and nearly slip from my barstool. I grab the handrail and make a last minute save, pretending that I was just shifting…oh, the deception dating brings about.

"Alcohol. I don't drink alcohol anymore."

"Is there a 12-step program involved or you just decided it wasn't for you?" He asks, sounding truly interested.

"Well, it wasn't serving me in any way and I have a low tolerance. I've even blacked-out, so I decided to stop all together."

Okay, stop talking, I tell myself. I can't believe I'm admitting all of this on a first date. It's like, it just feels right. Maybe that's why I've been alone so long? Because I wasn't ready to get serious?

Note to Self: Only ask questions on first dates. Reveal nothing of yourself.

"I don't really need it," I tell Alan, referring to the liquor. "I have just as good a time without it." Okay, enough already. I pause and then ask, "Does that bother you?"

Quit talking I tell myself again.

"No, not at all. As long as my drinking doesn't bother you, I'm good with it."

He orders a second beer and chugs it down before we enter the theatre.

We share a popcorn and I act like a lady—not the piggy I am—while eating it.

Alan holds my hand, and though I try, I can't control the clamminess. It's like we're never out of the teenage stage when it comes to a first date.

We enjoy the movie and though it's only 10:30, I want to get home. I have a big day planned for tomorrow with the shopping.

Alan takes me to the Port Authority to get my bus. I live in New Jersey in a condo with my friend, Dai. I commute into New York City most days though.

Alan actually gets off the subway and walks me to the gate.

"You really don't have to," I tell him repeatedly.

"I know that. I want to. I've got nowhere else to be," He says.

We hold hands all the way to the gate. When we arrive, my bus is already there, so I have to run to catch it.

"I'll be out shopping all day tomorrow," I remind Alan. "But I'll call you when I get home," I tell him.

I don't own a cell phone. I tried it once, but the damn thing kept cutting out and I got frustrated and threw it in the toilet and I never bothered to replace it. I know, I'm the only person on earth without one!

"Okay, I'll talk to you then," he tells me.

And then it happens. The Kiss. He kisses me. I am taken off-guard. It is an open-mouthed kiss, but no tongue and absolutely no reciprocation from me. I'm not ready. I'd like to do it again. Take Two please. And then I am off and on the bus. And I feel awful. How could I do that? I was just too nervous and there were all of these people and, and, oh, he hates me now! He probably doesn't want to take me now at all! What have I done?

Another sleepless night. This time no Bastard Casting People munching on me, but instead Alan blowing me kisses, one after another after another. I can't seem to catch a one.

Saturday is a blur of shopping, shopping, shopping. I think I hit every mall in the North Jersey area and then some. I'm exhausted as is my credit card.

I end up buying two dresses—both black, of course, not knowing which is more suitable since I don't have a girlfriend accompanying me. I called Anne-Marie and asked her to go, but it was last minute and she had a family obligation. So that left just me shuffling from store to store.

"What do you think?" I ask my roommate, male and older with little fashion sense.

"Nice." He states without looking up from his Gameboy—some things boys never grow out of...most things, in fact.

"Duh, you didn't even look," I say and snatch the toy away.

"Okay, let me see. Nice. You look nice. Stunning really."

"Okay, don't move, I have to show you the other one," I say and race into my room to change.

"Give me back my game then." He yells after me.

I change quickly and come back out. "Well?"

"Hmm...I think I like the other one better. This is nice too, but maybe the other one."

That decides it. I go with the second one and hand him back his toy.

As the day lingers on, I get more and more concerned. I may have nothing to be fussing over anyway. I mean I haven't heard from Alan all day. I'm sure he's supposed to call me and after the kissing debacle I am reluctant to call him. And I hate calling guys. They should call us. End of story.

Finally at 8:30 I receive a call. Alan.

"Hey, how are you?"

"I'm good," I say relieved to hear his voice, if only to tell me that he wants nothing more to do with me.

"What's up? Did you just get home from shopping?"

I laugh. "I was waiting for you to call. I thought you said that you were going to call me?"

"No, you said that you'd be shopping all day and that you'd call when you got in."

Reasonable explanation and of course I don't remember because I was so hyped up at the Port Authority I could barely breathe.

"Sorry about that. I didn't remember."

"No big deal," he says.

"Uh, about last night," I start. "I was just surprised and I didn't know that you were going to kiss me and I didn't mean..."

"Stop," he says. "I understand. You were in a rush and were nervous. Don't worry about it." After a pause. "So did you get what you need for tomorrow?"

"I think so. I guess you'll be the judge."

We decide to meet across the street from the reception hall. This will be a long evening. The bar, then the reception hall and then the actual award ceremony, which is held at another venue all together, and an after party at yet another locale.

So when I purchased shoes, it was even more of a big deal. See, it's only May and can be quite chilly at night and I don't like nylons with open-toe shoes—though Anne-Marie wears them all the time that way—yuck!—and I thought I should wear nylons to an event such as this, although I am now noticing that they sometimes go bare-legged at the Oscars, so I'm now re-thinking my opinion on this completely. So, I ended up buying the only dressy non-open-toed shoe I could find. Unfortunately, they are mules. It's not that I don't like mules, but with nylons...my concern with these, of course is that I may slide right out of them. I warn Alan of this on the telephone, so he can be ready to grab me and my shoe—in that order—should a situation occur (with me it does more often than not).

He laughs, "You women and your shoes. Okay, no problem. Got it. Save you then the shoes."

A sigh of relief, "Thank you. See you tomorrow."

CHAPTER 5

D-Day. I feel like I'm getting married. Except there are no throngs of people helping with my dress, fussing with my hair, or applying my make-up. I do speak with Anne-Marie before the big event though.

"So, you all ready, girl?" she asks.

"Not even close," I admit.

"What's the hold up?"

"My hair, my make-up, my dress...basically everything. I just can't seem to get it together. My make-up...ugh...I re-apply and re-apply and before long I'll be wearing as much as Tammy Faye. My hair doesn't want to cooperate. I bought these roses, they're black and they clip in my hair. I think I'm only going to be able to wear one though, since the other broke and I don't have time to glue it."

She giggles. "Just try and chill girl. You are gonna look fabulous. I know it! You'll knock his socks off!"

I laugh. Only Anne-Marie can get away with an expression like, 'You'll knock his socks off' and make it genuine.

I tell her, "You're crazy. Thanks for the pep talk. I gotta go or I'll be late."

And late I am. I get stuck in traffic on the George Washington Bridge. I have my roommate's cellular with me so I call to let Alan know that I'm running late and he should just go to the reception hall without me and I will join him there. I don't get him though. I leave three voicemail messages.

When I finally arrive, I am only twelve minutes late, so I decide to try the bar where we were scheduled to meet first. I feel self-conscious as I walk along 46th Street. It's May, a beautiful sunny day, late afternoon, tons of people out in cropped pants and shorts and here I am in a semi-formal. Self-conscious, uh, yeah.

I walk into Joe Allen's and make my way to him. He doesn't see me at first. He has his back to me, toward the end of the bar, talking quietly with the bartender. The place is surprisingly packed for such an early hour. The bartender motions him and he turns and sees me. It is my favorite moment.

He pauses, takes me in, all of me and then says in what I construe as a booming voice, "Turn around."

I blush. All of the patrons are now staring at me and awaiting my twirl. I abide and do a full once-around for all to see. He beams.

He says, "You're beautiful. I love the rose...the shawl. It's very Spanish" (just wait til he sees me Salsa!). People stare and we make our way out of the bar.

"I called to say that I was running late, but you didn't answer."

He pulls out his phone, sees there are three messages from me and smiles. "I didn't hear it."

We only have to go across the street to join the others. The others being the director, producers, and actors from the show. Before we join them, we stand outside the bar for a moment and look at each other. I don't want any awkwardness tonight. No Port Authority moments.

We come together. We kiss. A real kiss. I am completely present. I kiss him again. And again. And we kiss a final long, lingering kiss.

I suppose this is the moment that I fall in love with him. I'm not exactly sure why. I mean, yes, he's sweet and intelligent, and talented and funny. But surely there are many men out there like that. But they are not standing next to me. Alan is.

The reception hall is held in the home of a very exclusive restaurant on Restaurant Row, one I have never frequented before. It has two levels with a bar downstairs and a buffet and several rooms upstairs. We get drinks, mingle, and head upstairs.

"Oh, look, that's Kathleen Everglow," I say to Alan.

He nods. "Yep. And look who that is," he gestures toward an elderly couple, Mia Phillips and Jed Napson. They have been around forever. Broadway Royalty, that's what they are.

I take a seat on the padded bench that runs the length of the wall. Anticipating the long night in these shoes, I take advantage. Alan sits next to me. We enjoy our drinks and take it all in.

"Is this what you thought it would be like?" I ask him.

"Yeah, I suppose. It's all the same, really, isn't it."

I'm not sure what he means, but I nod my head anyway.

Suddenly, Alan gets up and kneels down in front of me. I look at him and wonder what the hell has gotten into him. As if reading my thoughts, he says, "I couldn't see you from over there."

"Well, we can go in there," I say and point toward another room down the hall.

He shakes his head. "No."

Though I am confused and embarrassed, part of me is flattered. The man is down on his knees in front of me in a posh reception hall. Even if I tried, I couldn't resist being sucked in by it all.

Soon we are carted off to the award ceremony, which is being held at the performing arts high school up town. They have all of the attendees board double-decker buses to be transported.

As I step onto the bus, Alan says, "Up top, up top."

"It's getting chilly though," I point out.

"I'll keep you warm. It's not that far. Up top."

So I climb to the top level, we take seats and watch the city below. Alan takes off his suit jacket and puts it around my shoulders. Half-way through the trip, he plucks a flower off of a passing tree and does a, "she loves me, she loves me not," the last leaf stopping, of course, on the "she loves me" part—couldn't have happened any other way…not on this night. I smile, my face aglow.

We await our turn to de-board. Alan is close behind me. I hear it, but it's when I feel it that I can't deny it—that is, my thong underwear declaring a 'SNAP'. I can't believe this. The man just snapped my thong. I turn and give him a hard pinch in the side—warranting an 'Ow'—nod my head in a 'serves you right' kind of way and make my way to the ground.

We have a full half-hour before the ceremony begins, so Alan makes a couple of phone calls—one to his mother in Florida...puts me on the phone with her. Then to his best buddy in Long Island...puts me on the phone with him. I am not at all comfortable with this. It's too much, too fast. I feel as if I've been with him for years and it's only been two, rather one and a half dates.

We start to our seats, but Alan grabs my hand and pulls me behind some rafters. He kisses me. And there I am making out with him, loving it, wondering why I have denied myself this pleasure for so long.

"I need to run to the Ladies before it starts," I say as I push Alan off of me. He is leaning on my body, my back up against a wall.

"Okay. Hurry up," he says.

I wipe his lips, taking my lipstick with me. I find the Ladies room, which is never hard to miss...just look for the line.

"Looks like someone's been doing a lot of kissing," the elderly woman in front of me says in my direction.

My face starts to redden and I turn away, hoping no one else will notice. The last thing I need is to look like a hussy tonight. Any other night...well alright.

The awards ceremony is much like the ones you see on TV. Too long. Alan doesn't win. Though he expected this, so no crushing defeat.

We walk to the After Party. Apparently these nights never end...either you've won and need to celebrate your victory or you've lost and need to forget it. Either way, a reason to party on.

"How're your shoes holding up?" he asks as we cross 61st Street.

"Pretty well," I say. "I only had one close call and I was able to slide back into it unnoticed."

The party turns out to be surprisingly tame. I figured there would be some juicy gossip for page six, but apparently the exhibitionists went elsewhere. Damn.

We take seats at a table designated for his group. I say hello to the producers, director, and actors, most of whom I have already met.

There is one guy, an actor it turns out, whom I haven't yet met.

"Alan, this your date?" he asks, gesturing toward me.

Alan nods.

"Yep. Rob, this is Samantha."

We shake hands.

Rob then says, "I thought you were gay."

He says this to Alan, not me.

"Uh, nope. I'm not."

Clearly.

Rob shakes his head, "Could've fooled me."

We all laugh.

The table nearly empties. People have gone for drinks or to congratulate a winner or possibly stop a non-winner from slitting his wrists. Alan and I sit with two others, who are seated on the other side of the table.

Alan looks at me, crinkles his nose and says suddenly, "Did you let a stinky one?"

What? What did he say! Did I...let a stinky one? My face heats from embarrassment, I say, "No. But I can't believe you just asked me that."

"Well, something smells a little foul." He smiles and then adds, "Invent nothing, deny nothing. That's the acting rule and that's the life rule."

CHAPTER 6

"Samantha, oh Samantha dear," a deep singing voice, clearly off-key wakes me out of my sound stupor. It's Dai, my roommate. I open one eye, see that it's 11:03, throw the covers off of me, leap up and dash into the bathroom.

It's not until I'm under the shower, head full of shampoo that I realize I'm off work today. I emerge ten minutes later, scrubbed clean, smelling of cucumber and avocado…makes me fear a giant weevil mistakening me for dinner.

I pad into the kitchen, dump some corn flakes and milk into a bowl, and head back into the living room. There sits Dai, at the computer desk playing a World War II game.

"Damn Nazis," he yells at the screen.

"They winning," I ask.

"Wie ein Held zum ziegen," is his reply.

I'm used to this by now. Dai speaks German, Spanish, some French, and is currently studying Japanese, so he often utters things that have absolutely no meaning to me whatsoever. I pretend they're compliments.

I shake my head and take a seat on the couch. I look at Dai for a moment and study him. He's one of those annoying people who think they know everything and even more annoyingly, often he does.

When I was in college, Dai used to like to quiz me. One day while I was reviewing for an exam in a history course, I mentioned that the Battle of Gettysburg was in 1864. He about had a coronary. Literally. His face turned red. He was unable to speak. I couldn't figure out what was wrong, but I had the phone in my hand dialing 911 when he finally found his voice and explained that Gettysburg was in 1863 and only a buffoon would think otherwise.

Salsa with the Pope

I look up. Dai is grinning at me. Oh boy.

"Good morning Dai." I say a little too friendly, trying to ward off the remarks that I know will be forthcoming. He can't help himself.

"Well, good morning to you too, Ms. Par-tay Girl. I see you brought home some lovely flowers," he gestures to the red roses sitting in the middle of the table. A parting gift from Alan last night. What can I say? The guy is good.

"Can I take this to mean you had a nice time?" Dai asks and then smiles his most sarcastic grin.

"Yes, it was very nice," I say.

"Getting married yet?" Dai asks.

He associates all good times with getting married. If I'm not getting married, it's not as good a time as it could be.

"Not yet," I answer.

"Oh, but there's hope. I can tell by your demeanor. In love already, huh?"

It pisses me off that Dai can read me so well.

"No," I lie.

I place my bowl on the floor so that Booty can have the last of the milk. She's our other roommate. Yes, we make a strange household, Dai the intellectual recluse, me the quirky actor, and Booty Miss, my sixteen pound feline whose favorite pastimes are drinking from the bathroom faucet and licking books.

Can't choose your family.

I lounge around the house for the better part of the day, stopping occasionally to work on my monologue for tonight's class.

It's my last Script Analysis class. The last time Alan will be my teacher. And though I've had all day to prepare, now that it's time to go, I'm late. I know, you're surprised.

I rush out the door only to have Dai call me back.

"Your mother. Sounds important."

I run back in, drop my black tote and grab the phone.

"Hey, what's up," I say a little more breathless than I feel, hoping that she will surmise that I am running out the door, too busy to be bothered by trivial matters...okay, it's mean of me, and a little manipulative...I admit it.

"It's these damn cats," she says.

I take it back. It's not mean or manipulative. It's necessary.

"What now," I say, feeling obligated to ask.

"Well, it looks like Flossy's in heat."

Good for Flossy, I think. I say instead, "Good for you," knowing that my mother has been trying to breed her two Himalayans.

"No, no, not so good," she answers.

I glance at my watch and sigh. I am confused. My mother has been trying to get these damn cats together for months.

"Why," I whine, not giving a shit, but knowing that this is the path of least resistance...otherwise, I could be on here playing word games for hours.

"Because Oscar De La Renta seems to have answered the call," my mother tells me frantically.

Ah, I get it. See, Oscar De La Renta is my mom's *other* cat, the alley cat (like a step-child, but not). Flossy is only to be bred by White Nugget, the Himalayan (the prince, not the gardener...get it?).

"Oh, I'm sorry to hear that, mom," I say using my best sympathy voice.

"Yeah, well, I'm not sure, so I bought one of those First-To-Know pregnancy tests hoping that they will work on the feline persuasion too. What do you think?"

She really doesn't want to know that I think. I think she's nuts. And despite my tardiness, I can't help but stop and visualize my mother on her hands and knees, pregnancy stick in hand, chasing Flossy around the litter box, in an attempt to get her to piss on a stick. *Right.*

"Ah, not sure mom. I'll ask around though. Sorry, but I really do have to go. I'll call you." I disconnect, but the image remains.

I race out of the apartment and hit the highway zooming. I make decent time, leave the car in a self-park and trot to class, adjusting my undergarments en route.

Salsa with the Pope

Damn panties…I'm not wearing a thong, but I might as well be, as this pair of bikinis has found residence in my crack and is hell bent on staying there. Ugh!

I am nervous in class. More so than usual. I want to do well and feel that if I don't, it's a reflection on Alan somehow. Not as his student, but as his girlfriend. His girlfriend? Already? Uh, oh.

I muddle through, perform my monologue, tell my damn husband that the jig is up and I will not be a punching bag any longer—well, words to that effect.

I am relieved and delighted when we all adjourn to a local pub for food and drink afterwards.

"Sam was my date for the Drama Desk Awards last night," Alan tells the group midway through mozzarella sticks and wings.

I beam. I can't help it. I really like this guy. I am seriously falling for this guy…I know, I know, I said I was in love with him—but that was just prattle, but this, this feels for real. No joke. Damn.

We finish our meal. Alan pays for us both—a definite 'girl-friend' sign—see, I'm not imagining it. He and I make our way to the door. He's going to walk me to my car to say good-bye. I am sad. He is leaving for Florida for a whole week and a half. Yep, tomorrow, he goes to visit his family.

Pam stops us at the exit.

"You're coming back?" she asks Alan.

"Yeah, I just want to walk Sam out."

Pam then looks at me and smiles.

"We'll talk." She says.

I almost ask her 'about what', but decide better of it.

I'm leaning up against the car, Alan hovering over me. His mouth on mine. I'm getting used to this. I really am.

"I better go and you better get back in there or they're going to start talking." I say in between smooches.

"Let'em talk." He says.

I pull away from him.

"So, you'll be back on the 20th?" I ask.

"Yep. But I'll call you from Florida."

CHAPTER 7

True to his word, Alan does call me. Every night for the entire ten days. And these are not just little chit-chats, these are four-hour conversations that last into the wee morning hours. Career, family, world views...we leave no stone unturned. These conversations delude me into thinking we know each other.

I reason that when you're on the phone with someone, you listen more carefully than when you're seated next to him...bodies touching, lips moving, mind distracted by musky cologne or tight-fitting Levi's.

It is Thursday. I am just falling into bed, my first time turning in early all week. Though Alan and I speak late as a rule, tonight is the exception, as he has a family outing. Thus, I feel safe to head to bed without fear of interruption.

The phone starts singing almost immediately. Obviously I was wrong.

It's Alan.

"I can't really talk. We're on our way out to dinner, but I wanted to let you know that I'm wearing my jacket. And I found it."

Huh? I don't have the faintest idea what he's talking about. Probably because I'm tired. I rub my eyes, take a sip of water, and think. Nope. No idea.

"What?" I say.

"From the awards. Your hair clip, the rose," he tells me.

Ah, the rose. It had fallen out of my hair while he was carrying me to my car—yes, at one point, he picked me up and carried me part-way to my car—I told you it was a magical evening. I had put the rose in the pocket of his jacket, which I had been wearing at the time.

"Oh, I forgot to get it," I tell him, wondering why this is so important that he needed to call me now.

"I thought you put it in there on purpose, so that I would remember you while I was away," he tells me.

I laugh. "No."

"You ruined it, silly."

His voice takes on a different quality, almost like he's angry. He then says, "It was so romantic the other way."

But not true.

I get off the phone quickly, claiming exhaustion, which isn't too hard, as I've racked up a whopping 24 hours of sleep in the last five days. I crawl into bed, get comfy and snug knowing sleep is only moments away…but it won't come. I've been dreaming about sleep all week and now, I'm wide awake.

I keep hearing the phone call in my head. Over and over again. Why would he be angry that I didn't leave the clip in his pocket on purpose? I ruined it? What the hell does that mean? Ruined what? His illusion?

This reminds me of the discussion Pam and I had earlier in the week. I was attending an audition for a new play LP is producing.

"You wanna go grab a cup of coffee?" Pam asked me as I was leaving the room.

"Now?" I asked.

"Well, we have one more person to see, but that won't take long. Unless you have someplace else to be…"

"No, I'd like that. I'll just wait outside."

After saying good-bye to Liza, Pam and I ventured to a nearby COSI and took a corner table.

"You did a really nice job in there today." She told me.

She had seen me perform the piece before, in class. That day, she came up to me and said it made her cry. Obviously it wasn't having that same effect on her today. Her eyes look dry as a bone.

"Thanks. It's kind of intense, but it seems to work. I actually adapted it from a book I read."

Our conversation lasted almost two hours. She talked about her life, LP, and her relationships. It was on her second cup of coffee that she told me, "I have to confess, I actually was kind of attracted to Alan. When I first met him," she added.

This completely took me by surprise, not so much that she was attracted to him, but that she was admitting it to me.

"Really?" I said.

"Yeah. You don't have to worry though, I mean I'm not into him at all...that way... now. Not that he would even think of me when you're in the picture."

"No, no, I don't...it's....I'm not worried." I took a sip of my hot cocoa. "Did he know you felt that way?"

"Uh, I pretty much made it known. I mean, after a while. He didn't seem to be responding to the signs...the flirting I was doing, so yeah, I finally just made an all-out pass at him."

My eyes grew big. Wow!

"And," I asked, "how did he react to that?"

"He didn't."

"What'd you mean, he didn't?" I said.

"He just...it was like he was asexual or something. He seemed to get this silent anger thing, but he didn't want to show it, so he just did nothing."

She brought her mug up to her mouth, but at the last minute decided against a drink and added, "You know, that's not fair. That's just my bruised ego talking. He was just not interested. Obviously. End of story. I mean we know he's not asexual...he's with you, and totally into you."

She smiled and took a sip of her coffee. "Have you talked to him since he left?"

I nodded. "Yeah. Every night."

"Every night?" She smiled. "See? What'd I tell you?"

CHAPTER 8

I am early for an appointment. For once. Don't know how it happened. And you wouldn't believe what it's for…certainly not something you'd think I'd want to be early for…it's my GYN exam. I've had it scheduled for months and I actually remembered—a miracle in itself—and I'm early. Ha.

As I sit reading *New Mothers* magazine—the choices are limited alright…it's either that or *Nine Months of Hell*—okay it's called *Nine Months of Bliss*, but I like to improvise…I'm about to be traumatized, alright…okay, I'm exaggerating. Though I do know women who act like going for your exam is like heading to the gas chamber…I'm not one of those…thank you very much.

In fact, I figured that this would work out pretty well, as Alan will be returning tomorrow and sex has got to be on the roster sooner or later. So it's always nice to have a clean bill of health regarding your tootle—remember, that's my vagina to all you purists out there.

"Samantha, you want to follow me." That's what Betty the nurse says. Obviously it's rhetorical. No, I don't want to follow you, Betty. But I do.

I stand on the scale and close my eyes. I do the same thing for horror movies. The sensations are actually quite similar. Nervous, scared, sweating…yep, very much the same.

"Okay, a hundred and…"

"AHHH, don't say it!" I tell Betty, wondering what is happening with her that she's forgotten the golden rule with me and the scale. We are certainly not on speaking terms, the scale and I. Betty…lest you forget.

"Sorry, sorry Sam, forgot."

She takes me to Room Three, places a paper napkin on the upright bench, instructs me to put it on with the opening in the front. Now what is the point of this exactly? I mean, that's like lingerie that covers only your elbows…it's hardly necessary.

I put the napkin on the window ledge and discard all my clothes—save my socks. Not only do they make me feel more secure, they actually do keep me a bit warmer. It's always freezing in these rooms.

I lie down, pull the sheet up over me, and stare at the cracks in the ceiling. I start to doze off. Betty stops this.

"Sam, uh, there's been an emergency. Dr. Katz had to go deliver a baby, so her physician assistant is here, if you want to go ahead and do it and not have to wait."

I look at Betty. First she almost tells me my weight—*tells me my weight, dammit*, and now the doctor had to go deliver a frickin' baby. What the hell.

"Okay, Betty." I tell her.

Let's just get this over with.

Tootle does not like to be exposed any longer than she has to be.

Almost immediately—what was she listening at the door—a young woman with bright orange hair—okay red, but it looks orange I'm telling you—enters the room. She wears large round spectacles and olive green corduroys.

"Hi, I'm Nancy Restard," she says and shakes my hand. Her hands are as cold as mine. I hope she warms them up before going pokin' in there.

"Hello," I manage.

And so it begins. Nancy takes a seat on the 'doctor stool' and Betty stands behind her, looking bored. I guess once you've seen one tootle, you've seen them all. Wonder why men don't feel that way.

I assume the position, sheet pushed out of the way, legs wide apart, feet stirruped, but no horse in sight.

"Okay, so you're going to feel a little pressure…that's my hand."

Her hand is still cold, even through the gloves. And tootle is not happy.

"And now the speculum."

Okay, my head is back, and as I'm not a contortionist, I cannot see what is going on down there. All I know is I feel the tightness of the speculum and then all the sudden, WHAM! The instrument literally ricochets out of my body and hits the wall behind Betty's head. Fortunately Betty has good reflexes or she would have been accosted by a flying speculum.

"What the hell?!" I say before I can stop myself.

Not that I should need to stop myself. This is a completely appropriate response to speculum ricochet.

"Oh, uh, I'm not sure what happened there. Uh, you're not hurt are you?" Nancy looks at me, like she's wishing and praying that I say, it's fine and tootle is in fact, in even better shape than before we started this whole debacle.

I nod.

"Let's just get this over with." I say in a low voice.

Nancy gathers a new instrument—no one wants a speculum that has malfunctioned, almost taken a woman's head off, and hit a wall—in their tootle.

"Okay, here we go," Nancy says as if we're starting a new hand of Uno.

I feel the speculum, the tightness, and although it doesn't recoil from my body at a high velocity, I can feel that it wants to. It is pulsing and bouncing against Nancy's hand. She is holding it in, but had she not been, it would fly out of me once again.

"Okay," I say in my most calm voice. "I need you to be away from me now."

Nancy seems to understand—perhaps she's had other speculum mishaps in her career—nods and exits the room. Betty and I look at each other in horror, then burst out laughing.

Gotta have a sense of humor about your tootle.

CHAPTER 9

Ten days have finally gone by. I am going to see Alan. Tonight.

I take over the left faucet and mirror at work and primp for the better part of an hour. Anne-Marie, ever-loving friend, finds me there just before I am about to leave.

"What in the world…are you still in here? You're going to be late!" She says when she spies me still standing in front of the mirror.

"How can I be late, when we're meeting here?" I point out.

"Ah, here, huh? Maybe I can meet Mr. Wonderful then?" She says teasingly.

"We'll see," I play along.

Actually I haven't even thought about anyone meeting him yet, though Dai has brought it up at least a dozen times since the first date. He fancies himself my stand-in father and likes to scrutinize—and does—each man I bring home. I was putting him off in the fond hope that Alan would get sucked into a black hole before that ill-fated meeting. So far, no luck.

"Okay, how do I look?" I ask Anne-Marie who is taking a load off in the only chair we keep in the restroom. Not really sure why we keep one in there, unless it's to put your papers or files on, like you have to go *right* then and can't be bothered going back to your desk to drop off files. No, you must pee now!

"The same as the last time you asked."

I give her a stunned look.

"Gorgeous of course," she yells and comes and gives me a big hug. "You just remember, he's the lucky one."

And with that we are off.

Alan is approaching the building when we exit. I see him two blocks up. All of the sudden there are rocks in my stomach. Dozens of them. They're doing a jig and I can't will them to stop. Oh, please, no getting sick. Not in front of Alan. Not on these shoes, even if they do have a tendency to give me blisters.

He waves his arm like he's a million miles away. I wave back. Anne-Marie steps to the side leaving us to make fools of ourselves.

First, there is the recognition, the reminding myself of what he looks like…dark curly hair, intense chocolate brown eyes—did I mention that I LOVE chocolate—and a dimple placed right in the center of his chin. His goatee covers it up, but I know it's there and it's in the knowing that I find sexy.

We embrace for a long moment and then look at each other and kiss lightly. We then kiss again and when he goes in for a third I am reminded that Anne-Marie is just two feet away. I look over at her and she grins and turns away. I take Alan's hand and pull him to her.

"This is Alan. And this," I say and pull her toward us, "is my best girlfriend, Anne-Marie."

They look at each other and shake hands. Something happens. It's instantaneous. It's like electricity…no, more like she is a medium and is getting something from his hand, some sort of premonition or intuition. And it's not good.

"Nice to meet you," she says and smiles.

But it's not genuine. Of this I know. I have known Anne-Marie for years and she is famous for her sunny disposition. She literally lights up a room with her smile and outgoing personality (no she's not Mary Tyler Moore—I told you, she's Hispanic). That's the upside. The downside is that when she is not feeling well, be it depressed or ill, it is very difficult for her to hide it. Similar to that happening, this is not good, yet I don't know why.

"Nice to meet you too," Alan says and I know, know somehow, that he picks something up from her too. Something that threatens him somehow.

I'm not sure what just happened, only know that it is not good, so I say, "Well, we better get going. See you tomorrow."

I hug Anne-Marie good-bye and Alan says, "Bye. See you again."

We begin walking downtown, holding hands and avoiding the topic of whatever just happened.

CHAPTER 10

I am at work the next day, trying to catch up on things…not sure how I got behind. I haven't missed any days. I've been here. In body at least. I guess that's it. You have to bring your mind along with you or you don't get full-credit. Now you tell me.

I look up and Anne-Marie is standing beside my cubicle, small grin on her face. She looks like the cat that swallowed the canary. Not sure why. Then it comes back to me. Last evening. She and Alan meeting. I had forgotten all about it. Sure at the time it seemed like a big deal, but that lasted all of thirty seconds.

Once we got to the Mexican restaurant—my favorite—and started catching up and staring at each other….rather Alan staring at me, I lost all awareness of the world around me.

"You do realize that you haven't looked at me once during this entire meal," he finally said.

I looked up at him briefly, averted my eyes and said, "What do you mean?"

He took my chin in his hand and held my face up to his, "What do I mean? This is what I mean. Are you embarrassed?"

Shit. Now what? Lie. "Of course not."

"Uh, huh." He laughed and then kissed me lightly.

What was it with this guy. I mean that I would be so embarrassed that I couldn't even look at him during dinner? That I couldn't eat in front of him? How was I ever going to bear his children? Or have sex with him, more importantly?? In the dark? Blah!

We walked to Westside Park and lay there on the grass with his jacket beneath us. His head lay in my lap and I ran my fingers through his hair—or tried to at least…got my fingers caught twice, but was able to get them out without yanking any curls by the root—thankfully. We smooched and breathed. It was so peaceful and relaxing. That is until we left.

As we made our way out, we ran into a colleague of mine, Roger Warner. I introduce the men, as proper etiquette demands, and thinking back to the introductions between Anne-Marie and Alan, I thought this could never be worse than that. But never, NEVER think like that, lest you a fool!

And all seems fine at first...they shake hands, say hello. But before I can get Alan out of there, Roger says...Get this...he says, "Oh, I'm so glad I ran into you Sam. Yeah, I heard that you'd met someone and were falling in love."

Murder. That's what I saw in my eyes right then. Me murdering Roger. Right there in Westside Park.

I smiled between clenched teeth and guided Alan off in the opposite direction.

"It's okay, y'know," Alan said after a few moments.

"What?" I asked, really hoping he was referring to something other than the encounter with Roger. Dead Roger. That's what I will forever refer to him as.

"What he said. If that's what you're feeling, it's okay. I'm good with it."

What exactly did that mean? That he was *good with it*. That he was good with me falling in love with him or that he was falling in love with me too?

I decided that clarification was not so important at that moment, so I just smiled and excused myself to the restroom, where I reapplied lipstick, which he kissed off moments later.

They really do need to come up with a kissable lipstick that isn't so dry that your lips feel like two-week old bologna after application.

I snap back into reality and see Anne-Marie still standing there.

"Earth to Samantha. Where you at, girl?"

I smile and stand to give her a big hug, our usual greeting. I'm glad to see that she seems the same. Not angry or resistant to me at all. Maybe I made the whole thing up. Maybe I was mistaken and there was nothing going on last evening when she met Alan.

"So," she begins. "How was last night? Your reunion date?"

I can't help but smile widely.

"It was wonderful. Really great. The whole evening. We just talked and ate."

Then I relay the incident with Roger and she laughs her ass off.

"I can't believe he said that," she finally says, eyes teary with laughter.

"Tell me about it. I really could have killed him right then and there."

I then tell her Alan's reaction and she seems to take it in, nods and then says nothing.

This is odd. I can't ignore it.

"What?" I say.

This is good, I reason, since she will tell me exactly what she feels in her own words with no prompting from me.

"What what?" She says.

Damn. That's even better and now I can hardly say, 'what, what, what'? I mean we just don't talk that way. Yes we are known to go, 'what what', but three 'whats' is one 'what' too many for sure. This puts the ball back in my court.

"Nothing. I was just wondering what was going on with you? What you were thinking?"

Okay, let's see what she says.

"Nothing."

That's it! She says, *nothing*. She says she was thinking *nothing*. Bullshit. I've known her way too long for her to be holding out on me. So I go for it.

"What is it? You didn't like him?"

Maybe I shouldn't have said it that way. It was prompting—exactly what I didn't want to do. And what if I was wrong?

"Not really." She says.

"What do you mean? You didn't *really* like him," I say knowing that I sound stunned, trying not to, although it's not working.

"Not so much."

I take Anne-Marie's hand and pull her into a conference room, shut and lock the door. This is serious business.

"What do you mean, you didn't like him much? Please cut the crap and just tell me why."

She knows I'm serious now. She looks away. After a moment she says, "I don't want to change the way you feel about him."

"Stop!" I yell. "We know each other better than that. Would you just tell me…"

"I got a bad vibe. Okay, I got a bad vibe, that's all."

She is now looking at me with pity. I hate that pity look from anyone.

"A bad vibe? What kind of bad vibe?" I ask.

"Sam, I don't know. It's not like I can see the future or something. I just didn't like the way he looked. Not his actual looks, but his mannerisms and the way he spoke. I could just tell that he wasn't sincere."

"That's odd since I was sure you were the one not being sincere last night," I say before I can stop myself.

"Well yeah, I mean he's your boyfriend. What did you want me to do? Tell him I could see right through him, so cut the crap." She slumps down into a chair. "I tried. I don't know what it is, but I just don't feel comfortable around him."

That quickly, she doesn't feel comfortable around him. It was like two seconds.

I am standing, looking out the window, wishing this conversation never started. Wishing I never introduced them.

"I don't trust him with you. I think he's going to hurt you. Use you…something." Anne-Marie's voice is quiet, regretful.

I look at her. I don't know what to say. I don't want to hear this. I can't hear it anymore.

"I'm outta here." I get up and walk out of the room.

Anne-Marie yells after me, "I hope I'm wrong about this."

CHAPTER 11

It is Friday night and I'm hopping around on one foot, trying desperately to find my other shoe while simultaneously putting on my jacket and heading for the bus.

"Samantha, what in the world are you doing?" Dai asks, as I hop by, the table jarring as I use it for balance.

"What does it look like? I'm trying to find my other shoe. Have you seen it?" I yell.

It isn't his fault. I know that, but sometimes I just get so aggravated with all of the comings and goings of my life that seeing Dai just sit there day in and day out, going out almost never, gets me angry. Like maybe I would like to do that sometimes too. But I wouldn't really. I would go nuts.

"I haven't seen your shoe, no. Maybe Booty has it."

Great. Now he's making jokes.

"Sure Dai, I'm sure she does."

I run into my room and drop down onto the floor a final time and try to see beyond the crap under my bed. I find my rollerblades that I haven't used in two years, a slew of old journals, and a pair of ripped stockings. No shoe.

"Oh, Saaammmmy, looky here," Dai sings.

"I don't have time for this," I say as I begin making my way back out into the living room.

Dangling from Dai's beefy hand is the mate to my shoe. Thank goodness.

"Where'd you find it?" I ask while shoving my foot into it.

"Around," is all Dai says. "What time is your bus?" He then asks.

I glanced at my watch and throw up my hands. "Two minutes ago."

"I'll take you in," he says and begins to put on his own shoes.

This is how our relationship has always been. Insulting, aggravating, annoying, tender, and supportive all at the same time. A strange team Dai and I, but somehow we make it work. In truth, I don't know where I'd be without him. He has been a mother, father, and mentor all in one. A truer friend could not be found.

I hope I'm as good a friend, but I fear it isn't so. I try, but sometimes my emotions, my own wants, get the best of me. Like today for instance.

I was picking up a few things at the store when a cellular phone began ringing. I was starting to get a little aggravated at the person who was not picking up her damn phone.

"Hello," I finally said.

Alright, I'm just not used to this damn thing yet.

"Sam, it's Anne."

Anne-Marie and I have been cordial, but cool with each other since our 'Alan discussion' earlier in the week.

"Anne-Marie, what's up?"

"I was just calling to see what you were going to wear tonight?"

"Well," I said, "I was thinking of wearing my navy turtleneck sweater and a light jacket. I don't want to look too flashy, I mean it is his family and I want to make a good impression."

Silence.

"Anne-Marie?"

Silence.

"Hello. Oh, these damn phones. See, this is why I never wanted to get one," I said as I pulled the phone from my ear and examined it for flaws. "They never work. Not really. Okay, for partial conversations, but what if you want to have a *whole* conversation? Then you—"

"Samantha, I'm still here," Anne-Marie finally said.

"Oh, where'd you go? This thing cut-out?" I asked.

She said, "No, it didn't cut-out, but apparently you are."

What the hell was she talking about? I was cutting-out?

Just then my brain blinked alive and I knew what she was talking about. Her brother's party. Tonight. It had been planned weeks ago, even before Alan and I started dating.

"Anne-Marie, I am so sorry. I completely forgot," I told her.

"So I see," she said with disdain.

"Your brother's party. I can't believe this. I totally forgot about it."

"So what are you doing instead?" She asked.

I didn't want to tell her, but I had no choice. I tried to sound less excited than I was.

"I'm going with Alan to his aunt and uncle's for dinner. This will be the first time I'm meeting any of his family and there's no way I can get out of it now."

Not that I wanted to. Maybe she didn't think he was right for me, but I felt just the opposite. And more so every time I was with him. We had something.

"I am truly sorry."

"So am I," she said. Then added sarcastically, "Have a nice time. I'm sure you'll impress the hell out of 'em."

I returned home, beautified, then headed for the city.

I am meeting Alan outside of his aunt and uncle's West Village Apartment. While I wait, I check out the neighborhood. God, it's gorgeous. Brick brownstones, quaint little shops, and small gardens abound. If only we could afford to live here. Someday. Someday, I tell myself.

I am nervous as hell. I want to make a good impression. I want to be smart and beautiful and have them accept me. But I'm scared.

Alan told me that they were both musicians and Kathleen had just gotten into banking. She spoke five languages and held a PhD, while his uncle was a musical genius. Great. A PhD and a genius. Nothing to be scared of...

"Ahhh," I leap what feels like three feet off the ground. Alan is behind me, unbeknownst to me, but now everyone, including people in New Jersey are aware of it.

I turn and swat him. "You scared the crap out of me."

"I noticed." He laughs. "Sorry. What're you so jumpy for?"

I tap-kiss his lips. "It's your family," I say, as if that explains everything.

"You'll be fine. Now, come on."

We enter the apartment and exchange introductions. Charlie, Alan's mother's brother, is shorter than Alan by a head with thick wavy gray hair. His face is pleasant, but it's his smile that wins you over in an instant. Kathleen is his opposite, tall and lean with short dark hair. She is a handsome woman dressed in business attire and low-heeled pumps. They're much younger than I anticipated.

"It's so good to finally meet you. We have been hearing so much about you," she says with a big smile.

I glance over at Alan, "Just good things I hope."

He gives a goofy look and says, "All good, except for that one thing, which we won't get into right now."

For one small instant my face falls and then I realize that he's teasing and I join the laughter and poke him lightly in the ribs.

"You're gettin' it," I say to which his response is, "Promises, promises."

I'm given the tour of the apartment, which doesn't take long as it's a small studio with a kitchen, bath and two adjacent rooms. We take a seat in the nicely furnished living area and have a drink before heading out for dinner.

The conversation runs from sports—Alan and Charlie are huge Yankee fans—to Kathleen's new Vice-President position and finally to music. I have nothing to contribute to this conversation…unless of course, they want to discuss '80's hair-bands.

Alan's phone rings repeatedly. He always takes the calls. He never leaves the room, but remains seated among us. Odd.

Probably out of not knowing what to say next, Charlie picks up a large drum, which I later find out is called a Conga, and begins rapping on it. Kathleen gets up and starts improvising on a flute. Alan gets off the phone and picks up the bongos.

Salsa with the Pope

Wow, dinner and a live concert just for me—now that's what I call entertainment. But it's not to be.

"Here, try this." Alan hands me a piece of wood and a stick.

"Huh," I say to him, trying to sound intelligent.

"It's a Cricket. You do it like this."

Alan takes the "instrument" from me and demonstrates.

He hands it back to me, I look at it more closely and decide that it's been misnamed—it looks much more like a snail than a cricket. I start to play it. Now we have a quartet of bongos, congas, flute, and cricket (snail). Not sure how pleasing to the ear we are, but it's mighty fun.

On our way to the restaurant, Alan and I walk arm and arm. He keeps playing with my hair, which is now getting longer as he talked me out of cutting it. He touches my face and kisses me full on the mouth. I'm embarrassed. His family is just steps ahead of us.

"You better be good," I say.

"Why? What if I wanna be bad?" He says.

I look at him. He's getting me hot.

"I love seeing you playin' the cricket in there. So cute you are. My little musical girlfriend."

He pinches my ass. He is clearly horny and here we are out with his family. It would have to wait. The weekend was coming though. *The* weekend that we had been planning since he returned from Florida.

Alan lives in Brooklyn in a small apartment with a roommate. He hates his living situation, and doesn't want to expose me to it. And since I live in Jersey with Dai, it's impossible for him to come home with me, so that left us in a bit of a quandary, as sex was going to have to be had at some point…wasn't it? So, he planned a weekend getaway for us at his best friend's cottage in upstate New York.

This would be the place that history would be made. Our sexual history. We would finally make love. I've fantasized about it and now it's finally going to happen. Just he and I in our naked glory. I know it will be wonderful. I mean how could it not be? I love him. He is so loving and sweet, so affectionate and caring, sex will just be the natural extension of this. I can hardly wait.

We catch up with Charlie and Kathleen just at they reach the restaurant. This little Italian place. Looks crowded, but I'm not bothered. It's like nothing bothers me when I'm with Alan.

Four different pastas, four different sauces and we share and pass around spoonfuls of each. Alan and Kathleen share a bottle of red wine, Charlie and I drink Perrier. We laugh our asses off. Until.

"Yeah, they're talking about another reading. A bigger one this time," Alan tells Kathleen and Charlie.

His play, *The Ghost of Dyckman Avenue* has already been through numerous re-writes and readings, but now they were attaching 'star' names to it and putting it up in a bigger venue, hoping to secure the needed investors to get it to Broadway.

Alan pushes his plate away and takes a long drink from his wine glass.

"Could I get a Sam Adams please," he asks a passing waiter.

Alan gets tense whenever the subject of his work comes up. And this is often. He talks about little else, and when we're out, we're always out with theatre people, so the topic seems inevitable.

"Maybe this time will be the one," Charlie says and pats Alan's hand.

Alan sighs. "Hmmm, maybe."

CHAPTER 12

I'm just stuffing the last items into my duffel bag when the phone rings. Again. Damn. I'm already running late. I got up in plenty of time. Plenty of time, but then my mother called and although I continued to get things together, you just can't focus on two tasks as intently as one no matter what anyone says. And now this. I grab the phone.

"Hello."

"Samantha. Oh, I'm so happy to hear your voice. I was afraid I might have missed you. Your mother told me that you were going out of town, but I wanted to wish you luck with your new fella."

It's my grandmother calling. Apparently word had gotten out that my cherry was going to be broken—again—this weekend and all of the female folk in my family were calling to congratulate me. Pathetic.

"Hey Gram," I say, knowing that I will now be at least a half hour late.

There is no getting off the phone quickly (in a polite manner) with my Gram. That's why I try to talk to her only four or five times a year. There's really no need to talk more because she has the tendency to have the same conversation each time you speak with her.

These conversations usually consist of gossip about the family, her indecisiveness about marrying again (she's 81)—though there usually isn't a prospect even remotely in mind (she's picky)—she wants a younger man, someone in his late 60's to early 70's with a full head of hair or it's not happening. And then there's our main topic of conversation. Sex.

I've grown used to it by now, but there was a time not so long ago that I thought I would have a coronary when my Gram started her ramblings about sex. I'll never forget it.

I had brought my then boyfriend home to meet the family. He, Gram and I had gone out to lunch and I was driving back to her place with Gram in the passenger seat, my man behind me in the backseat.

"I'm waiting to get these 'how to' videos," my Gram told us.

"'How to' what?" I asked (BIG mistake!).

"It's a tape on how to make love properly. Artie's havin' a problem, he can't do it the way I want him to, so it's gonna show him how to do it right."

Her man was 73 years old. If he didn't know how to do it right by now, I had little hope that a video was going to show him at this point.

"They even got a new thing on there called 'oral'," she continued.

My mouth dropped. I didn't know what to say. But I knew I needed to shut her up.

"You guys wanna borrow it?" she asked us before I could pull her plug.

I spied my boyfriend's face in the rearview mirror—a mixture of shock and amusement. I tried to give him an 'I have no idea' look.

"No, thanks Gram." I said politely.

"Yeah, I'll never forget that time I got caught, I was down in the floorboard when the cops knocked on the car window," she said as she motioned toward where her feet were resting.

That's when I knew that my relationship with my Grandmother had turned a corner. There was never another conversation that went by that sex wasn't a hot topic, whether it be if I was getting any and if it was good or the details to her sex life, which was always lacking by her standards. Not a typical chat most granddaughters would have with their Grams, but my Gram is anything but typical.

"Sammy, I am so happy for you. How long you been with this new fella?" My Grandmother asks me.

I shift the phone under my chin and try to zip my overstuffed duffel.

I say, "Awhile. A few months. It's going pretty well."

"And you haven't had sex yet?" She says, sounding appalled at the idea.

"No, Gram, the opportunity just hasn't presented itself," I say, not wanting to get into the whole living arrangement situation.

Though it was something I myself had been considering. I mean if we were only going to be able to have sex when we were away or at someone else's house, then we were not going to be having much of it at all, and that was going to be unacceptable. Maybe it was the 'Gram' in me, but I wanted to have it and more than once every month or so.

"Is he a big man?" Gram asks.

"Well, yeah, he is. Close to six feet tall. Dark curly hair, brown eyes, beautiful I think," I tell her, trying to anticipate the questions before they're asked.

"Oh, those are the best kind. Them good lookin' men. Have you seen him naked yet?" She asks.

Here we go.

"Uh, no Gram I haven't."

"You know Sam, I just mean so you know what to expect and all. You gotta watch, 'cause sometimes, you get a surprise!"

I manage to coax Gram off the phone, promising to call soon with all the details...*yeah, right.*

Still, I'm late. I call Alan to let him know. He's waiting for me at his best friend Gene's apartment on the Upper East Side.

I make my way over, the traffic pretty light for a Saturday morning. Thinking we're in a hurry (or is it just my libido that's screaming that), I leave the car double-parked, ring the buzzer and wait. Apparently, the guys have another idea, as they buzz me in.

Now, I've never met Gene before, though I've heard a lot about him. He makes money, that's made clear by the way he lives. Apartment in the city, cottage upstate, new car, yeah, he's living well. The way I wanted to be living in the near future.

The apartment is housed in a small brick building. Though a walk-up, it is well-maintained. This is made obvious by the fresh flowers and bowls of mints on each corner table at every floor landing.

As I near the end of my second flight of stairs and round the bend, I see the door is already open for me. It is red and heavy. I tap lightly on it.

"Come on in," I hear a voice say.

I go in, close the door behind me and take in my surroundings. There is a long corridor which leads in two different directions. One way goes to a small hall and bathroom while the other leads to the living area, bedroom, and kitchen. Since I don't expect them to be huddled in the bathroom, I take the second route.

"Hey there chicky," Alan says to me and gives me a hug and light kiss on the lips. "This is Gene, my best buddy."

I take his hand, which is extended and shake it.

He is the complete opposite of Alan. He is as white as cotton. Light sandy hair, glasses, blue eyes, medium build and height. He is pleasant. And smart. This I get right off the bat.

"It's great to finally meet you," I say.

"You too."

"This is a great place," I say as I look around.

The living area has an old oriental rug, which lies in front of a brick fireplace, that actually works. The room is furnished sparingly with only a couch, rocking chair, and old Victrola in the corner of the room. As I turn around, I see the kitchen, which is tiny, but holds its own washer and dryer. Wow.

"Let me give you a quick tour," Gene offers.

He shows me the route to the bathroom and bedroom, which is equally nice. It contains a full walk-in closet that has a second door that leads back to the other side where the bathroom resides. Nice indeed.

"Okay, if you're thinking of getting an apartment in the near future, I could live with this," I say to Alan when we return.

"I'll bet." He says and smiles. "Well, we better be headin' out."

I agree.

We say our good-byes to Gene, which include a hug for Alan and one for me and a promise to get together soon with him and his girlfriend, Jeannie.

Alan and I throw his bags into the trunk. I notice he has his laptop and printer with him. A working weekend?

We climb in and head toward our love shack in the woods.

Our journey upstate is pretty uneventful. We talk and sing along to Alanis Morrisette on the c.d. player. Old school, I know.

The closer we get to the cottage the more nervous I feel. I know this seems irrational. I have great feelings for this man and there is no reason to believe that will change. It's just that I don't want this to somehow not be as good as we're anticipating. I want to feel him next to me, inside me, around me so much that I think I might burst. He is the man I have been looking for…The One. No doubt in my mind.

Just relax, I tell myself. It's Alan. Nothing to be nervous about.

About twenty minutes before we arrive I mention his laptop and printer.

"Yeah, they want that re-write by next week."

Unbelievable. These people in these positions. They want to produce the same thing over and over again. They want carbon copies of what's already out there, so they are 'insured' to make money. But the public is fed up with that. We want something new. We long for it and these people need to stop worrying so much about their damned overhead and realize that they are dealing with creative people, whose life's blood is on those pages, on that stage, on that canvass. It's time they stopped fucking with that.

I don't want to start venting as it will only serve to stir things up, so instead I say, "Anything in particular they want changed?"

"They want a different ending," he says clearly upset.

At what point does it become their story and not the artist's to tell? These people are now dictating how many characters to put in a show, what 'can' and 'can not' occur in the story, and now, what the outcome should be. Ridiculous.

I look over at Alan. "I'm sorry honey," I say and take his hand in mine.

"Nothing for you to be sorry about. It's this fuckin' business."

We remain silent until we near the cottage. We wind up the gravel road and there it is, nestled between two other homes, several yards from each other.

The structure is small and painted yellow with white trim. It sits on a hill that overlooks a distant lake. It contains a small living room and an old-fashioned kitchen complete with old stove and refrigerator. There are two other rooms and a bathroom. No tub. Too bad. I love taking baths, but the shower stall will do just fine. Alan shows me the best feature of the house once we drop our bags into the first bedroom.

He takes my hand and leads me through the kitchen and out the back door. There we stand on an enormous deck. It's gorgeous. Beautiful stained wood with beams and steps that lead down to the backyard below.

"Took us three weekends non-stop," Alan says with pride.

"You built this?" I ask stunned.

"Yep. Me, Bobby and Gene did it all ourselves. Did nothing those weekends but work on this, drink beer and play golf."

A man's paradise.

"It's beautiful. Really amazing." I say as I walk along its perimeter, gliding my hand along the smooth wooden rail.

"Yeah. I love it here."

There's a barbeque on the deck with a table, chairs, and a chaise.

Alan comes up behind me as I stand looking down toward the yard and woods. He wraps his arms around my body.

"I think we should run to the store, grab a couple of steaks, some wine and juice of course," he laughs, "And maybe some corn on the cob and some dessert and make a feast for our first night here."

"Yum," I say before turning and planting a kiss on his cheek.

"But before that, I think we have some business to attend to." He kisses me softly, wetly.

I want him so much, but I feel so damn nervous. I pull away and walk into the living room.

He follows me.

"What's up?"

"I just need a minute. I was thinking that maybe we could...play Scrabble."

Okay, a crazy thought, the first to come into my head. Certainly not what comes to mind when one thinks of the term, 'foreplay'. But for some reason...the need to be in control, I guess. I need to make love when I'm ready, and though I've felt ready for weeks, now that the moment has arrived, I'm not. Not yet.

Having little choice, Alan pulls out the board and we set-up to play. We lay on the braided rug on the floor and begin. It is only ten or fifteen minutes later that I realize two things: one, he is clearly a superior player and two, that I am being a fool and need to take my man to bed.

I reach over and kiss him. I pull him up, scattering the playing tiles, and lead him to the bedroom.

There is nothing romantic about how we end up in bed. He doesn't slowly take my clothes off, I don't perform a strip tease...no, we both just shed our garments and jump in. I am scared. It is daylight and I am naked with someone who I adore, but who makes judgments about everything....including possibly my body, my breath, my level of experience. I don't want him to do that. Not now.

Alan starts kissing me and touching me and I start to feel a little more at ease. I am getting excited, but when I reach down I notice that he is no longer. He has lost the enormous erection that he had earlier. He is now not ready and I am. Fuck. What did I do?

"This doesn't usually happen," he says to me.

A likely story, my cynical self thinks, but maybe it doesn't. I have never in my life experienced this (rather, I've never experienced *a man* experiencing this), so I have no idea what I'm supposed to do...do I try to get him back up? Or if I try to do that and it refuses to inflate, will he get angry and blame me and become a serial killer? Okay, too much *Law & Order*.

I am embarrassed. Not for him, but for myself. I look at him and start laughing. Not at him. But at the situation. Oh God, if he's going to go serial killer, it's probably going to be right now.

I turn my face away, he pulls my face to him, kisses me and places my hand over his member. I begin to stroke him gently. I don't allow myself to think. I only allow myself to do. I kiss him up and down, all around and he comes alive again. He and I begin making love. It's a little uncomfortable at first, as I haven't had sex in quite some time (to my Grandma's shame, no doubt) and he's not exactly small. In fact, the damn thing is so wide, it's almost square-looking. I'm re-thinking my strategy...perhaps limp was the way to go here.

When there is no climaxing from either of us, Alan turns me over and takes me from behind. He comes on my back a short time later. He towels me off and we lay there in each other's arms saying little. What exactly is there to say? *I thought that would have gone better? I thought you mighta been going serial killer on me back there?*

Finally he turns to me and says, "You know, I sometimes think that it's easier to have sex with someone you don't know. I mean, that way there's nothing at stake. When you care about someone then there's a lot of pressure associated with the whole thing."

This statement sends my mind wandering in two completely different directions. On the one hand, I think it's ridiculous...just something to say when things have gone as strangely as they just have. If you care for someone, the pressure is gone. It is in the loving and caring that you are able to give yourself to another. That is the beauty of it.

On the other hand, I have to admit, this time it seemed more like pressure, though I haven't found that in the past. Okay I've only loved one other person, but we had great sex and I never felt pressure. It was simply the natural order of things.

The one question that keeps floating my mind though is, "Is he saying this is difficult because he's in love with me?"

It's as if he's reading my mind because moments later he looks at me and says, "You know, I'd be lying if I said that I wasn't falling in love with you."

My response, a nice long exhale.

We lay there a while longer and decide to take a shower and then run to the store for food. We cram ourselves into the tiny shower stall, intending to wash each other. I love a hot shower, so I have the water running pretty hot before we even step in.

Alan starts to kiss me. Oh, yes, this time will surely be better.

I don't even get lathered up before I start to feel ill. I try to push the nausea away. This can't be happening. Not when we have just made love. Not when he just told me he's falling in love with me. Not when…oh my God, I'm going to pass out.

"Hey, what is it?" he asks after I turn away.

"It's so hot." I manage to say.

He adjusts the water temperature, but it's too late. The bathroom is filled with steam and I must get out.

"I'm sorry," I say as I stumble out of the stall and away from the steamed-filled room.

He finds me a moment later in the back bedroom, lying on a towel.

"You okay?" He asks, water dripping all over the worn carpeting.

"I felt so dizzy…I'm so sorry, Alan. I don't know what's wrong with me. I don't ever get like this." I explain.

"It's okay," he says and brings a second towel to dry us off with. "No more showers together."

We change quickly, head to the store and return, our arms full of bags. I unload the groceries, while Alan fires up the grill.

The steaks are thick and tender, the corn sweet and buttery.

We talk and laugh much, the awkwardness of earlier events, seemingly behind us. Afterward, we begin to store the extra food in containers and clean-up the kitchen.

"Let's do this later," Alan offers while leading me back to my chair.

"Why? What did you have in mind," I ask as I sit down.

I take a sip of juice, attempting to extract some of the corn from my teeth. I know there must be half a dozen kernels stuck in between and they're making me crazy. I'm one of those people who carries floss wherever she goes and I'm in desperate need of a fix now.

"I just thought we could sit for a while or go out on the deck," Alan says looking directly at me.

I turn away. I feel embarrassed, having food in my teeth.

"What?" he asks.

"Nothing," I lie, still turned away.

"You're not sick again are you," he asks. The remark catches me off guard and I gasp at him.

"No."

I get up to run to the bathroom and take care of this once and for all, but am unable to pass. Alan stands in my path.

"Where you off to?"

"Bathroom," I say while trying to get by him.

"Pay the toll first."

"What toll," I ask, still trying to keep my teeth from view.

"A kiss, silly. Gimmee a kiss."

I can't kiss him. Not with corn in my teeth. Yuck!

"In a minute," I say and run pass him.

He catches up to me and drags me into the bedroom. He pushes me down on the bed. "Kiss."

I get up and try to pass him. "I have to go to the bathroom."

"I don't mind the corn," he says.

I laugh. I can't believe it.

"You, you knew."

"Yes, and I don't care. Give me a kiss or you're not gettin' outta here."

He continues to block my path to the door. I try to get around him time and again, but keep winding up back on the bed.

"I can't. It's yucky. I want to floss and then I'll give you all the kisses you want."

"Nope," he says. "Now. Now I want kisses."

I try to reason with him, "But don't you think it's nasty? It's gross."

He looks me in the eye, "No more than anything else. Now give me your lips," he lunges and I squeal and land on the bed again. This time he tackles me. I have no choice. I kiss him. And again. And again.

Then he says, "Okay, you can go now."

CHAPTER 13

Anne-Marie and I haven't spoken in over a week. It feels shitty. Especially because I am largely to blame—missing her brother's party. Time to pay the piper, I suppose.

I head to her desk, veer around the bend, but she's nowhere in sight. I peer into her attorney's office, still no Anne-Marie. I head to the loo. And there sits a teary-eyed Anne-Marie.

"What is it?" I ask, the silence of the past week already forgotten.

She sniffs, struggles with a smile, splashes a little water on her face and dries off.

"Nothing. Just a little stressed-out today," she tells me.

"Work?" I ask.

"Yeah, and, well, everything. No dates lately. You and I have been, well…"

I nod, turn away. I swallow my pride and turn to her.

"Yeah, that's actually why I was coming to find you. To apologize for missing your brother's bash. I just forgot. Plain and simple. I didn't mean to hurt you though."

She looks at me. Looks away. Seems to consider my words. She nods her head.

"I know that. It's just…I guess I feel like I'm losing you, and…"

"You're not. You never will. I promise." I hug her tightly and she reciprocates.

"You know what tonight is, don't you?" I ask her.

She shakes her head, thinks a moment and smiles. "Oh my gosh, I forgot. Are we going?" She wants to know.

"They called to confirm. I told them we were, though I wasn't sure if you were ever going to speak to me again."

She swats at me.

"You know, we're kind of even now." I grin wickedly.

"Yeah, how's that?" She challenges.

"Well, I missed the party and you missed Salsa and that…that caused me to step on Frank and break his foot. I mean, if you were there, it wouldn't have happened. Simple as that."

I step away from her before she has a chance to swat me again.

She laughs. "See you around five."

I nod. "Five."

Five comes quickly and things fall into their usual routine, this being our ritual outing. Every three months we go out for a big food fest, followed by a cleansing…yes, I said cleansing. As in, of the colon. Okay, it's not something pleasant to think about, I know. But it's still necessary. And there is an upside…it's the four times a year, we can binge on high calorie food without clocking extra miles on the treadmill or experiencing that hangdog feeling of guilt.

This time we opt for good ole' American food…burgers, fries, milkshakes, and banana cream pie…yum, but we certainly don't limit ourselves to that cuisine…Oh no. Next time it'll be Mexican, Italian, or even Chinese. Variety being the spice of life.

We unbutton our jeans (another necessity after this meal), pay our check and head to the Lexington Avenue Wellness Center, our cleanser of choice.

As we near 77th Street, I finish telling Anne-Marie about my weekend away with Alan.

"What do you think he meant?" she asks when I tell her what he said about sex with strangers being easier.

"I don't know. I was hoping you'd have some idea."

She looks over at me.

"An impartial point-of-view, I mean." I add.

"Impartial, huh?" She thinks for a moment then says, "He was probably just trying to cover for losing his erection, you know."

I nod. "See I wouldn't have even thought of that. You're probably right."

"Either that or he was having a hard time telling you how he really feels. That he was falling for you."

I sigh. "Maybe. Are you still convinced he isn't sincere? That he's going to hurt me?"

She smiles. "I'm not convinced of anything. You're happy. That's all that really matters to me."

We climb the three steps to the lobby, hit the elevator, and get off on the 5th floor.

Heidi and Christine, our colonisticians are ready for us. We walk to our adjacent rooms, give each other a little smile and go our separate ways, shutting the doors behind us.

The room is small and chilly, which only adds to my reluctance to ditch my pants. I have this same feeling every time I'm here and I've been coming here for what seems like forever.

Heidi is standing near the 'de-pooper' as I like to refer to it. She is preparing—what that entails I don't ask and don't want to know.

"Hey sister," she says, her disposition cheerful as always.

"Hi," I say and begin unlacing my boots.

"Have your Mexicana?" She asks, privy to my ritual with Anne-Marie.

"Burgers this time," I inform her.

I take my position on the cold table. There is a white cotton cloth draped over the steel, though it provides little warmth.

"You know the drill," Heidi says as I flip onto my side.

At first it feels strange, but after a few minutes, Heidi and I are so busy catching up on the last three months that I hardly notice that I'm lying on a steel table, naked from the waist down, with a tube sticking out of my ass.

In fact, if it weren't for Heidi's excited progress reports—"Oh, this one's a goody"—and subsequent high fives, I could probably go the entire session as if I'm at a café reuniting with an old friend. What can I say? I'm easily fooled.

Salsa with the Pope

And boy does Heidi love her work—and yes, I have questioned her about this, but some things are not for me to understand. Her passion for this job being one of those things.

It's been a little over an hour. I'm flipping through magazines of the self-help and alternative medicine variety, sitting in a chair in the lobby of the clinic. I've finished my cleansing, dressed, paid, hit the loo twice…still no Anne-Marie.

I get up, walk toward her door, thinking maybe something came up and she had to leave quickly, but the door remains shut and I am forced to believe that she's still in there. Hey, maybe she had a couple big dinners this week.

I sit back down, pick up a magazine, put it down and rifle through the remaining ones, looking for something "un-alternative" not in any way "self-help-like"…something more along the lines of Jerry Springer in prose.

A man, good-looking, construction helmet looking thing on his head, bat in his hands stares back at me. It's a split-page and the other side has the same man in a lavender pull-over and gray dress pants, smiling charmingly…yeah, if I was making what he was making, I'd be smiling too.

The heading, *Darren James, not all bats and balls* is splayed across the cover. Hmm, nice. Suddenly not so antsy about Anne-Marie's appearance. I settle into my chair ready to learn all about the Yankee hitter. But it's not to be as Anne-Marie appears.

She looks pale, exhausted.

"Hey. You okay," I ask, going to her.

She nods, gives a little smile and says, "Yeah, just tired. That really drained me."

"Literally," I can't help saying.

We both laugh and she swats me lightly with her hand, though I can tell her heart's not in it.

As we walk to the crosstown bus, Anne-Marie tells me that her session was really bad—the worst ever.

"I just couldn't go," she says defeated.

I furrow my brow and say, "I didn't know you had a choice."

"I know. That's exactly what I thought too, but Christine says it can sometimes be your mental disposition that's affecting it."

She goes on to explain that sometimes your own personality type—a tendency to talk and get issues resolved versus a tendency to get tense and hold things in—can affect how well a colonic can go.

"Damn," I say. "No wonder I do so well."

She looks at me and shakes her head. "And no wonder I don't."

Though Anne-Marie and I are close friends, we are polar opposites when it comes to what we share with others. I am an open book for the most part. Anne-Marie, on the other hand, is shut tight with a lock that few are afforded the key. Fortunately for me, I am one of the few.

CHAPTER 14

I am a nervous wreck. I am with Dai at LaGuardia. We're here to pick up my mother, who's coming for a visit. I'm actually surprised that she's making it at all, truth be told. I called to ask her to come a month ago and she insisted that she would not be able to make it—a combination of little money and very few vacation days left at her Insurance Adjustor job. During a subsequent conversation, Alan asked her again to come and she agreed.

Honestly, I'm a little pissed off. I feel like she respects Alan's invitation more than mine. And she hasn't even met him! On the other hand, I am very happy she's coming. Alan's having that huge reading of his play and he wants everyone here. My mother, his mother…yes, I am finally going to meet his mother. And that, more than anything, has me nervous as hell.

My mother and I are meeting him and his mother in the city this afternoon. I dress in a beige skirt, melon-colored top with matching sweater. My mother wears teal, which looks quite nice on her I think.

When we arrive, they're already waiting for us, seated at one of the outdoor tables. They have beverages sitting before them that although sweating in the heat, are barely touched. They're seated next to each other, hunched close, like two people telling secrets. God, I hope they aren't secrets about me.

They don't see us until we approach the table. Alan stands, kisses my mother on the cheek and kisses me lightly on the mouth. I introduce my mother and he then introduces his.

Gabriela is a woman in her mid-fifties. She still wears the remnants of the beauty she must have possessed in earlier life. Her hair is dark, tinted with highlights, her brown eyes lightened with make-up. Her smile is bright next to the tan of her skin.

"Sheryl, so nice to meet you," she says and shakes my mother's hand.

Then she turns to me. A pause. It feels like a century, though I imagine it is actually no longer than a moment. Is she scrutinizing me? Possibly.

"And Samantha. How lovely to finally meet you."

She smiles and then rises from her chair and gives me a hug. I hug her back and smile. This is Alan's mother. Finally.

"Oh, I'm so glad that we could all be here," I say feeling a little choked up.

Okay, I'm lame...it's no secret.

We all sit back down and Mom and I order drinks. A latte for her, a Shirley Temple for me. I'm feeling festive. I look over at Alan and we hold hands across the table.

The conversation is light and seems to cover a wide spectrum of things: the weather, Gabriela's home in Florida, my mother's job, the play, and then it takes that natural progression...to babies. It goes something like this:

My mom: Oh, well I would love to have a grandchild. Since, Sammy is my only child, she is my only hope. (A sigh and weak smile from me)

His mom: Oh, well I already have two—both boys and I would adore a little girl, yes, I definitely want some from my Alan (she pats him on the forearm and he gives me a 'deer-in-the-headlights' look).

My mom: Did Sammy mention that we have twins *and* triplets in our family. Several sets of them, in fact. (I give Alan a toothless smile that says, 'there's no stopping them now').

His mom: No, I had no idea. Oh, wouldn't that be wonderful. (Another sigh from me and under my breath I say, 'the only wonderful thing being only one labor').

We manage to get the moms out of there without having to find a baby registrar.

My mother confides that she thinks he's a gem. Now, wasn't that easy?

Salsa with the Pope

His mother and I seem to be a completely different story. I want to like her and I want her to love me. This meeting of the moms is truly the first time that I think that maybe, just maybe we are actually going to get married and have babies.

Yes, the thought has crossed my mind before, but this is the real thing. Alan actually made a comment to me after the meeting…something about his mother needing to be involved in the planning of our wedding and that I had to remember that. Of course…by all means…I'll remember.

It seems like only moments later and I am teetering on 14th Street in my 4" heels and black dress outside of a restaurant/bar called Alovera's. I am weeping. My mother comes over and guides me back to the little table just outside of the doors. We've just come from inside where food, drink and celebration were aplenty. Alan's reading was an enormous success. The best reading that his hotshot manager has ever seen. I am so proud of him.

I am unable to control my tears…Damn. I have been so emotional lately. Even last week, Alan and I were walking down Broadway coming from a movie—it's not like it was *Terms of Endearment* for God's sake…more along the lines of *Animal House*, but there I am balling. I couldn't help it. Like now. Can't stop. I am so happy. So in love.

"Thanks for coming out with me, Mama," I say and wipe my eyes with the tissue she handed me moments ago.

How come moms always have those things? Tissues, gum, safety pins. Does that mean that I will have to carry an even bigger bag when I become a mother? I don't think my back can take it. I honestly don't.

"I wanted to get out of there anyway. It's so hot," she says and fans herself with her hand.

"Yeah, it was warm."

She looks over at me.

"You alright now?"

I nod. "Yeah," I say a little embarrassed.

Most people don't get my emotionalism and I can't explain it to them. I don't understand it myself.

"Thanks. I guess I just felt so overwhelmed by the good news and it's really going to happen. It's going to Broadway this fall!"

"That's so great. I am so happy for you both," my mom tells me.

We sit a few more moments, then she puts her arm through mine and we walk proudly back into Alovera's.

CHAPTER 15

I'm neglecting my duties. To myself, that is. I joined the Road Runners—basically a group of masochists who get up very early in the morning and run through Central Park in the cold. I wanted to be a masochist too, but evidently not enough—I haven't even made it to one race. I desperately want to be in the New York City Marathon next year, but in order to ensure that, I have to run *nine* races. Yep, nine to go.

My attendance at auditions is slacking off too. I think the fact that Alan thinks that open calls are a waste of time helps to fuel my lax attitude. I don't completely disagree with him, but I don't have a hot shot manager nor am I preparing for my Broadway debut, so basically I need to take advantage of every opportunity.

The thing is, I feel that if I'm with Alan, I'm happy. I don't need my career the way I once felt I did. And I am always in the midst of things anyway…openings, readings, parties…they aren't *my* openings, readings, or parties, but I'm still one of the spectators, so I never feel out of the loop.

On the creative front, I am Alan's listening board. He calls me daily with any new pages he's written. I even brainstormed with him on *The Ghost of Dyckman Avenue* and made a major contribution. *I* helped *him*. And that made me feel good. Really good. We're two talented individuals, albeit one loads more talented than the other—I'll give you a hint, I'm #2 on the talent scale…and we're in love. Doesn't get any better than this.

I'm actually really busy these days. I just finished rehearsal—yes I'm doing a play reading—no, it's not for money or prestige, but it's something and I like it. It's kind of creepy. I play the racy, sexy split personality of the lead. Half a person. Full character. And though it's just a reading, this one is fully blocked—on its feet—so it feels more production-like than most readings I've done.

So I'm not completely lax in my commitment to myself...just not as invested as I once was. Which is fine. I'm going to be a wife soon and have other duties.

I'm rushing to meet Alan. I spot him a block ahead. He doesn't see me...has his head buried in *On Directing*.

"Hi honey," I say and give him a big hug.

"Hey cutie," he says and gives me a small peck on the cheek.

"Well, what's the word?"

"Uh, oh, it starts in twenty minutes."

"Sounds perfect."

We actually picked a movie to see today. Rare. Normally we just show up at the movie complex and see whatever works with our timetable. This means we see a lot of shit, though occasionally we do get lucky.

After the movie we head over to Ollie's for noodles. We order some strange concoction with pork, chicken, beef...basically everything they've got in the back. Except shellfish.

"You're sure there's no shellfish in this," I ask the waiter a second time.

A second time because the first time he just nodded his head and I wasn't sure if he was answering me or just having a pleasant day bopping along to a song in his head.

"I sure," he says, "no, no shellfish."

"Okay."

The waiter walks away and I ask Alan, "What do I do if you have an attack?"

Alan is allergic to shellfish and will swell up and die if he eats any. Actually even if he just touches it he has a reaction. Of course he's supposed to be wearing one of those medallions that says, "Hi my name is Alan and keep your shrimps to yourself" or something of the sort. Or maybe he's supposed to carry one of those shots...not quite sure.

"Just get me to a hospital."

"That's it," I ask.

"Yep."

He takes my hand and kisses it.

We close Ollie's. And evidently no shellfish, as Alan's face looks as big as always…which is big…don't get me wrong…we're talking a massive head…but no more massive than usual.

It's late. I'm so tired and I have rehearsal first thing tomorrow morning.

"I don't want to go to New Jersey," I whine.

I admit it. I whine. But it's deliberate, okay.

"Hey, Pam's out of town."

"Oh, that's right. Is someone staying there?"

"I don't think so. She told me we could use her place anytime," Alan says.

We hop on the train and are speaking to Abe, the doorman thirty minutes later. He hands us the keys and up we go. A free night with Alan. My tiredness is fading away. I have to take advantage of these times when we can actually have sex in a bed with no one around. It's like I'm sixteen again. I only look eighty.

We walk in. There are lights on.

"Is someone here, you think," I ask Alan. "Look," I point out a briefcase standing near her coffee table.

We check the entire apartment, making as much noise as possible—you don't want to find someone in a compromising position, especially when you've just walked right in on her. We find no one.

"So now what?" I ask.

"Maybe whoever it is just went out and is coming back." Alan says.

"We better go." I glance at my watch. "Shit. I'm stuck. The last bus left forty minutes ago."

"We'll go to Brooklyn, I guess." Alan says surprisingly.

"Really?" I ask, unable to hide my surprise.

"I guess so. What else are we gonna do?"

The entire subway ride there Alan repeatedly warns me about the apartment. It is "small, messy, tiny, a bachelor pad."

I don't care. I'm just glad to have somewhere to lay my head. I'm whipped. A little curious too, I have to admit. I mean after all these months, I'm going to get to see where Alan washes his hair and watches the Yankees.

As we get off the F train and start down Mason Road, he pulls out his cell phone.

"Hey B-man, it's me. Yeah, uh, I'm bringing Sam home with me tonight and we are two minutes away, so just wanted to give you a heads up. See you soon."

He disconnects and puts his arm around my neck and pulls me to him. He kisses my head three times.

"I don't care." I finally say.

"But I do." he says as we round the corner.

The block is very suburban, in the way that there aren't any apartment buildings, but rather rows of homes that have been turned into two, three, and four family abodes. Alan's place is half-way down the block on the first floor of a small white structure.

We walk into a haze-filled living room reeking of marijuana. This doesn't bother me per se, not that you'd find me tokin' up, because you wouldn't, but to each his own.

Alan makes the introductions then I take a look around. The living room is very tiny. It holds a lounge chair, a desk chair and two folding chairs. There's a large 35" television resting on an antique-looking table. I worry that the table might collapse, supporting the weight of the large console. An adjacent set of French doors leads to Barry's room, also small from what I can gage, but not unmanageable.

Alan's room is off the largest room in the apartment, the kitchen. He makes me sit at the dinette set and wait while he tidies his room. I spy the small bathroom toward the back of the kitchen. Yes, it's a tiny apartment, but not awful. It would be very nice for one person, or even a couple. For roommates, I can see how it could be a tight fit.

It takes almost a half-hour for Alan to deem his room safe for my perusal, so I go back into the living area and chat with Barry. He's a nice looking guy with thick blonde hair and

Scandinavian features. I can't decide if he and Alan make a better Starsky and Hutch or Hall & Oats.

I know little about Barry…he's an actor, has known Alan for years, and is just as big a sports fan. Barry's watching baseball, so I take a seat in one of the folding chairs and try to decipher what is going on. I don't think I've ever sat down to really watch a baseball game before.

"Now how come he didn't call him out? Isn't a foul ball a strike?" I ask more to make conversation than to actually learn.

"Except on the third strike, then fouls aren't counted as strikes." he says and takes a drink of his beer.

Alan joins us in the living room after several minutes. We finish watching the Yankee game, the two of them explaining the plays to me all the while. I'm actually kind of into it. I'm starting to understand it and Barry and Alan are taking turns asking me questions to see if I get it. I'm 2-6 on the questions, but I'm learning…I'm learning. And it's not like it's hard to watch. I mean the players aren't exactly unappealing to look at. More like Yum.

After the game, we say goodnight to Barry and head off to bed. I need some rest. Play rehearsal in just six hours.

The room is tiny. There is no bed. There is however, an air mattress pumped up ready to go. Alan puts the pump away by tossing it under his desk.

"Want to make sure there's enough air in there. Not sure how firm you like your mattress." he says to me and smiles.

"I'm not too fussy." I say.

He chuckles, shakes his head. I've never seen him embarrassed. Until now. I shut the door, take his hand and lead him over to the bed, which is actually a slow walk as my foot is resting next to it. I lay down next to him and undress him. I begin touching and kissing him.

"I don't care." I say as I look up at him.

"But it's ridiculous. And I never thought you would see this. I didn't want you to." he says and turns away.

"I love you. Not what you have or haven't got. And soon enough you will have it. And it won't change a thing."

Samantha Wren Anderson

    And so we make love on the air mattress like it's the King Size Sleigh Bed at the Four Seasons.

CHAPTER 16

I hate having my picture taken. Some people think that this statement goes against the very nature of my job—being an actor. I disagree. The two have absolutely nothing to do with each other. Except that actors use publicity to advertise their work. Other than that, nothing...okay, the 50 Most Pretty People or whatever, but other than that, nothing. Okay, even if it is slightly related, I DON'T LIKE IT, okay? I'm allowed an opinion, am I not?

So it stands to reason that I am not exactly jumping for joy about having my headshots taken today. In fact, between cost—we're talking over a thousand dollars for decent ones, and the whole having to lug your entire wardrobe, sit in a make-up chair for two hours and then actually pose, I'm debating if I'd rather take a guided tour of Attica—for those of you not from New York, it's a *prison*—come on, haven't you ever seen *Law & Order*!

The only reason I'm even doing this is that I got an awesome deal. Alan ran into a photographer, a friend of a friend...whatever...who said he'd give me headshots for $200 if Alan used him for his publicity photos for *The Ghost of Dyckman Avenue*.

Okay...I also need them. My old headshots keep warranting phrases like, "This you?" at auditions lately. They're six years old and my hair is shorter and red, not the long blonde it's become...so basically, it's time.

I'm in a cab heading crosstown on 36th Street. This guy has to be located west...very west, can't be near a subway. Though with all this crap, I probably couldn't have managed it anyway. My legs are killing me. I decided that I should go for a run before coming in, so that mentally I feel skinny. Don't want any headshots that say 'fat'.

I climb out of the cab and trip. "Dammit," I say louder than I mean to. I glance up at an old lady giving me a look and say, "What? Haven't you ever fallen before?" I jinx her. She trips and falls right there. I run away from my cab, leaving the door open and head for her.

"You okay?" I say as I approach her.

She's not moving. What have I done? I can't tell if she's conscious or not. Her face is still down on the pavement. I guess that would mean she's not. I mean, I love New York too, but to mate your face and this pavement for any amount of time is hazardous.

"Stay right here. Don't move." I say and then realize how foolish that sounds. Where is she gonna go? I run back toward the cab to get my cell out of my bag. Before I make it across the street, another cab comes racing by and clips the door that I left open.

"Shit."

I run faster to the cab.

The driver is now out of the vehicle cursing at me in Swahili and having what looks to be an epileptic fit. I grab all my stuff, best I can, and race back to the old woman.

"No, no, you come back here. You pay for this. You pay." the man is saying.

I look at him like he's still speaking Swahili hoping that maybe he'll go wherever it is they speak Swahili...

When I reach my destination, the woman has vanished. Where did she go? I re-trace my steps up and down the sidewalk, back and forth, but no old lady. I then begin to peer into car windows parked along the street, looking for a hidden camera...this could be one of those shows where they try to make the mark—aka me—look like a damn fool. It's going to be a very good episode.

I heave my belongings, which are dragging the ground pretty good and get to Mauricio's studio. I buzz. I buzz again. Come on. I'm on the run here.

The cab driver is still examining his door...or rather where his door used to be. The other cab evidently not only ripped it off its hinges, but took it too. I feel bad. But not bad enough to give him my information. The driver notices me just as the door rings open. I push my way through, closing the door in the cabbie's face.

I turn just as Mauricio approaches me. He is all smiles, on the phone, motioning me to drop my stuff on the nearby table. I nod, pretend that it's been a normal morning and that my legs don't hurt, I didn't trip, I didn't see an old lady almost die then disappear, and I don't have a Swahili cab driver after me.

The upshot? After all that, the headshots should be a breeze. And I should have a lot of different expressions to give him: terror, confusion, guilt. None of which are real good for headshots, but it's better than nothing, I suppose. Better than my normal deer in the headlights.

"How are you?" Mauricio says, his voice heavy with an Italian accent.

"I'm good," I lie. "Real good."

"I'll be with you in one minute. In the meantime, why don't you hang up your things and Butch can start your hair and make-up."

"Great." I say.

'Yuck,' I think.

I hang up my things, peering through the window shade occasionally, checking the progress of my cabbie. He is still there. Still looking at the damage. How long does it take to figure out that your door is missing? It's not like it's going to regenerate itself. Accept it.

"So, are we ready?" okay the accent isn't Italian, but homosexual. Heavy homosexual. And though that doesn't bother me, anyone who says "we" when they mean "you" reminds me of some aunt Betty who makes fresh iced tea (hate iced tea) and thinks masturbation is a car part.

I turn to see Butch, who is all of 5'5, 120 lbs. I hate it when I outweigh my stylist. My male stylist. I hide all of this—that's what makes me a great actor—and say, "Oh, you must be

Butch. Sam." I extend my hand, shake his, careful not to crush it, and take a seat in the chair.

I zone out. That's what I do when I have to deal with something I dislike. I try to meditate and pretend that it's not happening. I am impatient. And sitting in a chair while a man more effeminate than me heats my eyelashes and moans about the two sitcoms he's written with no industry interest is not what I'd call pleasant. So, two hours ten minutes later, when I am deemed 'aesthetically pleasing', I am all set to get this show on the road.

"Oh, you look marvelous. Truly beautiful. A picture." Mauricio tells me. Let's hope a picture.

"Now, what have you brought?" He says and begins to sift through my clothes. It goes something like this: "too flashy, color won't work with the background, fabric is too gauzy, too casual, too busy…" and on and on until we only have two tank tops left—one white, one black. I was told not to bring white or black, but fortunately I'm not one to listen to instructions.

"I guess we'll have to go with this," he says and hands me my white top. Sorry to disappoint. I don't bother to tell him that I spent a day shopping for this stuff with the headshots specifically in mind. Whatever.

I change. I come out. I sit on the crate—boy, talk about comfort. I pose.

"No, you're posing," he says.

Yeah, no shit.

"Sorry, was I not supposed to be."

"Right. Here, look this way, but keep your head turned that way. There. Oh, oh, Butch, her hair is in her mouth. Can you do something about that?"

And so it goes. An hour and forty minutes of this. I hope I'm getting something good, though I feel stiff. That's always a big no-no too. You want a natural picture. Not a cardboard cut-out.

"Oh, darn. Let's try it again. It's just not working," Mauricio tells me. After all this time, now he tells me it's not working. What's not working? My positions—not poses, my white top, my hair in my mouth…what?

Salsa with the Pope

"I'm not feeling it," he finally says and sighs.

He's not *feeling* it? Feeling what? I'm feeling something. It resembles anger.

"Um, could I just take a quick bathroom break," I say and escape.

I sit on the commode and breathe. In and out. In and out. I'm not sure what's going on out there, but it better be good. That's all I have to say. It's been a hell day, a *hell* day and I'm not leaving here without a decent headshot. I take one last deep breath and return to the torture chamber.

"Let's try this," Mauricio says. He contorts my body in such a way that I can't get it to stay that way without using my hands to hold my legs.

"Now, give me that smile. That sexy smile...no, you look like you're in pain." 'Yeah, there's a reason for that,' I want to yell, but I don't. I have such restraint. I silently give myself a gold star.

"This is just...not working," he says exasperated. Like he's the only one doing any work here.

I get up and go into the booth where Mauricio is sitting. And crying. He is crying.

"Mauricio, what's going on?"

"I'm just...I just don't feel it with you."

I don't give a rat's ass if you 'feel it' with me or not. I paid for headshots, you give me some friggin' headshots. Now. But I don't say that. I want to. It's on the tip of my tongue. But Alan is dealing with this person and to say that would also affect their relationship and I can't do that. It would be unprofessional. Exactly what Mauricio's being.

"What do you want to do?" I say, trying not to show my exasperation.

"You know, I'm under a lot of stress right now. My divorce, this damn business..."

"Mauricio, I'm sorry to hear that. Really. But what do you want to do about this?"

God get me the hell out of here before I kill.

"Well, why don't you come back next week and we can start over and I'm sure we can get some nice shots."

I don't want to do this again. Ever. But the prospect of getting out of here is too great, and since we're not getting anything of value anyway.

"Sounds good. I'll call you."

I pack up my belongings quickly and head out onto the street. Staring me right in the face is the cabbie.

"You need ride?" he says cynically, showing a full-set of teeth, some bleached, some gold.

"Actually, yes, I do."

I put all my shit in the trunk, sit with him in the front and begin to write down my information.

CHAPTER 17

I'm feeling a little nervous. It's Fourth of July weekend and I'm meeting Gene and Jeannie and heading up to the cottage to join Alan. See, I borrowed Dai's car and drove Alan up earlier in the week—so he could do some writing—and now we're all going up for the holiday weekend. The plan is that I will ride up with them and we'll all come back together.

Okay, seems like a good plan...a reasonable plan, except that I've only met Gene once and I've never met Jeannie and it's a two-hour car ride. Not to mention that I'm a neurotic, nervous person—okay, let's mention it—who worries she'll say the wrong thing or not say anything or more likely say too much. So when I meet them outside a café on the Upper East Side after work, I'm jittery to say the least.

"Hi there. How are you?" I say and extend my hand toward Jeannie.

She is lovely in that wholesome natural way. Dark red hair that catches the sun, more freckles than you could count in a year, and a smile that never leaves her face. The thing that you get right off though, is that she's self-assured (why can't I be that way?). She's not covering up her freckles with make-up—indeed I don't think she's even wearing make-up. She's celebrating who she is. And if you don't like it, well, tough noogies.

"Hey, Alan's girlfriend! Finally. I was beginning to wonder if you really existed, except of course that Gene said he met you. Once!"

She giggles this throaty, croaky laugh. She pauses a moment, waiting for me to respond I guess, and then I too start to laugh.

"Yeah, he keeps me pretty-well hidden." I tell her.

"Hey, there you are," Gene says as he makes his way toward the car, three coffees in his hands.

He kisses Jeannie on the lips and me on the cheek.

"Didn't know how you liked yours, so there's cream and sugar if you need," he says and hands me a cup.

"Oh, thank you," I say and add, "You didn't have to."

He looks at me, grins and says, "Stop."

I nod, though I really mean it. I don't drink coffee.

We get ourselves positioned in the Volvo and begin our journey. It's Friday night, the sun just going down, a beautiful pink and orange sky following us into the country. We make small talk about our jobs, aspirations, Alan.

"It's been over twenty years," Gene says regarding his relationship with Alan, as if surprised himself. "It's weird because at first it didn't seem like we would be friends. We dated the same girl even—at different times of course. Somehow, it still turned out to be cool though."

I like listening to Gene. He puts me at ease. I sit back, relax, and enjoy the ride. I note that the car contains every possible electronic device for an automobile on the market. There's the global positioning system, the satellite radio, and another contraption completely unidentifiable to me.

I also note that he and Jeannie are in physical contact the entire ride up…holding hands, a hand on the other's leg. It's like they're in-sync with each other. I hope Alan and I are like that too, but it's always so damn hard to know when you're in the relationship.

I fight the urge to doze off. I listen to the radio and comment on the beautiful scenery as we get closer to the cottage.

Finally, we arrive. It's dark now. A small porch bulb lights our way. Alan is at the door when Gene opens it. My heart stops.

Alan looks so sexy. I've never seen him look so hot. I can't help but stare at him. His curls are long, exactly how I like them. His face wears an expression of tiredness, but pleasure at the same time. He is tanned and wearing white linen pants, rolled up as if he's been walking on a non-existent beach. His white linen shirt falls open to expose a few dark hairs on his chest. As if embarrassed, he hurries to button the garment before anyone notices. Too late. I noticed.

I am filled with want. I want to take him right here. I can't even bother getting him into the bedroom and closing the door, save our friends from hearing our sounds of pleasure.

I'm lost in my own fantasy when I hear Alan say, "Sam. Samantha Wren," he calls me that often to tease me...like who could be teased about the middle name Wren...who couldn't?

"Yeah," I look at him, dazed expression on my face.

"What's up?" he asks and picks me up off the floor.

My arms go around his neck and I take a deep inhale. Oh, he smells yummy too.

"Nothing, I'm just....mmmm," I exhale.

"Weirdness," he states as if it's my name.

"You just look soooo good. So sexy, I could eat you up. Do you know that? Did you do it on purpose?"

He kisses me a few times and places me back onto the floor. He feigns like a woman, "These old clothes. Oh, come on, I just threw on whatever was on the floor."

But I can tell he's joking. He did this on purpose. To be beautiful. For me. And I love him for it.

"Shut up," is my response. "You're making me crazy and you know it," I tell him.

I go to touch him below the belt, but he teasingly pulls away just as Jeannie and Gene enter the room with the last of their duffels.

It's a fun evening filled with moonlight bee-bee gun shooting (beer cans off the deck—I'm not so good), whiffle ball (I'm pretty good...much better than I would have believed), and Scattegories. We indulge in barbeque chicken, vegetables (I steer clear of the corn-on-the-cob), and macaroni salad. We have fruit salad and toasted marshmallow smores for dessert. Fat and full we are. And Jeannie and the boys are puttin' the beers away too, so they must be ready to pop!

It is almost 1 a.m. when Gene finally announces that he's hittin' the hay. Jeannie says that she'll join him in a bit. This surprises me. I figured she would have gone in, even if she was just reading, just to be near him. I know I would have if Alan had wanted to turn in. Fat chance of that ever happening though. He is a night owl thru and thru.

"So, how's the writing coming along?" she asks Alan.

We three are sitting outside on the deck, fighting off mosquitoes, but still not wanting to give up and go in.

"Slow. It takes me a good two or three days to get in the groove, so I got going about Thursday and today was good, but now we're going back on Sunday and I don't have as much done as I would've liked."

It is nearly 3 a.m. when I finally give up and head for bed. Alan is still sitting at his desk, clicking keys trying to finish the first act. Again.

Jeannie left us about an hour ago. I had high hopes of making my fantasy a reality, but alas that doesn't seem to be in the cards. I go over to Alan and lightly kiss him on the top of his head. I start to walk away when he stops what he's doing, grabs my arm and pulls me back onto his lap. He kisses me on the mouth.

"I'm sorry, baby."

I hug him.

"It's okay. You're working and you need to get this done. I understand," I say and I truly do believe what I'm saying.

"I know, but I wanted to have sex and..."

I say, "We'll have sex tomorrow. I love you."

"Love you back," he says and releases me and picks up where he left off.

The next day I set off on a rigorous, not vigorous mind you, but *rigorous*—almost all steep hills—run, and then spend the majority of the day soaking up sun rays and reading a book on the deck alone.

Two other couples arrive, we all exchange pleasantries, share a meal or two, but primarily I keep to myself. I feel a bit awkward being the seventh wheel. Alan's in the bedroom writing and has been the entire day. I go in periodically to check on him, but I know that to be in there too much would defeat the purpose of him sequestering himself, so I try to keep my visits to a minimum.

Salsa with the Pope

I'm actually enjoying my time alone reading and just being mellow. I love to feel the heat of the sun on my body. It energizes and relaxes me all at the same time.

My only real concern is Alan. I mean he's always tense when he works, but I'm not usually around for the actual 'writing' part of it and the last time I checked on him, I was pretty sure he was going to throw something out the window. Since I didn't want that something to be me, I left him to his own devices. I am trying desperately not to take it personally, though that's difficult.

When he emerges for a snack and another beer an hour or so later, I try to keep it light. He comes over to where I'm lying on my lounge chair, utters a "Hello," kisses me lightly on the lips and scampers off. He stops to have a conversation with some of the others, who are busy planting herbs on the side of the house before going in. I can't hear their conversation at all, but I hear laughter. And I'm jealous. I won't deny it. They all get to laugh it up with Alan when he's clearly not in the mood for fun, but he's not going to share his misery with them. No, he saves that only for me. Lucky me.

The Genes and the others head over to the Hobarts for a barbeque in the evening. Of course we were to attend too, but Alan obviously had other plans. Like sitting in the hot bedroom—alone—staring at the same words over and over again. Since I was tired of the seventh wheel business, I opted to stay with him. I cooked burgers on the grill—he ate one two hours after they were made—and finished a suspense novel on the deck. Tomorrow has got to be better. Hope springs eternal.

Fourth of July. It's going to be a day filled with picnicking by the lake, riding bikes, canoeing and fireworks. I'm really looking forward to it, that is, until I spy Alan at the breakfast table. He looks like hell. Literally the devil. Red eyes, stubble, and hair that is sprouting in every direction, like horns. He holds a cup of coffee in one hand, his head buried in a notebook that rests on the table.

"Morning," I say to no one in particular.

There are two others at the table reading the paper, drinking coffee, eating fruit. They utter a hello. Nothing from Alan. I sit down and feel lost. All of the sudden I feel like I don't belong here. I mean I really like Gene and Jeannie, but they're busy trying to entertain the others. And what's with Alan? I know he has a re-write to complete. Oh, boy, do I know it…who doesn't know it? But what does that have to do with today. He already as much as admitted that he wasn't going to get as much done as he'd like. So give it up and join the human race, for God's sake!

I sit there a few minutes, say none of what I'm thinking and try to let my temper cool. Alan eventually lets out a frustrated groan and gets up, taking his notebook and coffee with him. He slams into the house. I sit a little longer, eat a few grapes, take a short walk around the house and then poke my head into the bedroom he's working in.

"Hey. You okay," I ask, just wanting to see what he comes up with.

"Hey."

He keeps staring at the keyboard, like he's going to make it type with his eyes.

"Anything you need," I ask, trying to be supportive, though not completely convinced it's warranted at this moment.

I approach him and touch his neck. It is slick with sweat.

"Nope. Just need to be alone."

"Okay. We'll, I'll just go and see you later."

And with that I leave the room.

The remainder of the day is just as tense. I go to the lake with the others, but find myself feeling isolated. I try to make conversation and join along, but I often don't know what they're talking about or am simply not interested. When Alan does eventually join us, despite the tension, I have to admit, I'm pleased to see him.

"Let's take the boat out," he says while grabbing hold of my hand.

Though he's here and trying to interact, I can tell there are remnants of frustration living not far below the surface.

"You know how to do this, right?" I ask, as we push the canoe out onto the lake.

Alan laughs.

"There's nothing really to it. We paddle and we move."

We begin paddling and traveling far out onto the center of the lake. It is a beautiful day and the water temperature seems just right.

"I think I'm going to head in." Alan says to me abruptly.

"Where? Into the water, you mean?" I ask.

"Yeah, why not? You stay here and then when I get back, you can go in."

"But how will you get back into the boat?" I ask, not akin to this idea in the least. We're way over our heads, nothing to hold onto even remotely near.

"I'll just climb in. It'll be fine."

And with that he dives out of the canoe. He swims along the edge of the boat and frolics around for a good ten minutes before preparing to re-board.

"Okay, I'm going to tilt the boat this way, so you need to move your weight to that end," he instructs before making his attempt.

I do as he says, but time and again, he is unable to make his way back in.

"Now what?" I ask.

"This time I'm just going to do it, okay. So, just stay to that side no matter what."

Again, I follow his instructions, but the next thing I know the canoe has capsized and we are both over our heads in the middle of the lake.

"Now what," I yell, my voice straining, my body paddling to stay afloat.

"We have to turn it over and get all the water out of it," he tells me.

"And how do you propose we do that?" I say with all the sarcasm I can muster, which isn't all that much, as I am treading water, holding onto a canoe that is doing everything in its power to sink.

I'm pissed, thinking of my hat and sunglasses—the third pair this month that I've lost. And this, this is what he calls a vacation. New Jersey's looking pretty good right about now.

"Not sure."

I spot a buoy with a dock several yards away.

"What if we pull it over there and then try to flip it over and get the water out? We can stand on the platform." I suggest.

"Okay. Let's try it."

We abandon our doggy paddle and begin swimming, guiding the boat for several minutes, finally reaching the platform. I boost myself up onto the dock and help Alan turn the canoe over. My God it's heavy. And then we have to really work fast to get the water out of there. It's weighing the canoe down, pulling it under.

It takes a good half hour, but eventually the canoe does seem almost back to normal...like it was run through a car wash, but no worse for wear. Alan takes it back to the shore while I swim alone.

By the time we reach the others, they are all packed up, ready to go back to the cottage. In fact, Jeannie and another girl have already headed back on bikes.

Alan and I speak little for the next couple of hours. We shower and get ready to go to the fireworks display at another lake. We pile into the car and ride with the others...still silence between us.

We stand amidst hundreds of people and wait for the magic to begin. I stand near Gene, who is holding Jeannie's hand. It makes me sad, to see them so happy. And to feel that my relationship is somehow off. I can't really put my finger on it. And when we're together and everything is going well...well, I am so in love with him and I am so sure about us.

But it's times like these that I question it...I question myself. No one is perfect. And there are always going to be things about the guys I date that I don't like...it's just a matter of deciding what I will and what I won't accept. And I just don't know. Where are we?

Alan comes to stand behind me and wraps his arms around my body. This is an unspoken apology. It is his way of saying that he is intense and he doesn't mean to take it out on me. But is this how it will always be?

CHAPTER 18

The day I've been dreading arrives. Well, not exactly dreading. I want Dai to meet Alan. But I want Dai to *like* Alan and I know that having both of those things happen is highly unlikely.

Not that Dai himself isn't perfectly likable and lovely. He is. Sometimes it just takes awhile for others to realize this.

He is also very protective of me. Overly protective. And when it comes to men, well, let's just say that I haven't dated one that passed all the tests. I mean they can be perfectly nice guys, and Dai will even own up to this, but that does not make them perfect *for me*. So, needless to say I am having high anxiety as the hour nears.

We are meeting Alan at a restaurant in midtown. It is going to be a dinner party of sorts with many people. This is done on purpose. So as not to promote an inquisition of Alan, I feel it will be easier for the two of them to meet during a function of sorts with other people. There will be plenty more time for them to get to know each other one-on-one, I reason.

I wear my white slinky dress. *Only* my white slinky dress. Well, I'm planning to wear sandals too, but other than that… My white dress, you see, is long and flowing with side splits and spaghetti straps, however, it is one of those items that doesn't promote the use of undergarments in any form.

Though I'm not one prone to going *neck-ed*, I find myself not fighting the notion. This after several attempts of trying everything from a white strapless bra (the stitching showed) to seamless panties (apparently not seamless enough) to pasties, which only stuck for 45 minutes (and I plan to be out a little longer than that).

I glance myself in the mirror. Not too bad. I look down at my feet, cramped into three-inch sandals and scrutinize my toes. Ten toes. Ten maroon toenails. Yes!

For some reason, I have been having a hard time keeping all ten of my toenails intact. I went to the doctor and explained that one day I noticed that my big toenail seemed to be loose. In fact, it was so loose that it came off in my hand about a week later. The entire nail! Like a press-on nail, but not. Though I believed this to be a rare and strange occurrence (me and my girlfriends were mystified by this for days), the doctor didn't seem to find it odd at all. He gave me some meds (pretty potent stuff apparently because I had to have my blood tested every six weeks to ensure that my liver wasn't being permanently damaged!), and miraculously it came back looking perfectly normal. This took several months of course, so I had grown kind of used to the nine toenails and one band-aid look of my feet (see picture opp. page). Also, it made a pedicure much quicker, leaving out an entire nail—and a big nail at that—but I must admit that I am much happier to have my ten toenails reunited.

"Samantha, lock and load," Dai shouts from the living room.

This is his way of saying it's time to go. Mind you, he starts saying this thirty minutes before we are actually leaving, so I try to pay little attention, as it just gets me flustered, thinking that it's time to go and why am I not ready yet? Of course Dai knows this. It's part of his game and he gets a kick out of it. I'd like to give him a kick!

"I'm ready. I'm just changing bags. Be right there."

I throw the remaining items from my dark bag into my smaller lighter colored purse.

"NOW, Sam. We're gonna hit traffic if we don't go now."

Salsa with the Pope

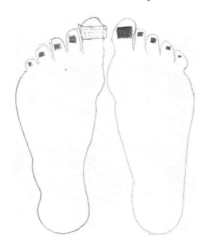

"Coming," I say as I race out of my bedroom, butterflies in my stomach, bongos in my hands.

Yes, bongos. I bought Alan a gift. Bongos. I saw them at a department store, believe it or not, and couldn't resist. I know they aren't authentic or great-quality, but it's the thought.

And truth be told, he is hardly ever not in my thoughts. I love him. Truly. Deeply. He makes me feel loved and cared for in a way that I have never experienced. And I love it. The feeling. The attention. The affection. He is the most amazing man I have ever known.

Oh, please, let Dai love him as I do (well, maybe not *as* I do, but rather, well, you know what I mean).

Remarkably, we don't hit too much traffic and are early for the dinner party. I leave the bongos in the trunk of the car and park a block from the restaurant in a garage. We head across 42nd Street. I am petrified nervous. Like for an audition, only I am not the one performing tonight. It's out of my hands.

Alan is standing outside talking with another guy. He holds a cigarette and as soon as he sees me, he discards it, knowing how I hate the habit and want him to quit. The guy is Peter maybe or is it Paul? I'm not sure. Vaguely familiar to me at best.

As we approach, Alan quickly finishes his statement, reaches out to me, plants a kiss on my cheek and goes to shake

Dai's hand. They act like they know each other already, that macho man stuff, playing cool, each knowing the other is sizing him up.

"Alan, good to finally meet you." Dai continues to shake Alan's hand heartily. "You too, Dai. Finally get to put a face with the voice."

We walk inside and Alan makes introductions all around. We each take a seat at a round table and the evening begins.

I share an appetizer with Alan, too nervous to eat anything else. Dai seems out of sorts, trying to make conversation though most of the chatter is about 'the business' (show business, that is), of which he has limited knowledge. Alan puts his arm around me and kisses me often on the cheek and ear. He compliments my dress, as do many of the others at the table. Pam, I am pleased to see, is there as well.

"That dress is stunning on you." She tells me from across the table.

"Thank you," I say. "I've had it a while, but it still seems okay."

I smile a little embarrassed. Alan brings this out in me. Embarrassment. Pride. At him. For being with him. Part of him.

The plates have been cleared. All except a couple of desert plates. Coffee cups linger, half full and lukewarm. I decide I better make my move. I whisper in Alan's ear, then tell Dai I'll be right back.

We excuse ourselves and head out of the restaurant. It is a warm night and I enjoy the small breeze that whips my dress up over my knees.

"Well, what do you think of Dai?" I ask as we head to the car for his gift.

"He's nice. Very nice. What I expected. Seems a little out of place tonight though," Alan says.

I agree, "Yeah, it's not his scene. But I'm still glad he came and you two got to meet at least."

We arrive at the car and I hand Alan his drums. He laughs.

"You are too much," he says and kisses my lips.

"I saw them and thought you might appreciate them. Sorry you have to schlep them home on the train."

"Don't worry about it. It's fine."

We walk arm-in-arm back to the restaurant. His hand trails toward my bottom and he slides it back up quickly and smiles.

"You going commando?"

I blush.

"Yeah," I admit. "I have no choice with this thing," I say and gesture at the white garment.

"I wish I'd have that known back at the garage," Alan says.

"Why?" I ask.

"Because I could have just taken you right there."

I poke him in the ribs.

"Oh, ya think, huh?"

He laughs.

"Yeah. Why not? We have to take advantage of our opportunities. Besides," Alan kisses my cheek, "You look absolutely beautiful in that dress."

Everyone is standing outside when we get back to the restaurant. Dai is busy chatting Pam up and I am grateful to have her here, talking something other than theatre. Some folks decide to head to a local bar, but Dai is tired and I don't want him to leave alone, so we say our good-byes and head home.

Once in the car heading up the Henry Hudson, I am tempted to ask Dai what he thinks of Alan, but instead I wait him out. I know he'll let it be known when he is ready.

"He's a nice guy." He finally says.

Not as upbeat a rating as I hoped, but not completely bad.

"Seems very intelligent. A little egotistical, if you ask me though," he adds.

Okay, I can accept this. He doesn't stop there though.

"He doesn't love you. Not yet anyway. You can tell. Body language."

This hurts. But I find comfort by reminding myself that Dai doesn't know everything. And to me, Alan's body language seems to say just the opposite.

Doesn't it?

CHAPTER 19

I am staying in the city. I love staying in the city. In the Village no less. At my girlfriend's girlfriend's apartment house-sitting. Well, actually cat-sitting. And at this moment, I am calm.

It is summer. Beautiful. I walk for almost two hours exploring all of the nooks and crannies the West Village has to offer. I have ice cream—chocolate chip—and buy sunglasses—yet again. I'm having a blast. And I'm calm. Though had you caught a glimpse of me yesterday, you would have seen a completely different picture.

See, this woman, Diana—she pronounces it Diiiieeeeee—aaaaa—nnnn—aaaaa—like she's some royal Dutchess with some accent from a made-up country—asked me to stay and watch Sttteeee—fffff—aaaannnn, Stevie, that's what I call the little critter, while she sees 'asssss—ooooooo—ccccccciiii—aaaaaattteeess' in Europe. Whatever. Who cares why. Just get out and go, that's my motto.

So, she leaves the apartment keys (the alleged apartment keys—I know, too much *Law & Order*) at a local deli. I am to go there and get said keys. I go.

I say, "Hi there, I'm here to pick-up the keys for Diana's apartment."

They look at me like I'm speaking in tongues, until I finally say, "You know, Diiii-aaaa—nnnn—aaaa," and I do my best impersonation of the phony Dutchess of Yuck. Presto, keys in hand.

I then return to the apartment, just around the block. I get my suitcase out of Dai's car, which is actually idling illegally near the sidewalk with him behind the wheel.

"What in God's name took you so long?" he ventures as soon as I'm within earshot.

I explain, he nods, laughs, smokes, but at no time does he offer to help with my bags. He has his limits, I understand. He did bring me all the way in from Jersey.

I unlock the building door, drag my suitcase in, go to Diana's door, insert key…it won't turn. I repeat the action for five solid minutes. I'm sure to bystanders the term "breaking-and-entering" keeps running through their minds…though technically, it would simply be "breaking," absolutely no entering going on here.

I return to Dai and report. He is forced to abandon the car—his second home—and shuffle into the building and show me what a buffoon I am, can't even open a friggin' door. Ten minutes later, we emerge, two buffoons, can't even open a friggin' door.

I load my suitcase again into the trunk of the car, pull out my cell phone and call Diana in Neverland.

"Diana, oh she's not here at present," I am told by her mother, who I am happy to hear, knows that 'Diana' has only three short syllables. I explain the situation and disconnect. It is two hours later before I receive a return call.

"Oh, Saaaaa—mmmmaaaaannnnn—thaaaaa, I am soooooo sorrrrr—rrrrryyyy. What about Steeee—ffffffff—"

I cut her off, sensing where this is going and truthfully, I'm getting worried she may just use all my minutes, she keeps talking with twelve syllable words.

"Okay, Diana, why don't these keys work?" I ask wanting to cut to the chase.

"Weee—llll," she begins.

I want to kill her. Simple as that.

"I actually got the locks chaaaannngg—ggeddd last week," she explains.

Hmmm….looks like little Stevie's going to be mighty hungry.

"So apparently, you left me the wrong key? Is that what you're trying to tell me?"

"It does raaattth—hhher look like that," she says and giggles.

Giggles. I will kill her.

Suddenly the giggle shifts and becomes a sob. She is crying. Loudly.

Okay. I didn't mean it. I won't kill her. I won't.

"Diana, I need the key. Can you overnight it to me?"

"You know whhha—aattttt," now it's not only long, but riddled with blubbering. Great.

"Calm down. I'll get in there. Somehow I'll get to Stevie. I will," I assure her.

Sniff. Sniff.

"Okaaa—aa—yyy, well, call the loooock—ssssmith. I haaaa—vvvvve his number somewhere and let him inn—ssss—tttall another lock. Now, don't yoooo—uuuuu worry, I'll pay for it, yoooooo—uuuuu won't have to."

Like I-I-I-I was wooo—rrrrr—ied about that? Do I look worried?

"Please, whatever you do, trrrr—yyyyy to be inconspicuous. The laaaaaaa—nnnnnnd—looooooo—rrrrrd is trying desperately to get mmmm—eeeeee out—I'm the ooooo—nnnnn—lllll—yyyyyy rent-controlled apartment leeee—fff—ttttttt in the building."

Sure, as inconspicuous as a man with a drill and a pick can be.

So, I proceed to call the locksmith, whom she swears she used last week, who swears he's never heard of her, and make arrangements for him to come out. The procedure is painless, the man obnoxious, the payment exorbitant.

As soon as I'm in the apartment, I call Diana, paying no mind to the six-hour time difference.

"Oh, wonderful news," she says in a speech pattern her mother would be proud of.

Note to self: Conversations with Diana are best while she's sleeping.

And so now all that nonsense behind me, I am ready to celebrate.

Yes, Alan is coming to stay with me tonight. We are going for dinner and then sex, sex, sex. I am psyched.

I return from my walk, shower, and ready myself. He arrives right on time, looking hot and sweaty in a beautiful pair of beige slacks and matching silk shirt.

"Hey Hot Stuff," I say when I greet him at the door.

"You're not kiddin'. I'm dyin', it's so hot."

"You want water?" I ask as I lead him into the small kitchen.

"Yep." I pour us each a glass and sit down.

"You can take a shower if you want before we go," I suggest.

"Nope." He says and pulls me on top of his lap.

He kisses me and then again. He is hot and wet, but I don't care. I am already dressed and ready, but soon it won't matter. We are in bed, naked, no covers, lying there after an unexpected (at least on my part) quickie. I look over at him.

"Hey Hot Stuff."

He looks my way.

"Yep," he says as he lunges for me.

I jump up as he begins chasing me out of the room and into the bathroom, where we shower and I ready myself a second time.

Dinner is at a delicious little Mexican place on Seventh Avenue South. We eat outside and Alan tells me about *The Ghost of Dyckman Avenue*, his manager, the investors…still not enough money for Broadway apparently.

I change the subject abruptly, not wanting a depressing evening ahead of us. The topic: past relationships…okay, maybe not a cheery topic, but I had to think fast, okay?

"How many girlfriends have you had?" I ask.

"Um, well, serious relationships, five or six I guess. I was engaged once."

I'm surprised to hear this. Apparently this was when he was really young, in his early twenties. He was already pursuing a career in the theatre, but this woman thought that too risky a profession, so she asked that he stop and get a real job. And he did! He quit the theatre! I can't believe it.

"But you love it. It's what you were born to do." I say.

He takes another bite of his taco and wipes his mouth before continuing. "I know. But at that time I thought that getting married and raising a family was more of a priority. So, I became a restaurant manager, a damn good one too, but it was a lot of hours, which left no time at all for this. Eventually I came to my senses."

He smiles a goofy grin, obviously trying to lighten the conversation.

"What happened?" I ask.

"To the woman? She cheated on me. It's funny though because later, I ran into the guy and he cheated on her too."

We pay the check and then begin walking the streets, just enjoying the night. I can sense pensiveness from Alan as we walk though. Perhaps he thinks he's shared too much?

"Hey, you alright?" I finally ask.

"Yeah, just thinking," he says.

"About?"

"I don't know. Work, I guess."

This again.

"Well, knock that shit off. This is our night." I remind him. "No thinking of work or money problems, or plot twists or—"

"I get the point."

We head back to the apartment after a quick stop at the corner bodega for chips, salsa, and playing cards. Once there, we sit on the bed, play gin rummy, nosh on chips and continue our heart-to-heart.

"I have intimacy issues." Alan finally says out of the blue.

"What do you mean?" I ask, really pleased that he's opening up to me.

"Well...I have a hard time with women. I have a bad history with them."

There are so many things that I want to say in this moment. I want to comfort him, tell him how it's different with me—with us—but I will myself to say nothing. Let him talk.

"I guess it stems from my mother not being there for me when I was little. I think I was three before I ever remember seeing her around. My grandmother from Spain, God rest her soul, raised me. She'd put me in front of the TV each morning, trying to teach me English because she didn't speak a word of it. My mother," he stops and lets out a long breath, "Who knows? She was too busy with her social life to give a shit."

I take a sip of Sprite and wait for him to continue.

"Now we're more like friends. And I'm glad. I care for her, but she and I had a real hard time of it and I hated her. For a long time. Truly hated her and told her so. It's only in the last few years that we've been able to bridge the gap at all. Gin."

He shows his four jacks and three threes. I put the cards aside.

"She loves you. She knows what you mean to her now." I say.

"Yeah," he agrees, "But the damage is done. That's why I told you not to worry when you met her. She's my mother. She's never going to be my mommy."

What a sad thing to say…to feel.

"So this makes you mistrust all women? I'm starting at a deficit from the get, is that it?" I ask, only half kidding.

He shakes his head. "It's not just her. I also had my first girlfriend cheat on me. With my best friend."

I feel the need to defend myself. "I'm not like that. I'm not them and I will never cheat on you."

"I want to believe that." He says.

Why is this suddenly coming up, I wonder.

He gets up and takes a bathroom break. I re-fill our glasses. When he returns, he looks tired and depressed. I hug him. I kiss his cheek, his hand.

"What an evening." I say.

"Yeah, sorry about all of this. If it bothers you…"

I stop him, "No it doesn't. I want to know." Didn't I?

"Did you ever see anyone about this? A doctor?" I ask him.

"A shrink, you mean?" he asks with distaste.

I nod.

"Once I saw a marriage counselor. The woman I was engaged to—she pushed me into it. One visit," he snaps his fingers, "never again."

Fear. He was scared. Scared of who he was underneath the macho, self-confident image.

Strangely after this conversation, I feel more connected to Alan than ever before. Maybe it's because I know he's as imperfect and flawed as I. Maybe it's because we're the same—both needing affection and love so much that we'll do almost anything to get it.

"I want love more than anything," I say to him as we lay in bed, his arms around me. "True, completely open, honest love. And I really think I've found that with you."

He shifts positions. "I don't even know what love is," he answers in an almost whisper.

I turn toward him, "What did you say?"

Obviously not what I thought I heard.

"I said," he begins as he raises himself up from the bed, "that I don't even know what it is. What is love? Can you tell me?"

I just look at him for a long moment.

What is it? Could I tell him? He has been telling me that he loves me for months. And now all of the sudden, he doesn't know what it is!

"What is wrong with you?" I ask, unable to mask the hurt I am feeling.

"Nothing is *wrong* with me. I just don't know…how do you describe it?"

I sit up, look at him, take his hands in mine.

"It's this. It's sharing and trusting and wanting to be with someone and caring what happens to them. It's all of it. If I ask fifty people on the street, I'll get fifty different answers. There's no set response. It's whatever it means to *you*," I tell him.

He nods.

I have to do it. I have to risk him saying it isn't true. Oh, please. Please don't say it.

I take a deep breath and say, "Why have you been telling me you love me, when now you claim to not even know what it is? Don't you dare say it if it isn't true."

He looks at me.

"When I say it to you, I think I mean it. It's what I think I feel."

I nod, slump back onto the bed, and wait for my heart to settle.

CHAPTER 20

I'm having a hard time concentrating on my work. Ever since my mom called earlier, I can't focus—not even on the menial task of doing a template letter. Brother.

It's been over two hours. I try her at work again—voicemail. I try her cell—voicemail. Damn.

What I do know is this...I got a call from my Mother earlier—first on her cell, the reception was poor—then on a landline. Though the reception was better, she got a call and had to go. She'll call me back. Hasn't.

The issue at hand is my cousin—a mentally handicapped man—who went in for emergency hernia surgery. This is not such surprising news, as this is to be his fourth surgery due to hernia. The problem however, is that it was discovered that this was an unnecessary operation, as he does not have a hernia. Apparently tests were not conducted and the Powers That Be just used his medical history as confirmation that it was indeed another hernia. Wrong.

This whole situation has my poor aunt riddled with anxiety. Not just because her thirty-eight year old retarded (sorry, mentally challenged) son just had an unnecessary hernia surgery, but also because while in the hospital he became adamant about seeing Dr. Gender.

See, my cousin is convinced that he wants to become a woman. Strange, you may think for a mentally retarded thirty-eight year old man, whose mental capacity is that of an eight year old boy.

He became 'woman-obsessed' (not in the usual way we mean 'woman-obsessed' when referring to the male species) about two years ago. He decided then to change his given name—Richard to Nellie Woman (not legally mind you, but rather within the family). From that time on, if you referred to him as Richard, he would look at you as if you had called him Chiquita Banana and declare that his name was Nellie Woman.

He has gone as far as having a description of the woman he wants to be...long flowing dark hair, beautiful brown eyes (his description, not mine), speaks well, and oh, she's a pilot...I wouldn't mind changing into her either, now that I think about it. Hey, if you're gonna dream, dream big, I say.

So we all go along with this, knowing full-well that it will never happen, he will never get the opportunity. Until now.

Now he is in the hospital demanding a sex change. They've had to sedate him, that's the last I heard.

The phone rings. I grab it.

"It's me. Sorry it took so long to get back to you. I had to turn off my phone. I'm at the hospital," my mother explains.

"And. How's Rich," I ask.

We only refer to him as Nellie Woman when he is within earshot. Otherwise, we revert back to old ways. I mean Nellie Woman isn't exactly a common name...even for a woman.

"We told him the truth. That they don't perform sex change operations at the hospital. At least not at this one."

"And he understood that?" I ask doubtful.

"Seems to've. Mind you, he's still a little groggy from the sedative. We did have to get the nurse to come in and confirm this to him or he said he wasn't going to leave."

I shake my head. Maybe with the money from a possible lawsuit for the unnecessary surgery, Rich can turn into Nellie Woman for real. Okay, maybe not.

That situation under control, I'm not so worried when I get the next call.

It's Alan's aunt, Kathleen, who tells me that she and Charlie spoke with Gabriela last night and they told her that they are sure that I am *the one*! That this time, it is for certain, no more women for Alan. It all stops here. With me. Yes!

After work, I am still running on that high when I arrive at Penn Station with my huge tote on my shoulder, a cake pan in my arms. I am trying to hurry, but my three-inch wedgies and my desire to keep the cake in one piece don't make it easy. It's my famous carrot cake, made for Mr. D., Alan's father. His birthday is today and we are going to Long Island to celebrate. It will be so nice to actually meet him and his girlfriend Barbara. Finally. It seems like every time we plan it, something comes up.

Penn Station is bustling with people, rush hour just beginning. I don't see Alan at first.

"Hey there Blondie," I turn toward the voice and plant a wet one on his lips.

"Hey. Whatcha got there?" I ask, indicating the drinks and small brown bag he holds in his hands.

"Just a little somethin' for the trip. Cookies. And coffee for me, and chocolate milk for you."

"Sounds yummy. Did you get the tickets?"

He shows me the tickets clutched in the hand that holds his coffee.

He takes a peek at the cake, samples the icing with his finger, utters an 'mmm', replaces the foil, and leads the way to our train, carrying our bags and treats as I trail behind.

The train is very comfortable and the ride is smooth, despite the throngs of commuters. Upon our stop, we gather our things and head for his father's apartment.

"I used to live here. When I was a teenager, this is where I lived." Alan tells me as we walk through the corridor of their building.

I can't even picture him here, in this apartment building. There is something so old-fashioned seeming about it. I instantly don't like it. The lobby. The way it looks. The way it smells.

When we round the bend, a man, who I assume to be Alan's father is waiting outside the apartment with the door open.

"Ah, you made it." He says and goes to Alan, giving him a huge bear hug, his grin wide.

Their bodies are like twins. Both tall and powerfully built, with short legs supporting longer than normal torsos. I feel like I'm intruding and perhaps I should wait back in the foyer by the mailboxes, but before I can make my move Alan speaks.

"This is Samantha. And this is my dad, Don."

Don and I shake hands and exchange pleasantries. Don then leads us into the apartment. It is nicely furnished, but small. Barbara makes her way out of the kitchen and gives Alan a big hug and introduces herself to me. She is a pretty blonde woman in her early fifties. She is dressed casually, her face made up nicely. I start to wonder if I should check my own make-up when Don says, "Well, we ready to go?"

Alan gets up, grabs his bag and leads us out of the residence.

We sit at the restaurant's bar for more than two hours. I am enjoying myself, save the grumblings going on in my stomach. The beer nuts just aren't cutting it. My desire for food takes a backseat when Don addresses me and starts talking about *The Ghost of Dyckman Avenue*.

"It's a true story, you know," he says before taking a sip of his vodka tonic.

"Really," I say hoping to entice him into opening up.

Though Alan told me about the basis of the play, I really am interested in what Don has to say. Don shifts in his seat and leans closer to me.

"Yep, me and my brother were on the outs for years. Not on speaking terms, nothing."

As he speaks, I can't help but take in his physical appearance. Salt and pepper hair, almost poker straight. This I learn is by design. The Spanish men in their family all sport the dark tight curls that I find so sexy, but Don, it turns out, straightened his years ago. His tanned face and eyes I have seen many times before. On Alan. Now I can imagine what he will look like in twenty-five years. Handsome, graceful, and strong.

I focus back on the topic at hand. Don is waxing poetic about Alan. His son is a great ball player, a brilliant director, great writer. Don's eyes light up and there's no denying his pride for his boy.

"My son is the best. There is no better. And he's a genius. They all know it. They're just jealous. He's going places."

We lift our glasses in salute.

CHAPTER 21

"Let's go Yankees," clap…clap…clap, clap, clap. "Let's go Yankees…"

I'm having a great time cheering our boys on. Yep, I've become a bona fide Yankee fan. Okay, this is only my first time at Yankee Stadium—so what! You'd never know it if I didn't tell you. I know all the players, the line-up, the positions and I understand three-quarters of the rules…the rest are strange rules that make no sense, so I disregard them anyway.

I take a bite out of my $6 hot dog. Tastes better than store bought—not sure if it's because I'm at the game or because I paid $6 for it, but whatever the reason, it sure is tasty.

We have great seats, right behind first base. Alan's manager scored them for us. Originally, it was going to be Alan, myself, his Dad and Barbara. But at the last minute, they couldn't make it—still not exactly sure what's up with that. So Barry and his new gal, Cindy came instead.

Cindy too, is an actor. She is petite with short blonde hair and light eyes. She is cute and sassy. Basically the female version of Barry.

Barry is sitting with us, but rooting for the visiting team. Of course every time he does this, he gets boos and shouts from our section. One guy even came down and got in his face—telling him to go sit with his losing team. It wasn't pretty, but the guy did eventually leave. Hallelujah.

"Next up, Darren James." The announcer's voice broadcasts through the loud speaker.

Cheers are heard all around us, with many, "Let's go Darren's," or "Go get'em DJ's."

Alan is among the shouters. He is a big Darren James fan—thinks he's not only a great ball player, but a humble one.

Darren keeps his private life private and is really focused on the game. At least that's what Alan told me one night while we were watching them on the tube.

Of course women also admire Darren—probably not for those exact traits—I would venture it's more along the lines of that smile, those dimples, and those buns—and I'm not talking hotdogs here…but that's just a guess. I wouldn't really know.

Darren earns strikes on the first and second pitches. He takes off his helmet, runs his hand over his almost non-existent hair, and replaces the hat. He then seems to focus on the wad of chewing gum in his mouth. Chomp, chomp, chomp.

Suddenly, he looks up toward our section. Our eyes meet, he smiles, winks, chomps his gum one last time and hits a homer. A home run.

Everyone jumps to their feet in celebration—all but Barry, who sits sulking, and Alan, who sits, a stunned look on his face. I look down at him.

"That was amazing…did you see it?"

Alan rises, nods.

"Yeah, great. Did he—was he…looking at you…no, I know, it just looked liked…"

I smile.

"Yeah, right. He always smiles, you know that."

"Yeah, but not the smile—the look…never mind."

"Most definitely he was smiling at you." Barry declares matter-of-factly from his seat.

I dismiss him with a wave of my hand.

"Nuh, uh, he was not. You're as silly as he is." I tell him, though I'm not so sure.

After hitting a pub in celebration of the Yanks victory, we make our way to Brooklyn. We hit the sack—a real mattress and box springs. Yep, that's right, a real bed. Alan ordered it through some ad so that we could rid ourselves of the air mattress.

The new comforter and top sheet of the set that I bought last week make their way to the dusty floor sometime during the night—or early morning more accurately. We don't go to bed in the night. EVER. We are always up well past midnight.

We are both awake now. It is almost noon.

Alan woke up around six with some epiphany. This happens often, but not to this degree. He was rummaging around for a pad and pencil to take notes before the thoughts left his head. Of course, these meanderings woke me out of my sound stupor. I ended up getting up, going to my tote and pulling out a pad and pencil so that the 'artist' could go to work. And boy did he go.

He was at it for almost two hours, reformatting a play, *Times of Confusion*, he had written two years prior. It was a collection of short one-acts and monologues, but his idea was to make it a full one-act play with all of the action happening simultaneously. Not an easy task, but a challenging one. I loved the idea.

After almost two hours of him tapping his head with the eraser-end of the pencil and me going through some of his papers, trying to organize him so that the next time he needed a pad and I wasn't there, he would have easy accessibility, we ended up back in bed.

We started to have sex, but his phone interrupted us. This has become such a common occurrence that I associate his ringing cell phone with my quivering clitoris. If his phone isn't ringing right before I orgasm, I just may not be able to come at all.

On the phone was his friend, Bobby from Long Island. He made it brief, but the 'moment' had passed and we both fell out almost immediately after he hung up.

Now it is past noon and I am starving. We get up, shower, and change. We are going to head into the city for a movie, a meal, and some supplies at Staples. Alan will need printer ink and paper if he is to begin a re-write on this play, which is exactly what he intends to do.

It's a nice day. We are on the subway into Manhattan. The F train. I like that we can enjoy some sunshine while we're on the bridge.

"Oh," I say to Alan, "I found some play when I was organizing your drawers this morning. It has your name on it, but I don't remember you ever mentioning it."

He looks up from the Post and thinks for a moment.

"Which one?" He asks.

"I'm not sure, maybe *Adolescence* or *Adolescents*."

He smiles and puts the newspaper aside.

"*Adolescents*. Yeah, that was my first play. The first one I ever wrote. It's not very good. It was a first effort, you know."

I poke him, "Oh, not so good, huh? Can I read it? Judge for myself?"

"Yeah, go ahead and read it. Take it with you if you want. I'll be anxious to hear what you think."

I look over the first few pages of *Adolescents* before turning in that night. It's funny and contemporary.

I keep telling myself *this is the last page, finish it later, go to sleep.*

But that doesn't happen. Not until I see the words THE END am I content to darken the room and sleep.

The next morning I can't wait to talk to Alan.

"Morning," I say when he finally picks up the phone.

"Morning," he manages, his voice sounding low and gravelly.

"Did I wake you?" I ask, knowing I did. He'll get over it.

"Of course not. I'm always up at 8:43. What's up?"

"I read the play. *Adolescents*." I say to him excited.

"Yeah? What'd you think?" He asks, seeming more interested in what I have to say now.

"I loved it. I really did like it and I can't believe you don't."

"It's not that I hate it. It's just my first effort and it needs work, that's all."

"Has it ever been produced?" I ask.

"No."

I think a moment then say as if it's a new thought, "Well, what about producing it?"

In reality, this thought's been floating through my head ever since I put it down last night.

"Barry has been after me to do it for a long time. He really likes it too. And there's a good role in there for you."

"Yes, I noticed that too," I say nonchalantly, though I've already put some lines to memory.

"But first, I would have to look at it and do some polishing. I don't want to spend too much time on it, but it could use a little re-writing."

"Of course." I say agreeable to any conditions.

"Okay. If we're going to do this though, you're going to have to help me."

"Absolutely. Whatever you need."

"I mean, you're going to have to help me re-write it."

I laugh. Yeah, right.

"You're nuts," I say.

"I'm serious. We will spend next weekend re-writing *Adolescents*. You and me. If you don't do this, I won't either."

Okay, this isn't a condition I expected. I can't believe he's serious. What do I know about writing? I make my decision right then and there.

"Done." I tell him wondering how bad can it really be.

Bad, okay, bad.

One week later, I lie on Alan's living room floor and stare up at the ceiling. Again. Still. I've been lying here watching a little gnat fly around for at least twenty minutes. It's not that I'm really into insects, I'm just trying to get my brain to focus. It is almost 1 a.m. and we are still re-writing *Adolescents*. Or at least trying to.

Alan sits on the couch and smokes. I hate it when he smokes, but he claims it is the only way that he can write. I'm not about to argue with him about it. Not this time.

"There has to be a reversal." He says as he exhales blue fumes.

"Huh? Translation please." I say still in a daze, staring at the ceiling.

"Whatever she is telling her has to reflect back on herself. It has to be the same thing that applies and what she is asking for has to be the opposite answer."

He calls that a translation...more along the lines of Farsi.

I try to play it off. "Ok-ay."

I begin to just throw ideas out. Not surprising, he vetoes them all.

"This is simply impossible. How can there be something that—"

He cuts me off.

"There is. I'm telling you there is."

I begin brainstorming again and no more than a half hour later I find it.

"It's her," I say, jumping up. "She is the reason he can't make it."

Alan's smile spreads across his face and I know that I have it.

"That's it. It's Oedipus. The answer to the riddle is himself. Excellent! See, I knew you could do it. Now, all we have to do is write it! But first, we need to go get more smokes."

We walk to the corner gas station, the only thing open at this hour.

"Do you believe it's true?" I ask as we walk.

"What?" He says.

"Like in the play, that you can only love or need one thing. If you are an artist, then it's that, but does that mean that you can't love a person just as much or is there always competition between the art and the lover?"

He knows what I'm asking. And I'm scared of the answer. I want to be the priority in Alan's life and I don't want anything to come before me. Before us. Not even his work. But I have my doubts.

"I believe that when you are with the right person, they mesh and become one thing. One great big beautiful thing." He says.

Good answer.

I nod.

Yes. I consider us that great big beautiful thing, especially at this moment, going for cigarettes in the middle of the chilly night, because we are writing a play. Together. Okay, I'm not really writing it, I know that, but I'm helping and it means a lot. A whole lot.

We hold hands on the way home and Alan says, "You realize you're going to be a very busy girl."

"What do you mean?" I ask.

"Well, you have *Adolescents* and then *Times of Confusion* should go up right afterward. You know, that great big monologue—it's seven pages long."

"So it's set? I'm doing it?"

I leap into the air.

"No other." he says and kisses my frosty lips.

Things really couldn't feel more perfect.

It is a long night of writing, but we muddle through.

I manage to get up and hit the office by noon. There is some miscommunication regarding my medical benefits that hits me almost immediately and I have to go round and round with several departments in the building in order to get it cleared up.

Oh, how I love red tape.

When I get home I am exhausted. I just want to go to bed. But that's not to be—I know this as soon as I open the door to the apartment—Dai is still up, perched in front of his computer, playing a war game. This is not the telling part. When he pauses his game and jumps up, that is when a signal goes off in my head and I know that bed will not be forthcoming.

"Samantha-son, you're home," Dai says as he makes his way to me. He has a silly grin on his face, his demeanor almost giddy.

"Hey, how are you?" I say as I give him a hug and go to throw my bag and the mail onto my bed.

"Good, good. Booty and I have been waiting for you."

Uh, oh.

"Oh, why?"

"Well, something came today that we ordered and we want to know what you think."

Two things you should know: one: Dai and Booty Miss, my cat, are now their own little team...I know this because Dai often informs me that Booty wants to know what I'm doing here, as I don't fit in. They are both old, gray-haired and retired; two: Dai has packages arriving daily from Japan. Everything from scrolls to shrines—we have now become 100% Japanese by association.

"Oh, okay. Uh, will this take long…it's just I'm so tired." I say to Dai.

I can see that I have hurt his feelings as soon as the words leave me.

"Okay, you know what, let's see it." I say hoping to ease the harshness of my last remark.

"Oh, goody," Dai says sounding like a child at Christmas.

He pulls out the most beautiful, ornate fabric I have ever seen. It is old-fashioned white, kimono-style, long with a wide puffy piping.

"It's for you. A wedding kimono for when you and Alan make it official."

Dai holds the robe open and I slip into it. It must weigh fifty pounds. No lie. Immediately, I feel a sense of regalness and power. Maybe this is all I ever needed to get over my insecurities. Forget the self-help gurus, just get a massive two-ton kimono to wash away your troubles.

"Dai, it's gorgeous. Really, really beautiful," I say as I examine the fabric. It really is lovely.

"It's stunning on you." he says and grabs the digital camera off of his desk. He clicks off a couple of shots before sitting back down at the computer.

I head to the full-length mirror we keep hidden in the hall closet. I admire my reflection, pose in each direction, and wish it were this simple.

I place the kimono back in its box. I go over to Dai.

"Thank you so much. It is truly beautiful. I really appreciate you thinking of me."

I give him a hug, and insist that he hug me back using two arms, instead of his customary one.

I sit on the couch, flip on *Law & Order* and decide that I'm not as tired as I originally thought.

CHAPTER 22

I am tired of inane conversation. I am tired of smelling garbage. I am tired of my ass feeling numb (because it is). I am tired of feeling tired.

I am sitting on cold concrete outside the Actor's Equity Building. My view is of three dozen garbage bags filled to the brim with, well...garbage. It is *pleasant* to say the least. But that's what happens to you when you decide to have Equity do your taxes for free. Oh, and when you wait until the last week to file.

Allow me to explain. Actor's Equity is the professional theatre union for actors and stage managers. I am a member, which on the surface would seem like a good thing (all Broadway, Off-Broadway, many tours and regional theatres are Equity, which means that if you are not Equity, you are ineligible to perform in the show). You can only join Equity with points (which are racked up from acting work), or if you happened to belong to another acting union (AFTRA or SAG), you can buy-in.

As a member of Equity, you are afforded a free tax service. This sounds great, but it is on the first come, first serve basis, so you need to be here early-on during tax season, or your wait could be mighty long.

Let me make it abundantly clear that I never, ever have waited this long in my life to file my taxes. In fact, I would venture to say that I am among the top 5% who file immediately upon receiving their W-2's, 1099's, and the like. Which leads me to why I am here on this God-forsaken concrete (did I mention that it's 3:50 a.m? Perhaps I was trying to spare you the unpleasantness of that awful truth).

See, I did not receive all of my 1099's. One company (who shall remain nameless...Dodge...) did not send me my documentation and not having any record of the actual dollar amount I collected from them, I was forced (or felt forced at least) to wait until the last possible moment when alas, I *still* did not receive it. But I have been assured by other Equity-ers (is that a word?) not to fret, the Equity tax people are awesome. I should hope so after this long, cold, numb-ass morning.

The good news is that I'm number 3 on-line...yes, two people showed up before 3:50 a.m. to stand in line. I should be in and out—*should* being the operative word—in no time.

At 8:30 a.m., we are permitted into the building. A nice warm building with real seats....heaven. At 8:31 a.m. they make this announcement:

"Please keep your line formation as you sign-in. Unfortunately, we do not know what time the first people will be seen, due to an unforeseeable computer problem with the system. Someone should be up momentarily to see if the problem can be fixed."

Before the kind woman who delivered the disastrous news can escape, someone in line blurts, "Wait a minute. I was here on Friday and the computers were down then. What gives?"

This question stirs us all up, as we've been on the sidewalk for hours waiting, apparently for something that was already known to be broken. A simple sign informing us of this couldn't have been hung? I am confused.

"Yes, they did go down on Friday and they are still trying to correct the problem."

Ah. Still trying to correct the problem. I should have gone elsewhere. I am just so tired of not having my acting expenses written-off every time I see a tax person, that this time I thought *I'll be smart and come to Equity where they specialize in writing-off acting deductions.*

I spend the next two hours on a carpeted floor getting rug burn, taking short naps, and listening to the rumors of what's going on in the computer room. #1 in line comes up to me and lightly awakens me.

"Is it time?" I say sounding as pathetic as I feel.

"No, not yet. Would you mind watching my bag for a minute?" he asks, pulling a cell phone out of the inside pocket.

"Oh, no, that's fine. Just leave it here," I mumble, still in my sleeping stupor.

"Thanks. I'll be back."

After forty-five minutes and no sign of #1, I decide that I can no longer wait and I must find a restroom. I take my bag, as well as #1's with me. I conduct my business on the 12th floor—apparently there is no bathroom on the tax floor—and return to find a still-missing #1. I take my seat along the wall and wait. But this time it is only two minutes and then a door opens.

"Bobby Pincher," the woman calls. #2 and I look at each other, not knowing what to do. We don't want #1 to lose his place—which could happen as you must be present when they call your name—but we don't want to not get in ourselves either.

"He's in the restroom," #2 tells her. "But I'm #2 and I'm ready," he adds.

"No, I'll just wait for him." She tells him and closes the door behind her.

"What'd you tell her that for?" I ask.

"Well, what was I supposed to say?" he asks me pleading.

"I don't know. Now, what?"

He nods. "We wait."

But not long. The door opens and the same woman asks #2 to come with her. He does and I position myself front and center. I feel like a hooker waiting to pick-up a date.

The door opens and a man, quite old with a wrinkled shirt appears. "Bobby Pincher," he grumbles.

"Uh, he stepped out." I reply in what I think is a clever response.

"He what? Stepped out?" Old Crabby says and pantomimes what I could swear is the international gesture for blow job. Maybe he thinks I *am* a hooker waiting for a date.

I say nothing. What am I going to say to that? 'Fifty bucks, baby'. No. I came here to make a hell of a lot more than that.

"Then, Samantha Anderson," Old Crabby says reading off a clip board and my stomach wretches. Damn. Why did I have to get Old Crabby. Where the hell is Bobby Pincher anyway?

I begrudgingly take my belongings—and Bobby's—and follow O.C. to his work station. I pull out my paperwork.

I say, "This is my first time here and I've had problems in the past getting my tax preparers to write-off acting costs, so I am really glad to be here. Could I ask you some hypothetical questions...kind of off the record?" I smile my most brilliant smile.

"This is an IRS Tax Office!" O.C. yells back.

I am stunned. Who the hell is this Crankster?

"Your paperwork isn't even completed." he says to me in a most crotchety voice.

"I am aware of that," I say pretentiously. "I wasn't sure what to do...I have a 1099 that I have no paperwork for," I explain.

"I can't help you then."

"You most certainly can. I called the IRS and they said to just estimate and it can be amended later," I inform O.C.

Just then Bobby Pincher has the balls to show up to claim his bag.

"I'm so sorry. Thanks a lot," he tells me and grabs his satchel and takes off to another cubicle.

Undoubtedly, the cubicle that has the nice tax preparer, who answers all hypothetical questions and speaks in a soft loving voice, not the scratchy out-of-tune record I'm getting over here.

"No rental costs, that's not good," he tells me loud and clear.

"Look, just do it, alright. You said I needed to be honest about every little thing and you won't answer any of my questions, so what do you expect!" I say my patience growing thin.

I hear a high-pitched voice on the other side of the cubicle. I don't recognize the voice, but I could have sworn she uttered Alan's name. Am I hearing things? I tune out O.C. and concentrate on the girl's voice.

"Yeah, it is the best news! I mean, I can't believe it. And this guy, Alan Da, Dala, well, he has a complicated last name, but anyway, he's really an up and comer, so to get this role, is amazing." She pauses. On the phone I suspect.

"It's huge. Like ten page monologue or something." Short pause. "No, they just called."

I take a peek around the corner.

"Where are you going? We're not finished yet." O.C. tells me sternly.

"Sure," I say and start around the corner. There sits a young (well young-looking, okay younger-than-me) woman playing with a ring around her finger. She blows a bubble, looks up and sees me.

"Oh, hey."

"Hi," I say, not sure what else to add. 'Did you just say that you're doing a part for a play called *Times of Confusion*, because if you did, it's my role and you're not' sounds about right, but I think better of it.

Instead I say, "I couldn't help but overhear you talking about booking a job. Congratulations."

"Oh, yeah." She smiles while putting her cell phone away. "Was I that loud?" she whispers. "Gosh, I guess I'm just really excited. It's a great role."

"What's the play?" I ask nonchalantly.

"Oh, it's a new one, um, *The Time of Confusing*, no, no *Times of Confusion*, that's it.

That's all I need to hear. I plaster a fake smile, don't hear her when she speaks again and make my way back to O.C.

"Oh, you decided to return. You people." he says and sighs.

"And you're a joy too." I say back at low volume.

My heart isn't even in my insults. Now, that's bad.

I take my paperwork to the counter, go back and drop a box of chocolates—a thank you—on O.C., to which he replies, "Oh, just what I need…" and quietly leave the Equity building, full of thought as to what just happened.

It is four hours later that I return to my life. The four hours spent walking aimlessly around Times Square, pushing tourists who can't seem to figure out which way to go and yelling things like, "Christ Almighty, go back to Kansas." It felt good. For a minute.

My mind kept trying to figure out how this happened. I came up with several scenarios...the girl was delusional and she made the whole thing up—including the telephone conversation; Alan was delusional and mistakenly gave my part to someone he thought was me; there are two plays written by an Alan Dala-something called *Times of Confusion*; I dreamt the whole thing, including Old Crabby (nightmare for sure). But none of them really resonate with me. The only thing that made any sense was that my boyfriend was a prick from hell who gave my part away.

He called my cell three times, leaving three messages, seeming more worried each time. Where was I? I felt like calling back and saying that I was having lunch with a woman who was doing a long monologue in a play called, you guessed it, *Times of Confusion*. I didn't though. I didn't call back at all.

CHAPTER 23

"So you haven't spoken to him at all?" Anne-Marie asks me the next day at work.

"Nope." I say before flushing the commode and exiting the stall.

"Well, how long you planning to keep this up?" she asks.

"Forever," I say and slump down into the chair in the corner. Don't think I've ever sat here before. Not a great view.

"Forever?" She says and laughs.

"I don't want to talk to him. Asshole." I play with my shoe, slipping it on and off. "How could he do this? And not even have the balls to tell me?"

"You've got to talk to him Sam. You can't just avoid him *forever*. You love him and to end it this way would be...wrong."

"I don't want to end it. But dammit, Anne-Marie, he hurt me. Bad."

I start to cry. Great.

Anne-Marie gives me a strong hug.

"Call him tonight and see where you're at."

I agree. Sound advice. But I don't get to call him because he is waiting outside when I leave work.

"Is your cell broken? I've been calling and leaving messages, but you never pick up. Are you alright?" He asks, worry furrowing his brow.

I feel torn between my anger and how concerned he seems. He pulls me to him and I am limp.

"What's the matter?" he asks, unable to miss my behavior.

"We need to talk." I say and lead us to the park across the street.

We sit beside each other on a wooden bench for several moments before I can find the words.

"Did you cast someone else in *Times of Confusion*?"
There. Direct. Honest.
"Of course I cast someone else. Many someone elses. There are eight roles in the play," he says and chuckles.
Oh, he's so funny. NOT.
I look him dead in his eyes, "In my role?"
The chuckling ends abruptly. He turns his head. I know the answer. He needn't say a word. I stand and begin to walk away. He grabs my arm.
"Samantha, where are you going? Don't...we need to talk, okay?" He says and pulls me back to the bench.
Should I stay or should I go (now I know how the Clash felt).
"Okay, talk." I say.
"Okay," he clears his throat. "I had a production meeting and they were holding some auditions for roles—"
"My role," I interrupt.
"Just, just let me talk, okay?" He tells me.
"Fine. Go ahead."
Oh, I can't wait to hear this one. I cross my arms and tilt my head....my open, optimistic pose.
"Stan and I were having some auditions for other roles, but there were a few people that were there for that role. Stan didn't know I had told you that you might be doing it, so—"
"MIGHT? MIGHT be doing it? Oh, no. Oh, no you don't. You told me I WAS doing it. WAS. There was no MIGHT about it."
"Samantha, I do not have all the power here. I can't just make all the decisions. Stan is co-directing, LP is producing, I can't just say what I want."
"Did you want her?" I ask.
"Who?" he says innocently.
"HER, the one who I just saw at Equity who got the role evidently." I inform him.
"Oh, you saw her. That's how this happened. I see now." He says and starts acting like I've done something wrong.

"Yes, I saw her and do you have any idea how much it hurt me to hear her say that she's doing MY role? The role you said I was doing?"

"Sam, they'll be other roles. You just weren't right for this."

"Weren't RIGHT? Weren't RIGHT for this? Are you fucking insane! Out of everyone who's read it, do you know that three of them, THREE of them came up to me and thought you wrote it *for* me? BASED ON ME! That's how NOT right I am."

I get up and begin walking away from him, forgetting my bag and having to go back and get it. Not a great exit, but can't have everything.

"So, that's it. You're not going to let me explain and you're going to let not getting a role come between us?"

"Alan, I thought we were a team. I try to help you at every turn...rather it's loaning you money or brainstorming ideas for your plays...I try. Because I love you and I believe in you. This...this cuts me to the quick because it means you don't believe in me." I am crying now.

He pulls me to him and holds me while I sob.

"And to find," sniff, sniff...I try again, "to find out," sniff, sniff, "this waaaayyy," I blubber onto his shirt.

Good. Serves him right. Hope I snot it up good.

"Baby, I'm sorry. I'm so sorry. I wish I could have made this happen for you. I wish I had the power to do that. But I don't. I don't."

He strokes my hair and I let it all out.

The next day I call Alan before I leave work. I need to clear the air and I hate to leave things unsaid. That's a thing with me—I feel nauseous when I am in a tiff with someone and I want it resolved ASAP or my stomach will just not level out.

"Hey, it's me."

"Hi. How you doin'?" he asks in a funny Brooklyn-Italian accent.

I can't help but laugh. He can turn it on when he wants to and it gets me every time. If I could just figure out a way for him to keep it turned on all the time, I'd be in heaven.

"I'm okay. You?"

"Why don't you come and see for yourself?" he suggests.

I acquiesce. Don't I always?

We meet up at the Bull Moose Saloon on West 46th Street. He is there with Albert and Barry watching a football game, drinking a beer. When he sees me enter, he puts his mug down and comes to me. He takes my bags and sets them near a barstool. He kisses me wet and hard on the mouth. I feel stunned a little when he releases me and looks into my eyes.

"Hi," is all I can think to say.

You'd think that we are beyond all of this, but we are *never* beyond all of this and I think it's what keeps me coming back for more.

"Hi," he whispers back. He stares deeper. He nods and says, "You okay?"

I nod affirmatively.

I'm not sure if he is talking about our argument or the kiss or the bruise on my shin that he doesn't even know about. But I'm okay. I'm with him.

I know that he likes things to move forward and doesn't like to discuss unpleasantness, in terms of our relationship, but I have to, must, and will discuss this issue between us. There is just no getting around it. And with our upcoming trip, I want nothing ugly between us.

I look up and Pam is coming out of the bathroom. I'm happy to see her. We walk toward the bar, and I hug Pam while Alan orders me a diet coke. We adjourn to a nearby table.

"How are you? I feel like we haven't had a chance to talk in so long. I mean we see each other, but it's always plays, and business and no girl talk," she says to me.

I nod in agreement and say, "Yeah. I didn't know you were here. Glad to have another female in the bunch."

"Albert called and asked me to join them and I only got here about ten minutes ago. I told Alan, no business talk. Not tonight."

I smile.

"Sounds good," I say and we clink glasses in salute.

"Have you read Nickey's new play," she asks me.

Isn't this business talk?

"Yes, and it's beautiful," I tell her.

I must admit that I do love that little bonus. Being Alan's girlfriend, I get to read tons of new plays and screenplays and then see the re-writes. I think I'm actually learning something here.

"I read it last week. Nickey is an amazing writer," I tell Pam.

She says, "Yeah, I'm really excited about the reading."

"Oh, yeah, when is that," I ask.

"A week from Monday," Pam answers.

Uh oh.

Alan and I were going to be in Florida a week from Monday. No problem, you say. Problem, I say. Alan is directing the reading. He obviously forgot about it. Typical.

Pam must be picking up on my dilemma because she says, "You okay?"

"Yeah, but uh, Alan and I are going to be in Florida that week."

She immediately gets pissed.

"I can't believe this. He does this shit all the time. He just doesn't ever consider anyone else. What is the matter with him?"

I have no response. He does disregard others at times. Hell, he disregards me at times.

"I'll talk to him," I say. "Please, Pam, don't say anything to him. Let me try to work it out and if I can't, then you can give him hell."

I join Alan at the bar. He is slapping hands with Gerry, congratulating him on a touchdown Dallas made. He sees me, puts his arm around me and starts planting tickly kisses on my ear. I smile and pull away.

"Hey, I need a word," I say trying not to sound too aggressive.

Salsa with the Pope

"Everything alright?" he asks as we step away from the bar. I glance back over at Pam, who is now in a conversation with Albert.

"Well, not really. You forgot that you have Nickey's play reading a week from Monday."

Alan looks at me puzzled.

"Yeah, so."

"So, we're in Florida that week."

He slaps his forehead with the palm of his hand.

"Fuck. Is it that week? Damn. I forgot all about it."

I nod, "I figured. What do you want to do?"

He looks away, his brown eyes moving and thinking, coming in and out of focus.

"I guess, well, can we call the airline and see if we can move our trip back a week?"

"We can see. We'll have to call them tonight. And your sister," I add, as her plans would now have to change as well.

"Okay, that's what we'll do," he says and pulls me into a bear hug.

And this is why our discussion of the previous events gets pushed back. Or so I tell myself. We are so caught up in rescheduling flights and speaking with his sister and having yummy make-up sex that we don't get to air-out our feelings about the plays, the definition of 'team' or the loyalty involved in a relationship.

CHAPTER 24

My ears are killing me. There is a sharp pain emanating from the inside of my ear canal and I can't make it stop. I wake Alan and share this with him.

"It's just the pressure from the plane," he explains in a 'don't bother me now, I'm trying to rest' voice.

"No, it's not," I argue. "I didn't have this kind of pain on the way down," I tell him.

"Come here," he says and pulls my head down to his chest and strokes my hair and face.

Like a child he is treating me, but it's okay. It's the only way he knows to try to comfort me and I must appreciate that. That he wants to make me feel better. Or that he wants me to shut up so he can go back to sleep.

I know we will be arriving at JFK within the hour, so hopefully the pain will subside by then. It doesn't. As it turns out, I have an inner ear infection caused by swimming in a pool followed by flying in a plane.

Note to self: Don't swim then fly.

I enjoyed Florida, which is saying a lot, as I don't really appreciate taking showers outdoors via humidity. Now, don't misconstrue, this wasn't Romantic Getaway Florida, this was Boyfriend's Family Florida, which is a whole 'nother thing.

I really like Alan's sister, Angela (maybe more than him). She's silly and fun-loving. She's also drop-dead gorgeous without seeming to be aware of it. I need to buy that girl a mirror.

Alan's mother, Gabriela was the one I was worried about. She hadn't seemed too eager to get to know me and I just couldn't imagine why. I mean, I'm, well...a lot of good things and her son says he's in love with me, so what gives?

Salsa with the Pope

Gabriela is an intelligent woman. I think she's had her share of rough patches in the past, but unlike so many, she's learned from her mistakes. She's got her shit together basically and I really respect that. She also paints. Who knew? Alan never mentioned that to me, but he rarely mentions anything that doesn't have to do with him.

I did still feel a little reluctance from her though. Almost like she needed to know without a doubt that Alan loved me and even more importantly, that I would become his wife, before she would fully accept me. I guess maybe she was just tired of getting to know Alan's women, then having them fall out of favor. Whatever. That wasn't going to happen with me.

Alan's step-father is a Spanish man set in his ways, full of wisdom, wit, and charm. He made me feel very welcomed with his easy manner and funny stories.

This all coming at the end of our journey. After our visit to see Mickey.

We were at Disney World for four days prior to going to Ft. Lauderdale. I've always wondered what the hype was all about. I mean, come on, an amusement park getting this much attention. But Disney is now its own city. It has resorts galore and theme parks out the butt. Quite spectacular, if I do say so myself.

I loved Epcot, going through and seeing all of the different countries. We stopped and bought Dai a few things in the Japanese section…plastic, unauthentic and overpriced, but a needed gesture.

We also had a lovely dinner in 'Mexico'. Alan knows it's my favorite and had made a reservation for a table along the river that runs parallel to the restaurant. You can cruise along in a boat, which we did. This could have been a prelude to an amorous trip, but remember, this wasn't about us, it was about family. His family.

Angela and her eldest son, Niles joined us at Disney. We were all sharing a room—expenses, you know—thus never a chance for lovemaking there. My hopes for sex in Ft. Lauderdale were dashed too, when it was decided that Alan and I would have separate rooms. Who decided this, I was not aware, though it wasn't me, to be sure. I thought perhaps we could make a game out of it and sneak into each other's rooms once everyone had turned in for the night, but alas Alan was not having that. What the hell was going on, I did not know, but damn, I wanted some sex!

Okay, there *was* one attempt at fornication. Alan and I went to Paradise Island one night and danced up a storm. For those of you non-Disney enthusiasts, this is an area of Disney that houses all of these different dance clubs. So you can do Disco, Grunge, Eighties Hair Bands, whatever lights your fire. We hit 'em all and had a blast. I drank so many cranberry and seltzers I thought I would pee myself, but poor Alan.

We thought it would be fun if I picked a drink for him at each club. They had maniac drinks with all of these different liquors and fruit juices at each bar, so I would pick what looked the most exotic and he would drink it. I don't know how he managed to still be standing at the end of the evening.

We were hot and sweaty and horny (hallelujah, horny) when we returned to the room, but alas, Angela and Niles were asleep in the bed next to us. So we headed to the shower, but that wasn't even remotely possible, as I stand 5'3" (on a tall day) and he is just shy of 6', so basically we either needed a ledge or a sick liking for penis/belly-button intercourse, which unfortunately neither of us have. So we take it to the bed and start trying to make love, ever so quietly. So quietly in fact, that we both fall asleep. Am I reduced to this? I'm not even 35 yet!

So, I was forced to get my thrills on the Tower of Terror and Oh, My, did I ever. I loved that ride. Rode it three times in a row and wouldn't have stopped, had we not had to get back to Angie and Niles. Next time, I promise myself endless rides.

Now I fidget in my seat, and count the moments 'til we deplane. Back in New York. Home, sweet home.

CHAPTER 25

My forehead is damp, my clothing starting to cling as I sit in the narrow hallway of Sundown Studios. There are dozens of us crowded into the tiny space. All here to audition for one of two things: a rap video or *Adolescents*.

Yes, that's right...I said, *audition* for *Adolescents*. Of course, I don't like this one bit. I am so often overlooked for roles cast by other companies and in bigger productions because they're "already cast" by people the director knew, dated, fucked or was affiliated with in some sense, that this one time, *this one time*, when I was going to be the 'in' person, I get screwed out of it.

Look, I'm not looking for a handout, but if that's how the business is run (and clearly it is—Tori Spelling—need I say more) then I want my share too. And this isn't Broadway for God's sake. It's an Equity Showcase, which essentially means, it's a non-paying union job...an oxymoron if I ever heard one.

Alan, of course, has assured us—his cast—that he will be present at the auditions (as playwright) and that he will "highly" recommend us to the director, an up and comer named Sandy Hodges.

Sure. Whatever.

I am seated beside Tom, a known-homosexual and wonderful actor. I only mention his sexual orientation because he seems to be having a rather allergic reaction to all of the scantily-clad women auditioning for the rap video.

I know this because he says, "Samantha, there are far too many breasts in here. Everywhere I look, it's breasts. Breasts bobbing up and down. Breasts bursting through tight stretchy fabric. Breasts everywhere."

Ah.

"What would you like me to do about it, Tom?" I ask.

"Not sure. Just letting you know not to get too close, as you have them too."

I look down and shrug.

"Well, not so much," I say before I can censor myself.

I must admit that lately I've become a bit obsessed with my breasts. It is true that I have always felt that I lacked cleavage. My breasts are so far apart, it's like I carry one on my back. As for their size, well, when I used to look down at them, they seemed fine. That is until one day when I was standing in front of the mirror at Alan's apartment and he came up behind me and pulled them up by adjusting the skin on my upper chest.

"See, if they were higher and a little closer together, they'd be perfect," he said.

That was when I noticed that he was right. They seemed to be fine on top, but then they somehow stopped short and didn't fulfill their roundness at the bottom. If they were 'lifted' then they would be perfectly round.

Alan has made comments several times in front of other people regarding my tits. This is always extremely embarrassing and once I got so pissed that I called him out on it, comparing his remarks about my breasts to a group discussion I would conduct about his penis...his square penis, lest you forget. He finally seemed to get the picture. He even hung his head in shame, which is exactly what he should do, though he never formally apologized.

But the damage was done...the insecurities already blooming in my head about my breasts.

Alan informed me that I had 'misrepresented' myself by wearing a padded bra (I told him from the start all about my breasts—shape, size, lack of cleavage, etc...how surprised could he have been). *Misrepresented?* I take offense at the word. Like every other woman walking around town isn't *misrepresenting* herself! Too bad society makes a woman feel that she has to *misrepresent* herself in order to compete in the 'pick-up' market. That or get surgery.

Which led me to Dr. Shapiro, a plastic surgeon at Hackensack Medical Center. I decided that I would "surprise" Alan with boobs…on me, not him. Like a birthday present for us both.

I made the appointment and actually showed up…I was having some nerves about the whole thing, but then I remembered that this was just a consultation, and nothing more. Talky, talky, which I am very good at, if I do say so myself.

"Well, I see here you are interested in Breast Augmentation," the doctor said as he opened the thin folder he was holding and glanced within.

"Uh, huh," was all I could get out. I was nervous, sweating.

"Okay, well," the doctor began then stopped abruptly. "Are you alright, Ms. Anderson?"

"I'm feeling, um, a little hot."

He got up and adjusted the thermostat that sat on the wall.

"See if that helps," he said and took his chair again.

"Okay, if you could just put on this gown then I can take a look and see what we can do for you," he said and smiled.

I nodded.

He left.

I changed, reveling in my nakedness…not because I think I'm a hottie, but because I was having some sort of hot flash. I put on the paper-thin gown.

Dr. Shapiro returned and examined my breasts. He made some notes and then said I could change and we could talk in his office just down the hall to the left.

I changed back into my clothes, feeling much better…no more hot flash.

As I walked to his office, I considered Dr. Shapiro. I actually liked him. He seemed sweet and we already had formed some sort of bond, him seeing my breasts and all. I made my way to his office.

"Okay, how you feeling?" he began as soon as I sat down.

"Much better. I think I was just…I don't know…nervous. Are most women who come here nervous at all?"

"Sure. Some are."

"Okay, as long as I'm not weird."

Like that was an indicator that I wasn't weird. We all know better.

"So, let me show you some pictures," Dr. S. said and turned his computer monitor so I could view some photos of another woman's breasts.

I wonder if she knows he's using her...does she get residuals?

"These are your breasts," he said to me.

I am confused. He didn't take any photos of me while he was in there. Oh my God. Is there some hidden camera in there? And I was doing the Naked Glory Dance and now they know it. I need to leave. NOW.

"Not your actual breasts, but breasts like yours. With the same issues as yours," he told me before I could make a run for the door.

I'm more confused. Now my breasts have issues?

"Um, issues?" I asked, waiting for him to tell me it's a turn of phrase, nothing to worry about.

"Yes. You have what is known as Tubular Breast Deformity."

"What?"

I smiled. Smiling makes things that you don't want to hear go away.

"It's just a fancy name for breasts like yours...kind of triangular shaped. Basically, your lower pole is constricted" (see picture opp. page).

If this was supposed to be an explanation that put me at ease, try again.

"I'm sorry, I'm confused."

I looked at the monitor and saw that the breasts *were* shaped like mine.

"See here," he pointed at the monitor, "you're lower pole is constricted...it's very narrow across. Now in order to perform the augmentation, we have to go in and cut that."

This didn't sound good to me. Not good at all.

"And how do you do that?" I asked, not at all certain I wanted to hear the answer.

"Well," Dr. S. said and pulled out a yellow legal pad. He used it to draw a picture of my breasts and their 'lower pole'. He showed how he would cut it.

"It's really not complicated, well, a little more complicated than a usual augmentation, but I've done it before with no problems whatsoever."

I took the drawing of my deformed breasts and headed to the parking garage thankful there was a reason, a *real* reason my breasts were like this. See, it's a deformity! I'm deformed, I wanted to shout, but didn't. I definitely knew they had cameras in there.

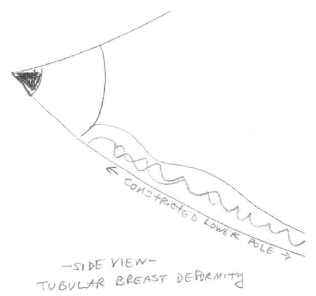

I decided against the surgery for several reasons. One being that they would be putting something foreign in my body (I still don't understand why they can't just suck the fat out of my hips—Lord knows there's enough there—and put it in my chest); two being that these implants were forever—not that they lasted forever, but that I would never be able to take them out and go 'au natural'—without looking like Droopy Saggy; and three being I have Tubular Breast Deformity for God's Sake and it's more complicated with having to cut ligaments. I mean this was *cosmetic*.

On my way home, I popped into Victoria's Secret and perused their selection of padded bras. They had your standard stuffed with cotton padding, one stuffed with what felt like sand pebbles (how comfortable was that going to be? and would I be making some strange bean bag sound when I walked?), one that was filled with water (I saw the Will & Grace episode...enough said), and one that filled with air when you pumped it.

Hmm, intriguing.

I took the pump-bra and gave it a test drive the following day. It filled just like a bicycle tire...and apparently was prone to leaks like one as well. I found this out the hard way as I sssssssssssssssssed my way out of a book club meeting, coughing frequently to cover the hiss.

Well, that settled it. I would remain the Cleavage-less Wonder. No boobs for Alan. Boo-hoo.

I am jolted from my obsessive breast thoughts by Tom being called into the audition room. I shift my position on the bench. I want to go home. I know I won't be going home with Alan tonight, as he will be here 'til the end, viewing all of the auditions.

It has already been two hours. I have been in the audition room five times. Sandy Hodges has called me in five times—to see what, I am not at all sure.

I mean she saw me do the entire play for her less than a week ago. Perhaps she has short-term memory loss? See, we had an informal reading of the play with "our cast" in their perspective roles in the hopes of avoiding all of this, but evidently, it didn't work.

I see Barry, who is going in next. Again. He is sweating buckets. I give him a thumbs-up sign and he sighs and nods. He seems very nervous. I understand. I mean I feel like I'm auditioning really well, but for fuck sake, it's a play that we've all worked on for months. We know these characters better than anyone in this hall. How can she even think of casting others?

Salsa with the Pope

Two more times in and I am dismissed. Damn. The longest audition I have ever had. How come I have to work harder for this one—the one that was supposed to be a given—than any other?

I go home. It is nearing midnight. I'm giving up on hearing from Alan tonight. I left him at the audition two hours ago, looking haggard and a little annoyed, but he couldn't talk. We kissed quickly on the cheek before I left.

Just as I'm pulling the covers up over me, my cell rings. It's him.

"Hey. How'd it go?" I say in greeting.

"Ahhhhhh," his response.

Oh, that good.

"Don't tell me," I say.

"No, it's all pretty good, but she just doesn't listen. She keeps asking me about other actors for your part, and I keep telling her that there are no other actors that I will consider for that role. She also doesn't want Barry and she has another girl just as good as Nikki, so it's kinda difficult. She even suggested Tom for Barry's role, and as great an actor as he is, he just isn't masculine enough. I mean that role is full of testosterone."

I laugh and repeat the incident with Tom in the waiting room.

Alan then says, "Exactly my point. So, we'll see. Nothing has been finalized yet. She and I are supposed to get together tomorrow for a meeting to go over our choices."

I don't envy him. I mean not only having to convince someone of something he feels strongly about, but having to give her equal respect, when it's his play.

"Go to bed, baby," I tell him.

"Okay. Hey, I love you."

"I love you, Alan."

CHAPTER 26

I'm getting off the elevator in Pam's building, making my way to her door. I can hear laughter. I knock lightly and walk in, the door ajar already. On the couch are Alan, Stan, and Pam. Liza sits in a chair adjacent to them. They are all sipping white wine and nibbling on something that looks like quesadillas, but I couldn't swear to it.

"Hey there, baby," Alan says as he makes his way to me.

He kisses me loudly, more noise than kiss, and pours himself more wine. He goes around to everyone offering a refill, but no takers.

"What's happening?" I ask as I take my coat off.

"Nothing. Just sittin' around bullshitting."

"You hungry? There's plenty." Pam says, gesturing toward the food on the table.

"No, I'm okay."

I want to know what's happening with the show, but at the same time, I don't want to look like I'm butting-in (though that's difficult, as I'm up to my neck in this play already).

I look at Alan, "How was your meeting?"

He shakes his head.

"Never happened," he says, mouth full of food.

"What do you mean?" I question.

"Sandy canceled on him and he hasn't been able to get a hold of her since," Stan explains.

"Left three messages. Haven't heard from her," Alan adds.

"How weird," I say trying not to sound judgmental, though I'm feeling a little of it creeping in. I mean she put us through the ringer at those auditions and now she can't be reached.

Liza smiles then says, "I know her. I've worked with her before and she's really good. I'm sure she's just crazy busy. He'll hear from her by tomorrow no doubt." I look again at Alan.

"So, what's the plan?"

I want to go home. To Brooklyn. To his bed. Our bed. I want to make love. It has been almost three weeks. Three weeks and no sex. And it isn't that we haven't seen each other or slept in the same bed. We have, but we're getting to bed at 4 or 5 in the morning and by then we're just too exhausted to even consider sex. So, this seems like the perfect opportunity.

Until Alan says, "Sit down. Relax. Take a load off."

I sit down, hoping it will only be for a few minutes. I don't want to rush out, but we can leave in a half hour or so and still make it to Brooklyn in plenty of time for sex.

Can't we?

Apparently not.

Fast forward two hours.

Liza and Stan went home long ago, Pam looks tired—it's common knowledge she rarely sleeps—and I'm ready to go and have been for more than an hour.

Alan is finishing the white wine off, talking to Pam about *Times of Confusion* when his cell rings. Alan says little, but looks uptight after the call.

He explains, "That was Gene. His uncle died tonight. Accident in Massachusetts. He's pretty wound up, wants us to come up for a while."

"Oh, that's awful. Where's Jeannie?" I ask.

"Out of town on business. He was pretty close to this guy. It was his mom's brother."

"If you think it would be better if you went alone, that's fine," I tell Alan.

"No, I told him you were with me and we'd be up soon."

Soon never comes. Alan hangs around speaking to Pam about grants, The Fringe Festival, *The Ghost of Dyckman Avenue*, anything and everything until it is after midnight.

His cell rings again. Apparently Gene got tired of waiting and called to say not to bother coming, he's going to bed.

I feel just awful. Not that I could have done anything about it really. But this is the one time, the only time, I've ever seen Gene ask Alan for anything. And Alan just sits there. He doesn't go when his friend needs him, but sits bullshitting, talking about himself and his own projects while his friend sits in pain two miles away. It is an act of selfishness that I wish I hadn't seen. So into himself that he would let a friend—someone he calls a brother—suffer.

The upside? I'm glad there won't be time for sex. I'm not in the mood anymore.

It is pretty easy to avoid Alan for the next three days. It isn't that I'm really trying to avoid him, but it just works out that way and I'm grateful. He has meetings and I have work and a girlfriend outing that I'm in desperate need of.

He and I speak a few times, just to check-in with each other and even though he sounds like the Alan I know and love, I have a hard time forgetting his actions regarding Gene.

Gene, however already forgave or forgot or both because he's back from Massachusetts and wants to speak with Alan about something very important this evening.

Alan thinks that Gene is going to propose to Jeannie, that he is gearing up for the big moment. I hope so. They're a perfect match and truth be told, I think it just might push Alan to make some decisions of his own....hint, hint.

Though Alan's told me time and again that he wants to take care of me and doesn't want to make a move until "we" have money, that just isn't important to me. Money or not, I want to get married and I think if Gene is ready to take the plunge, maybe Alan won't be too far behind.

I sit with Anne-Marie in a little pizza parlor near Times Square and stuff my face.

"Maybe he just doesn't deal well with death. Some people are that way," she says when I tell her what happened with Gene.

"It just put me off," I say between bites.

She nods.

"I know. I understand, girl. It would put me off too, but sometimes people react differently to things that they have no control over, you know?"

I suppose she's right.

"Hey, what, you're sticking up for him now?" I say teasingly.

"Never. You know how I feel about him. There's something not quite right there, I can't put my finger on it, but it's there. But if you're happy, then I'm not sayin' a thing. To me, it's all about you."

She gives me a hug and I know she's right. I have to be the one to decide what I will and won't put up with.

We all have our own thresholds and they're different. What one person will compromise in a relationship, another will not. I just have to decide what my boundaries are.

I feel that I'm the lucky one. That's what it boils down to when I analyze it. That I'm lucky to have someone like Alan. Someone smart and talented and funny and sexy. Someone that I can call my own. And he wants *me*. Samantha from Ohio. Samantha who doesn't feel that smart or talented or funny or sexy. So what is he doing with me?

And therein lay the problem.

I am giving Alan the power. I am no longer me because I am so busy being an extension of him. I am like an appendage of his, an extra arm or leg. Something he can move at will. And he does with his attitude and actions. They most certainly define my behavior. Because I allow them to. I allow him to. I am just beginning to see it. Well, perhaps only a glimmer of it. But I don't *want* to see it. I don't want my fantasy to end. I don't want him to not be perfect. So, I choose to look the other way. Don't look for it and it's not there. That's what I tell myself.

CHAPTER 27

I pass Barry on my way into the apartment he shares with Alan.
"Where're you off to?" I ask.
"Work." He says.
He plants a kiss on my cheek and continues on his way.
I knock on the door, Alan answers in a dirty tee-shirt and navy pajama bottoms, the cuffs rolled up to his knees.
"Ahhh, you dressed up just for me. You shouldn't have," I say.
"Smartass," he replies.
We kiss lightly a few times on the lips and he takes the groceries from my arms. Dinner is already simmering on the stove. Shepherd's Pie ready to bake and mashed potatoes. Yum.
"I was cleaning the bathroom and the floors, he explains."
Indeed it did smell lemony fresh.
"I'll just go grab a shower." He says and disappears into the bathroom.
I take a look around before putting things away. He has candles burning—we use them often when we make love—which was when? I can't even remember the last time. Maybe tonight I'll get lucky.
"Stir the meat or it'll stick," he calls from the shower.
I go and give it a few turns with the spatula.
"So did you finally speak with Sandy?" I shout into the bathroom.
"Yep." He answers and pulls the curtain.
He is dripping wet, the curls on his head, weighed down by water, spiral downward creating dozens of ringlets. His body's a large mass, that is until you get down to his bony short legs. They look borrowed from a twelve year-old boy. He carries hair on his chest, but he is no wolf man. Of that, I am grateful.

"Well," I say in anticipation. "What happened?"

Alan attempts to tie the towel around him, gets it three-quarters the distance and pads into the bedroom for some shorts and shirt.

"We're going a different direction." He finally says.

"What does that mean?" I ask.

This is getting me nuts, him being so evasive. He comes out fully dressed and hangs the towel over the shower rod.

"I spoke with Pam today and I'm not satisfied with the way this woman is running her operation. I mean look at it. I've left half a dozen messages and she calls only once and can only talk for thirty seconds…says she's in the middle of auditioning for another show she's directing. Fine. Then she's adamant about using some actors she's already affiliated with instead of using the ones I recommended and she just seems too damn busy. Not to mention that she sent some e-mail with some ideas for the play. I wasn't even sure we were talking about the same play, she's so far off my vision for this."

So he does have some authority…thought so. Why did he have to wait until now to use it? That's the question running through my mind.

He walks to the stove and stirs the meat one last time. He asks for the baking dish, which I hand him and he spoons the stew inside it and then places it into the oven. I watch him do this, anticipate his needs, wash the skillet and utensils and remain silent. He comes up behind me and wraps his arms around me.

"You're going to get to do this part. Don't worry," he says.

I turn to him.

"Now what?" I ask.

The play goes up in three weeks and he's firing the director. That seems reason enough to worry.

"Do you have someone else in mind to direct?" I want to know.

"LP is going to handle that. They understand what's happening with Sandy. Well, Pam understands and she's going to talk to Liza about it. I mean Liza is really gung-ho for Sandy because she's worked with her before, but she's just not right for this."

I shake my head.

"Do you know how bad this looks for us? It looks like you're firing her because she won't cast us. Like we couldn't get the job on our own, so you're firing her."

I walk into the tiny living room, just needing space between us. I know this play is a joke to him. But to us, Barry and me and the others, it's real.

"It should have been handled differently," I say as I walk back into the kitchen, wanting to make my point. "You should have either said we were the cast and that was the end of it or you should have had us audition without recommendation. But this, this is the worst it could possibly be." I tell him.

Alan sits at the kitchen table and pulls me onto his lap.

"I'm doing the role. I'm doing the lead," he tells me.

At first I am confused. *Him*? He's doing the lead.

"Did you hear me?" He looks at me with a grin on his face. I guess I did hear him. He's the lead in the play.

Part of me is dumbfounded, almost disappointed, like this is becoming a joke. The other part of me can't help be excited. Alan and I are going to be acting together on-stage as ex-lovers who are still in love. I have rehearsed the part with him so many times already that it just seems natural that he would do it, I guess. This character is based on him, so essentially, he is playing himself...not such a stretch, but they were having an awful time trying to find someone to fill the role. I mean, who but Alan, would Alan be happy playing him? Clearly no one.

After the discussion fizzles and we are simmered down, the evening turns wonderful. We eat too much Shepherd's Pie and ice cream, then play Scrabble and curl up on the couch. We even make love later that night.

Afterward, Alan says, "Oh, I forgot to tell you. I was right."

I look at him confused.

"Gene got a ring—he had it handmade. It's beautiful. And he's doing it this weekend. I tried to convince him to propose in front of her family—they'll all be together on Sunday, but his sister talked him into doing it on Saturday in Central Park. They have this whole elaborate scheme planned."

And so it goes. Gene and Jeannie are engaged on Saturday. A wedding date set for January. Alan is the best man. I am very excited for them. I am looking forward to their wedding, though it's eight months away.

CHAPTER 28

"One, two, three and four, now switch partners," Carlos is directing our Salsa class.

Salsa Wednesdays is Anne-Marie and my new day...and this took some doing as she loved our Tuesday class...rather she loved this guy, Jesus in it.

But I pulled rank and said, "Hey, I need you to come with me and if you would have broken some guy's foot and he would have asked you out and you would have felt obligated, I would have switched classes for you!"

Your basic guilt-trip, but it worked.

"Watch yourself in those," Carlos tells me pointing to my purple stilettos, as he walks the room.

Well, that's just great. Like he's blaming me for the Dweebie Whisperer Frank Oppenheimer's unfortunate mishap. The fact of the matter is the poor guy got his shoe caught under my elegant purple footwear and impaled his own foot. I was merely an innocent bystander in the whole ordeal...well, practically.

"Hello there handsome," I say to my next partner Dean.

It's funny that Dean's in this class, because he and I know each other from doing a play together a few months ago. He's here with his fiancée to learn Salsa before they travel to Puerto Rico on their honeymoon.

"Hey girl," he says and concentrates on his steps.

"You're getting good at this, I must say," Dean says and I glow.

Yes, I am. Maybe, maybe, I will finally be able to advance to Level Two.

After class, Anne-Marie and I make our way down to the street. The elevator is packed and we all smell like we've been, well...dancing.

"See you later," I call to Dean and Madge, his fiancée.

"Hey, you guys want to grab a drink," he asks Anne-Marie and I.

We agree and head to a nearby pub called O'Malleys.

"I just don't know if I'm getting it," Madge says as she sips her Guinness.

"You are. It just takes time," I assure her.

"Well, you look like you were born dancing," she says and I smile.

I feel guilty, can't even revel in my God-given talent that has taken several Level One classes. I let her in on my secret.

"You little sneak, you!" Dean says and laughs.

"Yeah, she's a born dancer, alright." Anne-Marie adds and we all crack up.

"So when's the wedding?" I ask wanting to get the subject off my non-born talent.

"A month." Madge tells me.

"Wow! Soon." Anne-Marie says.

"Yeah, time's flying by. And when are you and Alan going to tie the knot?"

"Ha, if I only knew. He wants to get this play up and running before he does anything else. Including get married."

"How's that going?" Dean asks.

"Well, the reading they had was amazing, but now it seems like everyone's dragging their feet. And there never seems to be enough money. It's not like the old days when one producer could do it all. Nowadays, it seems to take several of them." I say.

"That's right. I actually have produced a couple of things." Dean tells me and goes on to list two very successful Off-Broadway productions.

"Really? You were a producer on those?" I say stunned. He never mentioned any of this to me while we were doing our play.

"Yep."

"Well, would you be interested in reading Alan's play?" I ask, always ready to pounce on an opportunity.

"I haven't read anything decent in months. I'd love to."

We make arrangements for him to pick up the script the following day at Kiera and Jack's place, where I am housesitting.

I speak with Alan later that night, all's a go with Dean getting a copy of the play.

The next day, I awaken, straighten up the apartment and hit the toilet.

I haven't been feeling so great today....crampy. I'm feeling worse when I stand up and realize what I've just done. I've just gone to the bathroom. GONE, you know, #2 gone, and I'm at Kiera and Jack's. And Dean's on his way here.

The thing is, Kiera and Jack have an unusual toilet. I liken it to a woman's vagina. Finding that g-spot can be a mother, let me tell you, and if you don't flush it just right, caressing the damn handle this way and that for several minutes, you might never get rid of your...shall we say, undesirables.

So here I am moving it this way and that, up hard, and sideways soft...I must admit this forces me to have a little—I said a LITTLE—compassion for men during the sex act. I mean it can be difficult to hit your mark.

Shit (poor choice of words) Dean's going to be here and I'm in here making love to a commode. Unsuccessfully. Not exactly how I want to present myself. Let's just hope he doesn't have to go potty.

The buzzer sounds. Oh, no.

I give it one last yank and there she goes! I made her come! Or, flush, rather. Yeah!

I don't realize that I'm holding the handle of the toilet in my hand until the elation wears off a bit. Damn! Well, he'll just have to hold it. I tuck the handle under the sink, wipe my hands and make my way out to meet Dean.

I give him the play and we end up setting off for a quick bite...no mention of using the loo, for which I am immensely grateful.

I get a call late that evening.

"Wow. All I can say is wow." Dean tells me.

"You read it? You like it?" I say as excited as if I wrote it.

"It's beautiful. And funny. I really, really liked it."

"Oh, this is so great. So, now you and Alan need to have a meeting and see what's going on." I say.

"Yeah, sounds good."

So I hook the two of them up, pleased as punch with my matchmaking skills.

CHAPTER 29

Finally a good rehearsal for *Adolescents*. It's only taken ten days of rehearsals to come up with one good one. I guess I should be grateful. I'm just exhausted. The way it's been going, we rehearse for four to six hours with the new director, then we have to rehearse another two hours with Alan, so that he can remedy all of the mistaken instruction we were given.

It's called politics. Instead of just saying to the director, you don't seem to know what you're doing or seem to have a different take on the piece, they keep him on and try to fix things as they occur. I will say this for the new guy, he got us on our feet in one week flat. That's an amazing feat. So, he isn't all bad, but sometimes it just feels like we're doing two different plays.

Tonight though, we're putting all that behind us and celebrating. *Adolescents* is finally coming along and Dean and Alan have made a deal regarding *The Ghost of Dyckman Avenue*—Dean will be a producer on the project. Yeah!

The *Adolescents* cast is on its way to Trinidad's when Alan's cell rings. He stops walking and places his hand over his opposite ear, in an effort to hear more clearly. I continue to walk ahead with the others, until I realize that he's stopped in place, and isn't catching up. He slowly closes his phone and places it back into his jacket pocket. He just stands there and stares at the brick building beside him. I go to him.

"What's up?" I ask.

He looks puzzled, confused.

"Uh, my dad. My dad is sick. I have to go to Long Island."

I join the others for a quick drink before heading back to Jersey.

"He didn't say what was wrong with him?" Barry asks after I've explained about Alan's phone call.

"No, he doesn't know. Only that he's been admitted into the hospital for some tests. Apparently he passed out while getting up to go to the bathroom. He hit his head pretty hard and has a slight concussion."

The conversation shifts and we are back to bitching about the show and what we're going to do with the director. I bail after a half-hour. I want to get home and speak to Alan again. I'm boarding the bus when he calls.

"How's it going? How's your dad?" I ask immediately.

"They won't know anything until tomorrow when the person who reads the tests comes in. Until then he stays here. He looks like hell, Sam. Really old and worn-out."

"Well, he just needs some rest." I tell him. "It's been a long day for him. Is Barbara there?" I ask.

"She's been in the room with him the whole time. Won't leave his side."

"That's good." I say. "Do you want me to come out? You know I will." I say.

"No. I'm okay."

He lets out a sigh and I know that he is anything but.

"I'll call you tomorrow." he says and hangs up.

I sleep fitfully, have strange dreams about Alan's father and some milkman—don't ask, I have no idea.

The following day, I trek to work, try to put my time in, and wait to hear from Alan. I'm getting concerned. I leave a second voice-mail message. I head to rehearsal, hating that I'll have to turn my phone off, but having no choice. I try his line one more time.

He picks up on the second ring.

"Hey, I'll call you right back." He says and hangs up.

I contemplate waiting around, but then I'll be late for rehearsal and I don't want any 'special' favors because I'm the playwright's girlfriend, so I jump on the train, hoping to be off by the time he calls back.

No such luck. He calls while I'm in the tunnel. I try him again.

"Sorry I was on the train." I say when he picks up.

"That's fine." He says.

"So, what's happening? I've been worried."

He says, "I know. I've been on the phone most of the day, which is why I couldn't talk when you called." A long pause. "My dad's got cancer."

Oh shit.

"Where?" I ask.

Alan sighs.

"He has Pancreatic Cancer, which has already spread to his liver and lungs, so it's pretty bad. They said that he can start chemo and we'll see how that goes, but it doesn't look good. They're giving him eight to ten months to live."

I wait, thinking that maybe I didn't hear right. Eight to ten *months*? No, that can't be. When Alan stays silent, I feel the need to comfort him, but how? How do you comfort news like this? I try.

"Baby, I...I don't know what to say. I am so sorry, honey. This is just awful."

"Yeah, it's pretty bad. I've been on the phone with my mother and Angela, who is just freaking. Barbara is a total mess too."

"I'll skip rehearsal and jump on a train. I'll be there as soon as I can." I tell him. "No, that's not a good idea. I appreciate it, honey. I do. But there's nothing you can do and it's all I can do to try to keep it together here. My dad made me promise that I'd be strong and not break down. I have to keep that promise."

Why my presence would interfere with him keeping that promise, I have no idea. But I feel trapped. I feel that I have to acquiesce to Alan's wants now. What else can I do?

CHAPTER 30

Things just seem to go from bad to worse. *Adolescents* opens to shitty reviews. Alan gets a great acting review, but the play is panned as he knew it would be. I never have one good performance. I feel 'in my head' (death to an actor) constantly, like I'm being judged by each and every person that walks through that door as 'Alan's girlfriend' and not as 'Samantha, the actor.' This is a real problem for me. And it is my problem alone. No one to blame, but myself for this one.

And that's just the beginning.

Alan's father continues to deteriorate. The chemo had to be postponed, as he was undernourished. Thankfully, Mr. D. gained six pounds recently, mainly due to the weight-gain shakes that Alan serves him whenever he goes there, which is three to four times a week. Basically, Alan finishes the play and grabs the last train to Long Island and comes back the following day. He has been doing this for the past three weeks and he's exhausted and it shows.

This, of course, is taking its toll on our relationship. He's not only exhausted, but withdrawn and distant. We speak on the phone, but it's more out of habit than a need to talk. There is nothing to say. The play is awful, his father is dying, he is exhausted and pressured, and I am helpless to do anything about it.

Alan gets a call from his manager saying they need a new draft of *The Ghost of Dyckman Avenue* by month's end. That's just two and a half weeks away. Thank God *Adolescents* is ending. At least now he'll have a little more time.

In the midst of all this chaos, I book a staged reading of a play. The venue is this really reputable theatre and I'm psyched thinking maybe it could get a run there. Also, this is a victory all my own.

The reading doesn't turn out to be so successful. One, not too many people show up, though Alan does, sitting alone near the back. More importantly though, I feel ill a couple of hours before we go on. Some severe pains in my abdomen that come and go. They are so severe in fact, that I have to lie down on the dressing room floor before going on-stage. Could this be nerves? Though I've never had anything like this before, maybe since my crash-and-burn with *Adolescents*, I've lost my confidence.

I manage to get through the reading, but with much difficulty. When I join Alan afterward, he knows right away that something is the matter.

"What is it?" He asks immediately.

"You could tell? Some actress, I am." I say.

Despite my condition, we end up joining the cast for drinks and dinner at a local restaurant. I want the opportunity to speak with the artistic director and I know this may be my only chance.

I get through the dinner, the pains still coming intermittently. Alan and I go back to his place and straight to bed. I know that sex is not even an option, not only because of my stomach pain, but because Alan has become celibate in the previous weeks (which of course, means that I too am celibate). And knowing that he is sick with worry over his dad—who starts chemo this week—and that he is trying to get the re-write of his play completed, I feel like I would be putting unnecessary pressure on him by demanding sex. Besides, what's the point if he has to be forced into it? I know he'll come around. I just have to be patient.

That night, I awaken to a wonderful sensation. Am I dreaming? Yes, yes, I must be. Alan is making love to me. For sure I'm dreaming. He is showering my back with wet kisses. I don't want to wake from this fantasy. I want it to last a lifetime.

I open my eyes slowly to the realization that…oh my God, Alan *really* is kissing my back. It isn't a dream. He is so into it. I let him continue for several moments before reaching out and touching him. His penis is almost fully erect. Yes! Sex! Finally!

As I slowly begin caressing him, he stops the kisses and rolls over.

What?

I continue to try to stroke him, but to no avail. He is completely turned away from me now. I lie back down confused as ever. What just happened? If he was sleep walking (sleep-kissing?) and he woke up suddenly, then please just let him go back to sleep and let us continue where we left off...yes, I'll admit it...I am this desperate...I would rather have my man sleep-kissing me than not kissing me at all.

But this does not happen. We speak not a word. I toss and turn the remainder of the night, wondering if things are worse than I know.

The next morning, I get up quietly and slip out of the apartment, careful not to wake Alan...if last night is any indication, these days he's far more pleasant asleep.

Lately, every time I wake in the middle of the night, he is either lying awake staring at the ceiling or hunched over the side of the bed, his head in his hands. Damn. I don't know what to do.

I get to work without incident, do the usual and break for lunch around two. As soon as I finish my chicken fried rice, I feel ill...yeah, I know chicken fried rice can do that to you, but this is something different. Something worse. The same pains as the night before, but worse because they're accompanied by the cold sweats. I feel dizzy. Light-headed.

I throw off my huge platform shoes and unbuttoned my pants, the pains in my belly needing more room to grow. I start making my way around the bend, preparing for the fifty-foot walk to the restroom.

About four feet in I get an extra shot of dizzy and grab a filing cabinet for balance.

The receptionist, a dimwit to be kind, looks at me and says in a sweet lilting voice, "Sam, did you lose something? Do you want me to help you find it?"

This, because my head is bent down (can't pick it up or down I will go). As I try to nod to her, she keeps questioning.

"Is it a contact?" Finally a lightning bolt goes off in her head and she utters, "Are you sick? Do you need me to help you?"

Bingo!

She comes and puts her arm around me for support. We take two steps before I am out cold. When I come to, my pants have started to fall (remember, I had stupidly unbuttoned them), and I am muttering 'bathroom, bathroom, take me.'

So they wheel me in an office chair to the ladies' room, whereby I take to the cold tile like a baby to a mother's tit.

Before I know it, I have quite an audience, including Anne-Marie who informs me that the paramedics have arrived. Why? Apparently security got wind of my collapse and called them. I don't want to go with them. I will be fine.

My male boss comes into the ladies room and informs me that I should go to the hospital to be checked-out. I don't want to. This will pass. I look to Anne-Marie and she gives me the signal.

Damn.

Alright.

Anne-Marie and I ride in the ambulance, me on a stretcher-chair—cute little invention that combines the comfort of a stretcher with the ease of a chair. She says that she will call Dai and Alan as soon as we get to the hospital. I want her to call them, as I am scared, but then I remember that Alan is to go to Long Island tonight to stay with his father. His chemo starts tomorrow and he was planning to stay overnight. Nothing to worry about, Anne-Marie informs me. Just rest.

I have never been in the hospital before—and am not looking forward to a return visit either. They do every test known to man on me and I even get those sticky discs on my chest that take forever to come off—that sticky stuff is really sticky!. I end up being there over six hours, which I suppose is not uncommon…maybe even a record fast pace.

Dai shows up and gives his support, in the only way Dai can by saying that he needs to get home to Booty Miss, can they hurry this along.

Alan shows up right after him. I am so happy to see him. Every time we hug, my monitor goes off (he rings my bell, what can I say?). He can only come in to visit me for fifteen minutes at the beginning of each hour and then he has to go back to the waiting room. I tell him to go to his dad and he says that he'll go there tomorrow. Pam calls and tells him that she will sit with me if he wants to go to his dad. He tells her he is not leaving me. End of story.

The diagnosis is that I have gall stones. They recommend I see my regular physician (I don't have one) and tell us that they believe that the stones are innocuous.

Alan looks at the doctor who is informing us of this and says, "Uh, she just collapsed, so how innocuous could they be, really?"

After three consultations with three different doctors, it is concluded that I will have to have my gall bladder removed.

Removed? As in taken out? No longer a part of my body?

Ah. Wish I could say it sounded like loads of fun. Doesn't.

I contemplate seeing if a class-action suit can be brought against my office, as eight women have had their gall bladders removed since beginning work there. That is suspect to say the least, though we can find no common link (we drink spring water, not tap and many don't eat anything common to each other).

My surgery will be done in laparoscopy fashion, whereby they put three tiny holes in my abdomen and then "suck" my gall bladder out. Yuck.

I keep hearing how easy it is and how I will be home the same day and the recovery period will be no time. Okay, compared to the old days, whereby they split you open and you were in the hospital for six weeks recovering, I'm sure this is cake. But it is still surgery, lest we forget.

New York University Hospital, November 16 is the date. Seven weeks four days away.

I am scared.

CHAPTER 31

I wish *Times of Confusion* never came to be. Not that I don't like the play…on the contrary, I like it a lot. And therein lay the problem.

I wish Alan would realize what he's doing to us by not letting me do this role, or for not even putting me in the running. Fine, if he doesn't hold all the power. I can accept that. But for him to just cast me aside (no pun intended) I don't get it. The role is made for me. Everyone sees that. Everyone. Except him. He cannot see it. He does not want to see it. And I am a fool.

This because I continue to be there for him at every turn, despite my promises to myself. Despite my declarations to him. I even tell Alan that under no uncertain terms will I see the show more than once. I do not wish to be involved. I mean it when I say it.

But I cannot stand to see him in need and me not there. See, the press is coming one night, so he "needs me to be there". Then his famous actor buddy will be there another night and "it would be so great if you could be there". Then the possible producers who may option it Off-Broadway will be there the following night and "it would be wonderful, just for a little while, if you could be there."

And so it goes. I end up at every performance, save one.

I am even a reader for his callback auditions, help with publicity, and pitch-in to set-up the cast party. I am the All-Around Best Girlfriend two years running. And for what? I'm certainly not getting what I'm giving. And father sick and Broadway re-write be damned, I am getting fed up.

The shit hits the fan at the cast party when Alan and the young woman who played "my" role (she was good, I have to admit, but it was still "my" role) begin flirting with each other.

What the fuck? I get extremely pissed off, feign illness and set off to New Jersey alone. Before I manage to grab my bus, Alan is by my side, questioning my behavior. *My* behavior?

"You, you have a lot of nerve!" I tell him. "What—is this what she did to get the role?" I blurt out before I can stop myself.

He just glares at me and then finally, "You are fucked up. What are you talking about?"

"She's all over you. And you're ready to oblige her!" I yell.

"She and I aren't anything. She likes Mike, not me. You, you are… fucked." And with that he walks away. I run after him. I am going to have my say once and for all!

"I am the one overlooked, by my own lover. How can I ever believe that you think I'm talented when you give a role that's perfect for me to someone else?"

"Are we back to that?" He asks impatiently.

I shake my head.

I go in full-force.

"I'm the one who set you up with a producer, I'm the one who's playing Ms. Hostess for you at every fucking function you ever set foot in, I'm the one making sure you're dressed properly, know where you're going, have enough money—my money, thank you very much, I'm the one who's caught between trying to console you over your father, and not get in your way with the re-writes. I'm trying to read your fucking mind and getting NOTHING in return. I am that person!"

He shakes his head again.

I left my non-verbal communication rulebook at home so I have no idea what that means.

"I need to be away from you right now." he finally says.

Perhaps he was sensing the headshakes were getting lost in translation?

"No, I want this out in the open. I want to know what you're thinking." I tell him.

"No, no you don't."

And with that he walks away.

I am numb.

At first it doesn't seem like tears will come, which is fine by me. Who needs red, puffy eyes, a mascara streaked face, and a runny nose? Not I.

I walk to a nearby bench, plant myself and just stare. Eventually reality sets in and my stay of execution ends. I weep uncontrollably.

Just as predicted, my eyes are red and puffy, my mascara—long past streaking my pale face—lies on a tissue in my hand, and my nose runs incessantly.

Hey looking this good, maybe I can pick up a new guy on the way home. Preferably a blind one.

The next two days go along at a snail's pace…actually it's only been forty-four hours twenty-two minutes, but who's counting. Alan and I haven't spoken.

I yearn to hear his voice. To hear him read the new pages of the play, to find out how his father is feeling today, to hear him call me a nut and tell me that he "luves me" in that goofy cartoonish voice of his. I can't live without it. I don't want to live without it. And I will do anything not to.

Pathetic.

I call. I have to. We have plane tickets to Ohio for the following week—okay, it's not Florida, but my family deserves equal time—and my mother needs to know whether he'll be joining me. Okay, *I* need to know whether he'll be joining me.

"Let me call you back." he says when I ask.

Okay, I tell myself, fair enough. If he doesn't call me back or if he says no that he doesn't want to go, then I guess that will be the end of us. As easy as that.

But how can that be? After all of this, we could just breakup over something so silly. Okay, not silly. I don't think it's silly, but next to all that we've meant to each other, it feels ridiculous.

It takes Alan only thirty minutes to return my call.

"Don't cancel the tickets." he tells me.

"Are you sure?" I question.

I kick myself for probing further. He said, 'yes', leave it at that.

"I'll go with you." he answers.

"I love you." I tell him.
"I love you back."
And so off to Ohio we go.

From the start, the trip is riddled with mishaps. Alan leaves his cell phone on the plane and we have to hurry back to the airport, run around speaking with a number of people from different departments (who knew airlines had different departments?) before it is finally recovered. Luckily. Apparently it fell out of his pocket while he slept on the flight.

This leaves Alan feeling stupid and inadequate (not that it should—human beings make mistakes, but for Alan...well, he holds himself to a different standard—as if he should know better than the rest of us poor slobs).

Apparently the moon is in Retrograde Pisces (Alan's sign), because not a day later Alan leaves his bank card in an ATM and we have to sit on our hands until the branch opens on Monday morning only to be told that it's been destroyed. Bank policy.

Alan meets a few of my family members—thankfully only a few. And though it seems risky to introduce Alan to my Gram, I feel I need to do it anyway. I love her despite her eccentricities. And she's 81. When will an opportunity like this present itself again?

I dial her number, let the machine pick-up, identify myself and wait. The phone is picked up with a shrill, "Hello, Samantha. Where are you?"

"Hey Gram. How are you?"

"Oh, not too good."

"Oh, what's the matter?"

"Well, my damn arthritis is acting up again." she says and chuckles.

I didn't know arthritis could be so fun.

"I'm hoping we can get together. I'm in town." I tell her.

"Oh, well I don't know. I wish you would've told me before...given me some more notice, you know. Don't know if I can do it with my schedule."

"Well," I begin, but she cuts me off with,

"I'll have to see here now. Gosh, wish you would have given me some more notice."

Yeah, I heard you the first time.

"I'm sorry Gram. I really am. Things have been hectic. I-"

"No, I don't really think it's going to be possible."

I want to tell her that I have Alan with me. I figure a chance at a boyfriend interrogation might broaden my chances of us getting together. The problem with this, however, is that it requires me speaking and my Gram listening—neither of which is happening.

Even when I ask repeatedly, "Gram, could I just say something?"

She answers in the affirmative, but continues to talk saying things like, "Of course, say what you want."

I try, "Okay, but you're talking."

To which she responds, "I'm not talking. I don't talk. You can talk. I don't want to argue, but you go ahead and talk."

When I ask a final time to speak, she replies, "Samantha, I can't understand you...you're talking too fast."

"No Gram, you can't understand me because you're *talking*." Of course she doesn't hear this, because, yes you guessed it, she is still talking.

After five full minutes of this, I give up and disconnect.

She's probably still on the phone explaining how she's not talking.

Of course, the upshot of this is that Alan is spared the inquisition on his sexual history, penis length and girth, and dissertation on proper intercourse technique.

Part of me is grateful, but frankly at this point I would have gone for anything that would have gotten us back to the word S-E-X.

Finally, morning before our last there, I insist on having sex. It has been so long. He is hesitant, but I am adamant—he is not getting out of that bed until he satisfies me. Okay, satisfies is not quite the right word. Penetrates?

It isn't his fault. At least that's what I keep telling myself. He has a lot on his mind. Hell, I have a lot on my mind too. I'm going to have surgery, you know.

The sex is unsatisfying. And not physically. Alan can usually make me climax, but what I need is him. I need him to be present with me. Was he ever really present? Or was he just pretending? I start to wonder.

At the beginning I was so concerned about if I was good enough for him—in bed and out—that I could hardly focus on if he was really present when we were making love. And how does one really know if the other is *present*? I mean what is that? Obviously you know if the person is *physically* present (and if you don't, then I would suggest dialing 1-800-IAM-NUTS), but how do you really know if your man is *in* it? *With you*? If you aren't Kreskin (and last time I checked I'm not), then it's pretty tough.

I have high hopes for the end of our trip. I mean it's only five short days, so maybe we can salvage a nice finish. *Wrong.* "The finish" is spent playing gin rummy while waiting in Boston for our connecting flight to New York.

Mom and I wanted to take Alan to this great little restaurant in town, but when we got there, they weren't open. So Mom says she knows this other place. But she can't seem to find it. She drives round and round until finally we decide to just eat at some local chain.

This is all fine, except that it makes us late for our flight. Not that we actually miss the plane (which is the most aggravating part of it), but the airline refuses to put our luggage onboard due to some fucked-up policy. So we have to be re-routed (even though we are there and our plane is there too) to Boston before getting to New York.

Needless to say—but I'll say it anyway—Alan is pissed. Just the last straw on an already tense trip.

CHAPTER 32

"We've submitted you for a Bacardi commercial." a rep from Uniquely Talented tells me when I pick up the phone. She then proceeds to run down a slew of dates for which I need to be available.

"Four days?" I say, thinking there must be an awful lot of Bacardi that needs drinking.

She doesn't answer my question, but instead asks, "Are you available?"

"Sure." I say seeing no reason why I can't swig Bacardi for $150 a day.

Except of course, that I don't drink. But I'm an *actress*, which simply means I get paid to lie, so I'm sure I can handle it. I doubt I'll get it anyway. How many times have I been this-close to booking something only to have my rep call and say, 'They've gone another direction'—which translates to—'you sucked, and didn't get it' in this business.

Imagine my surprise when I get a call three days later saying I booked Bacardi.

"I did?" I say not believing my ears.

"Yep, the casting director will be calling to give you all the details," the rep from Uniquely Talented tells me.

"Great. Great!" I say unable to hide my enthusiasm.

We disconnect and I do a little jig around the office, chanting, "I'm Unique-ly Talent-ed, I'm Unique-ly Talent-ed."

I stop singing once I spy two of the mail room guys communicating via their eyebrows—fortunately, I speak fluent eyebrow—and what they're saying...well, let's just say, it has to do with *in what way* I'm unique-ly talent-ed. Adios celebration.

I make all the necessary phone calls that booking a commercial warrants—Alan, my mother, Anne-Marie, Dai...I stop myself from dialing Gram, knowing that she'll want me to raid the Kraft's Services table or get a cameraman's phone number—for her.

Just as I'm finishing with my mother—who is elated, she's telling her whole office—

"Mom, mom I have to go, I've got another call."

I hit the talk button.

"Samantha Anderson, please." a young woman with a twang says.

"This is she."

"Oh, hi Samantha, Urlene over at Casting Hundreds, how are you?"

"I'm good, thanks. You?"

"Oh, I'm doin' great. I'm callin' about the Bacardi spot."

"Oh, yes." I say excited.

I'm bouncing up and down, unable to calm myself when all the sudden I realize that I never read for anyone. I never auditioned, they just sent my picture in. How could they want me if—oh, no, not extra work. Oh, no please.

"Well, you need to be at the corner of Wall Street and Water Street Saturday at 4 a.m. Oh, and wear running shorts—be prepared to run two miles."

Silence.

"Hello?" she says.

I am numb. This can't be.

I find my voice, say, "I'm sorry, uh, Ms., uh, Urlene, I'm just trying to put this all together. I have a part in a Bacardi commercial and I'm expected to run two miles at 4 a.m., is that correct?"

"Yes ma'am."

"And Uniquely Talented is getting a 10% cut of my $150?"

"I would assume so, yes."

"Why do I need an agent for extra work?"

"Ms. Anderson, can I confirm you for these dates?" she says only concerned with getting the job booked, not concerned at all with my dashed hopes.

"Um, no Urlene, no, you can't. Sorry to ruin your day."

I replace the receiver.

These people are vultures.

I go home without telling anyone, save Anne-Marie about my non-Bacardi spot. How could this happen? We already celebrated, for God's Sake. That's like having an engagement party and then getting screwed out of the wedding.

I get into the apartment, not wanting to face Dai and give him the news. I get lucky. He's out. A rarity.

I go on-line and drown my blues at the poker table. I've been playing Texas Hold'em on-line for a few months now. My site is Poker Palace.com. My handle is Scooby-Doo. My limit is, well, it's for fun, so its limit-less.

"Damn. Trip eights." I say as the phone begins to ring. Saved by the bell.

"Babe, I think we're going to have to go upstate this weekend after all." Alan tells me without greeting.

"Huh?" I say, my face still stuck to my monitor. I need to win this hand! I'm all-in.

"The Genes, this weekend...what're you doing?" he asks.

"Damn. I just lost. I was all-in."

"I've created a monster." he says and chuckles.

So good to hear him laugh. Things have been tense since we returned from Ohio, but as long as it's just a phase, then I'm with him. I love him.

"Honey, focus. The engagement weekend." Alan says.

"Oh, well of course." I say in response.

I expected this. Why he thought he could get out of it, I have no idea. It's an engagement weekend for Gene and Jeannie being held at a friend's house upstate. Alan is the best man. No getting out of it.

"You have to go." I tell him. "You're the best man. It's expected." I pause. "I don't have to go with you." I say, wanting to give him all the space he needs.

"You crazy? I'm not going without you." he tells me.

I can't say how good this makes me feel. So wanted. He is trying.

I know that I'm not the only one to notice the changes in Alan. Many of our friends have come to me concerned about his anti-social behavior. I'm just one of the last ones to experience it first-hand…can't say that I'm enjoying it either.

"So, we'll go and make the best of it. When do we have to be there?" I ask.

Alan says we can wait until Saturday and then only have to stay one night.

I make arrangements with Dai to borrow his car and we drive up the following weekend. It's a nice drive filled with trees and farms, things you usually miss out on living in the city.

We arrive at the house, which is full of people. There are nine of them, mostly women that Jeannie works with. Everyone seems nice enough, but I feel a bit out of sorts. I mean, Alan will inevitably be hanging out with Gene and then I am left with all these women, none of whom I know, save Jeannie. The longer we're here, the more I feel I don't belong.

First of all, everyone is drinking. Heavily. From the moment we arrive. Morning, noon, and night. There are Mojitos, Sangria, beer, champagne, wine, and martinis. I am the only non-drinker.

And here Alan goes, being distant toward me again. Specifically to me, or so it feels. He is flirting with two other women—one of which he physically picks up and flips upside down (more action than I've seen from him in months), the other he pulls her pants down to reveal her tattoo (perhaps I should consider tattooing my entire body, enticing him to pull *my* clothes down—of course he claims to *hate* tattoos, so why he'd want to see one—except of course that it's on a part of her body that is not exposed to the general public—I don't know).

Look, let me make something clear here—I may be a mildly jealous person, but I can handle some innocent flirting from my man—if—*if*—I'm getting what I need from him. And in my book, not seeing his square penis in half a dozen weeks doesn't qualify as 'getting what I need from him'.

I don't want to cause a scene, it being Gene and Jeannie's engagement party—the longest in history—so I just distance myself from the group as much as I can. I write in my journal, sit by the lake, and cry. A lot. I hurt. I am scared. Of what I know I must do. Alan finds me by the lake after midnight.

"There you are. What are you doing out here by yourself?" He asks as if nothing's happened and everything is as it should be.

I try to hide my tears.

"Thinking." I say truthfully.

He sits down and tries to pull me onto his lap.

"Don't. Please." I say and turn away.

"I don't want you to be sad anymore."

I struggle to breath. My nose is stopped up. Attractive.

"I can't help it. This is awful. I've never felt so isolated in all my life. I don't get along with these people. And you, you are so...I don't know." I say it all in a nasally voice.

He shakes his head. "Look, I don't wanna be here either. But we have to make the best of it."

"Maybe I should have a few drinks to drown my sorrows." I say. "Seems to work for you." I add.

"Whatever."

"I'm ready to go. Maybe you can get a ride back with Gene." I say and stand.

His anger seems to dissipate and is replaced by guilt...as in guilting me into something.

"Don't leave me here. Come on, it's only one overnight." he says and takes my hand.

"I don't know, Alan. Maybe we, maybe we just aren't right...any more." I can't believe I said it. There is an instant pain in my chest.

"This isn't the time for this."

He shifts gears.

"Come on, we're gonna play poker, maybe it'll be fun." he says as he leads me back inside.

"Okay, it's poker time." Gene shouts when we enter. He is carrying stacks of chips and a couple of decks of cards, one of which is very worn.

"Come on, baby, let's show'em," Alan says, grabbing my hand and pulling me toward the table.

Salsa with the Pope

What is with him? Now, all the sudden I'm his baby again? What, he run out of women to molest? Did he not just hear what I said outside? He is like two different people, honest to God.

I get up begrudgingly. "I'm not really in the mood."

"Come on." Gene says as he divvies up the chips.

The game is Texas Hold'em and the players are Gene, Alan, Jeannie, Trisha, Natalia, and myself. Trisha is the hostess, this dingy woman from Jeannie's office who prides herself on having the correct place settings for each course...brother.

Natalia turns out to be this bitchy British woman. She is surly and snotty and I dislike her from moment one. She keeps stroking Alan about his poker playing—like he needs stroking—PUL—LEEE—ZZZZ!

I am in the game for only two hands. The second of which, Natalia goes all-in with a bluff—clearly a bluff. I counter her. A bad move—a move I would not normally make, but I want to put this woman in her place. Unfortunately, I am bluffing also and her nothing hand is bigger than my nothing hand. Alan puts his hand to his forehead, as if devastated by my defeat.

I muddle through the night, Alan and I sleeping in twin beds, the beds pushed together to promote closeness—the hostess possibly acting as couple's counselor—but it is unnecessary, as Alan comes to bed at 4 a.m. I'm still lying awake and he's still treating me like I have the Clap...so nothing new here.

I am so grateful when I wake and it's daylight. I can't wait to get out of here.

And after some pancakes and bacon, that's just what we do.

The drive back seems to get less and less tense the further we get from that house...maybe it was haunted. Alan and I hold hands and sing loudly to the radio. He abruptly turns the music down.

"You haven't forgotten about tomorrow, have you?" He asks.

"Of course I know what tomorrow is...how could I forget? Duh, the day I get more over the hill." I tell him, thinking maybe me turning another year older is prompting some sadness in me.

"And?" he prompts.

"Oh…and we're supposed to do something…aren't we?" I ask, confused.

"Of course we're doing something. I will meet you in the city tomorrow morning, 11 a.m."

"And where are we going?" I want to know.

"Not tellin'. Told you it's a surprise." He says and smiles, clearly pleased with his secret.

"Hmm." I frown. "Well, how should I dress?"

"Bring an overnight bag with you and something nice to wear in the evening. Casual in the day. And SEXY in the wee hours." he says seductively.

What the fuck? This guy is nuts. I love this man right here next to me. It's that other guy we left back at the haunted house that I want nothing to do with.

Traffic starts backing up. We exhaust our c.d. collection, remain at a stand-still.

"Must be an accident." I say.

"You know, why don't we pull off up ahead and that way you can just go to Jersey and I'll ride into the city with Gene and them. It'll just save you a trip." Alan says to me.

This is Alan's plan. For us to stop off and he get into the car with them and me to go on home. Now, if he was going to do this, why couldn't I just have left yesterday?

"Fine." I tell him.

And that's what we do.

Of course, as soon as Alan is with them, the party can begin again. They all go and have a nice dinner and play games and of course, drink. He has a great time. This he tells me later on the phone. Oh, goody for him. Prick.

CHAPTER 33

My birthday. The phone rings. It's Alan. He's calling early—well, early for him—to make sure I'm up and getting ready to meet him.

"I'm not." I inform him.

"What's up?" He asks in that patronizing, 'Oh Sam is PMSing voice'.

"Nothing. Just that I'm in a pissy mood and I don't want to go." I explain, thinking that should sum it up in a nutshell: You SUCK, this past weekend SUCKED, Dai and I got into an argument which SUCKS, and I'm old, which really SUCKS.

"Okay, well then what'd you want to do? Go to a show and dinner? Whatever you want honey, it's your day."

Oh, so there's my Prince Charming back from the dead. It's nice to hear him being sweet, but I'm skeptical, as Mr. Hyde seems to follow us wherever we go.

"I'll call you back." I tell him and disconnect. I need to mull it over.

I take a walk around the grand neighborhood of Hackensack. Actually, part of Hackensack truly is grand. There is this 'old money' section that is so beautiful. Old stone and brick homes that are enormous with manicured lawns, all of which are different, not like the developments of today. I wonder if I will ever own a home. I wonder if I will ever rent my own apartment. This gets me more depressed and knowing that it's my birthday, I can't have that.

I return home, make-up with Dai—which isn't such a big deal, as our argument was about milk—and call Alan. I tell him that I will meet him in the city in an hour. I know that this is a make-or-break event in our relationship. I know in my heart that if he doesn't meet me half-way—literally and figuratively—

then I will be forced to act. I can't really even bear the thought of that, so I put it far out of my mind.

I am actually on time meeting him. So unusual. Maybe I just don't care what I look like. No, I care. It's my birthday.

Gotta look good on my birthday, so that when people ask how old I am—and they always do, manners be gone—and I tell them way past 30 (well, maybe not WAY past, but still past) they can then reply, oh, you don't look a day over 25. Or they better say that, if they know what's good for them.

"I like that sweater on you." he tells me first thing. "It's a nice color for you."

Although I like the sweater too, I can't imagine gray being a 'nice color' for anyone (a cadaver maybe?). I take the compliment though (desperate times require desperate measures) and accept a kiss on the cheek from him. I do not offer my lips.

"You smell good too." he tells me.

I guess it's just taken him a year and a half to notice my perfume. Granted, it's not one of those overwhelming 'I can smell it six hours after you've left' scents, but a year and a half...perhaps I should ask for a refund.

We have a pleasant journey and actually have a lot of conversation. I know that Alan is really trying, as most of our conversation is chit-chat and he hates chit-chat. Why is that such a nuisance for him? Why is everything he does bothering me so much lately? Well, he hasn't exactly been a pleasure to be around these days. His father. His play. My surgery. My insecurities. I go back and forth. Who is to blame? Blame for what? I just don't know anymore.

The only time during our trip that reality rears its ugly head is when Alan brings up his father. He is to go there this week and may not be returning for a few days. Things aren't going well. The chemo is not taking, as they feared. My guilt surfaces.

It's all I can do not to apologize for not being a good girlfriend and not being there for him. The only real reason I don't, is because when I go to form the words, they make no sense. You *have* been a good girlfriend and you *have* been there for him, I remind myself.

We change the subject determined to hide all of our worries until which time they are deemed suitable for the occasion. A birthday? Definitely not suitable.

And so my surprise is revealed. Atlantic City. Whoopie. Actually it is kind of nice and to think that Alan made all the arrangements himself...well, there's a real gift right there.

The Borgata. The newest casino to hit AC. The room, palatial. The finishes, beautiful.

"Hello." I manage to say, almost dropping my cell phone in the process.

Alan is abruptly undressing me in a hasty manner, making phone conversation nearly impossible.

"Happy birthday, Sam!" Pam sings into my ear.

"Thanks." I get out before the phone falls to the floor. I grab it back up.

"What in the world are you doing?" Pam wants to know.

"Getting molested by my boyfriend." I tell her and laugh.

Alan motions for me to get off the phone.

"Ahhh." she says and giggles. "I figured some of that would be going on. Damn that was quick. Is it beautiful? Were you shocked?"

That he wanted to have sex? With me? Absolutely. I don't say that exactly, but opt instead for, "By what? Sex?"

She doesn't say anything for a moment, takes a deep breath and says suddenly, "Anyway, I was just calling about your birthday party on Friday."

"What, oh. Uh, well..." I say, my mind divided by my once-in-a-lifetime sex fiend boyfriend and how strangely she's suddenly acting.

"Can I call you tomorrow about it?" I ask.

It's really a plea, since I don't know when the offer of sex will be on the table again (my next birthday? the one after that?).

"Of course. Talk to you later, Sam. Or should I say Mrs. D."

We disconnect.

She is weird.

I look at Alan, who is down to his boxer-briefs and socks. Nice look. Really. He makes a face and fake-pounces onto me. We position ourselves on the king-size bed (yes, *king* size) and begin to make love. Alan is attentive, but I can tell he's holding back. It's so obvious to me. But he is trying and this is sex, so I don't want to ruin it by doing anything, especially saying something completely de-erection-izing like "Can I talk to you about something?" If ever there was an erect-penis-de-stimulant, that would be it.

I enjoy our time together. Mainly because I am close to Alan. Close in his arms.

Close to his lips and eyes and fingertips. I can lie on his chest, if only for a few moments.

Though our lovemaking lasts quite a while, when we are finished, I am not satisfied. I want to do it again. And again. It has been so long. I want to be next to him all night. I couldn't care less if we ever set foot on the casino floor. I want only him.

He suggests that we take a little nap, which we do. I hold out hope that we will resume our sexual activity after we awaken, but this is not to be. We shower and eat dinner at a charming little restaurant.

Once I see our table, the flowers, the meal, I know that Alan arranged it all. It is prepared without us ordering from a menu. A cake is presented afterward. It is lovely.

Alan excuses himself and I am left thinking of Pam's phone call. Mrs. D. That's what she called me. Oh my God. I am dense. Okay, I was in the middle of getting some much-needed nookie, so my mind wasn't exactly clear. But she said Mrs. D. He's going to propose. Oh, finally. Suddenly all of my reservations about our relationship vanish and I am ready and willing to become his wife. I want nothing more.

When he returns to the table I am suspicious. Wondering when he is going to do it, what the ring will look like. Will he get down on his knee? Has he already told my mother? Clearly he told Pam. Or someone did.

He sits down next to me, takes my hands in his and says, "Happy Birthday, Sam. I love you." He kisses my hands, then my lips lightly. "You look beautiful," he adds.

"Thank you. For everything, Alan."

We leave the restaurant and hit the casino floor.

Although I enjoy playing some blackjack, most of my time is spent in front of the video poker machines. Alan despises video poker. He thinks it is a waste of valuable poker time and money (statistically the most wasteful he states) though I have been awarded $1,000 for royal flushes on two separate occasions. Alan enjoys the real thing. Real cards. Real poker. Real sit-down for six-hours-at-a-time poker. And I don't join him on this—I would get my clock cleaned in thirty seconds flat. So I am very accustomed to him going to the tables overnight and seeing him in the morning. And I am fine with that.

But tonight is different. Alan plays *video* poker with me for hours. He doesn't *ever* leave me the entire night. This confirms what I already know...that my affirmative answer to his proposal will be the right thing. He loves me. I love him.

Suddenly, he looks over at me and smiles. He says, "You know I'm putting you in the movie, right?"

Alan's play, *The Ghost of Dyckman Avenue* was just optioned by a filmmaker, who wants him to write it in screenplay format. The opening sequence will be shot in Atlantic City. I guess being here triggered his thoughts.

I look up at him and smile sheepishly.

"Well, I knew you were starting the screenplay, but I didn't know..." I nod my head.

He smiles. "I'm not sure if you're going to be a Blackjack dealer or a crazy slot lady, but definitely you're in it."

He pulls me to him and kisses me full on the lips. I feel so wonderful in this moment. It's not about the movie really. It's about him believing in me. That's what it has always been about. Us being a team.

"Honey, I think I'm going to take a nice long bath. You go play some poker and I'll see you later." I tell him.

"You sure? I don't need to play." he says.

"No, go. I wanna take a soak. You go. I'll see you upstairs later."

I kiss him. Give his hand a squeeze and head to our room. I am elated. It's the best birthday I ever had. And we haven't even gotten to the best part yet. Wonder what he's waiting for?

CHAPTER 34

What transpires over the next two weeks I will never fully understand. At least not to my satisfaction. And that's sometimes how life goes. You want it to be like television, where at the end of the hour, the bad guy is caught and the good guys move on to the next case and we know exactly why, when, and how. We have *closure*. But life isn't always like that. In fact rarely.

Though wonderful, Atlantic City ends with no engagement ring involved. I am disappointed. Feel disillusioned. Can't figure out what happened, but plan on calling Pam to find out. It seems like she knows more about what's going on in my relationship these days than I do.

My birthday party is held on Friday at Stan's. Everyone is in attendance. Everyone except Alan, that is. He has the flu and sounds awful, so he opts to stay in. I miss him…feel a little empty. Partially because I think his flu is an easy out—it's not that I doubt he's sick, no, I know he is. But I feel like there is some distance starting to creep back in again and I don't like it. More importantly, I don't know what to do about it.

I make my rounds, listen to jokes, nibble on crackers with spread, and field questions about Alan's absence. But my heart's not in it.

I finally get Pam alone and pull her into an unoccupied room.

"How are you? A little sad Alan's not here?" she asks and smiles warmly.

"I suppose, but it's only one night. I'll survive." I put on my big smile. She smiles back and I clear my throat. I begin, "I wanted to ask you…you know when we were in AC and you said that…we'll you called me Mrs. D. and—"

"Oh. Yeah. Well…well, I was just teasing you, that's all."

I wait for her to say more. She seems awkward, like there is more to this. I wait her out. Finally, "I probably shouldn't be telling you this."

I give her a cold stone stare, which seems pretty effective because she starts talking.

"Alright...I heard that he was going to propose."

There. She said it. I was right.

She goes on, "He was talking about it with Albert and apparently he looked at rings, and he told him he was going back to get one for a big birthday surprise. I'm sorry, Sam. I shouldn't have said anything. I was just so thrilled for you and you sounded so happy."

"I was happy." I tell her.

"Doesn't mean it won't happen. He probably just needed to get the rest of the money. Those things aren't cheap." she says and smiles.

"No, no they're not." I agree.

We join the rest of the party, me feeling as befuddled as ever.

I see Alan only briefly that week, during the last playoff game for the World Series. The Yankees lose to Boston and Alan turns into an A-1 jerk. He is ignorant and yelling obscenities and I am genuinely concerned for his safety when he starts badmouthing two Red Sox fans outside the bar we're in.

I look at him squarely and say, "Don't be obnoxious."

I mean it. He needs to knock it off.

I go home with Pam that night instead of him.

Our subsequent phone calls are brief and empty.

On the following Friday I stay at his place—he is feeling a little better physically, but mentally, I just can't say. More of the same, I guess. We sleep awful. He has the window open, which freezes me to death and stuffs my nose, which leads me to snore, which in turn keeps him awake, which forces him to wake me up throughout the night with a roll-over request.

This cycle continues 'til the morning when I finally say, "I'm outta here."

I take the subway to Manhattan and try to think about what I'm doing.

I go to a movie, hoping to clear my head of bad relationship thoughts and then to an audition. It turns out to be one of the best auditions of my life. The artistic director is so friendly and you can tell that she wants you to do well—something very rare in this business. I call Alan afterward, but get his voicemail.

"It's me. Just wanted to check-in and see how you're feeling. Hopefully you're getting some rest. Talk to you later. Love you."

I am home an hour or so later, reliving my great audition with Dai when my cell rings. It is Alan. The conversation goes something like this:

Alan: Hey.

Me: Hi. How are you? Feeling any better?

Alan: Not really. (Long pause)

Me: That audition went really well. She was just so cool. I nailed it and it was cold, but she was just so… like she wanted me to do well. The nicest person.

Alan: That's great (though it sounds more like, 'blah, blah')

Me: (Pause) What's up?

Alan: I don't know. (Long pause) It's just, I…I feel like I want everyone to be away from me right now.

Me: Yeah, a lot of people have come to me and said that they could feel that. (Long pause). Does that include me?

Alan: I don't know.

Me: (Stomach starts doing somersaults) What are you saying?

Alan: I'm not saying anything.

Me: Are you saying that you don't want to see me anymore?

Alan: I didn't say that. I didn't call to break-up with you.

Me: (A moment's reprieve, but I can't just let this hang). What are you saying then? Do you want to take a break for a while?

Alan: No, we already tried that.

Me: (When the hell did we try that? Maybe that's why it didn't work—I didn't even know it was happening. Long pause. My heart pounds like it's going to come right out of my chest. My mouth is dry. I cannot speak. I cannot breathe).

Alan: I think we should stop seeing each other. For a while.

Me: (*For a while*, being the operative words and how exactly is that different from taking a break for a while??—which we apparently tried when I wasn't looking. I feel no relief, though one would wonder why, when things have been feeling so empty.) Why?

Alan: I'm just not happy.

Me: Because of me?

Alan: You didn't do anything. It's not you.

Me: (Oh, for fuck's sake, you're a writer, couldn't you come up with something better than that? I can't speak. I cry. I cry some more. I cry more than that. During this time, Alan stays on the phone. He is wanting to be there. I can tell. Though I don't know why. He tries to talk to me).

Alan: I'll be there for the surgery.

Me: No, no. I don't want you there.

Alan: I'll be worried. I want—

Me: NO! It will only make me more nervous. I can't be upset on the day of the surgery.

Alan: Okay. Whatever you want. (Long, long pause). We'll keep in touch. I want you in my life. I just, I just…

Me: (Still crying, needing to sob, but can't do it with him on the phone. I know we will work this out. He will come to his senses tomorrow or the next day or the day after that. Of course he will). I have to get off.

Once we hang up, I feel the separation immediately. I collapse onto my bed and I sob, sob, sob. Even though I know that tomorrow things will be better. He will come to his senses tomorrow or the next day or the day after that. Of course he will.

Dai comes to my room. He sees my state and pulls me out into the living room. I sit and explain, though my explanation is lacking since I don't have all the facts. Will I ever?

"He'll come around." Dai assures me.

And I believe him. Of course he will. I am too good to lose (aren't I?). We are a team. I'm going to be in his movie (aren't I?). We are a team. I'm going to be his wife (aren't I?).

We are a team. I'm going to bear his children (aren't I?). We are a team.

It is a blessing when sleep finally comes—though it is not for several hours. Several hours of sobbing and blubbering. Eventually I wear myself out much like an infant would.

I wake the next day. Waking is the hardest thing after a wretched night filled with wretched happenings. Waking confirms it happened. It wasn't a dream. The wretchedness is real.

Today is Sunday. I don't have to go to work. I don't have to do anything. And I don't. Nothing. But cry. Some more.

I speak with four people over the phone: 1) My mother, who now explains that Alan is egotistical and an ass and I can do better, but not to worry because he will come around. 2) Pam, who isn't even aware that Alan and I "aren't seeing each other *for a while*". When she finds out, she sympathizes, but explains that it's all about his father and he will come to his senses in no time. He can't live without me. It's obvious he really loves me. 3) Anne-Marie, who I cry to for an hour. She says she'll come to New Jersey, but I tell her that I would be really bad company, to which she says, 'Duh. I'm coming to comfort *you*, not so you can entertain *me*.' I love Anne-Marie. I convince her not to come, that I will see her at work tomorrow and she can save her comforting for then, as I have a feeling I will still be in need of it.

It's afternoon when the phone rings the final time. It's Alan. I am excited for the first ten seconds, thinking that he's come to his senses and things will be back on track in no time. When I find out he's only calling about these theatre tickets that we were suppose to use this weekend, I am crushed. Again. Why can't we still use them together, I keep wondering, but when he suggests that he take these and he will get me a new set, I see that he has no desire to even sit next to me in a crowded theatre for under two hours. He can't even stomach that. That's what my brain interprets. And it's ugly. So ugly.

Still, I know that tomorrow things will be better. He will come to his senses tomorrow or the next day or the day after that. Of course he will.

And though I tell myself this every day, it does not ever come to be.

The next month of my life is the most depressing time I can ever remember having to endure. The first part of the month is riddled with *hope*, which sounds refreshing as a spring morning after a long, hard winter, when in reality it is more like a time bomb, that can go off at any moment. See, *hope* is only good when things work out the way you'd *hope*d. When circumstances go against that which is *hope*d for, then your *hope*s are dashed and your life feels empty, useless and *hope*less. Thus, my life.

I e-mail Alan a heartfelt and very sincere letter. I write of our love, the good times, and our deep connection to each other. I remind him how great it is to have a partner who too is an artist (like there aren't thousands of those running around), someone to share your work, and brainstorm with. I tell him I miss waking up next to him and am dying to just sit and play Scrabble, make pasta, and hold each other on the too-small sofa. I tell him that I understand that he's just reacting to the pressure he's under with his father's illness and his work and that I can wait it out. Just tell me what to do, and I'll try, I tell him.

I get no immediate response. I wait. I get no delayed response. I wait some more. I get no response. I am baffled. This cannot possibly be happening. The man I love, the person I shared all of this time with, the person who was to propose just three short weeks ago ('was', the operative word) he cannot be behaving in this manner. It simply is not possible. But it is.

The second part of the month I spend trying to gear up for my surgery. It is just two days away and I am scared. Really scared. I have never had anything wrong with me. Never had a broken bone or even the chicken pox, so this under-the-knife stuff is scaring the crap out of me. I put on a brave front though and tell anyone who will listen that it's pretty much routine and I'll be back at work in a couple of days. No sweat. *Right.*

Already I look sick though. I don't bother with make-up anymore—I have no need—I am boyfriend-less and the last thing I want is another man looking my way. I'm in enough pain. The thought of wearing make-up for *myself* because *I* want to, never even enters my mind, sadly.

I lose twelve pounds, between feeling nauseous over the upcoming surgery and feeling nauseous whenever I consider the possibility that Alan and I will not be getting back together—it isn't that I'm near accepting this fact, no, even the slightest notion of it brings about sickness. I have no appetite. I only want to sleep. There is no pain in sleep. I want there to be no pain.

I briefly consider taking a handful of painkillers and sleeping my life away. Literally. Not that I consider myself suicidal. I think for many people experiencing despair, this seems like a viable solution. It's not that you don't want to live, it's that you don't want to live *like this*.

I get down on my knees and say a prayer. I ask that I be taken during my surgery if that is His will, otherwise, I will assume that I am supposed to remain on earth. That I am supposed to find a way to persevere and learn these hard lessons.

I get into bed, anxiously anticipating sleep and the end of my pain, if only temporarily.

CHAPTER 35

I sit in the large, cold room with Dai and Pam and await the inevitable. It is before 6 am and yet the room is nearly full. Full of people like me who are here to have organs removed, arteries cleaned, and devices implanted (the life-saving kind, not the bowling-balls-on-the-chest kind).

I haven't eaten or drank anything for sixteen hours—doctor's orders. I feel as if I could go forever without food—just not in the mood—but I would love a tall glass of water. Not happening though, so I try to push the image from my mind.

I am dressed in a black sweat suit. I purchased it especially for this day. I know that sounds kind of strange, but I wanted to feel taken care of and warm and toasty. I don't know, somehow the thick jersey fabric made me feel that way. It is my companion, my lover and my friend all in one.

"Samantha Anderson."

I look up. It's the nurse. The nice nurse with the strawberry blonde hair pulled into a ponytail. She has freckles all over her face, neck, and arms, which leads me to believe that her beautiful hair color is natural. Some have all the luck.

"Yes, that's me." I say, but I don't move an inch toward her. I feel cemented to the plastic orange chair beneath me.

"It's time." she says.

She says it in a sing-song voice, like what awaits me is amusement park rides and pink cotton candy. Either that or she's Irish. I'm going to assume the latter, that way I won't hate her for trying to make me feel good when there's no way in hell I'm going to feel good about going to have my gall bladder yanked out.

When I don't make a move to follow she says, "You should come with me now."

I smile.

"Must I?"

Dai pats my knee and says, "It's time kid."

"Oh, come on, you'll be fine," the nurse says and leads me by the arm. She then turns back to Dai and Pam and says, "She'll be right back."

We walk into the room and three more people are standing about. They are medical personnel all there to do something to me that I don't want done. One takes my vitals (I'm still alive. Whoopie!). Another assists me in filling out paperwork and going over my medical history, while a third discusses the drugs that will be administered.

After finding out that I pass out fairly easily and get motion sickness (only on long bus rides), he explains that there is a new steroid that makes the nausea manageable. Although it is a steroid, it is relatively (*relatively*??) harmless, as this will be a one-dose thing. This is a decision I have to make. Do I want it or not?

I am not in the mood to make any decisions. If it were up to me, I would leave right now and be done with the whole thing. He needs my signature on a paper authorizing this '*relatively*' harmless drug though.

Before I do anything, the door opens and Dai and Pam are there. The strawberry-blond nurse is with them.

"I thought you might like some company until you go in," she says.

I thank her and confer with my buddies on the drug. This doesn't help though, as Pam is completely against the steroid and Dai is for it. I feel stuck, even more so than before.

I like the looks of the Anesthesiologist so I go for it (okay, not the most sound deciding factor, but it was either that or eeny-meeny-miny-moe). I scribble my name (perhaps if there's a law suit, I can claim that it's not my signature) and three of the people in the room take their leave—the three that I don't know.

My nurse instructs me to change into my nightgown—AKA the paper napkin. I go begrudgingly into the adjacent loo and slip into it. I am freezing and lost without my mate, aka my sweat suit. I give it a warm hug and take a deep breath and join the others.

I sit. Pam, Dai and I chat about nothing. I am scared. Scared. SCARED. I don't want to go. I want Anne-Marie. She wanted to be here, but I told her no...that I could handle it—ha! Shows what a liar I am. And Alan. I want him here. I curse myself for not letting him be here. He would have been here. I would feel better. Maybe it would have been a step in the direction of our reconciliation. No. No, I tell myself. He knew this was coming up. He knew I was scared. And he did what he did anyway. He couldn't wait a few weeks until I got past this...no, he had to get away from me. So, no I don't want him here. YOU DON'T WANT HIM HERE, my mind screams from the inside.

"Okay, Sam, we're ready to start." It's my nurse.

She doesn't sound Irish anymore. She doesn't sound sing-songy. She sounds worried. Concerned. She knows something I don't. I start to panic. I can't hide it.

"You ready, kid?" Dai asks me.

Of course I'm not ready. He probably senses this, when I begin to cry. I can't help it. The tears roll down my cheeks and I begin to shake.

"Ah, you're gonna do great." Dai says and hugs me.

Pam then joins in the hug and we have one of those group hugs. This is pathetic. I buck up.

"Thanks guys. Thanks for being here. See you in a little while." I say and walk out with the nurse.

We walk no more than ten feet. Ten feet that ends at swinging doors. The same kind of swinging doors you see on those emergency room shows, except I am not being wheeled through them. They actually expect me to *walk* through them. There must be a lot of budget cuts at this hospital if they are having me walk myself to the operating table. I feel like Dead Man Walking.

The OR is cold and sterile smelling—rubbing alcohol, fake-lemon, and other chemical odors. There are a slew of people in here (you'd think one of them could have wheeled me in), bustling around getting things prepared.

"This all for me?" I ask. "You shouldn't have."

They laugh.

I give a fake laugh back and then add, "REALLY, you shouldn't have. You don't have to. How about we all go grab some breakfast and forget all this fuss?"

There is more laughter, but all of the sudden I don't feel like joking. I want out of here.

"Why don't you just hop up on the table," one of the technicians instructs.

I look at the operating table. I look down at my hips. My ass is wider than the operating table. I don't see how I am going to fit. Perhaps this is grounds for a dismissal.

"I don't think I fit." I say with conviction.

"Sure you do," I'm told by another of the team. "We strap you in."

Though I'm sure she meant that to be comforting, *not comforting*. Not comforting in the least.

They hook an IV to my arm and ask me to count backwards from 100. Oh, come on, they really do that…the last number I remember is 96.

The next thing I remember is what we call 'sleep interruptus'.

"Samantha, Samantha. Come on Saaamaanntha, time to wake up now."

I wake up to jostling. I'm being shaken awake. I am groggy. So groggy. I don't want to wake. This is one of the few times in my life when I genuinely don't want to wake up.

I know that probably sounds strange, since for most people every time their alarm rings, they don't want to be awaken. But for me, it's different. I would stay up 24/7 if it was humanly possible. See, I don't want to miss anything. I always feel like life is passing me by, so I don't want to sleep through something…anything. But this time is different. I *want* to sleep. I *need* to sleep. But apparently they see it differently.

"You have to wake up now. It's very important."

Okay, okay, I silently tell them. I'm awake.

My body feels like a hot dog snug tight in a bun. There is a soft plastic sleeve around each of my legs (to prevent blood clots I am told) and I am strapped to a gurney. This time I'm being wheeled, I am happy to report. Wheeled by two people I have never seen before. Or maybe short-term amnesia is part of the *'relatively'* harmless steroid. Either way, I am just happy that I don't have to hop off the OR table and find my own way to the recovery room.

I have lived a thousand days in a desert. That's what my mouth will tell you. That's what it's telling me. I have *never* been thirstier, even though I have uttered phrases like, 'Oh man, I'm dying of thirst' a hundred times. I was lying. I am now *literally* dying of thirst. No problem I remind myself, you are not in a desert. You have access to gallons of water. Problem: I am told, *'can't have anything to drink, may suck on ice chips though'*. Wonderful. Just wonderful. Ice chips that don't even begin to wet my dehydrated, parched, saliva-less mouth.

I am lying on the gurney, waiting to be moved. It is a long wait. Three hours. Patients are wheeled in, patients are wheeled out. I wait. A young guy named Brett comes to check my pain level every twenty minutes. The drugs do start to wear-off eventually, and I start feeling some pain. Ow. It's only when I move. Only when I breathe, try to talk, or suck on ice chips…basically, all the time.

"Okay, I'm going to give you a shot of morphine and that should hold you over until we get you upstairs," he tells me as he gets a needle ready.

"Which should be when?" I ask.

He injects the narcotic. I wait to feel better. Soon I do. It's fast-acting, I'll give it that.

"Someone will be along shortly," he tells me and begins to leave.

"What about my friends? Has anyone found them yet?"

I have been asking for Dai and Pam since I was rudely awaken over three hours ago.

"I'll check right now," he says and walks through the swinging doors.

It is almost a half-hour later, two more cups of ice chips later, that Pam and Dai come in. They had gone out for something to eat, thinking that I would be a lot longer.

"I have a small gall bladder," I inform them.

When I go to join them in the laugh, I can feel the pain. I have stitches holding together three holes in my abdomen. One high on my belly, one on my right side and one right inside my belly button. Attractive.

I am wheeled to a room upstairs. This is where the real fun begins. They evidently are short-handed again, as I am instructed to transfer myself from the gurney to the bed by 'simply' lifting my body up and sliding it over. *Right.*

I look at the woman giving me these instructions and wait for her to smile and tell me that she is kidding and the muscle men will be here in a moment to assist me. She neither smiles nor do any muscle men appear to assist me.

I nod an affirmative. It takes three attempts for me to actually get myself into the bed. I have never felt such pain before. It feels as if something is ripping me from the inside. I suppose the damage has already happened and I just aggravated it by using my stomach muscles. I had no choice though. No muscle men to assist me.

Dai and Pam are permitted to join me now (why they couldn't have been in here substituting for muscle men I will never know…stupid hospital policy). They sit down and we wait for me to 'recover'. How long this will take is anyone's guess, but Dai seems to think about eight minutes is suitable and tells me so.

"How much longer you think you're gonna be?" He asks.

"Uh, well, not sure what the criteria is, so couldn't really say," I mutter around a mouth full of ice chips.

"Well, I was just thinking that traffic's gonna get heavy soon and I would like to beat it, gettin' you home."

Before I can respond my surgeon walks into the room. She is not alone—the mean lady who made me move myself walks behind her. She is carrying a ginger ale. If she were bringing me a million-dollar check, I couldn't love her more! All of her previous sins—exonerated.

"Sip it," she tells me and leaves a straw. I do as I'm told, though I must battle my mouth that keeps ordering me to 'just chug it'.

"How ya doin'?" My doctor asks.

"Sore. Very sore." I tell her honestly.

"You did great back there. No complications, simple as can be." And with that she snaps her fingers.

"Good," I reply, completely occupied with my ginger ale. "When can I go home?" I ask between sips.

"Just as soon as you urinate and I sign your paperwork."

She turns and speaks to Dai and Pam, shakes their hands, comes back over to me and says for me to give her a call for a follow-up next week. I ask for any diet restrictions and she says, 'none'. None?

I spoke with all eight women at my job who have had their gall bladders removed and they all said that I would have to watch what I ate, no fried foods, no sweets or foods high in fat. My doctor says 'none'. Of course, I will go with the expert.

I am given two Percocet before finishing my ginger ale and making my way to the bathroom. Boy, that trip is a real workout. And a fruitless one, since when I sit on the porcelain, nothing happens. No urinating for me. I head back to my bed a broken woman.

"Sorry," I inform Dai. "Couldn't go."

He is not too thrilled, but what can he expect? I haven't had a drink in almost 24 hours, so why would I need to pee?

It's another hour before urine arrives. Pam has left, at my insistence. She was so good to sit here all day and since there was nothing else to be done, but wait for me to pee—jolly fun—I dismissed her.

Dai goes to bring the car around while I sit in a wheelchair and get pushed toward the exit. I don't make a bit of a fuss. You always see that in movies where the hero doesn't want to be in a wheelchair and insists on walking himself. Well not me! I am only too happy to sit here and be taken out. In fact, I would love it if he just pushed me right on to New Jersey.

Instead, I get into the car with Dai and make phone calls while he drives very, very slowly—at my constant insistence. I call every one of my friends, my mom and gram. "Piece of cake," I lie. "Ridiculously simple."

CHAPTER 36

The next three days are worse than the surgery. Much worse. Mainly because of the painkillers, believe it or not. They make me deathly ill and I vomit over and over again. Even after I have nothing left to throw up, I still retch, causing my stomach muscles to contract. Never a pleasant experience, but with stitches in your belly, it is almost unbearable.

Dai is good about administering to me, but what can he really do. He makes homemade chicken soup—one of my favorites, but I can't seem to keep it down. When all is said and done, one third of the pot ends up in the toilet.

I call my doctor, leave a message. When she returns my call, she is not concerned in the least.

"Oh, it's that Hydrocodone. Just discontinue it and take Advil."

That's her advice? No pharmaceuticals. Advil?

Since I have no choice, I do as I'm told and by day four I am feeling much better. Yes, I'm sore, but not so I can't move. The retching is over, and the constipation has ceased. What more can one really ask for?

I wake up late. I know it's late because of the silence. Oh, the Miracle of Silence. Today there will be no Japanese music, no Kanji, and no samurai lessons. Today is different. Today is Thanksgiving.

Dai went to Rochester to join his family at his sister's house. I was invited. I declined. I'm just not in the mood. In fact, to sit here, in the living room and just stare at the TV is all the excitement I can muster.

I go ahead and make my nachos, Thanksgiving dinner of champions. I see no reason to wait as I have missed breakfast

Salsa with the Pope

and lunch. Yes, I was tired. I plant myself in front of the television, but don't turn it on.

My mind wanders back to last Thanksgiving. My mom was visiting from Ohio and I was having my usual Friday Thanksgiving Dinner. It's a tradition—inviting all of my friends to a feast the day after, since most of them have family obligations the day of.

It is always a huge undertaking, this yearly occasion, not just for me, but for Dai as well. Basically, I am invading his space and he has to make concessions for that—mainly going through his mail that accrues on the side table—for nearly a year, shampooing the rugs, and getting dressed in real clothes (not that Dai goes around naked, but he is fond of shorts and sandals even in winter months).

I am the first to admit that I am not a good cook. Hell, I'm not a cook at all, but I love trying anyway. Thankfully Dai, and this particular year my mom was here to supervise the turkey making. I do many of the sides and appetizers myself though, and of course I make a ton of homemade desserts—my specialty.

Last year at this time, we are scurrying around, setting the table, finishing the side dishes, icing the cake. People are arriving and Dai and I are taking turns driving to the bus stop to fetch them. The last call is from Alan, he is at the bus stop waiting. Dai tells me that he will go get him while I jump into the shower.

When I emerge from the bathroom, hair still damp, make-up hastily applied, silky blouse sticking to my lightly coated sweaty back, eight guests are listening to music chatting about various things in the living area. I go and greet each of them, plant a kiss on their cheek, and give them a warm hug. I make sure they are settled. They seem to be. I glance around, but I don't see Alan. I hear Dai though, so they must be back. I excuse myself and make my way to the kitchen.

What a sight. Alan has on an apron that says 'KISS THE CHEF' (well, actually it reads ' ISS THE CHEF'—the K worn off long ago). He is instructing my mother as to the state of the sweet potatoes ("too hard; we're gonna have to mash them").

She eye-eyes him like the captain that he is and gets to work. Dai is busy making hot chocolates for two of our guests.

I make my presence known by clearing my throat in a presentational manner. All look up, see me and speak at once.

My mother says, "Ah, feel better? That looks nice on you, honey."

Dai says, "What do you think you're doin'? We aren't your servants, get a move on Samantha-son."

Alan says, "Hey baby."

He gives me a kiss.

Then another and adds, "You smell clean...nice and soapy."

I swat his behind, grab the two mugs of cocoa from Dai and head back out to the others.

The meal is not the best I've ever eaten, but it is delicious in the preparation, in the companionship, in the team effort. I enjoy every bite simply because of these things. Alan is given a round of applause for "saving the sweet potatoes" and making a lovely presentation of them.

It is three hours of food, frolicking, and fun. We embarrass one of my co-workers by making him sing 'Happy Birthday' to my mother a cappella (actually Alan threatens to go hug him if he doesn't sing and my buddy is really, *really* against hugs) and then there is the food fight.

This all begins when Alan puts a tiny bit of cream on the tip of my nose, while I am serving the desserts. Of course I retaliate and before you know it, we are rolling around on the floor, slathering whipped cream all over each other's faces. This is all caught on film, so a lovely display for the archives indeed.

It is late, past midnight when everyone leaves. Everyone except Alan, that is. He is staying over—the first and only time he will stay overnight with me at Dai's. My mother, Dai, Alan and I are traveling to Atlantic City the following day for the weekend. I am very excited.

My mother claims exhaustion and turns in soon after everyone's departure. Dai, Alan and I stay up chatting. I am wanting Dai to go to bed. I want Alan and I to have some time to

Salsa with the Pope

ourselves. We are sleeping in the living room on the futon, since my mother is in my room.

The three of us chat about everything from politics to Japan to movies. Dai has me get up and show Alan my practiced Samurai walk, which is very funny as I put a sword (a 'katana') longer than I am tall, into an imaginary belt and walk side to side, almost like a cowboy, but slower and more deliberate.

Dai yells things like, 'Chotto' (go slower); 'Abiyo' ('samurai spirit'); and 'Boshido' ('path of the warrior'). He repeatedly calls me a 'Baka Gaijin' ('stupid outsider'), which I am used to as he often addresses me as such.

We then play out the scene from *Dirty Harry*, the one where the robber goes into the diner and the waitress tries to warn Harry by putting sugar in his customary black coffee. I am playing the waitress, Alan is the robber, and Dai is Dirty Harry. It is a blast. We do the re-enactment three times, switching roles each time. I love it when I get to finally say, "Go 'head punk, make my day." It is decided (by me) that I am the best Dirty Harry of all. Of course our laughter wakes my mother, which is a sure sign for bedtime.

We all apologize to mama, say goodnight and go to our perspective beds. Alan and I then have sex on the carpet. We decide that we don't want to chance waking my mother again. It is short and sweet. We then curl up and take a nice nap, eagerly awaiting our trip to AC.

I wrap the quilt around me tighter and lie back, lost in the memory. It was this very futon that I slept with Alan. How had things gone so wrong? What happened? God, I wish I could go back, not just in time, but in *feeling*. The *feeling* of love and acceptance. The *feeling* of completion and security. Will I ever *feel* it again?

CHAPTER 37

I pull Anne-Marie by the arm all the way to the ladies' room. I need to talk. I am anxious.

"What is it? What happened?" She demands to know.

"Alan," I begin, but can't stop my voice from quivering. I try again. "I spoke with Alan."

Anne-Marie nods, "And?" She asks.

"We're going to meet. I played it really cool. I told him I want my stuff back from his apartment, but really, that might not even be necessary."

She looks puzzled, like she isn't following me.

I clarify, "Maybe he's finally come to his senses. Maybe he misses me and wants to get back."

Her expression tells me nothing, but I know that's a cover. Anne-Marie always thinks something, even if you can't read it at first.

"When's the meeting?" She finally asks.

"Tomorrow night," I tell her, grateful that it isn't tonight. I want to look my best, and my reflection in the mirror tells me that today that would not be possible with my ponytail of dirty hair, pale make-up less face and ratty clothes.

"How're you gonna play it?" She wants to know.

"I don't know," I admit. "I keep going over it in my mind and I guess it depends on how he is. If he's friendly or what."

She shakes her head.

"I don't know why you care if he's friendly or not. He did you wrong, bottom line. And to think that you're considering going back with him. What has gotten into you, girl?"

There it is. What she's thinking. Cover blown.

"I know what you're saying, but it wasn't all bad. It was mostly good and he was really pressured and…I just want to hear what he has to say is all."

She doesn't buy that though and lets me know it.

"He didn't even call you after your surgery, Samantha."

"But he called—"

"Pam, I know," she says before I can finish. "Him calling Pam and checking on you a few times on your surgery day was nice. Fine. But he never called *you* to let *you* know he was thinking of you or that he cared. And that is just plain wrong."

I let the sting of that wear off for a moment. I don't argue.

This is what our friendship is based on—honesty. Just a year ago, I was the one telling her that her relationship was abusive and she needed to get out. It was hard for her to hear, but eventually she saw it for what it was and left.

Why is it we women can't see what is really going on when love is involved? Why are we so willing to give ourselves over just to be loved? Don't we understand that we are worthy of it just by our mere existence? Just by who we are? I guess not. At least not yet.

Anne-Marie comes to me. She hugs me to let me know that she still loves me no matter what goes down tomorrow. She has my best interest at heart. This I know.

I spend my evening going through my wardrobe, trying to find 'Meeting After Break-up' clothes. I settle on black—good for mourning the relationship if I feel sad, chic and en vogue if I feel glad.

I get to work the next day, my heart pumping faster the closer I get to meeting time. I pull my compact out and glance one last time in the mirror before making my way out the door. I clutch my black tote tightly to my body, holding it like armor, as if it will protect me from any unpleasantness that results from my conversation with Alan. It won't. I know this. But I pretend anyway.

My stomach churns as I get off the elevator and walk toward the diner across the street from my office building. I haven't eaten since Alan and I spoke yesterday. I feared that nothing would stay down, so I figured I would just skip the involuntary binge/purge and simply not eat at all.

I don't feel ready for this, though I've had weeks upon weeks to think about it. What I would say. What I feel. What I want him to be held accountable for. What I want in the end. I take a deep breath and open the glass door and step inside.

It is a tiny establishment, with a narrow aisle leading to a large room on the south side of the restaurant. I look around, but can't make out anyone due to the dim lighting. They seem to be using only colored Christmas lights for illumination, leaving a nervous, shaky individual like me, basically in the dark.

I see his foot (when I trip and almost fall over it) before I see him. He is sitting at a table sipping a cup of coffee, reading a script (some things never change). I suddenly feel like I'm getting off an amusement ride…dizzy and disoriented. I feel my face heat up (due to embarrassment, no doubt). I feel my body turn to jelly, my legs no longer willing to support me. I feel these things all at once. Not exactly the impression I want to make.

I'm not sure if he senses this or if he is just trying to be polite, but he stands and offers me a chair, which I readily accept. We sit and look at each other for a moment. He looks the same. Big, dark curly hair, milk chocolate brown eyes, and a dimple in his chin that I can't see for his beard, but I know it's there and it's in the knowing that I find it sexy.

"So, how are you?" He finally asks as he puts his reading away.

I nod, unable to find any words for a moment. Finally I offer, "I'm surviving. And you?"

"I'm well. Doing really well."

The waiter comes and asks if I'd like anything, I order coffee (though I don't like coffee, so why—not sure) and he scurries off.

"You hungry?" Alan asks.

"Not really. You want something, go ahead," I say.

"I'm fine," he tells me.

It's awkward and not at the same time. Part of me feels so out-of-place, so uncomfortable. That is about my not knowing how he is going to react, what he is going to say or not say. The other part of me is so at home. I am with Alan. I could not feel more at ease. I want to go over and snuggle next to him. I want to read whatever script he's reading and compare opinions. I want to get out of this tiny little diner and walk to Brooklyn hand-in-hand, catching up on the past weeks all the while. It is a conflict within myself. One I do not know how to resolve.

We sit in silence for a few more moments and then Alan says, "I brought your stuff."

He pulls a shopping bag off the chair next to him and hands it across the table to me. I don't even bother to look through it. The gesture alone speaks volumes. I don't even know where to begin. But I do anyway.

"So, this is it? We're through?"

I say it with conviction, though I don't want to. I don't want to know what part of me already knows.

"You know how I feel." He says in response.

"I thought I knew how you felt. I thought you said 'for a while'. You wanted to stop seeing each other *for a while*. I guess you didn't mean that."

"I never said that," is his answer.

"Oh, yes you did. And you know what, let me just get some things off my chest right now."

I can't stop myself now. I don't want to.

"You could have been free from me, but to do the things you've done, the *way* you've done them has been beyond hurtful. You didn't have to do it this way, Alan."

He nods like he knows what I'm talking about. Know it or not, he's going to hear it anyway.

"You breaking up with me over the phone, after all our time together, after all that we shared…" I take eye inventory…they're filling up, but I will them to wait, just wait a moment before spilling out.

"You made me feel like day old garbage. Like some trash you were taking out to the curb. Something you had no more use for, so out it goes."

The tears trickle down now, but I don't care. I can't control them. I can't stop them. I take a breath and pick-up where I left off.

"You are a coward. For all of this time, you haven't picked up the phone once to see how I was doing. You didn't call me after my surgery, and don't you dare tell me that you knew how I was because you spoke with Pam! This is not about how I was doing. It is about you giving a damn…and clearly you don't."

My coffee arrives. I check to see how many patrons I have disturbed by airing my dirty laundry, but surprisingly there is only one gentleman sitting in the rear of the restaurant reading a newspaper. He seems unfazed by our 'discussion'.

"You're right," Alan says. "I was a coward. I just, I just didn't want to hurt you…"

"And you thought by breaking up with me over the phone and never speaking to me again, that would be the way to go. The 'no-hurt way'? Please."

He says, "I really do want us to be friends. I really do. I just thought that it would be better if I stayed out of sight for a while. Left you alone. I don't want to hurt you. I don't Sam."

I cry. I don't want him to hurt me either. But it's too late. And he can't remedy it here.

"I'm sorry I hurt you. I never meant to. But don't you dare say that I don't care about you. That's bullshit, Sam. You know that's bullshit." He picks my hands up off the table and gives them a squeeze.

His cell phone interrupts this gesture. He pulls away and mutters, "Sorry about this."

I nod and say, "Why should now be any different?"

He chuckles and picks up the phone.

After a lengthy debate on the phone with some PR person, he disconnects and explains that there is another reading of his play, with a name actress and her people are bugging the shit out of him. He is sick of her already.

I am sucked in immediately.

"I'd love to read the new version," I say.

"You should come to the reading," he says.

He gives me the date and time and I say that I'll be there before I can stop myself.

We spend the next hour catching up on what's going on with us. It takes me about ten minutes to fill him in on my life (or lack of one) and show him my belly scars—I've become quite proud of them. They are proof of my resilience. He talks for the remaining fifty minutes about all of his re-writes, re-writes, re-writes.

We both claim single-hood, which I must admit makes me happy. There wasn't someone else waiting in the wings, it was just circumstance, I tell myself.

He then tells me that his father is really bad off and he is going to be staying there indefinitely after the reading. I express my deepest sympathy, knowing that there is nothing I can say to make it better, nothing I can do.

We walk out of the diner together. We kiss each other on the cheeks. We say good-bye and go our separate ways.

CHAPTER 38

I'm just leaving work, heading to the train when the guy walking in front of me drops a folder full of papers, which spill out onto the sidewalk in every direction. I'm more than happy to help him, once I regain my footing. I don't even recognize him until I have several sheets in my hand.

"Here you go," I say.

"Hey...Samantha isn't it?" He asks. "Alan's girlfriend." he says in clarification.

I nod.

"Not anymore, but yeah, I was his girlfriend. I'm sorry, um, what was your name?"

"Rob. Myers."

He extends his hand, which I take in my own.

"Nice to see you." I say, then add, "I haven't seen you for so long. What's been going on?"

"A lot of the same. Auditions mainly. I did have a brief gig Off-Broadway last month, but it ended. Economy is really bad."

I nod in agreement.

"Yeah, the worst. I can't seem to book a job to save my life."

Unless of course, you count Bacardi. I don't.

Rob looks away and then says, "So, not to be too personal, but what happened with you and Alan? He seemed really into you. At least from what I saw."

I shrug. I don't know how to answer and say so.

"Not sure. Just...I don't know, things got really weird. His father's ill..."

"Yeah, I heard something about that. That's too bad, man. But to split because of something like that...that sucks."

I smile.

"Yeah, I guess. Hey, I seem to recall you saying that you were sure he was gay anyway."

That's when I had first met Rob, at the Drama Desk awards.

Rob laughs and nods. "Well, you gotta admit…"

"What?" I say as I let out a chuckle.

"Oh, come on. Don't tell me you don't think he seems a little…effeminate?"

I stop smiling.

"Are you serious?"

Rob says, "Yeah, man. I mean up until the Drama Desks I really thought he was gay. I never thought for a minute that he would show up with a woman. A date no less."

"What makes you think that?" I ask.

Rob shrugs.

"Takes one to know one, I guess."

I smile on the outside. On the inside, I am confused. I need to sit. I need to think.

Which is exactly what I do. And can't stop doing. All the way home. All evening. All night. All day. All night. All day. All night.

I finally pull the covers off of me and swing my legs out of the bed. It's 3:47 a.m. Am I really going to get up? I am. I do.

I walk to the kitchen, pour some OJ and go sit on the futon in the living room. I light two candles and don't bother with any lights. Don't want to wake Dai.

This is my third night in a row without sleep. I am exhausted, and yet I can't let my mind rest. It keeps going over and over what Rob said to me on the street the other day. I hate to admit it, but it makes some sense.

It puts so many little things in perspective. The photo albums at Alan's mother's (there are hundreds of pictures of a boy, tall and very thin with this big head of hair, dressed like the musical theatre king he is—I remember even making the comment that he looked gay); the inability to form true relationships with women (his step-mother—who had had a few too many at the time, and his mother both warned me about this in a roundabout way, but I didn't get it, I didn't want to—I was going to be the one to break the mold. *Right*). Then there's the fact that he loses interest in sex; and of course, the obvious—he's a playwright and actor (not to say that *all* male playwrights and actors are gay, but certainly there's no shortage).

Somewhere inside me, I know it's a true fit. And my heart is broken. This dashes all hope that we will ever be together again. In many ways, this is worse than him cheating on me with a woman. Fuck.

I understand why he had to get away from me now. I know that he could continue no longer in our relationship, one that was getting so deep, so complicated. He knew that I would know soon and then what?

I make a mental note to call my therapist—I haven't seen her in years, but I think that I need to now. I need to find a way to move forward. Without Alan.

These revelations don't stop me from attending the reading though. And not everyone is enthusiastic about my attending.

"I'm not sure it's such a good idea, is all," Anne-Marie says for the umpteenth time.

"I am fine." I reply.

Again.

I add, "I know them very well and I think I'll feel better if I go with people I know. It's the first time I'm going to be with him without being 'with him' and I'm a little nervous."

Anne-Marie retorts, "And you think by going with his aunt, uncle, and *mother* for God's sake, that's going to make it better!"

I look at my friend and can't help but laugh. She is the best.

"I love you," I say to her.

I give her a quick hug and dash out the door. I am running late already.

I haven't told Anne-Marie my suspicions about Alan yet. This has little to do with her reaction and more to do with not wanting to confront it myself. If I don't say it, it isn't true, my feeble brain reasons. But it's a lie and I know it.

I arrive at Kathleen and Charlie's place two minutes before we have to leave for the reading.

"Gabriela was meeting friends, so she left already. She said to say hello and she'll see you there though," Kathleen informs me while she puts on her coat.

Charlie then emerges from the bathroom, gives me a big hug and plants a tiny kiss on my cheek.

"You look great. Really," he says, all smiles.

They have been so wonderful to me since the break-up. We have gotten together a couple of times and they sent me this lovely bouquet after I got home from the hospital. I know they feel badly about the whole ordeal. Part of me thinks they even feel a little responsible somehow, that he would do this, especially to the girl they declared, "The One." It's not their fault though. We were all fooled. I am just grateful for their friendship and support.

We all walk out, chatting as we navigate the tiny streets to the reading.

"You nervous?" Kathleen asks.

"Yeah, a little." I answer honestly.

I wanted to get Kathleen's take on my thoughts regarding Alan, so I gave her a buzz earlier in the week, just to see if she thought I was in the right ballpark, knowing him as well as she does. I told her everything I had come up with, sitting in the living room 'til the wee hours of the morning. There was the homosexuality theory and my reasons for considering that. I also told Kathleen that I believed if Alan became privy to my suspicions, he would go and marry the first woman he met. Because that would be the ultimate in proving I'm wrong. Unfortunately, it wouldn't change anything. That's the thing about this—it's not a choice—you don't get to *decide* to be gay. Yes, you get to decide to act on it or not, but that still doesn't change the facts.

I also told Kathleen that I suspected Natalia, that woman from Gene and Jeannie's engagement weekend, would be at the reading. I just had a feeling, the way she kept saying what a great poker player he was and kissing up to him. Pul—leee—

zzzz. Of course, that would be right up his alley—someone to stroke his ego.

We arrive at the tiny theatre. It is old and quaint with a large lobby that leads to a narrow pathway into the staged area. We find our seats. I mingle about, seeing old friends, many of whom aren't even aware that Alan and I have stopped seeing each other. I don't bother to explain. Alan can break the news himself. Besides, this way I can still pretend to be the 'girl-friend'. The 'hostess'. Even knowing what I do, I can still pretend. If he can be a liar, why can't I?

I see Gabriela and go down to greet her. She and I hug. We don't speak about the break-up, but I know that she is addressing it in her own way. She feels bad, but doesn't know what to say. Nothing to say.

As I turn to go to my seat, Alan emerges from backstage, presumably from speaking with the actors. He looks up, sees me and mouths some words. I flunked lip reading 101, so I have no idea what he's saying, so instead I turn and ignore him.

I am strong. I don't need him.

It is time for the reading to begin. I shift in my seat. That's when I spot her. Natalia. She is there with another woman. Poor woman.

I glance at Kathleen, who gives a nod in Natalia's direction and whispers, "How'd you know?"

I smirk.

"I know him."

And so we sit through yet another reading of yet another version of *The Ghost of Dyckman Avenue*. I play a game with myself, silently mouthing the words, as I know most of them.

The reading goes fairly well, though nothing like the one a year ago. The ending is different. Part of it I like. Another part, I liked better before the re-write, but I realize that my opinions won't really matter anymore. I can just say, "Great re-write" and be done with it. No in-depth inquisitions about which lines I liked and which I didn't. This realization makes me both relieved and sad.

I go to stand up and join the others who are congregating on the stage in small groups when I see 'her' again. Who does she think she is, coming here? She is unwanted. I go to make my way to the stage, but before I can manage it, I am stopped. By her.

"Oh, hello Ms. Samantha," she says in her phony English accent (okay, so she's really a Brit…doesn't mean she's not phony).

I smile (with a clenched jaw).

"Hi. How are you?" I manage, feeling much like a person with Tourret's Syndrome, when the obscenities are about to become uncontrollable.

"Wonderful. Really enjoyed the play. He is such a gifted, truly gifted writer."

"Sure is." I say and silently congratulate myself for not punching her in the mouth.

"Big holiday plans?" she asks.

"Nope. Not a thing." I answer.

"Not getting together with your family?" She asks, sounding so concerned.

"Not this year."

"And where are they again?"

Like she ever knew where they were.

I feel like saying Riker's Island, but the truth comes out instead and I mutter, "Ohio."

"Ohio?"

She says it like I actually said Riker's Island.

"Interesting," she says before adding, "I'll be going to Paris."

Oh for fuck's sake…I will myself to gain control.

I say, "Oh, well, if you ever want to trade Ohio for Paris, anytime, I'm game."

Yes, lame, but not confrontational. I excuse myself and approach the stage.

Alan is wandering around. I join a conversation with Charlie, Gabriela, and a producer I know. We chat for a moment.

Alan comes over, says, "Hey baby," to me, plants a kiss on my cheek, kisses his mother's cheek and stands there between us, one arm around each of us. It feels good. I want to hold on to this feeling. In this moment, I know that he loves me. In this moment, he cannot be gay. In this moment, he wants to get back with me.

I know this because: a) he called me baby—my mind refuses to allow me to consider that he calls everyone, even his seventy-year old landlady, baby; b) he kissed me (yes, on the cheek—the same as his mother, and surely he doesn't want to 'get back' with her, but still) and c) he has his arm around me for several minutes—and his mother, I know, I know). Yes, it's love and we are headed back into each other's arms, my mind foolishly wants to believe.

It is decided that we will all meet at Delfino's, a nice restaurant/bar two blocks away. I go with Charlie and Kathleen and we sit at one of the two large tables they have assembled for our group.

I don't order food. I can only stay for a few minutes, as I have a bus to catch, and truth be told I don't want to overwhelm Alan. We cannot resolve our issues here, tonight, so it is best to make an appearance and then speak another day.

Alan shows up and goes directly to the bar—shocking. He goes from table to table asking different people their opinion on the play and making mental notes. I run to the ladies' room and when I return, he is sitting in my seat. He sees me, reaches out to touch my back lightly, but continues his conversation. Finally he looks my way.

"That's my seat," I say in a teasing way.

"Oh, I wasn't aware," he says, his voice sweet.

He gets up right away, but I shoo him back down.

"I should really go anyway. It was great. Really great." I tell him.

He remains standing and says he'll walk me to fetch my coat.

I give kisses to Charlie and Kathleen. I run to the other table and say good-bye to everyone. I kiss Gabriela on the cheek. We both well up with tears.

"I'm sad, seeing you," I say to her, as I know she will be returning to Florida and if Alan and I don't reconcile, I may never see her again. And we both know it.

"Of course you are. It's a sad time." She tells me.

I go back to get my coat and Alan follows. He helps me with my coat, always the gentleman. We hug. I kiss him on the mouth.

It is quick, the decision to do so. In fact, it seems so natural I don't even remember giving it any consideration at all. This must be how he felt at the Port Authority that first time, so long ago now, when he kissed me and I didn't kiss him back.

There is nothing, but flat rubbery lips in response. Like when you're a kid practice-kissing your hand. It feels like that, with a generous helping of humiliation on top.

I pull away.

"Take care," I say, though I can't look him in the eye. Still, I can't help but add, "Call me."

He nods in earnest. "I will."

CHAPTER 39

I grab the tissue box and keep it beside me on the sofa. These tears aren't stopping anytime soon. I blow and blow again making my head feel like it will explode from the pressure build-up. It doesn't. Damn, might have made all of this a lot easier. I glance over and she is still awake (sometimes they fall asleep, shrinks, but this one hasn't ever...that I am aware).

No, my therapist is actually exactly what I needed growing up—someone to cheer me on. She thinks I'm brilliant as an actor (though hasn't ever seen me act), a comedienne (she insists I should do stand-up), and a writer (she has read some of my short pieces, simply to get an idea of what is going on inside my head and she loves them).

She says she can tell that I am a wonderful entertainer because I never fail to entertain her every Monday morning 10 am. She doesn't say it quite like that, and though I do appreciate that she cracks up with laughter at times during our sessions (often while I'm crying), I just hope I'm gaining some insight. I just hope I'm getting over it. Him.

"You have to try to look at it from the other side," she tells me. "If I described the relationship that you described to me, you would think I'm a fool for being in it, much less for wanting it back."

I sit back and consider what she says. Sounds like Anne-Marie. Makes sense. And I tell her so.

I then add, "But even though you're right on some intellectual level, I still want it on another level. I love the cuddling and pasta-making and Scrabble, and the discussing plays."

She holds up her hand and says, "You aren't describing anything personal to *him*. You can make pasta and play Scrabble, and cuddle and talk about plays with anyone."

I never have thought of it this way. She's right. I can get it all elsewhere and not pay the high price…kind of like bargain shopping.

I hang my head for a moment, gather my thoughts and finally say, "I just don't want to do it all again."

The doc asks, "Do all what?"

"All of it. The meeting and getting to know someone, their faults and if you're compatible and meeting the families, and on and on and on…just to find out that he's another asshole who's going to break my heart…I just don't want to go through it all again. I can't."

I start crying again and am grateful the tissues are handy.

"I feel like it's him or no one because I'm just…" cry, cry, cry… "not willing to do it all again."

She lets me cry it out for a moment then says, "You don't need to think about all of that right now."

I argue.

"Yes, I do. I'm not getting any younger and I'm…I'm just…scared." I tell her, "The thing I realize about relationships is that with each break-up, you are less willing to give yourself to someone. You hold back more. You can't help it. Like, you know, when you're young and it's your first boyfriend, well, you'll do just about anything for that person. And I did. I really did. I was twenty then. And when it ended, I wanted to DIE. And it took me almost three years to be able to function again. So now it's years later and yeah, I've dated, but never felt like this. Like I did with Alan. And that's why I was so sure he was the one. Because it felt so right. And I gave all I had. Again."

I wipe my nose with the back of my hand, realize again that there are tissues and proceed to clean my hand off. I am anxious. My hands feel idle. They begin to shred the used tissues that sit next to me in a heap.

I glance out the window and say, "But this time I know I'll get over it. Somehow. Some way. I just don't want to though. And I don't want to go out with any other guy either. I don't want to go through all of this nonsense again. For what? It's all a bunch of bullshit and I just don't believe in it anymore! Break-ups destroy your sense of trust. They just do."

I start crying again, which gives her an opening.

"You're right. On some level, you're right. As time goes on, you are more alert, more aware of the choices you make regarding who you date and that. But this is not just a result of having your heart broken. This happens with everything. You're maturing. It is learning, as with everything. When we know better, we do better and as we get older, we hopefully are learning things that enable us to make better choices the next go-round. Some of these lessons are hard ones and they hurt. That is the nature of life. But, it doesn't have to be a bad thing. Though I can see how you might view it as such right now."

I know that she's right. But it's advice that I need to put in a compartment in my head for another time. A time that I can really listen and utilize her wise words. For now, I can only continue to wallow in my misery. Until the time that I deem it over.

CHAPTER 40

I am *so* not in the mood for this, but I have no choice. My very good friend, Faith, is having a baby—a miracle in itself because she wasn't even supposed to be able to get pregnant—and her shower is today. I have dolled myself up best I can and am walking there now.

Although I'm not really up to this because it involves couples and babies—things that elude me at this point in my life—I am very excited to see Faith. She's a wonderful person and we haven't seen each other in over two months.

She and I met in acting class five years ago. She is a former dancer, a former actor, a former personal trainer, who is now a life counselor. She is certified in everything from nutrition to herbology to aromatherapy (which gave her hives) to Creative Arts Therapy to becoming a minister. Yes, she is one well-rounded individual. And crazy, and fun, and did I mention crazy, and very, very 'out there' as far as spirituality goes. I have only met Brandon (her man) once, but he seems a perfect fit…even farther 'out there' than Faith (as impossible as that seems).

She recently told me that they were having a hard time deciding on a baby name, as Brandon kept insisting on Chinese names. 'We're not Chinese,' she told him. 'Yes, but I was in a former life,' he responded.

Suddenly single-hood doesn't seem so bad after all.

The first things I notice when I walk in are all the ribbons and bows and…boobs. Faith is this very thin woman with enormous boobs. Now pregnant, she is a very thin woman with a *tiny* belly and *enormous* (did I say enormous) boobs. I can't help but tell her that she could feed most of Nicaragua with those things. Floatation devices, my Lord.

I know a few of the women (and men—they are here too), and am introduced to the rest. Everyone seems very nice and friendly. There is one woman, CJ, who looks familiar, but I can't place her. She is a spiritual healer (only at Faith's baby shower—and on the reservation—would you meet a spiritual healer), who uses sound waves to heal your inner self.

I ask Faith, "Have CJ and I met before? She looks so familiar."

"No, but you probably feel drawn to her because of the vibrations she sent through me." Faith answers straight-faced.

What? I resist my usual sarcasm and tell her to go open her gifts. Now.

The shower goes well. They get some really nice stuff, enough to hold them until the child is nearing high school. I love buying baby clothes (what woman doesn't), so I couldn't help but get a cowboy outfit *and* a motorcycle outfit complete with leather jacket and black boots. Since I couldn't find these ensembles in 'newborn' I opted for 6-9 months, so I'll have to wait a while before seeing my new little guy all decked out on his Harley.

Dai has sent along a kimono and obi for the unborn child. It is gorgeous navy blue silk. Perhaps Brandon was also Japanese in another life or will simply think it's Chinese. Either way, it should make him feel right at home.

The shower ends pretty early. We all chip in with the clean-up and get ready to head out. Before we leave, CJ says a prayer for Faith and Brandon.

We all gather into a circle and hold hands, I between Faith and CJ. This is a prayer unlike any I've ever heard. It's not even in English—or no English I've heard before.

She begins reciting chants from Native Americans and the vibration is so strong that it jolts my hand. I feel something tight in my throat and when I open my mouth, I feel something come out of it. Something palpable, though when I go to look, there is nothing there. Exorcism anyone? I feel lighter in my body. In my being. I feel freaked out too.

As we're walking out, CJ says to me, "You alright?"

"Yeah, I think. You really, uh, kind of freaked me out back there," I chuckle, trying to blow it off.

"Yeah, I thought I felt something. You should come and see me. I do private sessions and usually just one does the trick. For whatever's ailing you."

She hands me a business card and we file out.

Scary stuff.

CHAPTER 41

I glance down at the directions, scribblings I can barely make out. All I see is the word *Parkway* about six times. It seems that traveling to Long Island requires one to go from parkway to parkway to parkway to parkway…can't they just call them roads or routes for cryin'out loud. Please don't let me get lost. Not tonight.

I turn onto the Sawmill Parkway at the last second by cutting off a red SUV. I give a small wave in apology, but the driver doesn't seem to accept it. I gather this from his middle finger response.

I take a deep breath and try to regain some control. I need to be as low-key and solid as possible. It will look bad otherwise. You know when you go to a funeral and people are passing out and throwing tantrums, well, I don't want to add to the mix. Not that I plan on passing out or throwing a tantrum. It's just been a while. We did speak on the phone briefly this week, so the ice has been broken. Kind of.

I was on the bus, traveling to work on Friday when my cell rang. When I saw Alan's number my stomach turned to jelly. It took a full three rings (one more and off to voicemail it would have gone) for me to steady my voice enough to answer. I think it woke at least two sleeping commuters before I picked it up.

"Hello," I said.

"Hi. It's Alan." He sounded dog-tired.

"Hey, what's going on?" I asked as casually as possible.

"My dad died early this morning."

"Oh, Al, I'm, I'm so sorry."

"Thanks. Just wanted to let you know. The funeral is Monday evening. I'll e-mail you the info."

"Of course I'll be there," I said. "Alan, if there's anything…well, you know, call me."

"Thanks, Sam. I gotta run, lots of calls to make. See you Monday."

And that was it. All business. I know he would have been that way if we were still together too. He's not so good with processing his feelings.

Dill Road. I make a left and see the large white structure on the right. I turn in and go around back to the parking lot. Another car pulls in beside me and Alan and his sister get out. We greet each other with hugs and kisses. Angela and I walk in together. Alan hangs back, seeming lost in thought. Or grief perhaps.

Alan looks the same to me. All except his eyes, which are rimmed in red. A combination of tiredness and tears I would guess. He is wearing black pants, white shirt and grey sports jacket. The jacket looks a little worn and a size too small. I wish I would have gotten him a jacket. He needed something comfortable for the funeral. I remind myself that that is not my job anymore—it never really was, I just took it upon myself to make it so.

Angela looks beautiful as always in a simple black dress. Her eyes are perpetually full of tears that spill out, but miraculously don't run her make-up (I'm not being shallow here…I'm just amazed).

I am wearing a black jacket, black blouse (that is so low-cut it keeps getting caught up in the jacket. This is bothersome because it looks like I don't have a blouse on at all. So every time I approach someone the first words out of my mouth are 'This damn blouse keeps opening up'). I also have on black pants—I wanted to wear a skirt, but didn't have one. Who doesn't own a black skirt? Pathetic.

There are several people here already, milling about, making small talk. I see Gabriela and head over to give her my condolences. I ask for Barbara, but am told that she had to be taken out. She will return in a little while when the service commences.

There are tons of people here from LP Productions. Pam, Liza, Brenda, Stan and more assemble in the foyer. I go over and we all hug and kiss, smile, chat, and try to be upbeat despite the circumstances of our meeting.

I take a seat near the back of the room. I look, but don't see Gene and Jeannie. Alan walks by and I stop him.

"Hey, how ya holdin' up?"

He sighs.

"It's tough, but I have to hold on for Ang and Barbara. It'll hit me later."

"Where's Gene?" I ask.

"They're on their honeymoon in Africa. Supposed to be coming home tonight, but I don't expect them to make it. We'll see."

I nod.

This is bad news. I want Alan to be comforted. I know that only Gene can do that. Not me, not Pam, not Angela or their mother. Only Gene. I want him here. Here for Alan.

I mingle with friends of Alan's I haven't seen for months. More than a couple aren't even aware of our break-up. When I inform them, they make comments like, 'What was he thinking' and 'He'll come around', all of which make me feel good, like maybe we have a chance, when I know deep down, that even if Alan proclaimed it, we don't. Perhaps he doesn't even know it. But he is not available to me. Or to any woman. Not now. Not ever.

I make my way to the powder room and when I return, my heart breathes a sigh of relief. I am overwhelmed. I start crying. I know it is silly, but I can't help it. I am so happy. Standing before me are Gene and Jeannie. I greet them. We hug and kiss. We hug and kiss again.

"I'm so happy you made it. Thank you. He needs you."

Gene goes to find Alan while Jeannie and I settle in for a chat. It has been so long and we have so much to catch up on…their wedding, honeymoon, jobs, my writing, acting, how I'm doing being single. We talk non-stop until the service begins.

I opt to sit in the back with LP, instead of with Kathleen and Charlie, who are sitting near the rest of the family. I am not family. I will never be.

The service is short and sweet. Angela speaks. She is wonderful and sincere. She is crushed at the loss of her father. Alan speaks. He doesn't shed a tear. He is holding true to his wish to be strong I suppose. A gentleman I have never met speaks. He seems nervous and stumbles on his words often, but he gets his message across and everyone seems in support of him.

When the priest returns to say a final prayer, my nose starts pouring blood. This is not uncommon, as in the dry winter months, I often get nosebleeds. And they're often at inopportune times—okay, like there could ever be an opportune time—but it's never at home watching TV, but instead at auditions, during work, while running—boy did I scare the hell out of the two people who saw that one—and evidently at funerals.

Not wanting to interrupt the service, and thinking that it will be ending soon, I try to hold my head back casually (casually?) and wait it out. Friends around me notice this and soon I have a fistful of tissues in my hand. Of course, they think that I am so shook up over Mr. D's death that I have caused my nose to bleed. Nothing could be farther from the truth. I am sad, but this is about the barometric pressure, not the emotions of the moment.

The service ends within ten minutes. My nose stops bleeding within eight, so I'm able to say my good-byes without further mess and explanation.

CHAPTER 42

I can't believe I'm actually doing this. I suggested it to my shrink and she said 'why not'. That surprised me. I was counting on her to talk me out of it. I figured she would be against anything that didn't deal with the psyche, especially something on the 'supernatural' or 'spiritual' level.

I walk up 116th Street. Boy, this isn't the Harlem of yesterday. Yes, the beautiful brownstones still adorn the streets, but minus the graffiti and boarded-up windows. Harlem is being restored and is more gorgeous than ever.

CJ's apartment is where she does her healing work. It is in a new building just above a health food store. Very mainstream. Harlem is now.

She buzzes me in and then gives me a quick tour of the apartment. A really nice two-bedroom, hardwood floors, spacious rooms. It's neat and clean. And going co-op in a year. By then she will be able to purchase it, she tells me. At what she's charging, she should be able to buy two, I think to myself, but don't say out loud. On second thought, if this works, I would pay anything. That is the bottom line.

I really know so little about this whole process. When I called to schedule—a call that took three full days, as I kept picking up the phone, dialing, and hanging up before she answered…I was scared I was turning into Faith. And if I ever uttered, *you know her through her vibrations through me* to someone, I would want to be committed. End of story.

But CJ assured me that there was nothing creepy about this. That I didn't need to bring anything with me, but myself and my willingness to rid myself of bad karma and of fear that was keeping my body rigid and preventing me from getting what I truly wanted out of life.

Okay, I brought that.

"So, you just lie down here."

I am on a turquoise covered daybed in the 'healing room'.

"There are tissues right next to you on the window sill, if you need," CJ tells me in her calm, clear voice.

"Am I going to need tissues? Is this going to hurt?" I ask, feeling panic creep in.

"You may or may not need them. Just depends. Sometimes things can get very emotional, so if you're an emotional-type person, then you may need them."

An emotional-type person? Me? She may need to go grab another box.

"I want to go over a few things with you," she says. "I channel other spirits through my being, so you needn't be scared, because I'll be right there watching the whole time." She points toward the ceiling.

"Huh?" I say as eloquently as possible.

"I will be channeling other spirits through my body. So if you hear my voice change or if you hear them refer to 'Moon Sun', that's my native name. There's no need to worry."

Worry? No, I'm far beyond worry at this point. How about *freaked*? She'll be up there, as in 'leaving her body' up there? And some other voice (but her body) will be talking about her, but using the name 'Moon Sun'? At this point, I would love to hear someone talk about knowing someone through someone else's vibrations.

Perhaps this is a mistake. I consider leaving.

"Samantha, you just need to lie down and relax. No harm will come to you. Only help. But it's up to you." She tells me in her regular voice.

I swallow. I swallow again. I nod.

I say, "Okay. I'm ready. Moon Sun."

The process is long and exhausting. We cover many areas of my life...my family—mom and dad, where many blockages and issues remain. We cover binge eating (a favorite of mine), Alan ('not surprising you picked someone unavailable, since your father too was unavailable' I am told), and fear, which covers the gamut of the remainder of my life. I cry and cry some more. I keep crying, even when I think I have no tears left. Where do they keep coming from?

The session consists mainly of CJ (or Moon Sun depending) asking me many specific questions and then doing a chant or prayer (in chant form) to alleviate the blockage or issue. She also goes through scenarios that I have lived through or 'what-if' scenarios that we act out while I remain lying still on the turquoise covered daybed. All of this is done in her normal voice or in a slightly lower, male voice. Surprisingly, I don't get too freaked out by this, as I am already invested in the process.

CJ makes me see things in a way I have never considered before. She really opens my mind and shows me another way of looking at things. It's the strangest thing I have ever done, felt, or been a part of, yet somehow it feels right. I can literally feel the vibrations through my body at times, and I feel so light and empty and carefree when we are finished that I am happy to pay her her asking price. It is worth every penny.

"You are so young to be getting to this level in your life," she tells me at the door.

"I'm not as young as you think," I say in response.

"Well, you're not fifty." She tells me. "It's very courageous of you. It usually takes people many, many years, even sometimes several lifetimes to get it right."

Though that thought seems preposterous to me, it makes me feel good. I smile, touch her hand, hug her once more and thank her sincerely for helping me break through.

CHAPTER 43

I guzzle the last of my Poland Spring and race into the apartment. I am late. I have been getting up to run several days a week and today, even though I overslept, I didn't want to forsake my run, so now I'm even later. I bypass Dai sitting at his desk doing Kanji.

"Ohayo Gozaimus Samantha-son," he says to me.

"Morning Dai," I managed while running into the bathroom to grab a shower.

The commute in seems to be less than usual...probably some little-known religious holiday.

I make a trip to the Ladies' Room first thing after getting to the office. I don't really have to go...I just want to admire my image in the mirror. I am wearing my brand new outfit (size 4 pants!! Okay, so they've changed the sizing chart and a size 4 is a former size 8—so what! A size 4 is a size 4, no matter what it used to be!)

I am going out with the girls tonight and I want to look good. The girls being Anne-Marie, Pam, Faith, and Kiera. Kiera went to school with Faith and I and we have all been great friends ever since. She is now trying to juggle her acting career, her massage therapy job, and her husband and new baby, whom I have declared my new boyfriend.

He seems to not have a problem with that, as he smiles whenever he sees me (okay, he's a happy child and smiles whenever he sees anyone, but I think I detect a special smile for me...okay, could be gas). Of course at eight months old, he can't avoid sex with me or overlook me for acting roles, so it's hard to gage how things are really going.

We've been trying to put together a girl's night for months. It is so difficult to find a night that we are all free. I haven't mentioned my healing session to any of them. This is certainly unlike me, but like the whole issue of Alan being gay, I don't want it to reflect badly on me. I know they're my friends and that automatically means that it can't reflect badly on me, but I don't want to be the girl who didn't know her man was into other men—I mean how tough can it be to see that? Tough, okay! Tough.

And I don't want everyone thinking I'm turning into Faith with this healing shit—though it really did work wonders. I am feeling so good. I'm exercising and writing and auditioning and basically running myself ragged, but it's all for me and it feels good. So, I'll just go and they can see for themselves how well I'm doing.

Satisfied with my hair and make-up, I return to my desk to answer personal e-mails and talk on the phone. Work can be so grueling.

The day seems long, as I have little work to keep me busy.

Finally, finally, 5:00 approaches and Anne-Marie comes to my desk to get me.

Ruby's Red on Nineteenth between Sixth and Seventh Avenues is the scene of the crime, or rather our girl's night out. We drink Margaritas, well, Kiera, Pam and Anne-Marie drink Margaritas…Faith (pregnant) and I (don't drink liquor) drink cranberry and seltzer and pretend to get drunk. We eat appetizers (those little fried foods that will put me right out of my size 4 pants if I'm not careful). We talk about everyone and everything (except Alan's gayness and my 'healing' self).

"You do look great, I have to say," Kiera says to me.

"Thanks. I feel great. Things are really starting to go my way," I tell them.

"Have you met anyone?" Pam wants to know.

"Nope." I say with a smile on my face.

"Still not over Alan?" Pam says.

"No, I am. I just don't feel that I need a man in my life…at least not right now. I'm just too busy."

"Oh, you better watch that. That's exactly what I said and now look at me. I'm 48 years old and alone. You don't want that Sam. Trust me, you don't."

224

Salsa with the Pope

I look at Pam. She is so sweet. So loving. So smart and friendly. How can she be alone? I always thought it was by choice, but I guess we don't always see what's really going on underneath the surface.

"You'll find someone. It's never too late." I tell her.

Faith pipes in, "She's right. When the time is right, when you least expect it, the Universe will make it happen."

"Well, we better be heading out of here." Kiera says suddenly.

"Oh, so soon. I mean it's only," I look at my watch, "after nine. Didn't you say that Jack was watching my little man tonight?"

Kiera smiles. "Yeah, he's watching him, but there's an..." she clears her throat "event here tonight and we need to make ourselves scarce."

"Oh, I didn't know." I say and begin to gather my things.

"You're not leaving. We are." Pam informs me as she puts on her coat.

She, Kiera, and Faith all stand up. I look to Anne-Marie, who has been pretty quiet all evening. I am confused.

"Do you know what they're talking about?"

Anne-Marie smiles slightly. She says, "You and I have a date."

I knit my brow. "I thought we all had a date...with each other. What—"

But before I can finish, an amplified female voice says, "Welcome to Ruby's Red. And to our nine-thirty Quick Date Event."

Oh no...

"But, I don't want to do this. I don't want to meet a man." I say in protest.

But no one, not even Anne-Marie, who is the one closest to letting me out of here, believes me.

"This is a sure-fire way to get over Alan." Kiera says to me.

"I *am* over him," I tell them.

"Sure." Pam says and begins to give hugs before departing.

225

"But, Pam, why aren't you doing this? You just got through saying that you're alone and you don't wanna be, so why not stay?"

"It's for 30-35 year-olds. Besides, I don't want to do this. It's ridiculous. And I'm happy with my life. Good luck." she says before kissing me on the cheek.

I say good-bye to Kiera and Faith, reminding them both that paybacks are a bitch and turn my attention back to Anne-Marie, who is sipping the last of her Margarita.

"Ready?" she asks with a smile.

"But why?" I say, my voice whiny.

"It wasn't my idea. They just thought that, well...this might get you back in the game is all."

"And you went along with that?"

Anne-Marie pulls her chair close.

"You gotta see it for what it is. It's just a game. Fun. It's not like you're gonna marry one of these guys. And we only have to talk to them for three minutes. Granted that will be three minutes too long for many of them, but it'll be an experience. One you can tell your grandkids."

She giggles.

I sigh.

Help.

Basically, I liken the Quick Date experience with getting my gall bladder out. Except that I liked that more.

It is on the ninth guy (there are thirteen total) that it finally happens. I have been through two accountants (one of which I almost fell asleep on—literally), an insurance salesman with eczema (I know this because he mentioned it while scratching his raw, red skin), three men that have been divorced a minimum of three times, a personal trainer who loved himself more than any woman ever could, and a chef who weighed-in just short of 350 lbs. It was time to get out of here.

As I sat and listened to #9 (a science teacher from Bed-Sty) I began gazing around the room, sizing up all of the lost souls. Sure, some of them are here to have fun and meet some new people, but more are here to meet "the one." It is pathetic.

It is the 'last picked for kick-ball' syndrome and it makes me sad.

I look up at the ruddy-faced guy in front of me, and although he is talking very animatedly, I can't hear him. It is as if someone put him on mute and I can only gage his meaning through his expressions and gestures, of which there are many.

Suddenly, I am awake. Something in me snaps and I am fully awake. Fully present. I am awake, present, and clear. Clear in my thinking. About my life. About what I want and what I don't want.

And I don't want this.

I stand and look for Anne-Marie. I am one behind her, but I am on the end now, so she is in the next row at the opposite side. I must go get her. Must tell her that I am leaving. I am not interested in this for my life.

As I pass, the number nine man grabs my arm.

"What…where, where are you going?" He asks.

I hear him. For the first time this evening. I hear his voice. It is shrill and full of insecurity and stammering.

"Away. This just isn't for me," is all I can manage.

I spot Anne-Marie as the buzzer sounds. This is our signal to go to our next 'date'. As Anne-Marie moves, she sees me, probably thinking I am headed in her direction because that is where my next station is.

I get her attention and mouth, "I'm leaving."

She shakes her head, not getting what I said. I say it again and this time gesture with my hand that I will be outside. She looks really surprised and maybe disappointed, but I can't tell.

She nods.

I say out loud, "I'll wait for you outside."

She nods and says, "Okay" quietly.

I am only outside for the better part of fifteen minutes when Anne-Marie comes out.

"Don't you even want to see your results? Who you're a match with?" She asks me.

"No, that's okay. I'm not a match with anyone I don't think. Because I'm just not wanting to be with anyone right now, you know?" I say to her.

"Yeah, I understand." she says.

We walk arm in arm toward the subway. After a few moments she says, "Hey, sorry about that. I know you felt put on the spot and I know that's not a good feeling...it was out of the goodness of our hearts though, not—"

I cut her off and say, "I know, I know. I'm not mad. I know you guys meant well. I'm just, I don't know. Hey, how did you score back there? Meet any Mr. Rights?"

She smirks, "Maybe."

My eyes grow big, my mouth opens, "Nahhh," I say to her.

"You never know." she says.

I am jealous. Not that she may have found a guy—that I wish for her every single day. Someone to make her happy. Someone worthy of this awesome individual. It is not that.

I am jealous of her carefree nature. How she is in such a good place. Such a good place that she can see this for what it is. Fun. Nothing more. Nothing less.

I look at her when we reach the N line.

"You want to get a drink?" I ask.

"Sounds good." She says.

We amble over to a sports bar, McNally's on the corner.

We grab the last available table and settle ourselves with two soft drinks.

I then begin to tell Anne-Marie the things I have been leaving out. Mainly, that I think Alan is gay and that I saw a healer.

"What, you're keeping things from me—that's my department." She says and giggles. "Seriously, why didn't you tell me? You know you can tell me anything, Samantha. I'm not here to judge you, girl."

I look at Anne-Marie's face, full of concern and compassion.

"I guess I just didn't want to face it. I mean gay is like...dead. I mean...you know what I mean. As far as our relationship goes."

She nods.

"I know, I know...are you sure?" She asks.

"Well, no. But..."

"And you're pretty much basing this on his past and that he and you broke up…"

"And that he stopped wanting to have sex and Rob…"

"And because Rob's gay, he knows. I'm not so sure about that. Yeah, I think there's something off about the guy, but gay? Hmm, not sure it's that."

The bar is fairly busy. Mainly due to the Yankees game playing on the flat screen above the bar.

I take a sip of my diet coke and glance at the screen. Darren James has just struck out.

An overwhelming sadness comes over me and I start to blubber.

"Hey, it's okay." Anne-Marie tells me.

When she sees that isn't working, she tries, "Okay, it's not okay, but it will be."

"It's not that," I start to tell her.

"It's…it's," my voice is thick from the tears, "The Yankeeeesssss."

I let out a big wail, which sends an older man, dirty jeans and work boots, over to our table.

"Eh, I know how you feel, but they still got a shot for the Playoffs…try to buck up." He advises me before giving my arm a pat and turning his attention back on the game.

Anne-Marie hands me a napkin and says, "What just happened?"

We both start laughing and I explain that I just got sad seeing Darren James because it reminded me of that day at Yankee Stadium. She knows all about that day.

She nods and tries not to smile, but fails.

I wipe my nose one last time and look up at her.

"What?"

She bursts out laughing again and I can't help but join in.

All the sudden the entire bar erupts in cheers and applause, as the Yanks score the winning run.

My working man benefactor looks over from the bar, gives me a thumbs up and a wide grin. I return the gesture, allowing him to believe my problems have all been resolved.

CHAPTER 44

"Bachelor number one, if you wrote a play and I was perfect for it, would you cast me...or feed me some bullshit about not being right for it?"

I hear myself say the words, but I don't know who I'm saying them to... 'You're not supposed to know' my mind reminds me. 'They're behind a screen.'

I get up quietly and tip toe around the pink partition and there is Alan sitting in seats one, two, and three.

Huh? I jolt myself awake.

I start to cry. Hard, uncontrollable sobs escape me. I start saying the word, 'Why' over and over again. 'Why did it have to happen this way?' my heart wants to know. My being wants to know. But my mind already knows.

I know that because I wasn't taking care of myself and I was only concerned with Alan, this relationship could never be. I was losing my identity more and more with each passing day and yet I was content to go on. As long as he was giving me some affection—love as I construed it—then I was all right. I was good to carry on. But that's not the way it's supposed to be.

I cannot hide behind someone else's successes and failures. I have to lead my own life. Live my own life. Find my own way. And since I was not doing that, I was not allowed to continue on my blissful identity-less path.

The sobs are now coming from a place within me that I didn't even know existed. It feels like the bowels of hell. So far down, so deep into my soul that my body is heaving and convulsing. I try to calm myself down. To remind myself that I am doing better. That I have analyzed and agonized and I understand why we're not together. But strangely, that does not help.

Not in the least. For some reason, when we talk about matters of the heart, there is a different set of rules that are applied than when we speak of anything else.

For instance, when I think of owning a nice car, say a Lamborghini, my mind understands that no matter how much I have my heart set on that car, if I can't afford it, then I can't have it. End of story.

But for some reason, knowing that Alan is gay (or even thinking it so), knowing that I lost myself in the relationship, knowing that it can never be, surprisingly, does little to ease the pain. I suppose that knowing all of this is somehow healing, but that process is so slow that the effects won't really be felt until much later. Only after I marry another, am living in Nebraska, with my third child on the way, will I suddenly realize, *I don't love him anymore.*

It's just all so fucked up. I have been feeling so good about myself and really getting myself together and it takes only one baseball game, one bizarre dream to wash that all away and put the pain back center stage. It's process and time. I know that. But only intellectually. And that doesn't stop the pain in my heart.

I get out of bed and hit the computer. No sense trying to go back to sleep. Especially if those dreams are the ones awaiting me.

I go right to Craig's List.

I admit it. I've become a Craig's List junkie. For those of you living on planet Zion who have not heard of this great little site, allow me to enlighten you.

It started on the west coast and now has listings for every major city in the world. It lists Real Estate, Jobs, and things to be bought, sold, traded, or given away. It is especially helpful to people like me who act and write and need pick-up jobs. And best of all, it's free.

I click the Etc. Jobs listing. I usually find interesting opportunities, though few I feel qualified to respond to—naked housekeeper and wet-nurse among the top two.

Today is different. Today, I have nothing to lose.

To my surprise, I get the job, though my experience is limited. The boss seems more interested in what I look like, than what my skill-level is—no real surprise there, as he's male—and straight, I surmise.

The following week, I buzz the #2 button that is labeled "Marketing Assistants" and wait. I am anxious. Nervous energy flows through me. I am wondering how I will do. I have been practicing for days. Even at the office, you will find me shuffling cards at my desk, going over my 'big blind' 'little blind' rules. And even though I have dealt poker for promo events many times, it has never been for real money. At a real poker club. A real 'illegal' poker club.

Okay, so the boss tells us that it isn't illegal. He says that as long as we don't rake the pot—take a percentage of the pot each hand—and don't serve liquor—we don't—then it isn't illegal. We are, however, charging time. It is $3-5 per thirty-minute playing time. Whether or not that is illegal, I'm not at all certain. I'm not confident enough to go ask someone at the local precinct though, that's for sure.

I am buzzed in, get into the elevator and press the button marked 2. The club occupies the entire second floor. It is a huge loft space, complete with tables, kitchen, several flat-screened televisions, video games, ATM, and many cameras to record the comings and goings of patrons. I will work on tips alone, so I am hoping that business picks up and we are packed soon.

I figure if I work three days a week here, keep my hours at the day job, I should have enough saved up to move out of Dai's by the end of the year. Granted, I'll be exhausted and it will be difficult to do any acting work, but I will manage. I always do.

Friday night. I am working at the club. I've just come from having an early dinner with Pam, who wanted to make-up for leaving me with those awful men at the Quick Date Event.

We enjoy two pasta dishes and catch up on things. I tell her about some co-workers who are getting married and she says that they aren't the only ones.

"Alan." I say, not wanting to hear the answer. Not wanting to know that he and that woman, Natalia, who he has known for exactly six months, are getting married.

She nods.

"Yep. It's strange too, Sam, because he is just so different with her than he was with you. There isn't any affection. It's like cold. Weird."

She takes a mouthful of pasta and looks around the room. Thank God, because my heart is beating a million miles a minute. I look down at my bowl to make sure it hasn't come right out of my chest and landed there.

Pam gazes down at her plate and says, "You alright?"

I nod, unable to say anything for a moment. Finally I say a little too loudly, "Yeah, I'm fine. Actually it's like closure, you know?"

"Yeah, it is. I know exactly how you feel." she says to me and puts her hand on mine. "If you need to talk…"

"Thanks," I tell her.

I proceed to talk for the next half hour about how I think Alan is gay and it makes perfect sense that he would pick an unattractive (easy to get her—the offers weren't exactly numerous), not in the business (lots of time away from her), rich (well, that's an obvious asset) woman. And I believe it. All of it. But part of me feels badly for Natalia.

I know. She's the enemy. But she's not. She's the naïve one. She doesn't know him like I do. She doesn't know that he can't connect to women, that he is self-centered, and an imposter. She'll know soon enough I guess.

I change the subject and we order a quick cup of tea before I have to head off to work.

Work. It's getting old. Working all the time, day and night. No time to hang out with my friends (or hanging out and falling asleep mid-way through), no time for auditions, or that little necessity we call sleep. Yeah, that's a big one. Sleep.

The talk with Pam leaves me feeling a little numb. I just have to get used to the idea is all. Alan is getting married…Alan is getting married…Alan is getting married…to someone other than me.

Part of me is relieved. The hope is forced to die. No converting him. No getting back with him, because there will be legal documentation that states that he is another's.

Of course the other part of me hurts. I feel like this stranger has come and taken my life away. Like she stepped in, pushed me aside and said, I'll take this and this and that. And in an instant, my life is not mine anymore, but hers. How did this happen?

I put it all out of my mind. I must focus on the cards. The cards. I begin counting my decks and arranging them rainbow style. I adjust my seat and wait.

The card sharks eventually start showing up and then it gets really packed. One of the busiest nights I can remember. We are shorthanded a dealer too, so I should do really well. I am working. I am focused. I am making money. Alan is the furthest thing from my mind. Until he walks in.

I do a double-take, thinking maybe this is another of those sick dreams where I will wake up sobbing. As bad as that is, I'd take it over this reality in a minute.

He doesn't see me at first. He is with Mark, an actor and buddy of his. Mark is a big poker player, so I guess he got Alan in—you have to be sponsored to get into a club—can't just walk in off the street.

I try to concentrate on dealing the hand. I almost forget to burn one before turning the River Card, but I remedy the situation at the last moment and then flip a nine of clubs. This gets an immediate response from the players at my table as a flush and a full house are now possible. All the ooohhhs and aaahhs draw attention to the table and that's when Alan spots me.

He is surprised. He is pleased. Why, I am not sure, but I have no doubt that he likes seeing me here. Dealing cards.

I try to concentrate, but it is difficult. I'll have a fifteen-minute break in one more hand, so just try to get through it, I tell myself. It is a quick hand, as everyone folds, save one older gentleman who gladly takes the measly pot.

I realize that I will inevitably be Alan's dealer, as we rotate tables every half hour. Unless that is, he keeps switching tables too. Maybe he will just leave. Anything, just don't make me deal to him. I will feel nervous and surely fuck-up and my boss will be none too thrilled. Especially on our busiest night ever. Please, I silently pray, please, don't make me deal to him.

Apparently God hears my prayer because I never have to deal one card to Alan. Apparently God also has a sense of humor, as the police bust us before I ever have a chance to deal one card to Alan. I am scared out of my wits.

"Please just remain calm and we will take you down and get this over with as quickly as possible," the hunky cop tells us.

I whisper to Elyuss, another dealer, "What will happen to us?"

He smiles and tells me not to worry.

"It's no biggie."

No biggie??

We're all put into the paddy wagon and driven thirteen blocks to the 2-9 Precinct. I am seated two people away from Alan. If I was closer I would belt him one. He's the reason for all of this.

If he hadn't shown up, I wouldn't have had to pray to God to not make me deal to him, and we wouldn't have been busted, I surmise. Ass, I silently call him.

We are placed in adjacent holding cells, one for each sex. I am put in with two female patrons. The men number over forty, so they're crammed in. I notice Alan keeps toward the front, not speaking to anyone.

I stand forward too, not wanting to stand too close to a woman, who looks like a man, who was here when we were brought in, and scares the holy hell out of me.

Alan looks over at me and says, "So you deal poker now, huh?"

He is smiling. I hate him.

"Uh, obviously." I say back as sarcastically as I can muster.

He wants to converse. Here. Now.

"Ever had this happen before?"

"No." I tell him. "You know what happens now?" I ask.

"Mark told me this happened once to him before and they just get you for a misdemeanor and send you home."

I look into his cell.

"Where's Mark?" I ask Alan.

"He left."

I nod. Great.

I look around and see no reason to hold my tongue any longer. I let'er rip. "So, I hear you're getting married."

He bites his lower lip. Nods. Says, "Yeah."

"Surprising and not so surprising." I say. "I mean not so surprising since you need to do something to get people off your back about me and surprising because you're gay."

His face registers nothing. As if it's been wiped clean. Clean of expression. Clean of comprehension.

Finally he says, "Nice thing to say to me. Especially considering I'm sitting in a jail cell. With fifty men. Nice Sam."

He turns and walks toward the back of his cell.

Fuck him!

"You say he gay, uh, huh, I like me a piece a him," Lola the cross-dressing she-male tells me.

It is three hours later before I can get a hold of Dai and have him come and post my bail.

The wait is spent, being a nervous wreck—I consider taking up smoking, but it's a non-smoking facility and I *hate* smoking; getting to know Lola; talking about padded versus push-up and the ill-fated pump bra with Lola; and playing gin rummy, as I still have my cards with me. They did frisk me earlier, but Hunky Cop said I could keep my cards. (See he could tell I was a good girl from the start).

An interesting evening to be sure.

I go over the evening's events, highlighting my conversation with Alan, as Dai drives me home.

"What do you think?" I ask him.

"I think you hit a soft spot. I think you should've known better than to do it then...not that it was a problem because of the men in jail with him, but because it was loud and uncalled for."

Dai puts his hand up in my face. "And before you say anything, I'm on *your* side here. I know you're hurt. He's just lost, is all."

Dai is right a lot of the time.

CHAPTER 45

The week Alan gets married, I have two dates. Not bad, right? I have two men who want me, not just one stuck-up, snotty foreigner—like what he has. Okay, that's harsh. I'm just having a hard time deciding between my two suitors, and that's making me cranky, okay.

I say two suitors, but there was actually a potential third. Yes, that's right, a potential *third* suitor…popular, I am.

I meet Belafonte on the bus. Okay, not a romantic setting, but he makes up for that with his tight tanned body, beautiful blue eyes and dark wavy hair. His accent, Columbian from his mother. His name, Italian from his father. With that combination, seems likely he would argue with himself, but I never heard him. Not once.

We make plans to go out four times. Yes, four dates with one guy. Would seem like we're starting a relationship…except that we never actually go out.

Our first date, I am just spraying a little perfume, adding some lipstick to my already made-up lips when Belafonte calls. Apparently his uncle has had a heart attack and was just rushed to the hospital. Of course Belafonte needs to be there, as this is his uncle from the old country, yada, yada, yada…you get the point.

Date number two, I get the call before I even towel-off from my shower. He has bronchitis. And he does sound pretty bad, I have to admit.

Date number three is an emergency with his company—he has his own—and he needs to view some property immediately. I don't really get the immediate part, as it's 9 p.m. on a Friday. Who views property at 9 p.m.? Apparently Belafonte does.

Date number four is the deciding factor. He could get hit by a mac truck and I still would expect to see him. NO excuses. He is late. I am pissed. The end.

So you see why I don't count Belafonte...technically, we never went out (though we did have some mad phone sex—that's not slutty, it's non-contact), and honestly, it's just too painful....so much potential and well...humiliation. You understand.

So let's pretend I didn't mention him, shall we?

Where was I? Two suitors. Two dates.

My first possible-husband is a chiropractor. Well, not just any chiropractor. *My* chiropractor. I end up seeing him when the physical therapy I'm getting turns out to be ineffective.

See, I was running a lot, trying to get my damn nine races in, so that I could gain entry into the New York City Marathon (a lifelong dream of mine, though for the life of me, I don't know why).

Apparently athletically overworking the legs, especially in a linear motion (ie. running in a straight line) tightens the Iliotibial Band (see picture below) that runs alongside the entire length of your leg...who knew? So, I am diagnosed with Iliotibial Band Friction Syndrome. What happened to the days of easy two-word diagnosis...broken leg, sprained ankle...oh, how I miss those days.

All I know is that I am in pain and having a hard time putting three miles in, which to a distance runner—which I'm not, but will refer to myself anyway—is pathetic.

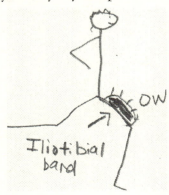

So when the physical therapy doesn't work, I am referred to Dr. Eric Robertson, a yummy dark-haired, green-eyed doctor—did I mention he's a *doctor* (at least that's what his business card says, though Dai insists that he's no *real* doctor) who has cause to put his hands all over my lower regions—medical reasons, get your mind out of the gutter, though I too have to admit that the thought does cross my mind as I lie on that tiny bench with him hovering inches above me, administering to my ailing leg.

The eroticism though, abruptly disappears when he begins the ART (Active Release Technique), which is some stupid alternative-medicine voodoo that maintains if you re-injure the affected part of the body, the body will go to that area and heal itself. *Right*.

There are dozens of professional athletes that swear by it. I'm no professional athlete though. Just skip the pain and give me the drugs. That's my motto. So, basically I lie there while the doc puts me into painful positions (sado-masochism anyone?). My only pleasure being him rubbing gel onto my leg, readying it for the pain.

It is after I have completed my five treatments—and feel no better mind you, though it is not uncommon for ART to take several days before the benefits are felt—and am leaving the office for the last time when Dr. Robertson (Eric, as he asked me to call him) jumps into the elevator with me.

"Going down?" he says and smiles.

I assume he means street-level and not to hell.

I nod an affirmative.

"So, I guess I won't be seeing you anymore. You'll be missed, I was getting used to having you around," he tells me before we stop on the ground floor.

"Oh, I'll miss you too," I say before stepping out. "Are you on a break?" I want to know.

He nods. "Coffee. Just want to grab one. Wanna join me?"

I do and say so.

We walk across Lexington Avenue, order a cup of coffee for him, a hot chocolate for me and find a quiet table toward the back of the deli. We chat about my leg, his family, the weather, and the upcoming holiday (Valentine's Day—ugh!) and how we will both be alone and how depressing that is (who knew that men got depressed on V-Day too!).

Before I know it, my voice betrays me and says, "Let's not let another Valentine's Day go by alone. How about a movie?"

I can't believe I said that! I, Samantha Wren Anderson, just asked a guy (no less my doctor, I mean ex-doctor) out.

He blushes, which makes me blush because I'm thinking conflict of interest or Hippocratic Oath—no that wouldn't be it—something along those lines though, but then he surprises me.

He says, "Definitely."

Not simply 'yes' or 'sure, why not', but *'definitely'*.

So we do go to the movies, and to dinner beforehand. And everything seems fine. No, better than fine. Good. Really good. That is up until the movie starts.

We are sitting there sharing some popcorn. The movie trailers begin. Eric is snuggling up to me, kind of putting his head near my shoulder. Then I start feeling something pulling at my sweater. When I turn to look, I discover Eric plucking lint balls off of me. And I'm not just talking one or two. No, more like dozens. And I can't get him to stop. It's like he's possessed. I try pulling away politely, but he just reaches further. There are no bounds he will not go to get to my bally sweater. Finally I lean over.

"Knock it off. Please." I say in my most firm chastising whisper.

Like a defiant child, he can't resist pulling two more (how many more could there reasonably be?) before acquiescing by sitting on his hands. Okay, strange.

Note to self: Check sweaters for lint balls before going to movies.

No more than two minutes later (okay maybe five minutes—we view three previews) he lay his head on my shoulder.

Suddenly he screams, "SMOKE."

Huh? I don't know what the hell he's talking about, but he scares the hell out of me and I leap up and look to see if maybe there's a fire somewhere. The only smoke I see is coming out of the ears of the people behind us, whose view is obstructed by my reaction to Eric's declaration. They seem unaffected by his outburst though, as if they're used to going to Bellevue's Tuesday Night at the Movies.

I sit down as quickly as I got up, and try to recover my composure. Eric is not having any of that though. He keeps sniffing and touching his nose.

Finally he says with a nasal voice—this due to him pinching his nose closed with his fingers, "You lied to me. You said you didn't smoke."

I cannot believe this. He is accusing me of lying. In a packed movie theatre. With his nose pressed closed by his fingers.

I get up, grab my bag and walk out.

He follows shortly after.

"What are you talking about?" I say when I see him behind me.

"You know exactly."

His nasal voice is making me nuts, so I wrestle his hand away from his face.

"I can't understand you with your nose plugged up!" I tell him.

He clears his throat, as if trying to conjure up some dignity, though there is none forthcoming. This I know for sure.

"I said that you clearly have lied to me. You smoke. I can smell it on you."

I start laughing. Wildly laughing. I can't help it. The guy's nuts. Absolutely nuts. And to think that I let him get close enough to touch my naked leg in his office. Scary.

My response really freaks him out. He tosses his hands up and walks out of the theater lobby.

I make my way to the ticket counter and exchange my ticket for the next showing and proceed to Starbuck's to wait it out.

This is on Tuesday. So you can imagine my reluctance to step out with Bachelor #2 on Friday. I am so reluctant in fact, that I turn him down flat the first time he asks. It is only after a second invite (and much prodding from Anne-Marie) that I decide to go for it at all. I mean it has to be better than Tuesday. Right? Not necessarily.

There are different levels of bad when it comes to dates. And there can be bad dates on the same level, with entirely different circumstances. So, no Chris (the Number 2 Man) does not scream at me in a crowded movie theatre (in fact, I refuse to go to the movies when he suggests it, saying that I had a traumatic experience there once and didn't know if I would ever be able to go again...okay, so I saw a movie that very same night...doesn't mean I wasn't traumatized).

Nor does he leave me with a threadbare sweater from pulling the fabric all night (I don't chance it—I wear a cotton blouse). He is good and doesn't do *those* things.

Instead, he takes me to a Chinese restaurant near my office (I see no reason to schlep all over town for a first date that I am already apprehensive about). We talk on the way about our jobs (he's a construction worker—hey I'm not a snob. I can date blue-collar and be okay with that), our aspirations (well, my aspirations...Chris seems to be plumb out of aspirations), but mostly we talk about our future children. This topic arises after we are already seated at the little eatery (otherwise, I would have veered off never to be found again).

Chris seems to think that I have the perfect nose for a little tyke. He goes on about this for a few moments, all the while reaching out to stroke my perfect schnaz, until I get tired of dodging his dirty fingers and excuse myself to the restroom.

I bring my purse and jacket along, hoping to skip out the bathroom window, but there is none to be found. I could have sworn there was a little window in here.

Note to self: Check first-date restaurant bathrooms to ensure escape route prior to date.

Forced to return to the table, I am already making up excuses to get out of here when I see Chris ordering from Kin, our waiter. Not only is Chris ordering for me—how could he even know what I like—he is doing so in Chinese. Not Mandarin or Cantonese mind you, but English with a mock Chinese accent. I am mortified.

It takes all of three minutes for me to feign illness (though truth be told, I'm not feeling so hot), speak with Kin privately and express my sincerest apologies, including a $10 tip, and race out.

My mind is made up. NO MORE DATES. EVER.

CHAPTER 46

I just want to sleep. Please. Just let me sleep. Sleep my life away. I don't want to talk to anyone. I do anyway.

"Yes, hello," I mutter into the phone, my voice thick with sleep.

"Samantha, this is your grandmall calling," she says in a loud, shrill voice. She then chuckles.

What is funny about her being my grandma (grandmall) calling? Well, come to think of it, just about everything. She is one crazy chick.

"Hey, Gram, what's up?" I say and try to physically get my body up off the bed.

"Well, I was just calling to see what you're up to. I made my will, you know."

"No, Gram, I didn't know."

"Yes, I did and I wanted you to know that I'm leaving you my organ."

Huh? I'm scared to ask which of her organs she's leaving me. Hopefully not her gall bladder, as I have little use for it now.

"Gram, uh, which organ did you, uh, have in mind?"

"Well now, Samantha, I only have one organ. The one in the family room. You know the one. Don't you remember it? It's been there since you were little."

I silently give a sigh of relief.

"Yeah, I know. The organ you used to play for us. Gotcha."

"Now, you are the only one of the grandchildren I am leaving something to. You know that? You are a good girl. We always talk and you appreciate me and I want you to have something special."

"The organ." I reply.
"Yes, the organ. You know how to play it?" She asks.
"I don't." I admit.
"How about the piano? You play piano?"
"Nope." I say.
"Oh, well, you'll just have to take some lessons, is all."
Sure thing.

The conversation goes from one thing to the next, though most of it I have heard before, so I can afford to find something to wear and make my bed while she talks. She then asks about Alan, if I've seen him. I tell her I think he's gay.

"Well, we need to find you somebody else. One that likes women. They've got them over there, don't they…men who like women?"

"Not too many." I tell Gram.

"Well, what in the world do you want a gay man for? He's no use to you."

Thank you Gram, for that sound advice.

I am thankful when the topic changes.

"Oh, I got them new pictures you sent me."

My new headshots. She likes to put them in frames for all to see.

"I can't believe you're not fat." she tells me.

I shake my head and laugh.

"Why is that Gram?"

"Well, you know, your aunt Billie, she's gotten even heavier and then Ron and Rita, they've lost a lot of weight, but they were big, you know. But you, you look good, Samantha. Not fat at all."

"Thanks, Gram. Thanks."

The conversation still in my head, I make my way to work. I call Anne-Marie first thing. Meeting in the ladies' room. It is during our conversation that I start to think I may never find someone to share my life. And I am truly okay with that. For the first time, I really feel like I am confident, I am attractive, and I can get along without a man. In fact, there are many perks to being alone.

I don't have to check with anyone about my comings and goings, I never have to compromise—about anything, and I don't have to pick up after anyone. It actually feels pretty good. I am sharing this philosophy with Anne-Marie, who is in the mirror examining dry skin on her chin.

"I can't believe I have this. I have never had razor burn before."

"It doesn't matter. You don't need to worry about a little dry skin." I tell her. "We are all empowering women. We don't care what the male species thinks of us." I add as I pull her away from the mirror and out to the lobby of our building.

"What's wrong with you? You're walking funny."

"Am I?" She asks and blushes. Her face is the color of a blooming poinsettia.

"What's going on?" I want to know.

She pulls me into an alcove and whispers, "Ted."

She giggles, as if there is an inside joke, though I am not in on it.

Ted? Who the hell is Ted? And why haven't I heard about him before. I wait her out.

She finally adds, "I met him at the Quick Date. I don't think you got to him. I asked him and he didn't recognize your description." she tells me.

"And?" I prod.

"And, well, we both were a match, so we've been e-mailing for a while and then he was out of town and finally we went out last week."

"Why didn't you tell me this?" I want to know.

"I just haven't seen you. You were off the next day and then the weekend. So I just haven't had a chance. I wasn't keepin' it from you, sugar lips." she says and laughs.

"Tell me why you're walking funny, *sugar lips*." I tease.

She giggles.

"Well, we really get along. We really just, clicked. I don't know. I can't explain it, Sam. It's like, he's who I have been waiting for my whole life."

"Slow down." I tell her.

"I know, I know. But I mean it."

I look at her. She is beaming. The happiest I have ever seen her.

"I'm happy for you." I tell her and give her a big hug.

"Are you sure? I mean, that it's not too hurtful for me to talk to you about this stuff?"

I give her a confused look.

"What? Of course not. You deserve to be happy. If this Ted person is who is going to help that along, then I am all for it. Now, when do I get to meet him?"

CHAPTER 47

I am binging on honey-wheat pretzels, a favorite of mine. I have eaten over half the bag and I don't care. I am frustrated and confused. And exhilarated. I have been forced by the fates (or my Higher Power, or God or CJ or Moon Sun or whatever you want to believe) to work.

I am writing a one-woman show. Something I have wanted to do for two years now, but never had the balls to attempt. Now, I feel compelled. There is nothing stopping me. No more excuses (no man and most of my girlfriends are too busy to get together—even Anne-Marie, now that Ted is in the picture), so it is time. Time for Sam to do for Sam.

I've been working on it for a couple of weeks now and things are actually starting to take shape. I have two How-To books (the 'how to write a one-person show' kind, not the 'grandma-sex' kind) to walk me through it and I have taken extensive notes, as far as the story itself goes. It makes me feel so good. Inside. Like this is what I should've been doing all along. It is difficult though. Don't misconstrue the rush with it being easy. On the contrary.

This work is the hardest thing I have ever done. I believe that is not only because it is something that matters to me deeply, but because it is a part of me. Of who I am. Of my soul. It is my guts.

I have designed a schedule that includes a two-hour writing session four days a week, one salsa class, four runs, work, and limited time for my friends. I find myself hanging out more with Brenda—a friend I met through LP Productions—than anyone else lately.

She and I have a lot in common too—both single women, in the arts, trying to make it in New York. Brenda is an Event

Organizer for the Arts, mainly theatre, so she sees a lot of plays and throws benefits, which I volunteer for when I have a chance. It's a good way to meet people and I usually enjoy myself.

I am now at one of these benefits, the second one this week. I am readying to leave, though the party has just begun. I helped Brenda set-up everything and she knows that being a Jersey girl, I am on a bus schedule and must skedaddle.

I run to the loo a last time. While in the stall, I hear two women enter, talking amongst themselves.

"I'm telling you, he didn't even see her. I barely saw her."

The other says, "Yes, but you don't know her. You didn't even know what she looked like."

"You're worry for nothing. Besides, he's your husband. He picked you. Isn't that enough?"

Woman #2 laughs. It's not a funny giggle, but rather a sad, ironic chuckle.

"I suppose. But you don't know this woman. What she would do to get back at him. She's even told people that he's gay. That's how—"

I open the stall and she stops mid-sentence. I am nervous. My stomach is in knots, but I wasn't going to sit in there and hide. I was finished with my business. I have a bus to catch. I'll be damned if I will allow this woman to take anything else from me.

"Excuse me." I say to her, making my way to the sink.

They both stand in silence for a moment.

Natalia finally speaks, "Well, I guess you heard."

"Hard to miss." I say to her.

"You know, you never cease to amaze me. The lengths you'll go to, to make him pay for not loving you."

I dry my hands on brown paper towels. I look her in the eyes.

"Has he started making excuses for not coming to bed yet?"

I walk out of the ladies' room and head for the exit.

I head home, unable to think of anything but what just happened. I hate it. I wish it hadn't happened that way. I convince myself, there was nothing I could do.

The next day, I hit the office and meet my best girl pronto.

"You said that?" Anne-Marie's eyes are big and excited. "I can't believe you said that! You go girl!"

She is congratulating me on my conversation with Natalia last night, though I don't feel much like celebrating. The entire situation is bad. And I don't want to rejoice in someone else's pain. I know that she wouldn't have been concerned if Alan had seen me if things were going well in their marriage. I didn't even know he was there. And I don't care. I honestly couldn't care less.

I look at Anne-Marie and she is still beaming. From the conversation? I think not.

"What's up?" I say to her.

"What'd you mean?" She asks innocently, her hands entwined behind her back, her eyes on the carpet below.

"What gives, girl? Something's happenin' here, now what is it?"

In one motion, she thrusts her hand at me, her eyes wide and animated. On her left hand is a diamond the size of Gibraltar. It is stunning, though not ostentatious despite its mass.

I look at her face. I nod my head quickly, as if to say, is that what I think it is? She nods back just as fast, indicating, yes, yes it is what you think it is. We both let out whoops and yelps and hug each other and dance around in a circle. Two girls going to the prom, that's what we must look like to bystanders.

I am so happy for her. She has tears in her eyes. As they slide down, she wipes them away with her bejeweled hand (though truth be told, Anne-Marie is rarely without a bejeweled hand—neck or wrist—she is a jewelry connoisseur with an armoire full to prove it).

"It's gorgeous. So...wow!" is all I can think to say. "When's the big day?"

"We haven't set a date yet, but, it's going to be soon. No long engagements for us. Ted wants us married soon. And so do I."

Salsa with the Pope

I really can't fault Ted. She is a good woman. He is one lucky man. He seems decent too.

I've seen Ted twice now. Once at a party at Anne-Marie's house where I got to talk with him for quite a little while and then he came with her to one of my plays. We all went out afterward, but it was hard to really have a conversation there. He seemed very down-to-earth though and very respectable. He is a veterinarian (not a doctor, but a close second) and a sex fiend (in a good way). I know this because Anne-Marie will come to work and moan (pun intended) about their constant sex-capades. I allow this to go on for about three minutes before piping in with my, 'I have no sympathy…it's been a year since a man touched me' monologue. She always gives me a 'wounded puppy-dog face' to which I reply, you know where you can take your wounded, woe-is-me puppy—to your vet!' We then both die with laughter.

Yes, I know…lame.

CHAPTER 48

I don't even know why I'm bothering to do my hair. The minute the humidity comes in contact with it, it will resort right back to Brillo pad status. To be honest, I don't even know why I'm bothering to go to this thing at all. I'm right in the middle of working on my one-woman show. And it's not like I'm in a party mood. I guess all of the wedding preparations for Anne-Marie have left me feeling a little lonely and sorry for myself. Exactly all the reasons Pam gave me *for* going.

It won't be so bad, I tell myself. I'll be with Pam and Brenda and Liza and Stan and hey, it could be a good time. Meeting theatre people, producers...famous people! Great. My hair will probably scare them all away.

I check my watch...time to go. Actually ten minutes ago, it was time to go. I twist my hair up, grab a clip and head for the train. It's in vogue to be late, isn't it? I think that's for the event, not the actual 'meeting your friends beforehand' part, but whatever.

I scrutinize my outfit the entire time on the subway. Dress is not trendy enough. Shoes are great, but are going to kill by the second hour. Hair...oh I don't even allow myself to go there.

I get out and rush upstairs. I made up time somehow and now I'm less than five minutes late. I don't feel so bad. When I arrive, we all have on black. Well, Pam and I all black and Brenda mostly black with a little purple. It's okay. It's New York, I tell myself. We walk down the block and I spy all of the limos and expensive sports cars. I feel underdressed all of the sudden.

"I didn't know this was this fancy." I say to Pam.

Brenda pipes in, "Oh, you're fine sweetie. You look great. Those people are just trying too hard."

Pam and I laugh.

Pam says, "They said semi-formal. We are semi-formal."

We check in at the door and I take in my surroundings. Awesome. A huge place. Gold and red walls. A bar that looks like it never ends. Food everywhere. Many small tables and an enormous dance floor. There are a few couples already dancing slowly to a song I don't recognize.

We take our programs (like a play, but not) and head toward our table. There will be Liza, Stan and two or three others at our table that I've already met, so I'm not so concerned. I stare at the other tables as we pass, hoping to see a celebrity or two. It's not like I'm that awestruck by them. It's just that they always look so different than on-screen that I find the comparison interesting. The things those make-up people can do!

There is one of the guys from *Law & Order SVU* seated next to a beautiful brunette woman; David Letterman; former Mayor Rudy Giuliani talking to former Yankees' manager Joe Torre; and some model, who looks familiar, but damn if I know her name. The table next to ours has the cast of *Wicked* and I notice a couple of actors I can name there.

Our seats aren't great, but not awful either. I think there are only a few presentations being made, so a view of the stage (which is behind the dance floor) is not that pertinent. And I don't care anyway. I'm just not in the mood.

We place our shawls, jackets, and the like at our seats and make our way to the bar. I order a cranberry and seltzer and go with Brenda to the buffet. I'm going to take full advantage of this spread. Not like usual, where I eat a tiny bit of this or that, trying to look lady-like. No siree, I am going to feast. They'll be lucky if I don't belch out loud. That is the kind of mood I'm in. Pissy.

I make small talk, I eat and eat some more and take everything in. Pam and Brenda have been dancing on and off all evening. Two of the men at our table, one I know, the other I do not, have asked me to take a turn with them on the dance floor, but I am simply not into it. I am polite (I hope) but firm in saying no.

Sometimes you tell a guy, 'no thank you' and for some strange reason, he hears instead, 'no, but ask me again…and again…and again'. Like you are just saying no and don't mean it. You have to negotiate with him for ten minutes when you finally end up saying in a thunderous voice—which many people claim is the volume of my normal speaking voice—*What part of 'no' do you not understand?* Of course by then the entire restaurant/bar/wherever is in on it and you end up looking like a real bitch. So this time, not wanting to reveal that I'm in 'real bitch' mode, I decide to be firm from the start, hoping that they get it. They seem to. Hooray!

It's getting late. I have already made three trips to the dessert table. I need to go before Jenny Craig is needed on my speed dial. I walk around our table to Pam, who is having what looks like a very in-depth conversation with Lloyd. I hate to break-in, but I must.

"Sorry guys, don't mean to interrupt, but I think I'm going to head out."

Pam's face falls like I just announced that the chemo isn't working and I will be dead by Sunday.

"Oh, you can't go already. It's early," she says spying for a clock somewhere.

This from a woman who never gets enough sleep and always looks like she's six blinks away from nodding off.

"It was great. I really did have a nice time, but I'm bushed and have to be up early." I lie.

"Well, okay. Oh, don't forget to say good-bye to Brenda. She's at the bar I think."

I turn toward the bar. There are hordes of people there. I am sure she will forgive me for not saying bye in person. I'll e-mail her later and say that I looked everywhere and came up empty.

Pam then says, "Oh, if you're going up there anyway, would you mind terribly getting me another glass of wine. Red please?"

What can I say? This woman has been a saint to me. She was there for my surgery, for my break-up, lent me her apartment countless times. Of course I don't mind standing in that long, winding, never-ending line for a glass of wine. Red. And I tell her so.

It takes a good ten minutes for me to even find the end of the line. It has swung back past the far end of the dance floor. Too bad I didn't bring a book with me like I do at the bank.

I'm there a good two minutes when a guy walks up behind me and says, "This the end of the line?"

"Apparently so." I say before censoring my bitchy tone.

What is wrong with me? Besides that I feel like I am struggling my life away, ALONE, men suck, and my child-bearing years are blazing by, nothing. Nothing at all is wrong with me.

I turn to apologize to the guy when a woman, well, not just a woman, a beautiful redheaded woman with perfect *everything* (she could sell her parts on E-bay and be wealthy enough to retire to the Cayman Islands) comes up and plants a kiss on the guy's lips.

"Hey. You guys made it," he says to her.

I feel like turning around and saying, 'apparently so', again but that would just be foul. I keep my head turned toward the dance floor and act like I'm interested in what's going on there, when I'm really just plain eavesdropping. What's a girl to do? Gotta pass the time in this God-forsaken line somehow.

"We just got here a few minutes ago. It looks like it's happenin' though. Glad we finally made it." She says and heaves an exasperated sigh.

Poor thing! She must have been getting made up for the past seventeen hours and finally now just broke free! I pinch myself in an effort to keep my thoughts pure, though I have little faith that it will work. Perhaps if I punch myself repeatedly in the mouth.

"You want a drink?" the guy asks her.

"No, Frankie already got us something. I was just heading for the ladies' room when I saw you here. Hard to miss you here. Even with all of these celebs."

Pul—leee—zzzz.

I threaten myself by making a fist and waving it in front of my face as a reminder.

"Okay, well, I'll stop by in a few," he tells her as she teeters off in her perfect silver sandals.

I could never wear silver. Too gaudy. But on her somehow, they look right. And not gaudy, just stylish. I hate people like that. Especially women.

The line has moved all of a foot and we still have at least ten more to go. I should apologize to the guy, but he probably won't even remember why. I hear him speaking again, but can't make out his words. I turn around and he has his back to me, talking to two girls, young women perhaps, but barely legal. I shift my weight. I still can't hear.

He hands them back something and then says, "Well, thanks a lot. Tell your Dad to stay tuned. It's just a slump. It's temporary."

What is he, some psychiatrist? Pul—leee—zzzz.

He turns back toward me.

"It's moving," he says to me.

I look at him confused. He gestures forward and I turn and see the line has moved ahead a few more feet.

"Oh, sorry." I say and move ahead quickly.

There, I apologized. Maybe not for the right thing, but it's still an apology. It still counts.

"I guess we all must be pretty thirsty to stand in a line like this." I hear him say.

Is he talking to me? I'm not sure. Should I answer and risk looking like a fool or just play like I thought he was speaking to someone else? What do I care? I was going to belch the night away and not give a damn, so what's with the reservations now?

"This drink isn't even for me." I hear myself say to no one in particular (just in case *he* wasn't talking to *me*, *I* wasn't talking to *him* either). But he answers.

"You're kidding, right? For your boyfriend? Husband?" He pauses and smiles.

I am tongue-tied. Before I can untwist my tongue and explain that it is for my very dear friend who is in desperate need of a glass of red wine, he says, "Lucky guy."

Salsa with the Pope

He looks familiar to me. I can see him more clearly now, as we have gotten closer to the bar and the ambient light. Who is he? Someone famous? Maybe I've just seen him around the theatre or he's an actor? No, that doesn't feel right. I'll have to ask Brenda—when I find her—if she knows.

"Nope, no guy. My girlfriend." I finally spit out a reply.

He smiles again. "Oh, you're here with a woman."

I nod. Then I realize what he is suggesting.

"Yeah, but it's my girlfriends. I'm not a lesbian." I say a little too loudly.

I know this because two of the couples on the dance floor lose their footing and stare at me at just that moment.

"Oh, I gotcha. You're here with a group of friends."

"Yes," I say clearly. "And you?" I add, though I don't know why.

I'm passing the time, I tell myself, knowing that there is more to it than that.

"I'm here with my friends and colleagues. The Yankees are big supporters of the foundation." He says.

"Yeah, they must be. I saw Joe Torre here earlier."

Before he can say another word, it's my turn at the bar. I feel shell-shocked, as I can't remember what I came up here to get in the first place.

"What can I get for you?" The bartender asks.

"That's a good question." I say trying to stall, in order that my brain can remember just that.

"Look, I don't have all day, I'm really busy here."

He says it in a slightly rude manner. He sounds like I've been feeling, so I try to cut him some slack, but before I can even empathize a male voice from behind me speaks.

"You don't need to speak to anyone in that tone. We're all friends here and I'm sure you're getting paid the same whether she speaks now or in thirty seconds."

It's the guy from the line—the Psychiatrist or whoever he is. I smile and nod at him.

"Red wine. That's all I need." I tell the bartender, suddenly over my amnesia.

Mr. Psychiatrist insists on leaving a tip for the bartender from both of us.

"Thank you." I tell him.

"No problem. He was just a little stressed. I can relate to pressure." He says and nods.

I smile and say, "Well, for everything. Stepping in and the tip and..." I'm rambling.

He smiles and looks down at the floor before saying, "Hey, I noticed you eyeing the dance floor earlier, how about we give it a shot?"

I wasn't eyeing the dance floor! I was spying on him and his redhead! I obviously couldn't tell him that though, so instead I say, "Um, I don't think so, but thank you."

He doesn't even bother to try to negotiate. He just takes the red wine out of my hand, places it on an unoccupied table and leads me onto the dance floor.

The song changes and it's Salsa. Someone's looking out for me. Though I really wasn't up to testing out my steps. Not here. Not now. Not with him. I'm not even sure if he's into it—I mean everyone doesn't dance Salsa, but I have nothing to fear (though scared I am) as he spins me around and we glide right into the tempo of the beat.

After a few moments I begin to give in and let the music and his strong embrace take hold of me. I can feel my miserable feelings start to dissipate. They're floating out of me, leaving me feeling light and exhilarated. I am actually having fun. I'm sorry to see the song end. Obviously he is too, as he shouts to the DJ to play another and to my surprise they acquiesce.

"Good one, Darren." I hear someone dancing near us say.

"Darren?" I ask.

"Yeah. That's me. Darren James."

I almost trip over my own embarrassment. Of course! You fool, I tell myself. This is Darren James! The Yankees. Darren James. That's like not knowing who the Pope is! I am dancing with Darren James.

Be careful not to break his foot, or you'll have millions of enemies for life, I warn myself.

Apparently this fear manifests onto my face because he suddenly says, "Are you alright?"

Of course I'm not alright. This I keep to myself. I say nothing.

"You seem a little distracted." He says when I don't respond.

"Yeah, I'm fine. I just really, I just…" before I can finish my thought the redhead returns and speaks in his ear.

How rude. He nods. Then says, "Um, I'm sorry, I don't know your name?"

"Samantha." I say. I sound far away like I have a bad cold.

"Samantha?" He asks.

I nod.

"This is Renee, Renee this is Samantha."

I nod and she waves. The three of us make our way off the dance floor.

Darren turns to me and says, "I have to go with Renee for a minute, but I wanna pick up where we left off."

"I'm sorry, but that won't be possible. I'm leaving." I inform him in my most uptight voice.

"Now?" He wants to know.

"As soon as I take my girlfriend her wine."

Oh shit, where was that wine? I could kick myself.

"Okay, well before you go, I wanna say good-bye, so I'll find you. Where are you sitting?" He asks.

I look around, but I'm not sure where our table is. I point in the general direction of where I assume it to be.

"Okay. I'll see you in a bit," he says.

I nod and set off to find my wine.

When I arrive where I think it was placed, it's not there. The line to the bar has died down a lot though so I go that route and get a second glass for Pam. The same bartender waits on me, but this time I know what I want without being asked a second time.

"Hey, sorry about before." He says as he pours the wine.

"Oh, that's fine. I've had bad days too." I tell him.

He re-corks the wine and places the glass on a beverage napkin.

"I can understand how being with Darren James could leave your mind a little scattered."

I can feel my bitchiness rise up, but I shoo it down before I speak.

"I am not *with* Darren James. Actually I didn't even know who he was, as crazy as that sounds."

"Okay, no need to get testy about it." He chuckles. "Boy, most women would be excited as hell to be dancin' with Darren James. They'd be on their cells all night tellin' everybody they know. But not you. I can see that."

I don't know what to say, so I settle for, "It's not you. I'm just not one of those women, that's all."

I leave a nice tip and take the wine to Pam.

By the time I find our table, I've seen Darren twice at his. He's having an intense conversation with another guy. Renee is also there, but doesn't seem to be participating in the conversation. I hope he doesn't see me. He may think I'm stalking him and that is just plain not true. Yes, he seems like a nice guy, good dancer, sexy, athletic to say the least, and rich as hell, but I am not falling for that. You have to keep your guard up with men like that...women crawlin' all over'em wherever they go. No, no. I want no part of that.

"I am so sorry it took so long," I say as I place the wine next to another almost full glass of red.

"You're still here." Pam says when she sees me.

"Yes, I was trying to get you some wine."

"And dancing with Darren James, don't forget." Brenda adds and snickers.

"Oh, that...well, never mind."

Pam smiles, "No, I want to hear. What's going on? Do you know him?"

I take a seat and give them the cliff's notes version of what happened. I then stand and grab my wrap and bag.

"Wait, you aren't going to wait for him to come and say good-bye?" Brenda wants to know.

"No. I'm sure he was just talking anyway. It's not like we even know each other." I say.

"Yes, but this is how relationships start," Pam points out.

Stan returns just then to the table with a full plate of food. This will be distraction enough to get me out of here.

"Good night." I say and kiss each of them on the cheek.

I make my way out of the club and am walking toward Eighth Avenue, thinking it will be easier to get a cab from there, when I hear my name being shouted from behind. I turn and Darren James is jogging toward me.

His expression is of a little boy—in a man's body. I'm not used to seeing him out of uniform (probably also why I didn't recognize him at first). He does clean up nice I have to admit. Charcoal gray suit (probably Armani), dark tie and big smile. He smiles a lot as he runs, which I find unnerving. As a runner, it is not often—truth be told *never*—that I feel like grinning as I exercise.

"Whew!" He says when he catches up to me.

At least I did him the courtesy of stopping when I saw him and didn't continue walking ahead. I congratulate myself on being a wonderfully sensitive human being.

"You don't listen well, do you?" He asks.

"What do you mean?" I answer.

"I said," he starts and then catches his breath, "that I wanted to say good-bye to you before you left. Now this looks to me like you left."

He smiles.

I smile.

"I didn't want to bother you. You seemed busy."

As soon as I say it, I regret it. It sounds like I was keeping tabs on him, when indeed I wasn't.

He says, "I was talking with a friend of mine. He needed to talk. You know, guys need to be heard sometimes too."

No I was not aware of this. But I don't share that with him, but instead say, "That's nice. That you were there for him."

"He's always there for me. That's what friends do."

"Yeah," I agree. "Well," I add, "I really have to get going. It was great meeting you."

"You too, except I don't even know your whole name. Samantha...?"

I grin, tell him my full name, including my middle name (why? I do not know this) and turn to go.

"Wait a minute." he says.

I turn back toward him.

He bows his head, as if shy and asks, "Are you married or have a boyfriend? I'm definitely getting a vibe here."

I sigh.

"No, I'm single. Heterosexual. But I don't…I don't have a notion that you're interested in me. I understand that you date celebrities and if you think that I'm just going to go to your place or my place or some, some sleazy motel, well…then you are mistaken."

I can feel my face getting flushed. Why am I even bothering to tell him this?

He starts clapping his hands.

"Well done. Now, I'm just curious, do you perform that little monologue for all the guys? Or is it just for the ones you're attracted to?"

I feel my face getting hotter. Thank God it's dark out.

"What gives you the impression that I'm attracted to you? Just because you're Darren James, you think that every person walking the earth with a vagina has to bow down to you. Is that it?"

I am shouting now. And I don't care.

His eyes lock with mine.

"Not at all," is his response.

He reaches into his pocket and takes out a card. He hands it to me.

"These are my numbers. Please don't give them out. I'd have to change them all again, and it's a real pain in the ass to do that. But I think I can trust you."

He smiles and winks.

It takes me back to that Yankee game so long ago. The wink.

I have always hated winking. It has always seemed skeevy to me, but on him, it's cute. Damn.

I take the card and look at it. It has the Yankees insignia on it.

"Thanks, but I can't call you." I tell him.

"Why not?"

"Because I don't call guys. Not unless we're in a relationship. I let the guy pursue me." I explain.

He laughs and says, "Yes, apparently you do. Okay, why don't you give me your number and I'll call you?"

I don't respond at first and I think he thinks that this is the end because he finally says, "Is it that you're not interested? That's cool. I was just thinking that we had a little thing, a little chemistry happening on the dance floor, but if you aren't into it or…" He turns to go.

"Give me another business card." I say, my voice stopping him.

He pulls another out of his suit jacket and I scribble my name and cell number on it.

"Here."

I hand him the card. I notice my hand is shaking.

It isn't because of him. It isn't because he's Darren James. It's because he's a man. An attractive man. In pursuit, if only for a moment, of me.

I finally say, "Call me."

He smiles. "Maybe I will."

CHAPTER 49

And maybe he won't. I never hear from the creep. Not surprising though. That type of guy is just bad news...even my therapist says that she heard some unsavory things about him. Whatever. Onward.

I'm rushing to the subway to meet Brenda. She asked me to join her for opening night of a play one of her theatre companies is producing.

I have on my standard black dress—more cocktail than formal—stilettos, and a wrap. I feel good. I look good. You know when you feel people (well, men in particular) admiring the way you look, though they pretend not to be looking, and you know they're looking, but you pretend not to notice (so much make-believe in adult behavior)...well, it's like that.

I notice one of the men in particular though. I know him. Can't place him.

"Sam? Samantha, is that you? Wow, you look great," he says, a wide grin on his face.

I smile.

"Thanks. How are you?" I say, hoping the answer will give me a clue as to who he is.

"Oh, pretty good. I ended up buying part ownership in a club, so that's something, I guess."

Bingo. A light goes on in my head. It's George, the manager of the poker club where I did that brief stint as a dealer. And then got busted.

"Really? Which club?" I ask.

"Poirot over on Fifty-Six and Seventh."

I shake my head, "Never heard of it."

Just then our train noisily arrives. We both squeeze in, as it's rush hour and there are hordes of people navigating their way through the city.

"So how long have you been there?" I ask George, who is resting his arm above my head, using the tallest bar for balance.

"Oh, a few months, I guess. It's cool. Better than the other place. Busier."

I am happy for George. He was always nice to me when we worked together. Our boss was a little strange. Not that he wasn't nice, but just a little off and that made me uncomfortable, but George was always there to calm things down.

"What happened with the other club? Did it close down after we got busted?" I ask George.

I never found out. I just left the business completely, knowing that I wasn't as good as the other dealers, knowing that I didn't want a rap sheet or mug shot to represent me.

"For a short time. But it's back now. Not very busy though. It just never caught on with the players for some reason."

My stop is next. I start saying my good-bye as I have to run out to avoid being late.

"It was so nice seeing you." I say.

George reaches into his pocket and pulls out a business card. This is no easy task, as we are crushed like sardines. He elbows a woman and she almost loses her balance and falls over, but in the end she is victorious.

"Here." he says a little winded. "Give me a call. We'll grab a bite and catch up."

I nod.

"I'd like that."

I pocket the card and push my way through the mass of commuters and out onto the platform.

I make my way up the stairs and to Brenda, who is waiting three blocks away.

It must be fate. At least that's what I tell myself. Because when I leave the gym two days later, George is standing there readying to cross the street. Thank God I took the time to shower and fix myself, as sometimes I'll just leave all stinky and head straight home. But not today. Like I said, fate.

"Hey you." I sneak up on him.

His startled expression turns to pleasant surprise when he spies me standing next to him.

"Well, hello there. You following me?" he says, smiling still.

"Strange, twice in three days, huh?" I say.

"Very. Very," he agrees.

When I discover that he's headed no place in particular—just to the ATM—we decide that we're hungry and we'll go find a little place to nosh and catch up.

We go to a specialty store/restaurant where they serve organic macaroni and cheese—whatever that is. George has had it there many times and swears it's delicious. It's also expensive as hell ($29 for a large plate of it, which he gets...I'm happy I only opt for the small portion at a mere $13).

I tease him about his very expensive dish (he claims he's never paid that much before, but I have my doubts) and he laughs and blushes too. He is a good sport, which for a ball-buster like me, is a good thing.

After filling our tummies and catching up on what's been happening in our lives, we venture toward the movie theatre to see what's playing. We both admit to being interested in seeing this horror flick that came out last week. It's playing in a half-hour...just enough time to run to the drug store and stock up on gourmet jelly beans and Butterfinger bites, the very things that will bankrupt me if I purchase them at the concession stand.

"Those are terrible for you." George tells me, gesturing toward my box of chocolate.

He's tall and thin. Says he thinks I'm thinner than he is (a BIG FAT lie), which I take to mean he's due for an appointment at the optometrist's.

"So what." I say in my most bratty fashion. I pay and then add, "And you're not getting any either, so don't even ask, Mr. Healthy."

George laughs and pulls my hair lightly.

I'm scared inside the theatre. Not because I think George will start pulling lint balls off my sweater or embarrass us both by yelling SMOKE at high volume, but because it is a horror movie. I'm scared for a reason.

I have a method for watching scary movies though, and it has never failed me. I cover my face with my hand, but I spread my fingers wide, so I can still see in between, like I'm spying on the movie. This way, it doesn't know I'm watching and it can't scare me...see, impressive, huh? And if, on those rare occasions I do get scared out of my wits, I can just close my fingers. It's full-proof.

I use my method many times during our flick and it works wonders—what'd I tell you? Besides, George is here and I can tell he'll protect me against the nastiness on the screen, if need be.

We are both pretty energized about the movie when we leave. I look over and George has his hand over his face, his fingers spread wide—he is using my method to mock me. I swat at him.

"What? I was just practicing!" He says and laughs.

We end our evening by going to grab hot chocolates at Starbuck's. Delicious.

"I have had oh, about 3,000 calories since I ran into you today." I tell George.

He is seated across from me licking whipped cream from his lips. See, he'll indulge, on rare occasion.

"Are you complaining?" He asks.

"Not a bit. Though I will have to not make this a habit." I answer.

"I was kind of hoping we could make it a habit." He says and looks away.

I feel my face get a little flushed. I nod. It's been fun. I've really enjoyed myself and I tell him so.

We make a date for Friday night.

A play. I want to go to a play.

CHAPTER 50

I am taking Anne-Marie out for a last hurrah before she gets married. We are still having the bachelorette party, but this is a private, just the two-of-us kind of thing. We are at Lombardi's cramming mouthfuls of delicious pepperoni, sausage, olives, and cheese into our mouths. We have said little since our pie arrived, too consumed with its enticing aroma and incredible flavor. Whoever said Lombardi's was the best pizza around didn't lie.

"Oh my God, that is almost better than sex." Anne-Marie says, putting her napkin down for the last time.

"Who you kidding? It's definitely better. I'd pick Lombardi's over sex any day of the week." I tell her.

"Then you been sleepin' with the wrong man." She says and giggles.

I don't laugh. I don't even smirk.

She notices.

"What's up? Everything alright?"

I thought everything was wonderful. I really did. I mean I knew when I first ran into George that I had never been *physically* attracted to him. But I also knew that sometimes the most unattractive men are the sexiest things to walk on two legs. Sometimes sexy has nothing to do with actual physical features. Sometimes it's the way he walks or talks or smooches (assuming you've gotten that far) or his passion about his career or family that make you swoon.

So I thought maybe, since George and I got along so well, that maybe that would happen here. I mean we have fun, enjoy talking and playing chess and cards and movies and eating and having real conversations and he laughs at my jokes—a real point-scorer with me. So, it seemed pretty good.

But then we dated a few more times and I found out that he doesn't like plays (huh? Is that possible?), can't understand why anyone would want to run a marathon ("You'll only hurt your leg more"), and gambles more than I'd like. He even fashions himself a professional poker player, something that I can never fully have faith in (but he hates plays, so how much faith can he really have in my career?).

The clincher, though, is the bedroom. We have had sex. Plain and simple sex. Not that I need it to be complicated, but I would like some passion. Some love. Some spark. Something to make it hot or loving or enjoyable. And I still haven't found it. And it's been three months.

I tell all of this to Anne-Marie. She takes it all in as we put on our coats and head out into the chilly night. We walk arm-in-arm, like a couple of old ladies, scared to fall on the hard cement and maybe break a hip.

She looks up after a couple of moments.

"Why didn't you tell me Sam?"

I am surprised by this question. It is about me. She and I. Not George.

"What do you mean?"

"Well, I've been going on and on thinking that you finally found a love match."

She stops and turns me toward her.

"Because you deserve it. You deserve to have someone that *does* make you tingle and feel special and passionate and all those things. And now you tell me you're just going through the motions and I have to ask myself why. Why didn't you tell me?"

I am struck by what she says. She has a way of putting things in perspective and making me see all of the obvious things I miss. Of course she is right.

"I don't know why." I tell her.

I start saying anything off the top of my head.

"Maybe because I wanted to be happy too. I wanted to be in love too, I guess."

I think about that for a moment.

"But I'm not. And I've known that. I never claimed to love him." I say in my own defense.

"No, you didn't." She says in agreement. "But you let me believe that you were happy."

I interrupt her, "I was happy. I have fun with George. It's true. I enjoy his company. But he's just not the one for me. And I'm actually okay with that, but I don't want to lead him on, you know?"

"You should talk to him, tell him." she advises me.

"I suppose." I say after a moment.

We continue walking east when suddenly she says, "You know what we should do?"

"What?" I want to know.

"Go to Sizzle."

Sizzle is this tiny dance club on the west side of town. They're known for their Salsa dancing.

"I don't know." I tell Anne-Marie in a whiny, 'I-don't-think-I'm-up-to-it voice.

"Oh, come on. It's just what you need. Besides, it's going to be one of my last nights of single-hood, girl. So you gotta do it for me, if not for yourself."

She sounds like a cross between a drill sergeant and a hip-hop gangsta girl when she gets going. What can I say?

"Oh, alright." I say and lead us back in the opposite direction toward Sizzle.

We stay clinging to each other the whole walk over. The wind is picking up and we have to tuck our heads just to keep from being blown over. We attempt conversation, but the wind and cold make it impossible to hear, so we opt for walking as quickly as two old ladies can and saving the conversing for inside.

Sizzle is pretty slow when we arrive. It's a Wednesday, and although it's Ladies' Night, the crowd doesn't usually get going for another forty-five minutes or so. At least that's what the bouncer at the door tells us. I have only been here once before. Anne-Marie used to come a lot though with her sister and her friends. Back in the day. B.T. (Before Ted).

We grab drinks at the bar—an OJ for me and a Cosmo for Anne-Marie—and take a nice corner booth on the mezzanine level. There is a tiny balcony with only three tables that sits right above the dance floor. It is prime seating and usually already occupied Anne-Marie tells me, but tonight we are lucky. Tonight we will sit in the best seats in the house. Not that we're planning on sitting much. No, Sizzle is all about Salsa, so I might as well take advantage of it while I'm here.

Within an hour, the place gets crowded. A large group comes in and basically takes over. Good that we have our prime seats.

Anne-Marie and I chat about the wedding, her brother, and my one-woman show, which feels stalled as of late, but I'm not giving up. I also have only one more race and I will be in the marathon next year. Yeah, finally. I know I can pull this off too...it's only a 5K.

An attractive man, well, attractive *young* man I should say, as he looks about twenty-two, approaches our table and asks Anne-Marie if she would be willing to dance with him, noting that he is not a Salsa dancer, but would love to try it anyway. She smiles, says something I don't hear and stands up.

"We'll see how this goes." she says in my ear before taking the short flight down to the dance floor.

"Keep your eye on me," she yells from below.

I nod and laugh.

It is not too long after, that a tall older gentleman comes and asks me to dance. I warn him that I'm not that good, but he smiles and says, "Come on," anyway.

We take a place on the floor not too far from Anne-Marie and her young escort. She doesn't seem to notice us. We finish the dance and complete another. It is fun, though this man seems too tall for my 5'3" body...actually he seems too tall for any woman in the place. It's difficult to reach his chest, let alone his shoulder, but he is good at leading, which is important in this dance.

When I go back to our table, Anne-Marie is already there finishing her Cosmo.

"There you are. I was lookin' but I didn't see you." she says.

I tell her about the man I just finished dancing with.

"Well, don't look now, but I spotted a couple of Yankees over by the bar."

I crane my neck, but can't make out anyone in particular.

"So. Even if he were here, he wouldn't know me from Adam."

She smiles.

"Don't be too sure."

Anne-Marie and I start letting loose and dance almost every song for the next hour. The crowd is mellow and fun, no one making trouble or being loud. We make our way to the ladies' room. Just as I step inside, a woman coming out almost runs into me.

"Oh, sorry," she says and giggles.

When she looks up I know her. Recognition floats in her eyes as well, but I'm not sure she remembers where she knows me from.

"Hey, you're…" she says and begins snapping her fingers… "Samantha."

Damn. The woman is good.

"I'm Renee," she says before I make an ass out of myself by having to rely on my poor memory. She offers her hand and I shake it.

"We met at that benefit," she starts to remind me.

I shake my head and say, "Yes, I remember. How are you?"

"Doing gooood," she emphasizes. "And you? How are you?"

I nod. "I'm well, thank you."

"Hey, DJ's here. I bet he would love to know you're here. You should stop by," she says and walks away.

Anne-Marie pushes me into the restroom.

"So, he is here!" She says excited.

We do our business and head back to our table.

"I'm not going over there." I tell her.

"Okay. I never said you should. But you should." She giggles.

I love her giggle. It is the sound of pure joy. Someone so caught up in the moment. So happy in this one instance.

"No." I tell her.

I am following Anne-Marie toward the stairs when we pass a couple of the players. Darren is among them. He sees me, though I am not sure he recognizes me. Damn him.

I tap Anne-Marie and walk over to Darren.

"Excuse me, care to dance?" I say.

My balls are the size of King Kong. I am a little nervous, a little shaky, but not as bad as I would have thought. Just didn't let myself think too long about it. That's the secret. Act before you think. Or make an ass out of yourself before you can talk yourself out of it, as I like to think of it.

Darren looks at me and smiles. He has the most perfect teeth I have ever seen. If he had not made it in baseball, he could have been a spokesperson for the American Dental Association for sure.

He then laughs, takes me by the hand, and leads me out onto the floor. We take our positions and begin to move. It is a slow rhythm. I like it. It lets me get used to feeling his hand on my back, his feet guiding us along.

"You surprise me." He says.

"I surprise myself too," I admit.

The music abruptly changes and we are forced into a much faster pace. I keep up, feeling only a little off, but that passes quickly enough. When the song ends, he offers to buy me a drink.

We head to the bar.

He says, "How have you been?"

I look at him.

"Do you even know who I am?" I ask.

It's been over three months. I look basically the same, save my hair, which has had a major growth spurt.

"Of course. You are Samantha Wren Anderson. The woman who stood me up on saying good-bye."

I am impressed.

I smile and nod.

"But you chased me down and remedied that. Or did you forget that part?"

"Yes, but I was getting the impression that something...wasn't quite right. Put it this way, I could tell that I was bothering you on some level."

I turn away and think a moment. I then ask, "Is that really what you were getting from me? That I was uninterested?"

He nods in earnest.

"Yeah. Or something along those lines. But that's okay. Whatever you need, you know."

He takes a sip of his drink, looks at me and says, "But tonight, you seem different. More at ease maybe."

"Well, *I* am the one who asked *you* to dance, so you can't be getting a 'blow-off' vibe now," I tell him.

He nods and smiles. Again.

I take Darren up to meet Anne-Marie, who is sitting with two men. One is the young guy she danced with earlier, the other I do not know. We make introductions all around. The guys bombard Darren with questions and accolades while Anne-Marie and I whisper to each other on the other side of the table.

"He looks good." she tells me.

"I know." I say nodding, my eyes wide.

Without warning, Anne-Marie announces that we all should dance. She grabs the guy I am not familiar with, pushes me into Darren and leads us all down the stairs. This is the beginning of a long night of continuous dance.

It is the time of my life. The fun I have been missing.

The night turns to day and I am still awake. I am still with Darren. We are sipping hot drinks from cardboard containers, watching the sun come up over the East River. It is chilly on the balcony, but I have a cashmere throw wrapped around me. I feel as if I'm basking on the beach in the Bahamas.

"It's really amazing. And something I never think to do. Then again, I don't have this view." I tell him.

He takes a sip and nods.

"I know. I'm really lucky. And I don't forget it."

Salsa with the Pope

He looks at me and smiles a little. I smile back. I don't even care that I look like crap, make-up smeared or faded, hair matted and uncombed. I am just here. Living in this moment.

"So, you like the balcony, the view, huh?" He asks.

"I love it." I answer.

"Finally found something about my apartment you like," he teases.

"I like a lot of stuff about it," I say, my eyes wide and playful. I then say, "You are so…so…"

"So what? I'm so what?" He probes.

"I never said I didn't like your apartment." I tell him.

"No, no, you just said that it was a little too…how did you say it…oh yeah, *ostentatious,* a little too ostentatious for you. A little too gold for your taste."

He looks at me with a straight face and I can't tell if he's kidding or not. I wait, but no sign appears.

"I'm sorry. I wasn't saying that it's not right for you, I was just saying that my own tastes run—"

He cuts me off with a chuckle and starts shaking his head up and down. "Oh, I get it. It's okay for me because I'm *ostentatious,* but you aren't, so for you, you prefer something a lot more…mild."

He looks at me still smiling. Damn. A thousand watt smile. Even at 5:50 a.m. I grab his hand.

"I'm sorry. It was rude of me."

He turns serious suddenly and says, "No. I want you to be real. I want to know what you really think. Otherwise, we're just playing and I don't want that. I don't."

I give him a hug. He is so strong. So tall. He could overpower me in a second, but right now he feels like a child. Someone who is in need of comfort and affection. Someone who is soft and delicate. Someone just like me.

When I pull away, he takes my hands and holds them in his. We sit like this for a while enjoying the sunrise and the awakening New York City streets below.

CHAPTER 51

It is two days later (okay one and a half). I haven't heard from Darren, though I'm not surprised. I've tried to block it—*it* being the notion that I could find someone right for me, someone suited especially for me—out of my mind. I've failed though, as I've spent the last day and a half doing little more than reliving the wonderful night we had. And it wasn't about sex because there wasn't any—not even a lip-lock. It was about fun. And really getting to know someone. I like him. Dammit. I like him.

I go to work determined to get my head back on business as usual. When I round the corner though, I can't find my desk. It's not that it's moved. I just can't see it. No, it's not a migraine. Not this time. It's simply buried. Under no fewer than eight vases of flowers.

All shapes and sizes, colors and fragrances. They are gorgeous. My cubicle is now a florist, though I will sell not a one. No, these are all for me. For my own pure enjoyment.

"Nice flowers," a co-worker says as she passes by snickering.

Most will think that I either had sex last night or at the very least gave a very good blow job. For this many flowers, several very good blow jobs. Not true. But I'll never tell. Let them think what they will.

I call Anne-Marie and ask her to come to my cubie ASAP. When she arrives, she can't stop laughing.

"Sam, oh my God, where did they all come from? Darren James." she whispers, careful not to spread our meeting around.

I haven't told anyone. Not even my mother. No reason to. It would just turn humiliating when I never hear from him again. But now…well, I'm not even sure they're from him. I've not been able to find the card. Though there hasn't been a man around in months—save George and who else could afford this exotic assortment of flowers? But who knows? A secret admirer? A mistaken delivery? Either way, I'm thrilled.

"I love these." Anne-Marie is saying. "I wanna call the florist and be sure that they include these for the wedding."

Anne-Marie speaks about a deep purple and lavender specimen that I have never seen before. It is stunning with its leafy, soft petals and sharp, symmetrical edges. Looks like it comes from someplace exotic, like Fiji.

"Here, I found it." Anne-Marie says and hands me an envelope.

It is not the normal size flower card envelope, but rather a business-size envelope. I guess when you send this many flowers, you have a lot to say.

I open it up and inside is a note that reads, "Just making contact…not looking for a homer. See you on the 12th? Hope to. D.J."

Inside I find two tickets to the Yankees game against Boston on the 12th. The 12th, the 12th? Why does that date sound so familiar? Before I say it aloud and stick my foot way in, it comes to me. Anne-Marie's wedding! It's the 12th. Just a couple of weeks away.

"What's it say? What's it say? Is it from him?"

She is more excited than I am. Okay, maybe not.

I nod, "Yeah. I think at least."

I hand her the note, she reads it and frowns.

"Oh, Sam, I'm so sorry. It's on the same day as the wedding."

I say, "Don't be silly. It's a baseball game. You're getting married. It hardly compares."

"Hey, maybe you can invite him to be your date at the reception? I mean the game says 1:00, so you'll do the church alone, which is fine since you're in the wedding party anyway, and then maybe he can join you later? What'd you think?"

"I think you're nuts. I can't ask *him* to be my date. At your wedding."

"Why not?"

"First of all...it would just be weird. We barely know each other. It's your wedding. He's Darren James. No. Too weird. Besides, he has a game. And I already have a date for the wedding...have you forgotten?"

I refer to George, who has left no fewer than six messages since our last meeting. I haven't had the heart to call him back. I don't know what to say.

Anne-Marie puts her hand up to her mouth and says, "Oh, shit, George. I forgot all about him. Have you spoken to him?"

I tell Anne-Marie about the messages and ask her advice.

"You've got to talk to him, girl. Putting it off is only going to make it harder. On both of you. Besides, you don't want anything coming between you and your new man here."

I purse my lips and say, "You're nuts. There's no new man. He sent tickets to a ball game. Big deal."

"And about fifty different kinds of flowers don't forget. You think he does that for just anyone?"

"He could." I argue. "He can afford it," I add.

She shakes her head and starts walking away. "Call George," she instructs as she disappears around the bend.

I can only busy myself with work for so long. I can only stop and smell the roses—(and the daisies, tulips, carnations and God knows what else) for so long. I can only avoid making these calls for so long.

My hands are shaking. My stomach is swirling. Damn. I hate this. I don't want to be nervous. To call a guy. To call George. To call Darren. Why is life so difficult?

George answers before the phone even rings on my end.

"I was getting worried. Where have you been?" is his greeting.

"Busy. That's all. I've been busy."

He tells me everything that's been going on in his life since we last spoke. I let him ramble on. I am grateful actually. It postpones the inevitable. I should probably do this in person.

I am contemplating this when he suddenly says, "Sam, I think we should stop seeing each other."

Huh? Since I was having my own internal conversation, I'm clueless as to where this is coming from, or if indeed he actually said what I think he said.

"Could you repeat that?" I ask.

"I'm sorry. I know it's kinda out of the blue and all, but I just, I care too much about you to just keep going on like this and I don't want you to hate me and I know I should probably do this in person, but to be honest, I don't know if I could handle seeing you upset. I mean, I'd probably take you back and that wouldn't be good for either one of us so, I just want to do what's best and—"

I cut him off. I've heard enough.

"It's fine George. Really. I'm fine. And thank you." I tell him.

"Are you sure you're alright?" He asks.

"Absolutely."

I get off the phone and grab Darren's business card, which has been sitting on my desk staring at me for the past six hours. I am starting to think that it can talk. Okay, I'm mental.

I take a deep breath and dial. The phone rings twice, then voicemail.

"Hey, it's Darren, leave me a message."

Beep. I clear my throat. And again.

"Hi Darren, it's..." clear my throat again "Samantha. Anderson. Just wanted to say thanks for the flowers—I think they were from you—they're beautiful. Really. Thank you. Oh, and thanks for the tickets to the game. I would love to go, but my girlfriend is getting married and I'm in the wedding, so there's no way I can swing it, but thank you so much, I really appreciate it. Okay, well, keep in touch and thanks again."

I disconnect, relieved. I have done my duty. With both men.

My phone rings no more than two minutes later.

"Hello."

"They were from me. Glad you liked them." Darren's voice is so relaxed and masculine.

"They're beautiful. How did you know where I worked?" I ask.

He chuckles. "Oh, a little birdie told me."

"Who?" I demand.

He laughs again harder and says, "I'll never tell."

"That's not fair."

"Are you complaining? Already?" he asks as if we actually know each other and can speak to each other so frankly.

"Maybe." I tease.

"What are you doing right now?" He asks me.

"Getting ready to leave work."

"You need some help with all those flowers?"

I say, "Well yeah, if I was taking them home. I was just going to leave them here, thinking there would be no way to get them back to Jersey."

"Do you want them home?" He asks me.

"If I had a choice, sure."

"Okay," he says. Then adds, "I'll be right there."

He disconnects before I can respond.

Right here. Now!

I race to the ladies room, do a quick make-up redo and brush my hair. I pull two lint balls from my sweater and think of Dr. Robertson. I smile.

When Darren arrives he's not alone.

"This is Paul," he says in introduction.

We shake hands and Darren explains. "You have two choices," he says to me.

"You can go with Paul here, who drives that white van out there."

I look out the glass door and indeed there is a white van with a dark logo on its side I can't quite make out.

"Or we can just send the flowers with Paul and he will take them to your place in Jersey and you can ride with me," he points to a small sporty car parked directly in front of the van.

"Well, can he handle all the flowers? I mean, I don't want Dai to have to come down and get them." I tell Darren.

"He won't. Trust me."

Without saying a word Paul goes to the back of the van and gets out several cardboard containers. They have holes in the bottom to hold things in place...like flowers. Oh, I get it now.

"Are you sure he'll take them all up?" I ask Darren again.

"Absolutely."

I don't even know where we're going. We're in Darren's car though, driving up Sixth Avenue. My senses are on overload, as my head is full of the scent of leather from the upholstery, the musky fragrance of Darren's cologne, and the sound of the soft music coming from the stereo.

"You hungry?" He asks.

I don't feel hungry. I feel so overwhelmed with everything else that is going on, my mental being feels so satisfied, even spoiled, that I feel full.

"Well, what'd you say? I'm starvin'."

Well, if he's starving, I don't want to interfere with that.

"Sure, why not." I come up with.

We end up at a little Italian restaurant on the Upper East Side with the words La Trattoria among others etched on their sign. Darren is apparently a regular (or they just know him from baseball?), as they address him by name, shake his hand and give us a beautiful corner table. Darren introduces me to the owners, who are a little Italian man and woman with thick accents and warm smiles.

We are not seated two full minutes, when a little boy from across the room approaches the table shyly and asks for Darren's autograph.

"Hey, how you doin'?" Darren asks the boy, who's strawberry blonde hair and freckles glow with excitement.

"Good," he says.

Darren asks for the child's name—Joe—and then makes the autograph out to him.

The boy then places another book in front of Darren.

"Could you...for my brother. He's not here tonight. He's going to be so sorry he didn't want to eat with us."

Darren takes the book and says, "Sure. What's your brother's name?"

"Patrick."

"Why didn't he want to eat with you?"

"He doesn't like to come out with us. He's fourteen and thinks he's all that," Joe says.

I stifle a giggle.

Darren finishes, hands the book back to Joe, smiles and says, "Okay, there you go."

"Mr. James? Kick Boston's butt." Joe says as he turns back to go to his table.

The entire restaurant seems to be aware of Darren and the goings on at our table. I'm not sure how I feel about this. I like my privacy. Especially when I'm with a guy I don't know. Basically, I'm neurotic enough. Don't need the added pressure of everyone watching.

"This how it always is?" I ask.

He looks at me as if confused.

"People always coming up to you? The autographs and pictures," I say.

"Yeah. A lot. But I'm used to it. I don't mind it much. I can't." he says.

"Why?" I ask.

"Comes with the job. I get to do what I love. I make a lot of money. Some of these kids look up to me. I can't not be there for them. I just couldn't do that."

Damn. I like him more and more. Bad, Samantha, bad, I tell myself.

Dinner is delicious. I eat only a small amount though. Just not hungry.

Darren signs several more autographs and poses for some camera-phone shots with some giggling teenage girls. They're children, I remind myself. Yes, children with tanned thighs, bouncing bosoms, long flowing hair, and not a wrinkle to be found. CHILDREN, I scream in my head. I'm fine. I'm fine.

We do manage to get a little conversation in between the eating and the signing. We chat about baseball, something we really haven't spoken much about surprisingly. He tells me that it's all he ever wanted to do. He loves it. He never tires of it. Ever. He says that he thinks when he is forced to retire, he will become a coach, an owner, something. He can't imagine his life without it.

I tell him about wanting to be in the theatre. I tell him that it's all I ever wanted to do. I love it. I never tire of it. Ever. I tell him that if I don't start making a living at it soon, I may shrivel up and die. I can't imagine my life without it.

Surprisingly, Darren doesn't drink alcohol. He is surprised to hear that I don't either. I suspect that he thinks I am just saying this to be like him, to appear to be more compatible, but once I go over my history with alcohol and my reasons for abstaining, he seems convinced.

The conversation turns lighter later in the evening, as we share an apple cobbler.

I start giggling and have a hard time controlling myself.

"What?" He asks.

Every time I start to tell him, I start laughing uncontrollably. Finally after he says he doesn't want to know, I get it together and begin.

"It's just that, when we met, the first time months ago, I didn't know who you were. I thought you were a psychiatrist."

I can't help but start to giggle again. This time, he starts laughing too.

"What the hell? Why would you think I was a psychiatrist?"

"Well, you were helping your friend and then there were those two women in line at the bar with us and I thought you were dispensing psychiatric advice or something. I have no idea."

I start laughing again, but it's more controlled this time.

"You are nuts. And yes, as a psychiatrist, that is my medical opinion."

He shakes his head and laughs.

"That is so funny...you don't even know why that's so funny," he says after a moment.

I look at him with question.

"Tell me."

He laughs.

"My dad, he is a psychiatrist."

"No!" I say.

"Yep," he tells me and takes a drink. He then says, "How could you not recognize me? Not a Yankees fan, huh?"

"Oh, do I detect a little ego there, Mr. Yankee?" I say playfully. "Yes, yes I am a fan, as a matter of fact. And yes, of course I'd seen you before, but you just looked different to me. I just didn't get a good look at you. It was dark in there and I wasn't used to seeing you in regular clothes, so I guess I was just thrown, that's all."

I am sorry to see our meal end. Our evening end. He asks if I'd like to come to his ostentatious apartment for a while. I am tempted, but I decline, saying I have to get up tomorrow and get some things done. It's true.

Tomorrow I am seeing an apartment. I am moving back to Manhattan. Finally.

Darren drives me to Jersey and drops me at my door as promised. He lingers, caressing my face with his hands.

When he goes in to kiss me, I am ready and eager. Our lips part and meet each other. It is a soft, moist kiss. The perfect first kiss.

I thank him for everything and head in to share my adventure with Dai.

CHAPTER 52

When I said that I was seeing an apartment today, perhaps I wasn't painting a clear picture. Perhaps a little embellishment on my part. I am seeing an apartment, but more accurately I am seeing a room *within* an apartment.

It's quite a large apartment, with six bedrooms, or rather six rooms used for bedrooms, and five roommates. My room is a good size too...almost the size of my studio on the east side when I lived in the city years ago. And that's no embellishment.

I take the apartment...rather the room. It's within my budget, in a safe neighborhood—the Upper West Side—and makes me feel independent.

I move in on a Saturday, have Dai come and help me with curtains and appliances—I'm not thrilled with the way the kitchen is run, so I set-up a microwave and a small refrigerator in my room. The place comes together and I am very pleased.

I meet my roommates in phases, as they never seem to be in the same place at once. There is Sirus, the man who owns the apartment. He actually is only there periodically—when he feels the need to spy and see if any of us—all female—are lounging about scantily clad. I know, that part's yucky, having a perv for a landlord. But I keep my door shut and locked and never run around in my nighty.

I meet Carol one day while going through the mail.

"You must be the new girl, I'm Carol," she says and extends her hand.

She is older than I anticipated, I would guess late forties. She is tall and very thin, with stringy blond hair. When she smiles, her two front teeth show a large gap between them.

"Hi, I'm Samantha," I tell her while shaking her hand.

"How do you like it so far?" she asks.

"I like it. I'm pretty set-up and it's an easy commute to my job, so it's workin' pretty well."

"I've been here four years." She tells me. "I'm in there," and she points to the room behind us, the one separated by a partition from Sirus' room.

"How do you like Sirus?" I ask.

"Oh, he's just an old pervert. Nothing to be scared of though. He's weird, but fine."

Glad to hear that. The 'fine' part, not the 'pervert' part.

"What do you do?" I ask, always loving to hear what people do in New York. It's usually some lame job, while pursuing some dream job.

"I work for Ford." She says.

I work that over in my mind for a moment. Ford car dealership—surely there's one in the city somewhere, but I can't imagine many people buying cars. Ford Model—well, she just wouldn't qualify, would she? Perhaps they've lowered their standards? She does have the build for it, I have to admit.

"Ford Model." She offers.

"Oh, you're a model?" I say, trying to keep the shock out of my voice.

She shakes her head.

"Comedienne."

I didn't know Ford did Comediennes.

"Oh." I say.

"I work for Ford as a receptionist. But I'm a Comic. I'm doing a show at Caroline's on Thursday. You should come. I think everyone here is."

And so I go to Caroline's on Thursday with the other roommates, Sirus, Barbara, Christine, and our newest girl Crystal…every time I say girl, it sounds cathouse-like. But nothing like that is going on here. Really. Well, not that I know of.

We don't have a great time, as Carol, the Comedienne seems to forget that in order to be a good Comedienne, you need to be funny. That's the one requirement. We try to laugh—empty hollow chuckles—but then everyone around us starts looking at our table as if we're nuts, as they know she's bombing. Poor Carol.

The evening does give me a chance to get to know my other roommates though.

Barbara works for Fox News and boy can you tell. She is the most conservative woman I have ever met. What she is doing at Sirus' I have no idea. She seems ready to make a move though.

"I'm in the small room off the kitchen...the servant's quarters." She tells me, while sipping a gin and tonic.

"Oh, yeah. I don't go in the kitchen much." I admit.

"Yeah, I'm so tired of being in that cramped space. I need to get out. I think I'm getting a promotion and that will be the end of my days at Sirus'. Hallalujah."

She toasts herself and takes another drink.

Christine moved in just weeks before me. She is a nice girl, who like me, likes to run. She is French.

"Oui, I am wondering...you see Sirus looking at you...like...not mannerly?" She asks me almost first thing.

"Like how? Mean?" I say.

"No, no, not mean. Like, how do you say...uh, sexy?"

Oh, shit.

"Oh, you mean, like he's a pervert? Like he wants you?" I ask her.

"Like he wants everyone." She says in a thick accent. Obviously perverted looks are universal.

I haven't had any personal issues with Sirus. However, I did come home from work last week to find him with ten or twelve teenage girls, all in uniform, in the foyer. Before I could utter a word, he advised me, "Please call me Lawrence Cubana."

I looked at him with a confused 'whatever' look on my face.

"We're conducting an audition here." He said to no one in particular.

"Now, who's next...uh, Nancy Walter," he said reading off a clipboard.

The young girl stood up and proceeded to sing that 'Sun' song from *Annie,* the musical. Please make it stop.

I went into my room, unsure what I should do. I mean he couldn't be doing something inappropriate with a dozen girls and get away with it, could he?

The most disturbing thing that happens in my days at the apartment has to do with our newest roommate, Crystal. From the moment she arrives, things just aren't right. She claims that she recently got into a car accident, in a cab, and has some memory loss as a result.

I can believe it…that or she's just plain nuts.

Crystal shows us photograph albums and in them, she looks like a different person—her hair is burgundy, and she is very thin and muscular. In person, she is part blonde/part brown haired with a softer, heavier body. She claims these photos are only two months old. I think she's just trying to show off; trying to act like her body is still that tight. That or it's the Madonna influence.

Sirus claims that Madonna used to live in this apartment…in Crystal's room. He says she used to watch his children….yuck, that means someone actually had sex with him willingly. So, maybe, just maybe Crystal is pulling a Madonna and trying to re-invent her look? Okay, maybe not.

One day I come home from work and find a note on my door: ROOMMATE MEETING. TONIGHT 7:00.

I meet with the others and I learn a few things. Crystal tried to hang herself in the shower today—not sure that would have worked, as she is at least 5'7" and our shower rod stands at about 5'8". Also I'm told that she's locked herself in her room and refuses to come out.

"So, what do we do?" I ask.

"Try to coax her out I suppose." Carol says.

"Sirus is having a fit. He called her parents and is trying to get them to come and get her." Barbara informs us.

As if that wasn't bad enough, a couple of weeks later, I get home and my door is open, hanging on a hinge.

"What happened here?" I demand to know.

"The fire department was here. They kicked it in, thinking that's where Crystal was. She tried to kill herself again. Pills this time." Barbara tells me.

"Did they get her?" I want to know.

"See for yourself," she says and walks away.

As if on cue, Crystal makes her way out into the hall. I only assume it's Crystal because of the room she's exiting. Otherwise, she looks nothing like herself. She looks like her old self—burgundy hair, thin, sinewy body. How the hell did she do that? She's only been in there for two and a half weeks.

"Sorry about your door, Sammy." she says as she saunters down the hall.

What the fuck? This place is a freak show. I've got to get out.

And so I do.

I start looking at places immediately. But it's a jungle out there, let me tell you.

I am exhausted. This is the fifth apartment I have seen today and so far, there have been no winners. Though, next to Sirus', they do all seem to be lacking…in suicidal roommates, perverts, and conservatives…which is a good thing.

I just don't want to make the same mistake again. Granted, the main issue isn't the apartment amenities, it's my deficient salary. But what can I do? I've got to find something.

"Look, if this is like the others, then let's just skip it," I tell Francis, my guy from NYAR.

"It's lower. It's lower. Let's just take a look." he tells me.

I grab him by the arm, "How much lower?" I want to know.

Before Francis can come up with another line of bullshit, my cellular rings. I release his arm and hunt through my bag, trying to feel where the vibration is coming from. I catch it on its last chorus.

"Hey," I say to George, whose name is displayed on my read-out.

"Hey Sam, how's it going?" He asks.

"It's going," I say exasperated.

I am following close behind Francis as he enters the building of our next showing.

"I was just thinking, you know, I feel real bad about the ways things went with us and I really appreciate you being so understanding and I just, well..."

"George, I'm fine. Really. Are you okay?" I ask, detecting something in his voice.

"Yeah, I'm cool. I just, well...I wanted you to know that I'd be happy to go with you to Anne-Marie's wedding. I mean I know it's this week and I don't want you to have to go alone. And I think we'd have a pretty good time together."

"Oh, George, that's sweet. Really, it is. But it's not necessary," I tell him.

"Well, you don't have another date, do you?" He asks.

"No." I tell him.

Unfortunately, I'm telling the truth.

I mentioned the wedding to Darren, but it seemed too much with his game earlier in the day and he really likes to focus and not have anything that could affect the way he plays, so there was no way I could insist or get angry. But I am content to go alone. At least I was.

Now I feel almost obligated to take George just because he wants to do this to allay his guilt about the ways things went down with us. I see no harm.

"So, what do you say?" George asks me.

"Sure. Why not," I tell him. "It'll be fun."

I put my phone away and scan my surroundings. The apartment is on the first floor, in the back—two strikes against it right there. I glance over at Francis, who is cowering in the corner of the room.

"The tub is in the middle of the kitchen!" I scream.

"Yes, it's an older building, but well within your price range," he says from a distance.

My response is to walk out of the apartment, out of the building, and out to find another realtor.

CHAPTER 53

I am standing by the bar, waiting for a cranberry and seltzer, watching everyone do The Electric Slide. How this became a wedding favorite, I'll never know.

The day has gone relatively well thus far. I didn't fall coming down the aisle, George has been an apt escort, and I haven't spilled any drinks on my lavender-colored dress. But the night is young.

"Uh, could you make that a Sprite?" I ask the bartender. No need to tempt fate.

I look over at Anne-Marie and she is laughing, her mother and sister beside her. They all are holding flutes of champagne, having just shared a toast. She looks radiant. Even more than usual, which is bright, let me tell you, luminescent.

George returns from the men's room and stands near me at the bar.

"They're going to do the flower throwing soon," he says.

"Oh, the bouquet. Don't want to miss that," I say sarcastically.

Truthfully, I have never liked that part. It feels so out-of-place to me. I mean there is this beautiful ceremony, often in a church—a serious event in one's life to be sure, poignant toasts and a first dance.

And then there is this flower tossing, which feels more like roller derby, putting women in serious competition with each other—and it's not playful...whoever told you that lied...I once saw a woman get an eye taken out during one of these 'friendly' bouquet tosses. Who needs it? It's not like it's going to actually seal your fate to be the next to get married. And who says that getting married is that great of a thing anyway? I mean it never mentions the 'to whom' in the fate of getting married next, now does it?

As if reading my mind, Anne-Marie runs over and grabs my hand.

"Come on. I'm going to throw the bouquet and I want to make sure you have a prime spot. Front and center."

I groan.

"Oh, come on now. It's time you and your man," she glances back at George, "and I don't mean him, start getting things moving."

I shake my head and say, "Anne-Marie, it's only been a little over three months, four weeks of which he was out of town. How quickly do you expect things to go here?"

"Well, we have to be grateful for that—him never seeing that hole you were living in. Still, never hurts to do all you can. Come on."

She leaves me in the middle of the dance floor. She signals to the DJ to announce the event. He does. Woman flock ohhhhing and ahhhing all the while I talk myself out of putting my finger down my throat and sharing my appetizers with these overly eager women.

Anne-Marie takes her position at the top of a staircase.

"Ready?" She asks the masses.

They all shout yes.

I purse my lips and yawn.

She tosses in my direction, but it is too high and climbs way over my head. Fine by me. I don't hear much shuffling and fighting surprisingly, so I suppose one woman was the definitive winner. When I casually look back, I can't see the woman holding the bouquet, only the hordes of others who are empty-handed.

Then all of the sudden I hear, "That's not fair. You're not supposed to even be down here."

Another voice says, "Yeah, this is only for girls."

"We need a do-over," another says.

I still can't see what's happening, but then I hear, "Hey wait a minute. Aren't you Darren James?"

Oh shit.

Salsa with the Pope

I excuse and pardon my way at first, but that quickly turns into pushing and shoving as the women begin to horde around Darren. I can't see him. But I know he's here. I can smell his cologne.

"Excuse me," I say to a woman I've never met before.

She is dressed in lemon yellow chiffon...most likely a guest of Ted's, as Anne-Marie has enough sense not to invite someone who would wear lemon meringue as a dress. She gives me a dirty look, I force my way around her and get to Darren.

He is on the floor trapped, two women on top of him, one with her hand reaching for the bouquet that he still holds, like it's the final out of a World Series game. I have never seen him look so haggard...not even in that last game to Boston where he hit the stands running.

I bend to help him up and Anne-Marie gets there at just that moment—apparently she knows a shortcut—and escorts us both out, telling the vultures—I mean women—that she will re-do the bouquet toss in just a moment.

"Are you alright?" I ask Darren when we get to the small room adjacent to the lobby.

Darren is trying to brush crushed flower pedals off his dark suit. In reality, Darren is wiping crushed flower pedals into his dark suit. They streak the fabric white, pink, and lavender.

"Here, let me do that," I say.

I try to lightly whisk the flowers away, but the damage has been done.

"I'm sorry. I should have called," he says quietly.

His face is flushed. I'm not sure if it's embarrassment or adrenaline from the bouquet fight. Apparently his instincts just kicked in and he went for the ball...bouquet, rather.

"No, no, it's fine. I'm just sorry you got bombarded by those scavengers out there...don't you know the bouquet toss is the sole reason single women come to weddings?"

He smiles. His first of the day. It makes me feel like everything's going to be all right.

George rushes in then and says, "Oh, there you are. What was that about? Some lady out there is swearing that Darren

James stole the bouquet from her. You're right Sam, women do get crazy at the flower-tossing."

"Yeah," I say and look at Darren. He says nothing.

I introduce the two men. George seems surprised. Not only by Darren's appearance, but that the 'crazy lady' wasn't crazy after all.

They shake hands. George tells him what a great ball player he is and how big a fan his sister is (George actually hates the Yankees).

I then say, "Would you excuse me just a moment. I'll grab some club soda for your suit…maybe we can still salvage it."

I leave the two men talking, Darren seeming more like himself, though clearly he is out of his element here. Not just because of the whole bouquet-debacle, but because he doesn't know anyone. And everyone knows him.

I run like the wind. Still not fast enough. Anne-Marie is coming down from her do-over throw and spots me.

"How is he?"

"His suit looks ruined. Some of the flowers got stuck when those women were trying to wrestle the bouquet from him. He wiped them into the fabric, so I'm going to try to work some magic with club soda, though I doubt it'll help."

"You left him all alone?" She asks.

I shake my head.

"No, George is in there with him."

She looks at me like I'm insane.

"You left George in there with him?"

I look at her, not following her reaction.

"Yeah, why?"

She clears her throat then says, "Well, for one thing, he hates the Yankees."

I dismiss her by saying, "Oh come on, Anne-Marie. He's certainly not going to tell him that. He's not a complete idiot."

"And then there's the fact that he's here with you. George is your date. Or at least *one* of them."

I look at her, my eyes grow wide.

I race back to the room empty-handed, the club soda long forgotten. I get turned around twice in an attempt to find

Darren. This is due to the throngs of people, mainly men, who have formed what resembles a ladies' room line outside of the small room where I left George and Darren.

I excuse and pardon my way through the line, best I can. I am told by more than a few that there is 'No ditching' and 'Cutting the line will result in removal from the event.' What the hell is going on here?

When I finally get to the door, it is jammed with people, as is the room. I push my way in.

"Hey, lady, wait your turn."

I turn to the man and say as politely as I can manage, "We need a minute."

I shove him and the others out, promising them it will only be a moment and they can resume their activity.

I turn to George.

"Would you mind," I say and gesture toward the door.

"Sure, no problem," he says and slips out into the crowd.

Finally it is just Darren and I.

"What do you think you're doing?" I say to him.

"What does it look like? I'm signing some books, taking a few pictures...making some fans happy."

"Not here you're not."

He furrows his brow, as if he's completely confused by my response.

"What's up Samantha?" he asks.

"Darren, this is a *wedding*. My girlfriend's *wedding*, not some Hall of Fame ball signing."

He nods his head. Looks at the floor.

"Well...I should go. I guess your invitation was just what I thought it was."

"What are talking about?"

"Come on, Sam. We both know you only invited me here to show me off. It wasn't ever about anything else."

"That's bullshit, Darren. I would never do that."

"Oh, no. Then why do you have another date?"

His face is tense, his voice stern. He is angry.

I nod my head.

"Darren, this is all a big mix-up."

"I'd say so," he says not too kindly.

He pulls his suit jacket off the chair it's hanging on and begins to put it on.

"Darren, look…I invited you here because I wanted to be with you. With you. Not your groupies. I wanted you to be my date. Not because you're the Great Darren James, baseball extraordinaire, but because you're Darren. The sweet, generous, sexy man who can dance a mean salsa."

I turn away and add, "I had my suspicious about asking you."

Darren is now seated on a bar stool, ruined jacket resting on the empty bar. He is looking at me intensely, as if what I tell him may change his life. He remains silent, allows me to continue.

"Only because I didn't want what just happened to happen."

I sit on the stool next to him and look over at him.

"I wanted this to be Anne-Marie's day. It *is* her day. And no one, not even Darren James should be able to take that away from her."

He thinks for a moment, licks his lips, nods, then says, "That's not what I was trying to do."

"I know."

"It just happened. Like a few people, then a few more, and I don't like to turn them away. I think that's being—"

"I know. But there's a time and place for it. And even though it seems like everyone thinks that time is *any* time, it's not."

He thinks for a moment. Nods his head.

"You're right. I apologize."

I look at him, take his hands in mine.

"Good, now that we got that cleared up."

I stand and try to pull him to his feet. He's not budging.

"Not so fast," he says to me in a firm tone.

"What now?" I ask, wanting the night to just end.

"You still haven't explained George to me. Or his role, rather…as your date."

So, he wasn't going to let that slip by. I sit back down and begin to explain.

"When you told me that you wouldn't be able to come to the wedding, I was disappointed. But I was good with it. Then George called and he just sounded so...I don't know. Like I was doing *him* a favor somehow, by letting him bring me."

Darren seems confused. I feel confused. I try to clarify.

"He felt guilty. He didn't know that I wanted to end our relationship too, so when he did it so abruptly...basically he thought he was leaving me in a lurch, without a date, so he asked to come along. And I didn't see the harm."

I look at Darren. He doesn't seem to subscribe to my 'Didn't see the harm' theory.

"You couldn't come. I was essentially just doing a friend a favor. That's all."

It seems like an hour, though I'm sure only moments have passed. Moments of silence.

Finally, "Do *me* a favor...keep those favors to a minimum, huh?"

I smile, nod my head and go to where he sits. I stand between his legs and wrap my arms around his neck. He wraps his arms around my body. We hold onto each other.

Darren pulls back and says, "I thought I would surprise you. We had a good game, 4-1, and I really wanted to see you. Then I remembered about the wedding and thought, what the hell."

"I'm glad," I tell him.

"Right," he says sarcastically.

"I am. I really am."

"You are, huh?" He smiles, "And about the autograph signing and that I got a little angry...you happy about all that too?"

"It's going to happen."

"What?"

"Arguments. Misunderstandings. All relationships have them. Can't be helped."

"So, this was our first fight, huh?"

I smile.

"Of sorts."

"I have a hot temper, you should know that," he tells me.

"I don't," I say teasingly.

He laughs.

"Uh, huh. You didn't seem so cool back there a minute ago."

"Well," I say, "You said you wanted the real deal and not someone just trying to play nice."

He looks at me with a feigned surprise expression.

"I said that?"

I stick my tongue out at him.

He laughs. He offers his hand.

"Care to dance?"

I take his hand and we make our way to the dance floor.

CHAPTER 54

"This is so...beautiful. Are you sure that's the right price? Per month? Not per week, right?"

I am talking to Lenny, my new realtor. Darren gave me his name.

"Yes, Miss. It is correct."

Something is amiss here.

"Uh, Lenny, how long have you known Darren?"

"Oh, Mr. James has us help many people." Then adds as if he's just remembered my question, "For a long time."

"He's had you help many people? Help them find housing?"

I am confused. My usual state these days.

"Mr. James very kind man. He always help people."

"How?" I want to know.

"Many way. He give them money for house."

"And how does that work?" I ask, my suspicions growing.

"Well, after down payment, exactly $1250 a month."

"Wait, what down payment? I'm not purchasing the apartment." I tell him.

"Oh, of course. The $10,000 down payment Mr. James gave for your house."

"What, what $10,000?"

Lenny seems to sense that he has let the cat out of the bag somehow and tries to back pedal, but I won't allow this to happen.

"Are you telling me that Darren James gave you money for my apartment?"

Lenny is trapped in a corner, a caged animal cowering with nowhere to go. He looks the other way.

I demand, "Lenny, what's the story?"

"Miss, I cannot lose job. I not know that Mr. James not tell you that he was helping you with your apartment. If he find out, it could mean a lot of trouble for company."

Not to mention for him.

"Okay, Lenny tell me what the story is here and I'll make sure no one is in trouble, okay?"

Apparently, Darren called Lenny's agency and said to show me higher end properties—ones that I can't afford, but to lower the rental price and he would make up the difference. He gave them a $10,000 retainer already. I guess he has done this in the past with others.

What others? Women? Well, it's time he realizes I'm not one of them. Okay, it's true, I need to get out of Dai's—I'm back there temporarily. Okay, I'll admit, it's a nice gesture. Still, I'm going to kill him.

I leave Lenny, promising him that no harm will come to him or his agency. I jump on the #4 train and head to Yankee Stadium. When I arrive an hour and ten minutes later, practice is in full swing and I can't get into the stadium.

"But I'm here to see Darren James," I tell the bully-looking man in a security uniform.

"So are all of those people," he tells me and gestures to a mass of men and women standing by a set of closed double-doors.

"When practice is over, you'll probably get a glimpse of him from there. He'll even sign your book. He's good about those things."

I nod my head, "No you don't understand. I *know* him. I need to speak with him as soon as he's finished. I won't disturb his practice, but it's imperative that I see him."

He chuckles. "Sure lady. You and everyone else."

I wait the hour until practice ends. I refuse to stand in line though, so I sit on a cement bench, numbing my ass, reading my suspense novel, waiting.

Finally, a player I know walks by. I flag him down. Luckily, he recognizes me from that first night at Sizzle.

"How you doin'?" he asks.

"I'm okay. A little chilly. A little tired, but all in all, okay. And you?"

"About the same," he says, then adds, "You here to see the man?"

"Yes, but that man," I gesture toward the guard, "wouldn't let me in."

"Oh, well, that's his job and if Darren didn't leave no note saying it was okay to let you in, then he don't know nothing about who you are. Come on, I'll take you," he says and leads the way.

I follow and resist the urge to stick my tongue out at the guard and say, "na, na, na, na, told ya so, told ya so!"

Darren is just showering, so I wait in the small lobby area. He doesn't even see me as he walks out.

"Excuse me," I say.

He turns, then grins as recognition settles onto his face.

"What are you doin' here?" He asks.

"I was in the neighborhood and thought I'd drop by."

"In this neighborhood?" he asks concerned.

"Yeah, I was seeing some apartments. Ones that I can afford. On my own."

He misses my meaning, too concerned about the possible locale of my new home.

"Here, in the Bronx? Didn't you call that realtor I told you about?" he asks.

I nod, "As a matter of fact, I did. And he showed me some beautiful places. But they were far too expensive. Even if he said they weren't."

Darren is catching on now. He doesn't know how to react.

"So, you know?" He finally says.

"Yes."

"And you're not too happy about it?"

"Right again," I tell him.

"Sam, you gotta understand that I just want to help. It's not something you need to worry about. You work so hard, your job and your shows and your writing, and you still don't even have enough to pay your rent, and that's just not right.

People gave me a break early on and I just want you to have one too. That's all."

He is so earnest. So honest and good. I just want to hug him. I do. He pulls me closer, holds me tighter.

"So, you understand?" he says finally.

"Yes, I understand. But I still can't accept it. You understand that?" I ask.

He shakes his head, as if to say I'm crazy or stubborn, or both.

"Okay," he finally says resolved, "But if you change your mind…"

CHAPTER 55

It is late. Darren just left. He has an afternoon game tomorrow and then he leaves town for almost two weeks. That part of his job sucks—he's gone probably half the year. But in the larger scheme of things, I think it keeps things fresh and allows each of us our own time—something I have to be forced into.

That is what I have learned about myself. That when I am in love (did I just admit that), I want to be with the person all the time. I can't help it. I don't understand people who aren't like that either. I mean, if you love him *like that*, then it's inevitable that he will make whatever you're doing better, (okay, unless you're out with the girls man-bashing, then he's just a target, but otherwise...).

This was the first time Darren's been to my new place. I spent three full days setting everything up, asking Dai to put in dimmer switches, shelving, mound wall hangers for just about everything. I bought him a really nice steak dinner last night to say thank you. He is the best!

Darren arrived, we ate a delicious meal of Ruben sandwiches, chips, and pop (that's soda to you East Coasters out there). We made out on the couch (aka, the bed), but still no sex. I'm getting concerned. I mean it's been almost four months (does that sound slutty? Of course it isn't!!) and we still haven't consummated the relationship. I refuse to worry about it (which is self-help talk for 'I can't stop thinking about it'). It'll happen when it happens.

I gaze around the room. Okay, the apartment is tiny. But it's mine! It has one room, a separate kitchen and a bathroom with a full-sized tub (a must!). A total of about 350 square feet of mine-ness. I consider having a house-warming, but I figure it would take too long, what with having to have two people come in, party for a spell, leave and call the next two in…only in NYC, ya know."

This I have to remind my mother every time she comes to visit. We always end up having the same conversation that goes something like this:

Mom: You're paying $1195 a month for a room!

Me: It's not a room Mom. It's a studio.

Mom: In Ohio, we call that a room, Sam. And for $1195, I could almost afford two homes. Do you know I only pay $800 for my mortgage and we have a three-floor house?

Me: Yes Mom, I know. I've been there.

And so it goes. But I am content. I am in the city. No more commuting. I have my own space. Dai can puff away all he wants (not that he was asking my permission before, mind you) and I don't have to worry about my dates accusing me of the heinous crime of smoking. Yes, life is good.

I pull out the bed and turn out the lights. The phone rings. I flick the light back on and grab it.

"Hello."

"Sammy, I hope it's not too late…it's Brenda."

"No, I'm up. What's going on?" I ask having no clue why she would call so late.

"Well, I'm just walking home from a meeting with Daniel Sanderson, you know that guy I told you about, the one looking to produce something…I mentioned your show to him and I just happened to have a copy of the script with me…"

My stomach turns from tranquil to tumultuous roller coaster.

"Brenda, tell me you didn't?" I say to her.

"What? Oh, come on Sam. You have to have a producer or we're never going to get it up and running. I'll do all the bulk work as producer of course, but we need cash, Sam. Cash. And we have it! He read some of it and he really liked it and he wants to produce it! He wants it! Now," she continues as if it's all a done deal and I have nothing to say about it. Maybe I don't. "He has a space reserved for September 8th through the 29th, so we need to be in there for rehearsals by the 24th of August…so any re-writes would have to be done—"

Salsa with the Pope

"In two and a half weeks," I say finishing her thought.

"Exactly." She says pleased with herself.

"Brenda, I don't know if it's going to be possible to do that," I say, thinking that two and a half weeks is on the same level as, say, *tomorrow*. I mean it's true I have been working on this damn thing for what feels like years now, but these things take time.

"There are problems in the second act that I haven't even figured out how to fix," I tell her.

"Sam, listen to me. This is an opportunity of a lifetime here. People with money don't just come crawling out of the woodwork, you know that. We've got to take this chance. We have to. I know you can do it."

I stay on the phone saying nothing. There's nothing to say. She's right. An opportunity like this is once in a lifetime. If I don't take it, I will never forgive myself. I know that.

The reservations are only fear. Fear of not being able to finish in time. Fear of not knowing how to finish. Fear of not being any good. But what? Am I going to spend my life living with fear and letting it win? I can't. I have to try. I have to.

I tell Brenda I'll do it. She whoops and yells, cheers and hollers and I join in, giving little consideration to my new neighbors at all.

I spend the next three days doing nothing but working on the one-woman show. I go through my mail…receive a postcard from Anne-Marie. This is the third one. This time, Madrid. Last time, Milan. The first time, London. A honeymoon in Europe…must be nice. Actually, I am so riddled with fear about the writing that I would go anywhere—North Pole, Iraq, Mars…it all sounds good to me right about now.

The play is coming though, I have to admit. I found the issue in the second act that was causing problems. The thing is, that I need it in there, but it has to be placed differently. I'm stuck.

I take my computer off my lap and put it on the couch, screen facing in. I don't even want to look at it right now.

I make a tuna sandwich, drink lemonade by the liter and watch two re-runs of *Law & Order*. I've seen them all. More than once even. But I still can't stay away. Worse than cigarette addiction I imagine.

The phone rings just as McCoy is giving his summation. Damn. I love this part. I reach for it, not even noticing who it is.

"Yeah," I say, not in the mood to talk to anyone.

"Hey," Darren says.

Except him. I'm always in the mood to talk to him.

"Hey yourself," I say, my disposition suddenly sunny.

"What's up?"

"I'm just finishing a sandwich, watching television, trying to escape my writing. What's up with you?"

"Oh, not a lot. Practice, practice, practice and then we leave in an hour for the game. Gonna watch?" He asks.

"Try and stop me," I say wanting it to be the truth, but knowing that it's likely I will be in the midst of an affair with my laptop.

"I hope so. You sound like you need a break," he says.

"Yeah, I do. But no can do."

I go on to tell him the good news/bad news about finding the problem in the second act.

"Congratulations!" He says sounding like he means it.

"Thanks. It is good I guess, but I'm still worried that I don't know exactly how to fix it."

"You'll figure it out."

He says it matter-of-factly, like there is no doubt.

"It's not easy." I tell him.

"I know that. I'm not trying to downplay the work end of it. I'm just saying that I know you can do it, because I know you. I know you want this. And I know you're good."

My heart hears his words. My eyes fill with tears.

"Thank you." I simply say, knowing that those are the words I have been needing to hear my whole life.

"Hey," he says. "Skip the game tonight and get to work, girlie."

CHAPTER 56

I am wearing my sexiest clothes, which to be honest, don't really warrant any whistles or hollers or whatever it is they do these days when a sexy woman walks down the street. I mean it is red silk, low-cut, and clingy, but that rates just above mediocre with today's generation. Basically it would have to be cut down to my navel, slit up to my chin and see-through to garner a 'sexy' title. Why not just wear cellophane? I check a last look in the mirror. I like what I see.

I walk up the subway stairs, my mind distracted with Darren. Finally, at long last we are going to see each other. It's been two weeks. I've missed him so much. Yes, I had work and the play to occupy my time, but I missed him all the same.

I gaze at the newsstand as I walk by, not paying much attention until I see the headline. *DARREN JAMES BATTING FOR THE OTHER TEAM?*

At first I am angry. What in the hell are they talking about, he's a Yankee 'til the day he dies. When I near the rack and skim the article though, I see that they aren't referring to baseball at all. Uh, oh. Oh God. Please no, not again.

I buy the paper, not bothering to collect my .75 cents change. I lean against the nearest building and pull open the section. I read it. I read it again. I am confused.

The article basically says that Darren has been getting very 'chummy' as they call it, with a new teammate, Juan Carlos. There are two photos of them at various events, patting each other on the back or huddled close talking. There are three unnamed sources that say they have seen Darren in compromising positions with other men during his past eleven years on the team. Not much proof of anything when you think about it.

My first instinct is to throw this piece of shit newspaper into the nearest receptacle. But I can't stop the little voice inside my head that keeps reminding me of two things...Alan—and my apparent affinity for picking gay men—and the fact that Darren and I haven't had sex. *Not yet, but we will,* I keep wanting to yell back at my little voice.

I look down at my red silk and want to cry. I feel stupid. What was I thinking? That I could just find a great guy and make him mine in the blink of an eye and float off to Never, Neverland. *Right.* I feel like just going home, picking up a pint of Ben & Jerry's, and turning off my phone...no need, it'll probably never ring again anyway.

I lean against the wall and think a moment. I lean and watch the people passing, on their way to meetings, dinner, the dry cleaners.

I am feeling sorry for myself. No. No more. I can't do this. I can't run away. I have to go tonight. Even if it's the last time I ever speak to him. I have to go and face it.

I begin walking the two blocks, look up, and shake my head. I just can't get used to this big apartment building in the sky. This large, *gold*, luxury apartment building. I take a deep breath. I walk in, say hello to Brad the doorman and go up the forty-two floors to the penthouse.

When I arrive, soft music is playing, a wonderful scent I cannot quite identify fills the place, and Darren is nowhere to be found. I call for him, but nothing. Finally I go to the master bath, and voila, I hear him singing a chorus of *New York, New York* through the closed door.

I am tempted to enter, take my clothes off and throw myself into the shower next to him. But considering my journey over here, I reconsider. Be patient, I tell my extra-horny, extra-uneasy self.

I tiptoe out to the living area and take in the surroundings. There is baseball memorabilia everywhere the eye can see. Not just about him either. He has Mickey Mantle and Joe DiMaggio, Babe Ruth. There is an entire cabinet full of Bubble Yum Bubble Gum too. I'm talkin' dozens of boxes. It's gum their chewin' these days, not tobacco, I remind myself.

I follow the winding hallway into the kitchen to see what smells so delicious. As soon as I take the lid off the pot, Darren comes around the corner.

"You made it," he says and smiles.

He is dressed in jeans, a white tee-shirt, and lose-fitting sweater. His hair is wet and possibly combed (though he keeps it so short, it's often hard to tell), his face clean-shaven and pretty. Just the way I like'im. Just the way Juan Carlos likes'im??

He comes up behind me and puts his arms around my middle. I stiffen up, he senses this and I am forced to let go. I allow myself to fall back into his body for a moment.

"What's this yummy stuff you've got cookin' here?" I ask.

"It's a recipe of my mom's. I just hope it's gonna come out okay. I've never made it before, but if it comes out half as good as when she makes it, it'll be tasty. If not, well…there's always pizza."

I laugh, turn to him. Kiss him. Kiss him again. We walk to the couch, sit and begin making out.

"I missed you." he tells me.

"I missed you too. I hate it when you're gone so long."

"I told you, you can always come visit me," he says.

"You know I can't. Especially, not now."

I don't even realize how much I've missed him until we get comfy on the couch, sprawled out, bodies intertwined, feet bare. This is the way things are supposed to be. I can feel it.

"How's it comin'?" He asks.

I tell him all my progress (and stalls) on the one-person play. I sigh.

"I only have four more days. I've got to get it done."

"You will. I know it. You know it."

He gets up and goes to the kitchen to check on dinner.

The meal is delicious, the recipe a hit. I stuff myself. He stuffs himself. We decide that we should watch a flick, and allow our bellies to settle before dessert.

"Did you make dessert too?" I ask when he mentions it.

"Kind of," he answers, sly look on his face.

Pride and Prejudice is our choice—okay, my choice. It is so good. And romantic. And long.

It's three hours later and the topic of sexual orientation hasn't come up. I spy the newspaper tossed on the couch. It's my opportunity. I must say something.

"So, you made the front page," I say to him in a joking (not joking) way.

He is in the kitchen pouring drinks.

"Oh, that crap again. You know, they print that kind of stuff every three, four months. And it's not just me. Many of us have been labeled 'gay.' Good thing I can handle it. There are a couple of guys who have a tough time of it. I mean they get PISSED and want to kick some ass."

"Can you sue?" I ask.

"It's been looked into, but there's always the First Amendment issue and then we have to watch ourselves, because they don't want bad publicity for the Yankees, so it's a touchy issue."

I shake my head, "No truth to it though?"

He looks at me as if I have six eyes.

"Of course not. Why would you even ask that?"

"Well, I mean, I...of course know that it's, I mean...well, I don't KNOW for a fact, I mean we haven't exactly—"

"Sex?" he says before I can stumble out of the conversation. "Is that what you were going to say? That we haven't had sex?"

I wait a moment, thinking that maybe he will need to go to practice soon, get a tooth pulled, something...nope.

Realizing that he's not going anywhere I say, "Well, yeah," elongating the words, shaking my head, wishing I were anywhere but here.

Darren approaches me. I am scared. I don't know what he's going to do. Is he going to pretend I am a ball and hit me (of course not!), pretend I'm a man and kiss me (Sam! I silently yell at myself), throw me out over the balcony (now, there's a definite possibility).

Before I can decide and make a run for it, he is here. All 6'3" of him. Smooth, dark, handsome, looming over me and my red silk. He doesn't say anything for a bit, just seems to be checking me out, rubbing up against me with his body, touching my face with his fingertips. When he gets close to my lips, I open them slightly and he pulls my lower lip down with his thumb. He takes his tongue and licks the inside of my lip slowly at first and then all of the sudden inserts it into my mouth. I have only one thought. Yes!

Darren gets down on his knees and teases me without even bothering to undress me. He then makes his way back up to my face, caressing it softly.

All the sudden, he grabs my hair and whispers in my ear, "Is that what you want, little girl? You want me to sex you up? Huh? Huh?"

Oh My GOD.

"Uh, huh," I moan, thinking that not even Woolite can save my red silk from this wetness.

Before I know what hits me, Darren picks me up and throws me over his shoulder and carries me to his bed. He flings me down and mounts me. He lets his tongue do some heavy overtime before allowing his member entry.

It stuns me at first. It's been so long and I was so anticipating this moment that I feel I will come immediately. He senses this and slows down, saying, "Uh, uh, uh, not yet, baby. Not yet."

Our sex turns to love making before long and Darren is caressing me and kissing me, making me hotter than I ever thought I could get. The bed sheets are soaked beneath me.

I shift. I get on top. I look down at him. I start pumping him. And more and more, faster and faster until neither of us can take it anymore. We exhale and our bodies explode together.

I fall down onto him. He wraps his arms around me and we sleep, contentment between us.

Two and a half hours later, I roll over and find the bed empty. I hit the bathroom then pad into the kitchen and find Darren fussing.

"What in the world?" I ask.

"Dessert." He says, and licks whipped cream from his fingers.

He brings a single plate of chocolate cake, whipped cream, cherries, hot fudge and vanilla ice cream into the great room. He spoons a little of each and holds it up to my mouth. I take a bite. And another. Excellent, but I have dessert of another kind on my mind.

I get up off the couch and begin pulling the tee-shirt I am wearing slowly up over my head.

"You hot, cause I can turn down the heat?" Darren calls to me teasingly.

I then seductively pull my panties down and say in a breathless voice, "Yep. So hot in here."

He quickly puts the plate onto the coffee table and chases me into the bedroom for round two.

CHAPTER 57

I look at the caller i.d. and turn the ringer off. I can't believe I'm doing this. I can't believe I'm turning the phone off on my boyfriend. I have no choice though. Darren has called three times today. And yes, it's true that normally I would be thrilled by this, but today, I can't be bothered. By anyone. No man, woman, or child. I have to finish this damn play *today* or I am through. That's the bottom line. I even had to let voicemail pick up a call from Anne-Marie, who just returned from her honeymoon last night. It makes me feel guilty, but if I don't shut them out, I will not make it to the first reading tomorrow with a completed script in hand.

I throw myself into a hot shower, trying to wash away all of the bad feelings. It's just this damn play. Everything else is going great.

Darren and I had another wonderful night, making love 'til the wee hours of the morning—when I should have been here working on this God forsaken piece of shit writing—but really it was good (and not just the sex) because we aired a few things out.

As we lay there, catching our breath, readying ourselves for sleep, Darren says out of the blue, "You really thought I was gay?"

This completely catches me off-guard, as I think our several marathons of sexual activity would make this conversation moot.

I roll onto my side and look at him. I smile a little.

"Not really," I say as sincerely as I can.

It's not like I'm lying. I didn't actually believe he was gay. I rather believed that God disliked me and was punishing me for unspeakable acts, of which I knew nothing about.

"Didn't seem like that to me," he says.

"Well," I begin, "it was a lot of things. Not even you, really. I mean my history with Alan and…that article just threw me for a loop and then, well…we hadn't made love and I wasn't really sure why."

"Why," he says to me, "is because of you."

I wait for him to clarify.

"You remember when we first met? The first time? You ran out and then said all those things about me wanting to take you to my place or a hotel? You remember that? Well, I was just trying to tread lightly. I didn't want to scare you away, Samantha."

He runs his hand over his hair like I've seen him do a hundred times during games.

"I can't believe it. It's what you asked for and then it comes back to bite me on the ass," he says ironically.

I can't help but laugh.

I then say, "Oh, does my poor baby have a boo-boo on his whittle be-hind."

I use my best baby voice, as I wrestle him onto his stomach and begin pinching his bottom.

Yeah, okay, that was worth it, and not only because of the conversation.

As I rinse off I realize that I have a lot to be thankful for. I have a great man in my life, I received my confirmation about the New York City Marathon (now all I have to do is train for the 26 miles—piece of cake—*right*), and I'm working on a major project and though it's scary as hell, it's what I've always wanted, so yeah, I couldn't ask for much more. Possibly sanity. But, not much more than that.

I turn the nozzle to ice cold and give myself a spritz before exiting the shower. This wakes me up. I'm ready to work. I dry off quickly, throw on my robe, and go directly to my laptop. I do not pass the fridge, I do not collect a snack or cool drink.

It is almost five hours later when I finally finish. I will need to look at it again in the morning before the read-aloud, but I am done. I did it. It is finished. I can't believe it. I actually wrote a play! I actually did what I set out to do. I am so proud of myself.

I go to the phone to share my news with the world. I don't even notice that it's after 1 a.m. until the phone begins ringing on the other end. I disconnect quickly, hoping I didn't wake anyone. I turn my ringer to the 'on' position and play back my messages.

First it's Anne-Marie telling me she wants to meet for lunch or dinner. We have lots to catch up on. Then it's Darren saying to give him a buzz. Then it's Darren again saying to call him. Then it's Darren again saying he's getting worried, to call no matter what time it is.

I push #1 speed dial. It rings three times. He answers groggy.

"It's me. Sorry to wake you, but you said to call no matter what time."

"Yeah, yeah I did," he almost whispers.

"Well, I'm okay. You get back to sleep. Sorry I woke you."

"You finish?" He asks.

"I did."

"Good for you," he says and disconnects.

Is he angry? I can't tell. But, I'm not going to bother calling him again to find out though, because that would surely make him angry and then I'd have created my own answer—the one I didn't want, so I'll just have to wait until tomorrow.

I set my alarm for 8, pull the covers up over me and pray for sleep.

The alarm sounds, I jump up quickly, get ready for my day. I leave the apartment, head to work…work being the show, the rehearsal, the theatre…something I have longed to say my entire life.

Brenda, Daniel, and Tim the director are going to be there. I've never met Tim or Daniel as they reside in Los Angeles, so my nerves are in full-swing. I will be reading the piece aloud for the first time and getting their feedback on re-writes, which isn't helping the anxiety one bit either. I pray there will be only a few suggestions, nothing too earth shattering to the piece, but

I don't want to speculate. Doing that will only get me in trouble.

I feel groggy. I'm not a coffee-drinker, but there are days—this one—that I wish I were. I need something to pick me up. How about adrenaline?

I walk up the subway stairs and silently say a prayer that they're running. The MTA workers were threatening to strike, which equals a nightmare for all involved. Can't drive, can't take the train or bus...might as well stock up on dry goods or hiking boots, because it's either walk or go nowhere.

The streets are flooded, the result of early morning rain—buckets of it—combined with the four inches we got during the night. I'm glad I'm not driving in this, though walking in it is no picnic either. I do have on my handy-dandy black rubber galoshes though. They're great, though they don't prevent drivers (aka shitheads) from hitting every puddle and pouring dirty cold water all over me. Just the way I want to look for my first rehearsal.

When I arrive, I look soggy, like my cat looks after I've tortured her with a bath.

"Hey you," Brenda says as I take off my wet stuff and place it on the coat hooks near the door.

"Hey," I say and give her a not-so-close hug.

"You're soaked." She informs me.

"Uh, yeah, pretty much. You seem dry though...how did that happen?"

"Well, I've been here about 25 minutes and it wasn't coming down too hard then. And I had my umbrella with me."

She gestures to a pink and purple tent, turned upside down, drying out, near the front door. That would explain it.

"That thing's enormous," I tell her.

"Yeah." She smiles as if she's proud. "And I'm dry," she reminds me.

I go into the bathroom to freshen up. I dry my head on the only towel I see, which has probably been sitting here since God knows when, but whatever. My hair's not going to know the difference. I smooth out my smeared mascara and re-apply

Salsa with the Pope

lipstick. I change into the sweatshirt I brought for working-out this evening. At least it's dry.

I join the others, who are seated in the front of the house. That's what they call the theatre...the house (fancy, huh?). Brenda makes the introductions. I shake both Tim and Daniel's hands firmly. I won't be intimidated, though I don't sense a need to defend myself. Daniel is older, feigning excitement and ignorance at the whole process of doing a play. His expertise is finance (providing it, that is), while our expertise is spending it.

Tim is younger, very attractive and distinguished, even in his early thirties. He is clearly a homosexual...see, I am getting better at this. Didn't take me two years to figure it out. Marked improvement.

We take seats, they in the first two rows, me on the stage, which is elevated and dark. It is an old space, musty, and damp, but not without character. It surely has potential and I intend to use it to its fullest.

The play runs exactly 79 minutes. This is an extension of 3 minutes from the version they had prior to my arrival. I found a couple of jokes this morning and thought they would lighten the piece up a bit...it could use it.

The play is primarily about my relationship with and the subsequent death of my brother many years ago. So not exactly light fare at the theatre. But even in tragedy, there is humor.

Upon saying the words, "The End," I feel lighter. Lighter, fresher, accomplished in some way. It is as if this play, art, piece, tragedy, whatever you want to call it, was living inside me up until this very moment. It needed to be purged in some form. And now it has been. Even if they hate it, it is out of me and has become someone else's burden.

Brenda begins clapping, the others join in almost as she stops. I nod my head, feel my face flush, climb down to join them.

"You may want to stay up there," Tim says as I near him.

"Oh. Okay," I say, having no idea what he has in mind.

"I would like to go back and see how we can re-work a couple of things," he tells me as I take my seat again.

"Okay," I say, still having no idea what the specifics are.

He proceeds to have me re-work four areas of the piece. I try very hard to give his ideas a try. I mean you never know. Two of his thoughts I find very helpful, one I could go either way, but one—this last one—I am extremely resistant to.

"Tim, I really don't think that that's the way to go here. Not at this particular point. I mean, if that's what's going on, then why would she be so heartbroken in the first place?" I say to him, trying to get him to give this one up, as I am not going to compromise here.

"Samantha, I really think this will give it a lift. Just try this...try this," he says and proceeds to re-write my words (need I remind him that *I'm* the writer, *he's* the director) and he gives me a line-reading (a huge no-no in this business) to boot. I take a deep breath, try to focus and really try it, though I know that I can't. I know they know that I can't. That I'm not really trying.

"Try it again. Really try to make it work," Tim is saying to me, as if I have a choice. As if I can will my being to say something false and inaccurate. I try. And again. But it's false and we all know it.

"I just think if you work on that..." Tim is telling me.

"No." I finally say firm and loud.

"What?" He says, as if he's never heard the word before.

"I said, no Tim," I say in a softer more understanding voice. "I can't, no, I won't do this. Not here. Not at this juncture in the play. It needs to be this way. Otherwise it will read phony and I won't put my work up there, knowing it is riddled with falsehoods. I'm sorry."

I don't wait for a response, but instead jump down from the stage and hit the bathroom. Brenda comes in a short while later.

"It's good, Sam. It's really good."

I flush, come out of the stall, face her.

"I'm sorry. I don't want to put you in an awkward position in there," I say to her sincerely.

"What? Oh stop being silly. I agree with you. Daniel too. Tim is just doing an ego-director-thing. Don't worry. It looks really good. If you work out those few other things he suggested, then it's going to be brilliant."

She gives me a hug and I feel better. Even vindicated in some way.

I go straight home after rehearsal.

It's late, already after 11. I am dog-tired. And I still have to work on these re-writes. I have to have something to show for tomorrow's rehearsal. I want food, sleep, and a shower. Okay, skip the shower. I'll settle for food and sleep.

My cell rings just as I'm putting the key in the lock of my building. I rummage through my bag until I find it. It's Darren.

"Hey," I say, sounding as tired as I am.

"Hi. How'd it go? You home?" He asks.

"Just walking in the door now. It was rough, but good. You? How are you?" I ask.

"Yeah, I'm in the car, driving home. Thought maybe I would stop by for a kiss beforehand."

"No," I say sounding sterner than I feel.

"Oh, okay." He says recovering quickly.

"Honey, I'm sorry. I didn't mean it that way. I would love to see you. You know I would, I just, I'm whipped and I have some work to do on the script before tomorrow morning's rehearsal, so I just can't."

"I understand," he says, clearly sounding like he doesn't. "Maybe tomorrow," he pouts.

"Perfect," I tell him.

I begin work on the script, but fall asleep within an hour, having almost nothing completed. I wake to my alarm and realize that I have slept with my glasses on, pencil in hand, pages strewn across the bed. Not exactly the bedmate I had in mind.

I throw myself into the shower, forsake my workout, knowing that I will have to use the time to come up with something before I leave for rehearsal. I work fervently; feel as if I have a little something…not enough to walk into that theatre my head held high, but what can I do. It's what I have.

I hand a set of the new pages to each of the four people—we have a fourth person with us today, Billie Myers, who will stage manage the show. They look them over, seem pleased and ask for the others.

"Oh, uh, there are no others. Not yet, at least. I worked until I fell asleep last night and worked more this morning, but it's just going to take some time. Not a lot of time, mind you, but a little more time."

I'm nervous, though I hope I don't sound it. I want to appear professional. Like I have the right stuff. I have the right stuff, I remind myself.

Tim looks at me and says, "Good, because we don't have a lot of time. We need the new pages complete and ready to go by Thursday. That's it. We have to get to staging then. Oh, and how are you coming with your lines?" he asks me.

"Getting there. Definitely getting there," I lie.

Rehearsal is a lot of nothing. I keep wondering why we are here having a discourse on the recent popularity of the one-person play (obviously because it's cheaper to produce) when I could be home writing, Tim could be home directing (something) and Daniel could be out producing (or spending, or something). But no, instead we are all sitting around, wasting time. After a few hours of this, and a lunch that is catered in, I decide to take the plunge.

"Well, I think I'm going to head home and get to work."

I gather my things and ready myself.

"Oh, well, I suppose we're done here," Tim says, as if he needs to be the one who does the dismissing.

Trying to appease him I say, "If there's nothing else?"

"No, no, I think it's good that you take this time and get some stuff done. We have a lot of work to do and not a lot of time," he says.

I agree heartily.

I am home less than an hour later. I have set-up my workstation and prepared myself for a long evening of suffering.

My door buzzer goes off. Damn. I get up and flip on the TV, turn to channel 502 to see who's standing in the lobby. Darren. Shit. I buzz him in and go to the door.

He comes in with a bottle of sparkling cider and a single red rose.

Salsa with the Pope

"Well, look who's here?" I say to Darren. The word 'unannounced' attaches itself to my greeting, but it is for my ears only. How did he even know I'd be home?

"I thought I'd drop in."

He kisses me. He tastes good. Almost fruity, but mild. I kiss him again, try to figure out the flavor, give up and invite him in.

"Sorry I didn't call. Was on my way home, thought I'd give it a shot, and surprise! You're here!"

"It's good to see you baby." I tell him.

He notices my workstation and looks at me, confusion on his face.

"You're working? Again?"

I sigh.

"Yep. Tim wants some re-writes and then I have to get off-book very quickly or we're going to be in trouble. Basically, this is my life for the next month."

Darren nods his head, pensive and heavy.

"What?" I say.

"Nothing. It's just…we haven't seen each other much lately. And I'm going on the road tomorrow, and then when I get back you're knee-deep in this, and then I go away again and it's play-offs and I thought you were going to get to come and visit me this time. But now it looks like you're gonna be stuck here."

He sits on the edge of the sofa, defeated, like a little boy who's lost his dog.

"I'm sorry," I say to Darren, though I know there is little truth in the words. He knows it too.

He says, "Are you?"

I sit down next to him on the couch.

"Darren, look. I have wanted to do this my whole life. I have worked my ass off and now I'm finally getting my chance. And I've got to put everything I have into it. You know, I'm surprised that you don't understand that."

I get up from the couch, pace, and sit back down on the arm of the chair.

"I don't like not seeing you. I hate it. But I can't be in two places at once. I can't be at your place making love, and here on my sofa learning lines. It's just not possible."

"So, what are you saying?" He wants to know.

"What? I'm saying that right now, I have to do this. I can't see you right now," I tell him.

He gets up suddenly, like someone's jabbed him with a cattle prod.

"Okay. Good enough." he says.

No venom, no shouting, just matter-or-fact. He makes his way to the door, opens it, walks out, and shuts it softly behind him.

CHAPTER 58

I look up and see Pam at the entrance. I wave to her and she begins walking my way. I'm seated at a table by a window at Café Blanc in the Village, drinking a fruit smoothie. I'm celebrating.

The project is finished. Well, the project isn't totally finished, but several goals have been met. Goal one: the writing is finished, to everyone's satisfaction, including mine—almost. Hard to be *totally* satisfied, but I'm damn close. Goal two: the learning of the lines, also completed. Goal three: the staging, this too is rehearsed and ready to go—well, it better be, as we open *tonight!*

Basically it has been three weeks of pure hell. Pure hell, pure exhilaration, pure torture, pure excitement, pure fear, pure enjoyment. If I didn't know it before, I certainly do now…sadomasochism really is my life's theme.

Pam comes up to me and gives me a frosty peck on the cheek.

"You're cold."

"Yeah, it still hasn't warmed up out there," she tells me and chuckles.

We've had an unusually cold autumn.

"Or have you been so wrapped up at the theatre" (she over-pronounces it and says thee-a-ter—with a British dialect to boot) "that you haven't noticed?"

"Maybe." I tell her. "Maybe."

We order soups—butternut squash for me, split pea for her—and salads and catch up. She is dating a Wall Street broker named Ken, who she knew years before, but ran into at a dance recital and now they've been getting together regularly for the past month and a half.

"Good for you!" I say enthusiastically, meaning it.

"Yeah, I'm happy," she admits and smiles widely.

I tell her all about my production, leaving out the details of the story, though she knows what it's about. She's coming tonight and I don't want to spoil it completely.

"And Darren? How's he?" She asks between spoonfuls of soup.

"Haven't heard from him."

"Huh?" She asks.

I tell her about our last meeting in my apartment and how he just left.

"And I haven't heard from him since." I say.

"That is so odd. Have you tried to call him?" She asks.

I confess that I haven't.

"And why not?" She wants to know.

"I don't know. No time really. And what do I say? I mean, I don't want to hurt him. I don't want to get hurt. I—"

"Do you love him?" Pam asks me.

I think for a moment, though I know the answer right away. "Yeah. Yes, I do love him."

"Well, then there's nothing to discuss. There's nothing that can't be worked out here. Just call him. I'm sure he would love to hear your voice. Besides, he probably could use a little distraction from the game…have you been watching?"

"No." I admit.

"Well, it's not going too well. Didn't see the game last night, but if they didn't win, they're out."

Shit.

I feel badly for Darren. I feel shitty because I didn't even know they were doing so poorly. But I've had my own stuff to worry about and if I didn't take care of me, then no one else would have.

Yeah, I've been really wrapped up with the show, but that doesn't mean that I haven't thought about him. Because I have. A lot.

I tried to convince myself that we just wouldn't work out. He's a star ball player. I'm some girl from Ohio. But that didn't work this time. My being wouldn't listen to that shit. Not this time. Not ever again.

I need to call him. Even if he tells me to buzz off, even if he's married to another, I still need to call. For me.

We dig into our salads and Pam reaches into her bag and hands me the entertainment section of the newspaper.

"You ready for this?" She asks.

I look down, don't see anything at first, and then, wow, at long last.

There is a short article discussing the opening of a new play on Broadway. *The Ghost of Dyckman Avenue.*

"He did it. Finally." I say.

It's been over four years. He's been trying to get this thing to Broadway for more than four years. From what I've heard, it's not even close to the original play he wrote all of those years ago. But so what. Good for him. I can't be upset or jealous or angry. Only happy. And sad. I wanted to be the one to share this with him. But it wasn't meant to be. Clearly it wasn't. And now I have my own project up and running. Maybe it's not Broadway, but it's mine.

I look up at Pam, tears in my eyes.

"Good for him." I tell her. "Good for him."

She nods, takes a bite of salad, dabs the Italian dressing from her lower lip and says, "I heard he's taking his mother to the opening."

I nod, "Well, of course she's going to be there."

Pam shakes her head.

"As his date." she informs me.

I frown, not understanding.

"Natalia out of town?" I ask.

"Natalia and Alan? They split a few months back. Last time I saw him, he was with some other woman...Silvia something, but now apparently that's over too. Don't know what's going on with him. Maybe you should give him a call. I mean you're both single now."

I give her a look that say's *when pigs fly.*

She takes the hint and changes the subject.

Pam and I finish our lunch, cutting it short, as I have to get back to the theatre.

I go in, run my lines, then lie down for a short nap.

I awaken suddenly.

I vomit.

I lie back down.

Hit the toilet again.

Lie back down.

I vomit for a third, and hopefully last time tonight. I go on in 35 minutes and I'm ready to get into my costume and don't want any mess on it, if you know what I mean.

I lie down, try to meditate and remind myself that I am a professional—I try to keep the laughter in my head to a minimum when I recite this. I can do this. I can. I will be great. Those are my friends out there. They love me. They will love the show. No worries...no worries...no worries.

Tim approaches me quietly and whispers, "You feeling alright now?"

Unfortunately he was giving me a final bit of direction when my last bout of heaving began.

"Yeah, I'm great." I say convincingly.

I've turned into a great liar. Which makes me a great actor, I tell myself.

Tim leaves, I warm up, change clothes, and drink a little water. The house is open and I can hear the audience filling up the space. We are sold-out, a 199 seat theatre too, so I am very pleased. My mom couldn't be here tonight, though she plans to come and bring her sister next week. That will give me time to perfect the show and get in the groove.

Billie comes in, gives me my five-minute warning and places another box of flowers on my dressing room table. There are several boxes, notes, vases, cards...I haven't bothered to open a one. Too nervous.

I go to the bathroom a last time. No need to pay homage to the porcelain bowl, which gives me confidence that I am ready for this.

Billie meets me in the hallway, "Places," she says.

Shit.

I follow the glow tape, stand in front of the chair placed center stage and wait for the lights to come up.

CHAPTER 59

It is the best day of my life. Bar none. I have never felt so good. So alive. So empowered. So *talented*. Yes, tonight I feel talented. Tonight Spielberg could call and I wouldn't be surprised.

I'm looking over the flowers, the cards, the well-wishings backstage, having just sent Brenda, Daniel, and Tim to the restaurant where we're having our after-party. I will join them soon. I just want to be prepared to thank those that sent things, and having not even looked at them, that would be difficult.

I take off my costume (simple black on black), hang it up on the rack and throw my jeans and sweater on. I am putting on my boots when I hear a noise in the theatre. I think Billie already left to join the others, but now I'm not so sure. I walk out, don't see anyone at first, but it's dim and hard to see into the house.

"Billie, that you?" I call.

No response. I hear the noise again though.

"Anyone there?" I ask, a little shaky.

Suddenly there is loud clapping, whistles, a 'bravo'.

I wait.

Darren walks down the aisle.

He is dressed casually in jeans and a blue sweater. He is smiling. His eyes look glassy, like they're carrying tears or maybe it's the faint lights. I can't tell.

"You scared the crap out of me...what're, what're you doing here?" I say, coming toward him.

He shrugs, says, "Wanted to see what my competition was."

I smile.

"No competition." I tell him.

He reaches out to me, pulls me to him, kisses me on the mouth. I kiss him back, full of hunger. We seem out-of-control, unable to get enough of each other. We devour each other, pull at each other's clothing, end up on the bare, dusty floor.

There are no words spoken. Only groans and noises. Like animals that haven't eaten in days. Or people who haven't fucked in weeks.

He comes inside me, I wrap my legs around him, my jeans down past my knees, his sweater rubbing my face, making me itch...I don't care.

We finish as quickly as we began. For the first time, I notice the floor, dusty with cobwebs and scattered dirt and debris.

"Gross. How long since they've cleaned these floors?" I say as I try to get up.

Darren pulls me to my feet and we adjust our clothing. I look at him.

"Hi," I say, as if just seeing him for the first time.

"Hi," he says back, giving me that dazzling smile of his.

I go to him, kiss him, hug him. When I pull back, he looks into my eyes.

"You were amazing. Amazing."

"You saw the show?" I say surprised.

"Yep. Sat right there," he points toward a seat near the back of the house.

"I didn't know." I tell him.

"You made the right choice. Heavy competition." he says and laughs.

"No, no competition." I swat him. "Just work. You know how that is," I tell him.

"Yes, yes I do." He says and suddenly seems down.

"What? You okay?" I ask.

"Yeah, just...we're out. We lost last night and that was the end."

"I'm so sorry Darren." I tell him sincerely.

"Hey, there's always next year, right? Besides, now I can get some rest and maybe take a nice vacation some place warm, and do some extra time at the foundation."

Darren runs a foundation for children. It's a program to keep them off alcohol and drugs. He often goes there on the weekends to help out. He's very hands-on—one of the many things I like about him—especially when his hands are on me.

"Interested? When the show's over, of course." He is saying.

"Vacation? You and me? Hmm, I need to think about that. Okay," I say immediately.

I look at him. I know I am home. This time, it's for real.

"You know...I love you. I really do." I tell him.

I can say it. Now. I can feel it. It's okay.

"I was hoping...I love you, Samantha," he finally says.

CHAPTER 60

Time is flying by...I can't believe that three weeks is already up, like that. My show is closing. Tonight is the last performance and bye-bye Samantha Play. It's not the only show in town closing either...I just heard that Alan's play got notice. After only three weeks.

It got decent reviews, but can't seem to pack the house, so they now have three more weeks to pull in a crowd or bye-bye Alan Play. That sucks for him. It really does. After waiting so long and suddenly in one instant, poof, and it's all gone.

No word on perspective producers interested in taking my show to Broadway, but I wasn't expecting that. In fact, we've done better than we ever thought we would. We are coming out ahead. Not just even, but far into the black. I am really excited about that, as is Daniel. He mentioned taking the show on the road, and I just may take him up on that.

But not before Barbados. That's where Darren is taking me next week. Ten days of pure bliss. I cannot wait!

I am struggling to open the theatre door, as I am carrying a garment bag with my outfit for our closing party, my black tote, and a slew of little gifts for everyone. The gifts are more a token than anything, but it was important for me to do it. Everyone on this production has helped to make my dream come true, and I'll never forget it.

My cell starts ringing, but it's impossible for me to get to it. I head to the dressing room, set all my wears down and inspect my phone. One voicemail. When I listen, I am truly surprised. It's from Alan.

He wants to come to the show tonight, but doesn't want to make me uncomfortable, so if I don't want him here, I should call and tell him. Otherwise he will be here.

I sit on the old, lop-sided sofa adjacent to the dressing table. It looks as musty as the dirty floor in the theatre, its cranberry color long faded and even worn through in spots. I contemplate. Should I call and ask Alan not to come? I weigh the pros and cons.

Pro: Alan is having a hard time right now, with his play, and presumably his marriage, so he probably could use the distraction and what does it matter to me?

Con: Alan is a real critic, so he'll probably make me more nervous, though that is my issue and I have to get over that. I actually think I am over it, just using it as an excuse.

Pro/Con: Darren will be here, but that shouldn't be an issue. In fact, Alan is a huge fan.

So, why not? He can't hurt me anymore. I am in love with another. Someone who can truly give himself to me. Someone who is not reserved and isolated. Someone who is not gay.

Decision made, I go about my business, preparing for the show. It's going to be a great evening.

And it is. I think it's my best performance to date.

I take a second bow to a standing audience. The applause is thunderous and full of love. I can feel the love. The respect. Truly. I brush the tears from my eyes, spot my mother and aunt who are crying too—despite already having seen the show last week—and blow them a kiss. I want to remember this night forever. Don't think it will be possible to forget.

I run off the stage and into Tim's arms. He hugs me tight and whispers, "We did it. We did it." He then looks at me and says solemnly, "You did it."

I nod, crying harder now. I break away and scurry to the dressing area. It feels like the safety zone. A place I can let it all out and not have to make apologies, modifications, or excuses. I can just be.

When I close the door behind me that is exactly what I am anticipating, but not at all what I get.

"Aaaaaaahhhh," I scream, startled by the presence of a man. Not just any man. Alan.

I try to catch my breath and say, "You scared the shit out of me. What are you doing here?"

He looks thinner. Older somehow. He shifts his body, always playing the cool customer.

"Sorry. Didn't mean to scare you. Just didn't know if I'd be able to get you away from all of those people. Your fans," he says teasingly.

I pour myself a glass of water from the pitcher sitting on the table and steady myself. I gesture toward Alan. He shakes his head, "No, thanks."

He stands as if in deep thought a moment and then says, "You nailed it. It was right on. I was hoping."

So I met his approval. Finally.

Ironically, it was only when I didn't give a shit, when I didn't need his approval that I got it. If I were still scared and nervous, wanting so to please him, it wouldn't have happened.

I smile, say, "Thanks. That means a lot," knowing that although it's nice, it will never mean what it once would have.

He shifts, paces a bit and then returns back to the same spot he stood before.

"I guess you heard?" He says to me.

I raise my eyebrows, not exactly sure what he is referring to.

"The play...it's closing."

The play being his play I assume.

"I heard it was on notice, but hadn't heard anything else," I tell him.

"Notice," he says mockingly, "is just another way of saying, you're out, pack your things and hit the road."

"I'm sorry Alan. Truly I am. I know you worked so hard on it. And for so long. And the reviews seemed to be better than you thought they'd be."

"I only thought that when it was *my* play. The play I wrote wouldn't have gotten such great reviews, though the reviews didn't help much anyway, now did they? No, *this* version, well, it's pretty much cookie-cutter, same shit as everything else...I take it you haven't seen it then?"

I shake my head, "No, I've been here every night rehearsing or performing since you opened."

It is the truth, but I wouldn't have seen his play anyway. I don't think I could have sat through it, knowing where it came from, how they made him sell his soul just to get it to 44th Street.

"Good thing," he tells me, "you wouldn't have recognized it."

I nod, saddened by the whole thing.

"You know, it's just not my year. I mean, first the play and now Natalia…well, I guess first her then the play, but it all becomes one thing, you know…one horrible, awful mistake."

He seems to be rambling now. I sense that maybe he's been drinking. Or perhaps he is just so distraught at the state of his life that he seems inebriated.

He sighs, sits on the worn sofa and puts his head in his hands. I've seen him do this a thousand times, yet it has never impacted me like it does now. I kneel next to him.

"Alan, it's going to be alright. All of it. It is."

I sound convincing. To me at least.

When he speaks, it's as if his words are being spoken by an old man, his throat gravelly and dry, his speech choppy and severe.

"My play, closing…Samantha, my work…the most important thing to me…it is destroyed. I have allowed these people, these bastards to destroy my art."

He pauses, then, "My marriage…is over. Natalia filed for divorce last week. We're through. I've hurt someone else. Another in a long list of casualties."

He looks up at me then. His eyes pierce mine, as if seeing right through me. They are scary, yet calming and hypnotic. I cannot look away.

"I never, never meant to hurt you. You know that, don't you? I need you to know that, Sam."

"Alan, you need to get some help. Why won't you let someone help you, for God's sake? Your fuckin' pride…it's killing you. Look at you, it's killing you."

I am now shouting. Trying to get through to him. I can't bear to see him this way.

He starts weeping, hard sobs escape from a deep, dark place, buried for God only knows how long. I go to him, wrap my arms around him and hold him. I say nothing. He keeps trying to talk, apologizing, saying how fucked up he is. I just keep holding him. The crying stops abruptly and he pulls himself off of me. He looks at me and caresses my face. He pulls me to him and kisses me on the mouth. It is a hard, unconvincing kiss. I push him away instantly.

"Alan, no."

"I need you." He says.

"No, no." I repeat it again and again.

To him. To myself. The time for this is long over.

Though you would think that part of me would feel vindicated—the way we always imagine it will be when we're dumped—*you'll be sorry…just you wait and see, you'll come crawlin' back*…I feel none of that. Only pity.

I look at the rumpled mess on the couch. I loved that. Once upon a time. But that time is over. I lie Alan down, pull his cell phone out of his pocket and call Gene to come and get him.

This of course makes me late. Late for my own party. Damn. After throwing myself together and waiting for Gene to collect a distraught Alan, I arrive outside the party a bit breathless. As I near the entrance, I see Darren pulling his coat on and heading in the opposite direction.

"Hey there, big boy," I call after him, so glad to finally see him.

He turns, sees me and says, "You talkin' to me?"

Kidding. At first I think he's kidding.

"Don't see any other eligible men out here," I say in a put-on southern accent.

"Oh, well, try your dressing room, could be one there."

And with that, he storms off down the street, jumping into a cab before I can even respond.

I chase the cab, thinking maybe I can catch it at the light, but the light goes green and it speeds off, leaving me behind, breathless and confused.

I pull my cell out of my bag and try Darren's number. Voicemail. I slam the phone shut.
"Shit!"

CHAPTER 61

I scurry down the street as fast as I can, having no particular place in mind, only knowing that I can't go into that party. My own party and I'm a no show. Can't be helped. I need to be away from here. Away from him. *And* him. Far away. To think. To sort my thoughts.

The tears start falling as I near the avenue. I will them to stop. PLEASE. Just 'til I can get myself back to my apartment. Then you can wail and thrash about all you want, I promise myself. I round the corner in search of a cab. Not a one. Surprising for this hour on a Sunday night.

I start walking aimlessly. I can't believe this. For this to happen and...well, there's a Starbucks. That's something you can always count on. No matter where you are...Harlem, on a deserted island off the coast of Antarctica...there's a Starbucks and somehow that makes me feel a little better. I'll just pop in for a cool drink, sit down and calmly figure this out.

I open my bag for a tissue and items start popping out all over the sidewalk. My hairbrush, perfume, and two tampons make their way out before I can stop them. Of course, what one would call 'a nice breeze' comes along at just that moment and carries one of the tampons off down Chambers Street. I recover the remaining items best I can and wipe my face on my sleeve. These are party clothes that will never see the party, I reason, so who cares about a spot of snot on my jacket.

Just as I am approaching my salvation—aka Starbucks, a tall lanky gentleman in a tux approaches me.

"Lose this?" He asks.

His accent is British. He is holding up a tampon...presumably the one that got away.

"Never seen it before," I mumble, continuing to walk.

"Oh, come on now, saw you goin' after it like it was your long lost chap," he tells me.

"Look, mister, I don't know who you are, or what you want, but I don't have a need for a used tampon."

"Well, it doesn't exactly look used, now does it, in the traditional sense I mean."

He displays the wrapped tube between his fingers, as if it's the next item up for bid at Sotheby's. I turn away disgusted, more because of his maleness than because of the tampon. I mean it's just a tampon. My tampon. Rather, my former tampon.

I look straight ahead and continue to put distance between us.

"Just...buzz off."

Okay, admittedly lame, but in a pinch, it still carries some punch—no?

"Ah, come on now, I've come all the way from England to meet a woman just like you," he shouts to me, arms raised over his head, as if ruling a field goal kick as good.

"I doubt it," I say under my breath, though were I in a better mood, I might pursue that thought.

He is tall, dark, and handsome. I just happen to have my fill at the moment with tall, dark and handsomes. Nope, no room on my dance card for another. Perhaps if he returns in say...2025. I should have this all sorted out by then.

I walk into Starbucks, survey several empty tables and breathe a sigh of relief. The last thing I need is to be crammed into a corner seat with someone's elbow and cell phone conversation inhabiting my space.

Note to Self: Sunday nights at Starbucks, practically empty.

I order a Venti Vanilla Crème and take a seat at a small table in the corner. I dump all my stuff into the chair opposite and heave my body down, as if it weighs 500 lbs. That's what it feels like. Like I'm lugging around two tons of shit.

I take a long swig of my drink, allow the sugar to hit me and consider...how did this happen? What have I done to deserve this?

Salsa with the Pope

I contemplate this all for a while. For exactly how long is anyone's guess. I feel numb. Like all of the sudden, I couldn't move if my life depended on it. How long have I been here? An hour? Two? Feels like days. I pull my watch out of my bag and see that it's almost 11:30. Time to go.

I stand, steady myself, gather my things, and then realize I must dump all my trash first. I gather the remnants of three Venti Vanilla Crèmes (what can I say...I was thirsty) and schlep to the trash receptacle.

Through the window, I see Darren walk by...or someone with his short hair-cut and boyish good looks. I run closer, stare out, and confirm that it is him. Not sure how to handle this, but before I even get a chance to decide, he spots me and comes in.

"Thirsty?" He says when he sees me holding the three containers.

I walk back to the table and set them down. I purse my lips, say, "Maybe," in a bratty tone and continue to ready myself to leave. "Why are you here?" I ask him.

"Why are *you* here?" He counters.

"I asked you first."

I can be as childish as a three-year old sometimes...like now, for instance.

"Looking for you. Daniel called—had gotten my number from your mother, said you never made it to the party, so they were concerned and figured you were with me. I confirmed that you were and then came to see what really happened to you."

I nod, say, "Nice story. What do you care?"

"Good question." He answers. He thinks a minute and repeats, "Good question. I really don't know. Besides I love you and don't want to be without you, I really don't know."

He gives a tiny laugh, full of irony, not humor.

"You always seem to be with some other guy though and this time, well...this time it being your ex, it just...it didn't sit well with me is all."

I sit down at the table and gesture for him to sit too. He does, but I can't see him over the mound of stuff on the table.

He pushes it down, but it refuses to stay that way. We move my stuff to another table.

"Darren, I love you. Just you. Only you. There is no other guy. None. Period. You're it. Not even Alan. That's over. It's been over a long time."

I sound like a recording. Like I was here learning lines.

I pick up one of the Vanilla Crème containers, and try to suck a drop from it, but it's dry.

"I'll get you one, you want one?" Darren asks.

"No, no I'm good, sick actually. I just...I just want you to understand. Alan...he's having a really hard time right now. That's all."

"And the kissing?" He asks me.

"There was no kissing."

He starts to interrupt, but I talk over him.

"There was *one* kiss. One kiss. Initiated by him. Stopped by me. Immediately. I don't want to kiss him. I want to kiss you. Only you. But I'll be damned if I'm going to turn people away, who are in my life, who I care about, because you have a jealousy issue."

He thinks for a moment, nods his head.

"Okay. I guess if you can handle all the female fans," his voice is now lighter.

"Groupies," I say.

"I prefer to call them female fans, but whatever...if you can handle all of that, I will handle ex-boyfriends. But no coming on to you."

"No, no coming on to me."

"You sure he's gay?"

Was I? What proof did I have? My instinct. My heart.

"No, I'm not." I finally admit.

Maybe it was just an excuse, a way for me to get over my hurt. If he was gay, there was a *reason*—a reason he had no control over—he couldn't love me. I guess I'll never know for sure.

We stand, dump my trash, gather my things, and grab a cab headed for his Upper East Side Gold Ostentatious Apartment Building.

340

CHAPTER 62

I hop into the car and kiss the driver.
"Hello sexy," I say to him.
"Hello," he answers.
I throw my few packages into the back seat. There is a new navy suit for his mother, a set of crystal, a new briefcase for his father and a coffee table book. We are headed to Darren's parents' house for dinner tonight and I didn't want to go empty-handed. It's not that I haven't spent some time with them in the past, but usually it's a quick hello/good-bye or we sit together at a baseball game. But a real dinner. At their house. Never before.
We speed down Varick, cross on Grand Street, and park on Prince. Nice neighborhood, Soho.
"So, what's here?" I ask Darren as he gets out of the car.
"Just somethin' I wanted to show you...get your opinion on."
We walk hand in hand, looking at numbers on buildings.
"It's this one," he says and points to a large gray commercial building. Darren holds the door for me, buzzes #3 and we are allowed entry.
We take what resembles a freight elevator to the third floor. When the doors open, we are in a large room. An enormous loft-space.
"This is huge." I say as we enter.
Lenny, the realtor is here, clipboard in hand.
"Mr. James, nice to see you again. And Ms. Anderson." He says and turns to me.
He shakes both of our hands and leads us in.
"It's spectacular. Really it is," I say. "What's it for?" I ask Darren.

"Living. I was just thinking maybe I'm getting a little less ostentatious in my old age and maybe it's time for a change."

I inspect the space, which seems to go on forever. It is drab and empty. But if someone actually moved in here, what you could do. The possibilities are endless.

"So what do you think?" Darren asks me when I return to he and Lenny.

"Well, I don't know. I mean it's big, that's for sure. And you could really fix it up. But do you want something this big?"

"Well, I was thinking that I might not be living alone. Forever."

He smiles and takes my hand and starts swinging it back and forth.

"I mean eventually, I would like to…have a family," Darren chuckles and looks at me.

"Uh, huh. You are moving way too fast for me." I say and smile.

"Oh, come on. Don't tell me you haven't thought about it."

I sigh.

"Of course I've thought about it. Once maybe."

"See," he says as if he's won an argument.

"See what? Just because it's entered my mind doesn't mean that I'm ready to take the plunge," I tell him.

"So you're saying, if I got down on my knees right here and asked you to marry me, you would say no."

Darren drops to one knee in front of me. My face flushes. My heart beats. I look to Lenny, who is calculating something and seems completely oblivious to what's going on around him. I shake my head.

"I can't. It's too soon."

"You're scared." Darren tells me.

"No I'm not," I lie.

"Of course you are. Chicken. Scaredy-cat, scaredy-cat, Samantha's a scaredy cat."

"If you think you're going to bully your way into a 'yes' you can forget it," I say and walk away.

Salsa with the Pope

Darren approaches me a few moments later. I am standing by the window, yards away from Lenny and his calculations.

"I'm sorry."

I turn to him.

I say, "No, you're right. I'm scared. I'm scared."

He moves my hair away from my face.

"Don't be. I'll get'cha. You'll come around."

I smile, nod.

"Yes?" He asks, smiling widely. "Is that a 'yes'?"

"Maybe." I counter.

CHAPTER 63

Barbados is wonderful. The bluest water I have ever seen. The clearest water—I could see the ocean floor. The warmest seawater I have ever felt. It is gorgeous. We have so much fun.

I really get to know Darren...little things that you get to know about a person only by spending time together. There are little annoyances...mainly people wanting his autograph, picture, conversation. He is very good about that always, and here is no exception. It's something I will really have to get used to, because I don't see it ending anytime soon.

I just finished unpacking my things and am sitting on the couch, trying to muster the motivation to tackle my bills. I have decided to stay in my apartment. At least for the time being.

I'm going on tour with my show for the next six months, so I see no need to hurry into Darren's place, when I will just be leaving anyway. Besides, I want to take it slow. I do. I love him. Nothing is going to change that. I just want a little more time to ensure my independence, because nothing can threaten that—not a marriage, a baby, a career-change—nothing. I can see that now so clearly.

I go over, gather the bills, the stamps, envelopes, the calculator and park myself back on the sofa. The buzzer rings. I turn the TV to channel 502 and Anne-Marie's profile appears. I jump up, buzz her in, and open the door.

"Oh, my gosh, you're here." I say to her as she approaches my open arms.

We hug long and hard.

"And you're back and I didn't want to wait. It's been too long already."

She's right. It's been hard to find time to get together with our schedules. I'm so happy to see her.

"You want tea, something?" I ask.

We settle on lemonade and shortbread cookies.

We eat and drink, catch up.

Finally, she says, "I have news."

"What news?" I say excited.

"I'm going to be a mommy."

The news hits me hard. It is wonderful. It is beautiful. It is a miracle. Anne-Marie had problems in the past, with her first marriage, but now all that is behind her.

I stand, go to her, hug her, kiss her, hug her again. We both cry, laugh, and cry some more.

"You are going to be the best mommy." I tell her.

"I hope. You know, I've been around kids my whole life…first there were my little brothers and sisters and then my sister's kids, but now…I'm really scared."

She starts sobbing softly. I put my arm around her and guide her back to the couch.

"Why? You're going to be amazing."

"I just…I just don't want to mess them up, you know?"

"Anne-Marie, no chance. No chance. We're all human. We make mistakes. But mess them up? No way, girl. No way."

CHAPTER 64

It is the night before I leave on my tour. First stop: Philadelphia. Okay, so it's not exactly a million miles away. I'll still be away though and working and I'm excited, though I will surely miss my life in New York. Especially Darren.

Not that he's going to be around much. He leaves for Spring Training in Florida next week. We will actually overlap there for three days. Three glorious days, though we will both be working and distracted. At least we can eat together. And sleep together. Though I'm not so sure how much sleeping will actually be going on.

I am running to meet everyone at Sizzle. We are having a party there. Salsa and food and all my friends. I'm excited.

I feel so good. Really good. I am happy in my life. My career. My relationships. Even my past relationships.

I read that Alan has a new play opening Off-Broadway in six weeks. Good for him. He too needs a fresh start. It's almost like everything has come full-circle.

Last week at the drug store, I ran into Natalia. I wanted to run away, as I saw her long before she spotted me, but I needed the items I was getting and it was time to face up to this (whatever *this* is) and move on. We were in the checkout line before she noticed me.

"I suppose you're gloating, behind those sun shades." She said to me, two behind me in line.

"Hardly. Just covering my pale, make-up less face." I told her.

"Well, he's all yours now. You can run back to him."

I allowed the person between us to go ahead of me. I placed my basket on the carpet and turned to face Natalia head-on.

I lifted my 'sun shades' and said, "I don't want him Natalia. I haven't for a very long time. And believe it or not, I am sorry that it didn't work out for you. I want him to be happy. Despite it all, all I ever wanted was his happiness. Unfortunately, he's not able to deal with his own issues, which makes happiness an illusion for him. But it's not about you. It never was."

I replaced my glasses, picked up my basket and proceeded to the checkout.

When I left the store, she was outside, waiting for me.

"I'm sorry."

I turned to see who she could possibly be speaking to.

"I'm talking to you," she said when I looked around. "I just loved him so much and now, well...he's a hard man to love."

She said it. I nodded. I couldn't have said it better myself.

I was almost home, standing at 82nd and Broadway impatiently waiting to cross the street two days later. I trotted out, debated going against the light, and returned to the curb. No sense trying to make it in these heels and falling or worse, getting run over. As I stood there shifting from foot to foot, partially out of excitement, partially out of a blister forming on my pinky toe, I smelled a familiar cologne come up along side me.

I turned and saw Alan, dressed in a suit, silk shirt, and tie. He never wears ties.

"What's the occasion?" I said to him.

He turned, saw me and a smile crept to his lips.

"Hey."

"Hey there yourself."

After a moment of neither of us speaking, I ventured, "I heard about the new play. Congratulations."

"Thanks Sam." He said.

He seemed more nervous than I had ever seen him.

"Going to celebrate?" I asked, hoping this time to get some answers.

"Got a date," he finally admitted sheepishly.

I nodded.

"Good for you. Who is it this time? Oh...Silvia isn't it, oh no, um, Bernadette maybe?" I asked teasingly.

"Frank," he answered and began crossing the street, leaving me—something I've never been accused of in my life—speechless.

Acknowledgments

There are so many people that have made this book—and frankly my mere existence—possible. For My Maker who is up there looking down upon me keeping watch, I am eternally grateful. And to all of the following watchers on this earth, in no particular order:

Mama—I love ya. Thanks for being my Woman Extraordinaire! Thanks too for reading all my stuff and encouraging me to keep going. Your input was invaluable. Lastly, thanks for making me a reader!

Dave, my Dandy Man—you are the father I never had, but always wanted. I love your kindness, spirit, generosity, and cat-whisperin' ways (otherwise how would I ever know what my furry babies were thinking!!). Simply put, you are the best!

Anna R—to merely call you a best friend would be a gross understatement. You keep me grounded, you show me the other side of things (which as it so happens isn't so difficult since we are polar opposites!), and you remind me to find my joy in all that I do. Thank you for finding the super-secret formula for keeping me on the straight and narrow and walking upright (at least most of the time!).

Karen KC—I feel so lucky to call you a great friend. You've got my back (and everyone else's who has ever met you!) and are always there to lend an ear and share some good advice. Your creative nature helps inspire me to go to greater lengths, to try greater endeavors, and I am so full of gratitude for your vision.

Joe C—One word from you and I can see myself in a whole new light. Write a play, a movie, a one-woman show—with your encouragement, it all seems possible. I thank you for making your daily life an inspiration to all artists everywhere. How lucky I am to call you my friend.

Barbara T—Your encouragement and support have helped to get me to this point. Thank you for always lending a hand and giving such sound advice in my times of need. You are a true friend.

Neil O—We both know this would not be happening without you. I so appreciate your guidance and support in this endeavor I knew absolutely nothing about. You are generous and thoughtful with your time and resources and I could not be more grateful.

Ronnie and Ginny B—I love you guys! Thank you both for all your encouragement through all of this. Ron, thanks for reading an earlier draft and telling me that it held your attention (not that you're into women's fiction or anything!!). Gin—thanks so much for all your time and effort on the original cover! That truly was the inspiration for this one! You both make me wanna find someone and put an end to my decades of singlehood!

Bill G—Thank you so much for being a reader and sharing all your insights into the publishing world! I so appreciate your encouragement and your writing too!

Stephen B—Design Master! Thank you so much for coming up with a great website (and cover for the 'other' book)! But mostly for being patient with a crazed-maniac such as myself! I know I can be a lot to handle at times (did I just admit that!)

Alison W, Susan H, Vanessa B, and Paige K—My LA crew! I love you ladies. Thank you so much for making your own dreams happen and in doing so teaching an old woman like me that I can do it too!!

About the Author

Samantha Wren Anderson is an actress and writer residing in New York City, who has found life as a single woman in the Big Apple has fueled many an amazing tale. Anderson bounced around the country as a child, calling Ohio, New Jersey, and California among her many homes. After college, Anderson packed a bag and with barely enough to cover a month's rent, headed east and has never looked back. She also publishes under the name Cat Acewal. Visit her at www.samanthawrenanderson.com

Made in the USA
Middletown, DE
22 September 2015